The Angina Monologues

The Angina Monologues

Rosamund Kendal

JACANA

First published by Jacana Media (Pty) Ltd in 2010
Reprinted in 2010

10 Orange Street
Sunnyside
Auckland Park 2092
South Africa
+2711 628 3200
www.jacana.co.za

ISBN 978-1-77009-812-1

Set in Ehrhardt 10.5/14
Printed and bound by CTP Book Printers, Cape Town
Job No. 001210

ISO 12647 compliant

See a complete list of Jacana titles at www.jacana.co.za

Rachael

1

'Ah, well, if that's your problem,' the male voice on the other end of the grubby telephone receiver said slowly, 'then it's not really a problem at all. You see, there's a perfectly good borehole outside.'

'I'm sorry?' Rachael asked, not immediately understanding how the presence of a borehole solved her dilemma in any way.

'There is no problem with the accommodation,' the man answered, slightly irritated now, 'because there's a borehole for water at the bottom of the garden.'

The implications of the man's rather annoyed response dawned on Rachael in a moment of ominous clarity.

'Do you mean to tell me that I'm supposed to get my own water from the borehole?' she asked. Incredulity turned her usually well-modulated voice into a high-pitched squeak.

'Yes, so you see that there is in fact no problem. Goodbye.'

Rachael heard the mechanical click of a telephone receiver being placed in its cradle. The man had hung up on her. Anger superseded alarm and she punched the redial button. There was absolutely no way that she was going to spend the rest of the year in a house without piped water. There must be some alternative accommodation. She was, after all, only a couple of hours north of Durban. She heard the beeping tones of the number being redialled and then the telephone was answered, almost immediately, by the same man to whom she had been speaking previously.

'I was speaking to you a moment ago about the intern doctors' accommodation,' Rachael said.

'I'm sorry,' the voice interrupted her, 'but it is now four o'clock and we are closed. I cannot help you.'

'But I've just been discussing this with you, not even two minutes ago,' Rachael spluttered. 'You can't do this! You can't leave me in a house without running water. I don't know how to pump water from a borehole; I don't even know what a borehole looks like. For goodness sake, this is absolutely ridiculous. It's inhumane. You must be able to do something. I refuse to spend the year like this.' But the man on the other end of the telephone had obviously replaced his receiver; Rachael found herself shouting at the empty echo of her own voice. She slammed the telephone down, livid now, then picked it up again and pressed the redial button once more. This time the recorded voice of an answering machine responded to her call and advised her not to leave a message but to try to call again during office hours.

It was now four o'clock on the thirty-first of December. Rachael would only be able to call again in two days' time, on the second of January (presuming, rather optimistically, that the human resources department of the hospital would not regard the second of January, as well as the first, as a public holiday), and until then she would have to live in a primitive hovel with no water. Rachael briefly considered the option of walking across to the administration block to see if the useless idiot with whom she had just been arguing on the telephone was still in his office, but then realised that option would, in all likelihood, be a futile exercise. It would probably take nothing short of a loaded gun to his temple to make him do something about her complaint and Rachael was not in the habit of carrying firearms around with her.

Her short burst of fury spent, Rachael collapsed onto the edge of the sagging bed next to which she had been standing and started to cry. Suddenly everything was too much for her and she wanted to escape from the uncivilised place in which she now, through very little choice of her own, found herself. She could think of nothing better to do than jumping into her car and driving the fifteen hours straight back to the comfortably furnished flat that she had left behind in Cape Town. She had expected her intern year to be difficult, especially after she had received the curt, impersonal letter from the Department of Health notifying her that she had not been placed in any of the locations on her list of choices but had been assigned to a rural hospital in KwaZulu-Natal. What she hadn't expected was to have to pump her own water. Surely pumping one's own water went far beyond the call of duty.

When, two months before, in October (she remembered that it was October because she had bought herself a bunch of sweet peas as a good-luck charm before going to the post office), she had collected the registered-mail official document informing her that she would be doing her internship in Prince Xoliswe Hospital in Tugela Bridge – an institution she didn't know in a town she had never heard of – she had vacillated between accepting the post and leaving South Africa. Now she wished that she had not been so naive and idealistic as to have chosen the former.

Puffy-eyed and disillusioned, Rachael looked around her at what was supposed to be her accommodation for the year. Apart from the worn bed on which she sat, the only other piece of furniture in the bedroom was a small chipboard bedside table, on which rested the generic government-issue telephone that she had recently been using. Even the light bulb hung bare from the ceiling. The rest of the shack (she didn't feel that the prefabricated building in which she was supposed to be staying warranted being called a 'house') was similarly bare. The kitchen-cum-lounge contained a metal sink, an old Defy oven, a bar fridge that a previous resident, either in an attempt to cheer the place up or in a moment of manic psychosis, had decorated with luminous orange stars, and a single, stained seventies-style armchair. A broken spring in the cushion of the chair poked up through the mustard upholstery, giving the piece of furniture a decidedly hostile appearance. The bathroom contained a toilet (currently without any water in the cistern) and a shower. If Rachael had had any idea of how spartan the accommodation would be (she had been assured in her letter of appointment that she would be provided with basically furnished lodgings), she would have organised for her furniture to be moved from Cape Town before she arrived at Tugela Bridge. She thought longingly of her comfortable leather couch, her convection microwave, her plasma-screen television and her imported teak dining-room table. Strangely, even though she had only arrived at Tugela Bridge earlier that afternoon, Cape Town, and even Durban, already felt worlds away.

She had flown to Durban on the seventeenth of December, the day after her graduation from medical school, and stayed with a cousin for the ten days that it had taken for her car to be freighted from Cape Town to Durban. Even after her car arrived, she had delayed leaving Durban for as long as possible, not only because she enjoyed the company of her easy-going, party-loving relative, but also because she was dreading finding out exactly how rural and backward the place she was supposed to be spending the next year actually was. Rachael was by upbringing a procrastinator; she had never wanted for anything in her life, and so she lived under the illusion that if she just waited long enough, somebody – usually her father – would sort out her problems for her. It had never really entered her mind that things might not go exactly the way she wanted them to (which was entirely reasonable, since they had done so for the first twenty-five years of her life). Even on the morning of the thirty-first of December, the last day before she officially started her internship, she had half expected to receive a text message from her mother telling her that her father had managed to organise an intern post for her at Groote Schuur Hospital in Cape Town. When the message had still not arrived by mid-morning, Rachael realised, with a harsh and unwelcome introduction to reality, that it probably was never going to come and had reluctantly embarked on the two-and-a-half-hour trip into the unknown.

Contrary to what she had been expecting, she had actually enjoyed the drive to Tugela Bridge. Initially she had been nervous about the journey because she hadn't known the roads at all and because she wasn't used to travelling alone, but the closer she got to her destination, the more confident she felt herself becoming. She had found the vegetation that she drove through unusual and beautiful: first the quivering lime-green of the sugar-cane plantations, and then the lush overgrowth, the twisted trunks and the thick canopies of the pockets of preserved coastal forest. Dotted intermittently along the side of the road were clusters of mud huts with reed or tin roofs. So pastoral were the scenes she passed that they could have been painted but for the movement of chickens pecking in the yards in front of the dwellings or of a lone goatherd urging on a group of scrawny yellow-eyed goats. By the time she reached Prince Xoliswe Hospital in the small town of Tugela Bridge, she had been filled with a benevolent self-satisfaction bred from the confidence of having successfully completed her first independent journey and the belief that she had arrived at a suitable destination upon which to bestow her recently acquired medical knowledge.

Her good mood had been abruptly terminated when she found the human resources department, where a fat, sweaty woman, who appeared to be able to speak English but not to understand enough to answer Rachael's questions, had given her a key to the prefab that was to be her accommodation, a bleeper with a three-digit number tippexed on its base and a copy of a call roster, which indicated that Rachael was to be on call on the night of the first of January.

The prefab, when she eventually located it a couple of hundred metres west of the main hospital building, had not looked too bad from the outside. There was even the remnant of a potted geranium at the front door, forgotten by a previous tenant. It was only once she had opened the screen door and run to the bathroom to empty her painfully full bladder that she realised just how awful the year ahead of her threatened to be. The toilet had not flushed when she pulled the chain; it had simply made a hollow, burping noise. She had lifted the lid of the cistern but had found it empty and disturbingly dry. When she had turned on the shower tap to try to collect some water to fill the cistern and an anorexic-looking brown trickle had emerged from the spout, she realised that her prefab had a water-supply problem. Which had led to the unsuccessful telephone call.

Thinking of the call triggered a fresh flood of tears. Rachael indulged in a further ten minutes of misery before realising that time would probably not sort out this problem (the little she knew about boreholes excluded them having a timer or being automated) and that, realistically, her father would be unlikely to be able to do anything about her lack of running water from two thousand kilometres away. The realisation should have made her feel more

5

overwhelmed, but instead it left her with a newfound if inexplicable determination. It was a strangely empowering sensation and, because in the past she had always had someone to fall back on, one she could not remember having experienced previously. She pulled her carefully straightened dark hair into a ponytail, wiped her eyes and nose with a piece of toilet paper (ironically, she had found a quarter of a roll of single-ply toilet paper next to the defunct toilet) and sat down to determine her plan of action.

She had one of two choices: to get into her car and drive back to Durban, then take the first flight she could back to Cape Town, or to go in search of a borehole, which she knew would prove problematic since she had no idea what a borehole actually looked like. After some deliberation she settled on the borehole quest rather than the return to Cape Town, mostly because she would rather face two days without running water than two weeks of her mother's smirk. (Rachael's mother had never condoned her decision to do her internship in South Africa; she had wanted Rachael to emigrate to the United Kingdom or Israel as soon as possible, before South Africa ended up going the way of Zimbabwe.)

Rachael scrunched the used piece of toilet paper into a ball and threw it into an old shopping packet and then made her way out of the screen door in search of the borehole. Mentally, she imagined a borehole to look something like a well. Unfortunately, even her idea of what a well looked like was skewed, as the only well she had ever seen was an illustration in a children's fairy-tale book. What she eventually found, and presumed by default must be the pump for the borehole, was a long, metal lever set in a cement base. Next to the cement base were two large green water tanks. Tentatively, she pulled down on the lever. It remained fixed. She pulled a little harder but the lever still refused to budge. She swung on it with her full body weight and the earth emitted a shuddering groan. She released the lever and it returned to an upright position with a squeal. She pulled down again and then helped the lever up. Down and up, down and up. Groan-squeak-groan-squeak. The more she moved the lever, the more momentum it seemed to gather and the easier the pumping became. She smiled; the whole borehole thing had been far less painful than she had imagined it would be.

She had just started to establish a rhythm when she saw a movement out of the corner of her eye and turned to see a black man in blue overalls watching her quizzically. She realised with horror that she should probably have made sure that, before moving it, what she was pushing up and down actually belonged to the borehole. Swiftly she jerked the lever to a halt. She felt like an idiot; perhaps she had been working the irrigation system for the hospital grounds or, even worse, pumping the bellows for the hospital incinerator. She glanced at the hospital fearfully, part of her expecting to see a cloud of smoke billowing from the roof. She didn't know why she had jumped so happily to the conclusion that the lever pumped water from the borehole simply because of its proximity to two green tanks.

'Um, hello. Is this the borehole pump?' she asked the man anxiously, presuming, because of his outfit, that he was a hospital groundsman. He nodded slowly and she smiled with relief. 'I'm just pumping some water,' she said. 'I'm one of the new doctors working here this year.'

The man nodded and Rachael smiled politely again. She waited for him to leave, but instead he squatted down against the low brick wall behind the pump, lit a hand-rolled cigarette and followed her movements with apparent interest. Rachael pulled at the lever hesitantly, unsure of whether she should continue pumping. She needed the water but she felt uncomfortable with the man watching her. She was suddenly conscious of the fact that there was nobody else around, and that she was wearing diamond stud earrings and a tanzanite pendant necklace, and that her expensive new cellphone was protruding from the back pocket of her jeans. Perhaps the man was sussing out her valuables, biding his time before sticking a knife to her throat. She didn't want water that badly. As she was about to stop the lever and flee back to her prefab, the man untwined himself from the mottled evening shadows and stood up.

'Next time, I pump for you. Twelve rand,' the man said, stubbing his cigarette out against the wall. He walked away before Rachael could ask him why he hadn't bothered to tell her earlier. Obviously, she had inadvertently been providing his evening's entertainment. The only witness to her embarrassment was the thin wisp of smoke, strangely sweet, from his discarded cigarette stump.

Rachael turned back to the pump and pulled at it with renewed vigour. Although it was past afternoon, it was not yet dark, and the air was still warm and humid. She felt beads of sweat form on her forehead and then become heavy and trickle down into her eyes and onto her cheeks. She didn't know for what length of time she needed to pump in order to fill the green water tanks, so she just carried on pumping. The rhythm became almost hypnotic. The muscles on her back and shoulders burnt, and the salt from her sweat stung the blisters that had formed and burst on her palms, but the exertion felt inexplicably good. She transferred all the anger and frustration that she had felt over the past twenty-four hours through her arms and into the lever. The force of it, and the rhythm and the repetition, were cathartic. It was as though she was emptying herself of emotion, thrusting the thoughts and feelings that limited her far into the bowels of the earth. Eventually, when her skin had risen in the bumps of a hundred mosquito bites and darkness almost shrouded the movement of her arms, she stopped pumping. She slowly walked back to her prefab, picking her way half blindly over the unfamiliar terrain. She felt lighter, almost ethereal, without the burden of her emotions anchoring her to the ground.

Rachael pushed open the front door, which she had forgotten to lock, and fumbled in the dark for the light switch. Eventually she found it and flicked it on. The naked bulb hanging from the ceiling buzzed slightly and then filled the room with a harsh light. Rachael walked across to the sink and turned on the tap, praying that her pumping had been successful. After a series of splutters and one rather disconcerting explosion, water spurted forth from the tap. She cupped her hands beneath the spout to catch the stream. It was cold as it splashed on her skin, colder than she had expected. Gingerly, she lifted her cupped hands to her mouth. The water tasted earthy, slightly brackish and delicious, far better than any bottled water she had ever drunk. She brought some more to her mouth and then splashed it on her face and the back of her neck.

She turned off the tap and started laughing. She had done it; she had pumped her own water. It was bizarre that she had never before felt such a sense of accomplishment, not even after passing her final medical exams. She lifted her arms and spun around the prefab's kitchen-cum-lounge. The exercise, the endorphins, the cold, cold water, must have made her high. She couldn't remember when last she had felt so carefree and so simply happy.

Later that evening, Rachael's phone rang. Rachael watched her mother's name and picture flash on the screen of her cellphone, hesitating before pressing the green answer button. She didn't feel like talking to her mother right then, but she knew that if she didn't respond her mother would persist in calling her until she did. Reluctantly, she put the phone to her ear and greeted her mother.

'You've been doing what?' her mother screeched against the background of a New Year's Eve party. 'I'm going to speak to your father. I'll make sure he fetches you tomorrow. We'll have you out of the country by next week, my girl. No child of mine has to pump her own water. I'm not going to say I told you so, but you should have listened to your silly old mother. This country is going one way fast, and that's down. The sooner you get out, the better. I've been speaking to your Aunt Hilda. Do you know what happened to her hairdresser's son's girlfriend?'

'Mom, calm down,' Rachael interrupted her. She knew that once her mother started complaining about South Africa, she was likely to carry on her tirade for at least half an hour and Rachael didn't have the energy or the inclination to listen to thirty minutes of urban-legend horror stories. 'It's fine. I've come all this way; I might as well give this place a try. Besides, I'll look like a real idiot if I give up before even starting my internship properly,' she said with as much conviction as she could muster. She sounded far more positive than she felt, far surer of her decision than she was. Her mother muttered something about her being her father's child and then wished Rachael a happy, and wet, New Year before putting the phone down. The last thing that Rachael heard before the line went dead was the clinking of champagne glasses.

Rachael realised that, having been caught up in the distraction of her water crisis, she had forgotten it was New Year's Eve. This wasn't exactly her idea of a New Year's Eve party: she was sitting on her own, without a drink, without even the television to count the year down with her, eating a partially warmed-up ready-made meal from the carton. Tears of self-pity pricked her eyes. She had never been alone on New Year's Eve before. She thought briefly of the New Year's Eve party of the previous year: she had been in Athens with her two best friends from varsity. They had seen the New Year in at the foot of the Parthenon, beneath brilliantly coloured flowers of fireworks, and had then gone on to dance the rest of the night away at a trendy club. It was so far removed from her current situation that she almost felt as though she was imagining it, as though she was caught in a Cinderella-type fairy tale. She pushed aside the rest of the lukewarm meal and delved in her handbag for the slab of chocolate that she had bought earlier at a garage quick-shop. She had debated before buying the chocolate, but her self-discipline had eventually given way to her addiction, and now she was glad that she had succumbed. Slowly she peeled off the silver wrapper, then broke off a block of chocolate, letting it melt in her mouth. It would be pointless to try to stop eating: as the thick, creamy sweetness dissolved between her palate and her tongue, she knew that she would finish the slab. As she crumpled up the empty wrapper, she promised herself that she would never spend another New Year's Eve alone again. She threw the remainder of her meal into the plastic bag that she was using as a makeshift bin, changed into her pyjamas and then carefully unfolded her aching body onto the sagging bed, trying to work out why she was not in her car driving to Cape Town so that she could fall asleep on the specialised chiropractic bed that she was used to sleeping on.

2

A loud bleeping sound woke Rachael. Still half asleep, she grabbed at the telephone next to the bed and then at her cellphone in search of the source of the noise. Neither seemed to be causing it. She was about to stumble through to the lounge to see if she had inadvertently activated the alarm on the old oven while warming her food the night before when she remembered the bleeper she had been given the previous day. Someone must have paged the incorrect number. She buried her head in her pillow, deciding it was best to ignore the noise. She had just slipped back into semi-consciousness when the bleeper went off again. She grumbled and pulled the duvet up over her ears. It wasn't even eight o'clock yet. It was only after the pager went off for the third time, and Rachael knew that she was too wide awake to go back to sleep again, that she decided to answer it. She picked up the telephone and dialled the four-digit number that was flashing on the pager screen. The call was answered almost immediately by a sister in casualty. Rachael explained to the sister, as politely as could be expected of someone who had been prematurely woken up by an incorrect page on New Year's Day, that somebody had bleeped the wrong person. Three times. At half past seven in the morning.

'You aren't Dr Lipawski then?' the sister asked, clearly as confused now as Rachael had been a few minutes earlier.

'Yes, I am,' Rachael answered, suddenly anxious. The worrying thought that perhaps somebody had actually been paging *her* entered her sleep-befuddled mind. Perhaps she had misread the timetable and was supposed to be on call. She leant down over the side of the bed and found the roster among the wad of paper that she had dumped onto the floor in her state of exhaustion the previous night. She checked the date: she *had* read the timetable correctly. She was not on call. A Dr Zamla was on call. Reassured, she asked the sister what she wanted.

'You're supposed to be working with Dr Singh today,' the sister said. 'We've got patients waiting.'

'But I'm not on call,' Rachael explained, waving the photocopied call roster in the air as though the sister could see it. 'Dr Zamla's on call today. I'm only on call tonight.'

'Did nobody tell you?' the sister asked (rather too gleefully, Rachael thought). 'Dr Zamla doesn't do calls.'

'I'm sorry?' Rachael asked.

'Dr Zamla doesn't do calls,' the sister repeated. 'Whoever's on in the evening usually stands in for his day shift as well. They should have told you.'

'So does someone do my night shift then?' Rachael asked, confused.

'No,' the sister said patiently. 'You do both shifts.'

'But that means I end up doing a twenty-four-hour shift,' Rachael objected. The sister's reasoning made no sense to her whatsoever.

'Yes, that's how it works. I'm sorry you weren't told, but you need to get here as soon as possible please. It's getting busy,' the sister said, putting the telephone down.

Rachael wondered why she had decided the night before to stay at Tugela Bridge. She cursed the impractical, romantic notions that she had had. This confusion over the call roster was probably just a foretaste of what the rest of the year was going to be like. What the sister had said was completely illogical. If Dr Zamla didn't do calls, why was his name on the call roster? Rachael checked her watch and realised that she didn't have time either to ponder the logistics of the call list or to wallow in remorse over her decision to stay at Tugela Bridge; if she was supposed to be working, she was already an hour late and it was only her first day.

Rachael checked the call roster one last time to be sure that she hadn't missed some obvious explanation for why she would be working for twenty-four hours and not for twelve, and then climbed stiffly out of bed. Her body was sore both from the unaccustomed exertion of pumping water and from spending a night on an unsprung mattress. She walked to the bathroom and turned on the shower tap, praying for water to emerge. It did and she quickly immersed herself in it, unsure how long the luxury would last. She wondered whether the shower water was the result of her efforts the previous night or if the man with the sweet-smelling cigarette had subsequently been working the pump. She towel-dried her hair and put on a pair of charcoal slacks and a pastel pink blouse. Out of habit, because it was what she always did after putting on her clothes, she opened her make-up bag. Her fingers hesitated over the bottle of foundation. The sister had said that patients were waiting; morally, it didn't feel quite right to make them wait longer while she spent time on something as trivial as putting on make-up. The situation presented Rachael with a major dilemma: she didn't want to keep sick people waiting, but she also hadn't ventured out in public without make-up on since she left school. She even wore foundation, mascara and lip gloss to gym. And she never, ever went out without blow-drying or straightening her hair. She was so embarrassed by her curly hair that she had managed to mislead even her close friends into believing that her hair was naturally straight. But blow-drying and straightening her hair would make her at least another half an hour late. She decided on a rather unequal compromise and quickly slicked some gloss over her lips. As she stepped out of her prefab to walk across to the hospital, she couldn't help feeling self-conscious, almost naked. As she closed the screen door behind her, she reassured herself that it didn't matter what she looked like, because she knew nobody working at Prince Xoliswe Hospital. Nobody that really mattered, anyway.

Rachael could see Prince Xoliswe Hospital from her front door. It was a four-storey, red face-brick building, separated from the doctors' accommodation by about two hundred metres. There was a well-used path that led from Rachael's prefab to the main hospital block and, as Rachael started walking along it, she wondered how many doctors had walked this path before her. It made her feel, at least briefly, as if she was part of a bigger story than her usual small narrative. Overgrown shrubs and bushes encroached on the path from either side and brushed against Rachael's legs, making her glad she had worn long trousers. She wasn't used to the Natal vegetation. In the Cape, the hospitals at which she had worked had always had a slightly barren, windblown look. Here things grew. The soil was rich and red and crumbly, not like sand at all but rather like mud or clay. The plants were thick and verdant, almost parasitic in their desire to thrive. Creepers with dark, waxy leaves choked trunks and sent feelers down branches. Even the air was different –

wet, clingy and thick – so that by the time she reached the hospital she felt as though every exposed inch of her skin was covered in a fine film of sweat. Yes, it was beautiful, but it also frightened her: she sensed that accompanying such a wild, throbbing life force was an equal violence. Death, she felt, was close by: in the rotting vegetation, the bloodied soil, the shadows behind the leaves. In KZN, she thought, life cycles were fast-forwarded.

The path ended at the hospital parking lot. Rachael walked across the hot tar to the main entrance of the hospital. Patients loitered at the front door: a man with a bandaged head talking on a cellphone; a pregnant woman sitting in a wheelchair eating a banana; an elderly man leaning against a patch of sun on the wall, holding a drip stand in one hand and a cigarette in the other. Rachael made her way around the patients and entered through the glass sliding doors. A paramedic carrying a bloodstained spinal board walked out through the automatic doors as Rachael walked in. He nodded briefly to her as they passed each other.

Inside the building, signs directed Rachael to reception. Everywhere there were patients waiting, milling around. Rachael suddenly felt claustrophobic, as though her senses were being bombarded. Images burnt onto her retinas like photographic stills: a blood-soaked dishcloth wrapped like a makeshift mitten around a hand; a woman wiping her infant's soiled bottom with a corner of a faded red sarong; a threadbare handkerchief trying to disguise a grotesquely swollen mouth. Rachael knew that with her white skin, her chic pants and fitted silk blouse, she looked out of place. She wished she had worn a doctor's coat over her clothes or that she had had the sense to wear a less conspicuous outfit. Walking past waiting patients, she wanted to hide her diamond earrings and tanzanite necklace and designer watch, not so much because she was worried they would get stolen but because she felt embarrassed, even guilty, displaying such wealth amid such abject poverty. She felt eyes bore into her, judge her, as she made her way as swiftly as possible to the reception area. The woman behind the glass-fronted admissions desk directed Rachael to casualty and she walked quickly towards it. She wanted to get away from the eyes of the crowd in the foyer.

14

The other doctor on call in casualty was already busy seeing patients when Rachael arrived. Rachael remembered her name from the call list: Dr Singh. She was a short, slight woman with straight black hair plaited into a long rope down her back. Her face was perfectly made up: black kohl lined her dark brown eyes and her lips were plump with tinted gloss. She wore a white coat over a smart navy dress and gold earrings dangled from her earlobes. She was busy writing notes in a patient's file and hardly looked up when Rachael introduced herself.

'Sorry I'm so late,' Rachael apologised, suspecting that her tardiness might be the reason for her colleague's indifference. 'I didn't realise I was supposed to be doing Dr Zamla's call,' she explained. Dr Singh acknowledged the apology with a curt nod and then, without once making eye contact with Rachael, showed her around the casualty unit. It was a long, rectangular room divided into six adjoining curtained examination cubicles. Each cubicle contained a doctor's desk, a chair and an examination bed. At the end of the unit, closest to the entrance door, was a nursing station. On the other side of the room were two doors, one of which led to the doctors' office and the other to the sluice room. Dr Singh showed Rachael the pile of folders belonging to patients waiting to be seen.

'You pick up the top file,' Dr Singh explained in a voice barely louder than a whisper, 'and then ask one of the nurses to call the patient in. The patients wait on the benches outside casualty. You can use any open cubicle to see your patient in. If you have an emergency or you think a patient needs surgery, then you need to call the community service doctor on call. Beds seem to be a problem here, so you should limit admissions only to patients that really need it.'

Rachael wanted to ask Dr Singh for more information. She wanted to know what the nursing sisters were like, who the community service doctor on call was, whether the interns got tea and lunch breaks, where the toilet was (and whether it had a water supply), but Dr Singh had already picked up a file and was leading a patient to a cubicle.

Before beginning to see patients, Rachael went to put her bag down in the doctors' office. The office was a square room with a desk against one wall, six decrepit chairs arranged into a squashed circle in the centre of the room, a sink piled high with unwashed coffee mugs, and a sideboard cluttered with a kettle, toaster and microwave. Stuck to the wall above the kettle was a list of the names of the doctors who had paid their monthly contribution to the purchase of tea, coffee and milk. On the brief tour of casualty, Dr Singh had mentioned that the morning handover round took place in the doctors' office. The following morning, Rachael would be expected to present to the other doctors the patients she had admitted during her shift.

Thinking of the next morning's handover made Rachael acutely aware of the irreversible reality of the situation. She was a doctor. She would have to decide, entirely on her own, who warranted admission to hospital and who could be discharged. There was no practice run, no room for her to make even the tiniest error in judgement. It all felt like a horrible mistake. She was not ready to be a doctor yet. She wondered how she had passed her final exams, why her professors had let her out of medical school. She wanted to go back and tell her examiners that they had slipped up. She looked down at her feet, at the pair of designer shoes that she had bought specially for calls because they did not have high heels. Doctors didn't wear pink polka-dot patent leather pumps. She put her bag next to the telephone on the desk and walked back into casualty. Quickly, before she had time to doubt herself any further, she picked up a file and called in her first patient. She would just have to trust that, somewhere in the recesses of her grey matter, she had enough knowledge. Her only consolation was a quote she remembered from one of her lecturers at medical school: *The most important skill that you can leave medical school with is the ability to admit ignorance.* In the worst-case scenario, Rachael thought, she could always ask someone for help.

Rachael's first patient was a fifty-year-old Indian man with a balding dome, heavy blue pouches under his eyes and an apple-shaped waist. He followed her slowly into the examination cubicle. Walking at his side was a small, bird–like woman that Rachael presumed was his wife. She had a red *bindi* in the middle of her forehead and wore a grey sari that swept the ground with each step that she took. Rachael extended her hand in greeting to the patient, but she couldn't bring herself to introduce herself as Dr Lipawski. It sounded too fraudulent. So she just shook the man's hand and said hello, hoping that he would realise that she was the doctor by virtue of the stethoscope around her neck. As she gripped the patient's hand, Rachael noticed that his skin was cold and slightly clammy. She asked him how she could help him, and the man told her that he had a severe chest pain that had started about an hour before. He had taken a Disprin and one of the tablets that go under the tongue, as his family doctor had told him to do, but neither had alleviated the chest pain. Rachael asked him a little more about the pain and he described how it radiated down his left arm and into the left side of his jaw.

'It's like a pressure poking on my chest,' he told Rachael, 'like an elephant's standing on my chest. It's very heavy, doctor. My chest is very heavy.' Rachael told the man to lie down on the bed and tried to contain her alarm. The man was obviously in the throes of a heart attack – anyone who had ever watched an episode of *Grey's Anatomy* would be able to recognise the symptoms – and Rachael was supposed to treat him. She was no longer the student, moving politely to the side to observe as the doctor took over the management of a critically ill patient. She *was* the doctor and she didn't have the vaguest idea of where to start. It was as though all she knew of acute myocardial infarctions had suddenly been moved to a remote part of her brain. The knowledge had to be there somewhere because she remembered studying it, but it was all at once terrifyingly inaccessible to her. She couldn't even remember the name of the tablets that the man had described putting under his tongue in an attempt to relieve his pain.

Rachael started panicking. She was stupid to have believed for one moment that she could do this; she wasn't cut out to be a doctor. Not in a million years. Her father had been right: she should have studied business, not medicine. At least then she would only have been responsible for people's money and not their lives. She felt her heart rate accelerate and the palpitations brought her harshly back to reality. Her patient was having far worse palpitations than she was; in fact, his heart was in imminent danger of ceasing to beat if she didn't pull herself together very quickly. She took a deep breath and exhaled slowly, as her yoga teacher had taught her to do under stressful circumstances. The well-meaning yoga instructor had probably not had quite these exact stressful circumstances in mind when she prescribed the relaxation technique (Rachael had rather got the impression she had been talking about traffic jams or shopping queues), but the breathing worked to calm Rachael. She needed to go back to basics, she thought. In their third year her class had been taught a mantra to help them to remember the basics: *History, exam, special investigations.* She would take a medical history from the patient, then do a clinical examination. She knew she was capable of doing that, at least.

She picked up her pen and asked the patient what past illnesses he had suffered from and what medication he was currently taking. She noted his answers carefully in the file. Next she asked him what previous operations he had had and what his smoking and drinking habits were. It was while she was asking him about his parents' and siblings' health that she noticed that her patient was starting to become breathless and that his skin had taken on a greyish tinge. He also appeared not to be concentrating very hard on the questions she was asking him but rather to be gazing fixedly at the lamp usually used to illuminate the cervix during vaginal exams which someone must have left burning. When he asked her whether she believed in God and an afterlife, she decided that the basics would have to wait. She really didn't want her first patient dying on her, especially since he had been in her care for only a few minutes. It was relevant that the man's father had had high blood pressure, but at this moment it was definitely not a priority. She told the patient's wife to call her immediately if her husband's condition changed at all and ran from the cubicle to find help, in the form of either the nursing sister or Dr Singh.

18

While she was looking for her colleagues, Rachael tried to remember something, anything, about the management of acute myocardial infarctions. A mnemonic popped into her head: MONA. Morphine, oxygen, nitrates and aspirin. She wondered why she had remembered it only now, once she had left the patient's bedside. At least she would have something to start doing when she returned to the patient (assuming he was still alive). She found the sister, a large black woman with a cheerful face that was starting to show the beginnings of a beard, changing a patient's catheter in one of the other cubicles and introduced herself.

'Oh, the doctor that didn't know she was supposed to be working today,' the sister said, slightly sarcastically. Rachael had no difficulty in recognising the voice that had woken her up earlier that morning. The sister chuckled to herself and then said something in Zulu to the patient, who started laughing. Rachael felt herself blush and wished that she understood the language. The only word she had recognised was Zamla, the surname of the doctor whose call she was doing. She was about to try to justify the morning's misunderstanding to the sister when she remembered why she was standing outside the cubicle.

'Would you mind helping me with my patient?' she asked the sister. Rachael consciously tried to make her request as polite as possible and to keep her tone humble. She didn't want to antagonise the sister by coming across as an overconfident, arrogant new intern. 'I think my patient's having an MI.'

The sister looked nonplussed. 'Which cubicle?' she asked.

'The one on the other side, in the middle.'

'Oh, cubicle five,' the sister said. Rachael hadn't realised that the cubicles were marked. 'The numbers are above the cubicles,' the sister added, as though reading Rachael's mind. Rachael looked up and saw the numbers, glaringly obvious. She felt herself blush again. No doubt the sister now thought her not only unpunctual but also dim-witted.

'I'll be with you as soon as I'm finished here,' the sister said, dismissing Rachael with the tiniest hint of a smile. Rachael rushed back to her patient. He looked, if possible without being dead, even more distressed than when she had left him. She searched through the trolley in the cubicle for a drip needle and a bag of intravenous fluid. It took her only a couple of minutes to find everything, but it felt like hours. On the bed, the patient had started groaning softly and his skin was wet with a film of sweat. It was obvious that his condition was deteriorating rapidly. Rachael realised that she couldn't afford to spend so much time trying to find simple things, like needles and alcohol swabs. Even minutes were precious now. She wished that she had taken the opportunity to spend some time in the casualty unit the day before, instead of pumping water, to learn where everything was kept.

Rachael stood next to her patient's bed and asked him to extend his arm. She took her tourniquet from around her stethoscope and placed it just above her patient's elbow. The lettering on the tourniquet spelt CRESTOR, the name of a drug manufactured by the pharmaceutical company that had sponsored Rachael's final-year graduation dinner. Each of the new doctors had received a tourniquet as a gift. Rachael had hardly imagined then that the first time she would be using hers would be on a patient having a heart attack. Even in her state of panic she couldn't help thinking of the irony of the situation: the drug advertised on the tourniquet was used to lower cholesterol, imperative in preventing heart attacks. More ironic was the fact that, owing to its cost, the drug itself was not available in Prince Xoliswe Hospital. Rachael wondered whether her patient would be lying on the examination bed in front of her now if he had been able to afford the drug. She felt for the vein that the tourniquet had brought to the surface of the skin and then inserted the intravenous needle. Once she knew that the needle was in the blood vessel, she removed it, leaving the plastic catheter behind in the vein. She attached the bag of saline and let it drip through slowly, one drop at a time. The last thing she wanted to do was inadvertently to give the patient too much fluid; his already failing heart wouldn't handle being further overloaded.

The sister, finished at last with the man that she had been catheterising, entered the cubicle, and Rachael could see by the way her expression changed that she immediately perceived the gravity of the situation. 'I've just inserted a line,' Rachael said hurriedly. 'Do we have oxygen that we can put him on?' The sister nodded and connected some piping with a mask on the end to the oxygen valve at the wall. So far, the patient had had three parts of MONA: the aspirin and the sublingual nitrate that he had taken at home, and the oxygen. Rachael had the presence of mind to realise that she should probably confirm that the patient was actually having a heart attack before administering morphine. Up till now, she had been basing her diagnosis solely on history and clinical findings.

'Can we get an ECG?' she asked the sister.

'I'll get the machine for you but you'll need to do the ECG. We don't do them; it's not in our job description.'

'Sure,' Rachael said. At the hospitals in which she had worked as a student, the nursing staff almost always did the electrocardiographs, but she decided not to mention that. Luckily, Rachael had taken the time to learn how to do an ECG.

Once the sister had brought the machine into the cubicle, Rachael helped the patient to remove his shirt and then attached the electrodes to his chest. He was hairy and his chest hair, in combination with the film of sweat that covered his skin, made sticking down the electrodes difficult, and Rachael ended up having to shave little square patches of hair off the patient's chest in order to get a decent connection. She turned the machine on and waited for the tracing to be printed. It confirmed what Rachael had suspected, that the patient was having a heart attack. She checked his blood pressure, then requested that the sister give him two milligrams of morphine and some intravenous nitrates.

Having done as much as she felt capable of doing (all four parts of MONA having been successfully ticked off), Rachael decided it was appropriate to admit ignorance and contact the community service doctor on call to help her with further management of the patient. As she left the cubicle she caught sight of the patient's wife standing at the head of the bed. Her hand was resting lightly on her husband's shoulder, but this seemed to be more for her own reassurance than for his. Rachael realised with dismay that she had not yet told either the patient or his wife what was going on. She didn't really have time to do so now, either. The patient was still far from stable. She urgently needed to get hold of a more senior doctor to take over from her. But the patient's wife had caught her eye and was looking at her with an expression of desperation. Rachael shifted her gaze, trying to avoid the woman's unspoken plea, but she knew that it would be cruel to ignore it. She hesitated for a moment and then walked over to the head of the bed.

'Is he going to be fine, doctor?' the patient's wife asked, before Rachael had time to say anything.

'I hope so,' Rachael said, realising almost immediately that it was a stupid thing to say. Although it was the truth, it made her sound uncertain and out of control, neither of which was likely to instil in the patient or his wife any confidence in her abilities. 'I mean, I'm sure he'll be fine,' she corrected herself. 'He's just had a small heart attack,' she continued, talking to the patient's wife. It felt easier to break the news to her than to the patient himself.

'A heart attack?' the wife interrupted, almost choking on the words.

As the woman repeated the phrase back to her, Rachael realised that the inferences of what was being said were very different for the wife and for Rachael. To Rachael, the phrase 'heart attack' was simply the lay term for myocardial infarction; the words carried ramifications of possible complications (of which death in this case was definitely one), decisions on management, and adjustments in risk factors. To the patient's wife, they probably implied a whole lot more. They could mean the loss of a spouse, companion, lover; they could leave children fatherless and parents childless; they could imply financial ruin and destitution for the family left behind. To the patient's wife, implicit in the words must surely be an inevitable finality. Rachael wanted to explain to the patient and his wife that this was not necessarily so and that he was still far from the Hollywood portrayal of a fatal heart attack, but she knew she didn't have time to do so. With every moment that passed in which she didn't get help from a more experienced doctor, his chances of survival diminished. She explained to the patient and his wife that she was going to call a more senior doctor to take over further management and rushed from the cubicle.

The harried voice of the community service doctor on call answered Rachael's page. Rachael's explanation of the situation was followed by a brief silence. 'I presume a myocardial infarction does qualify as an emergency?' she volunteered into the void.

'Well, it depends,' the community service doctor answered sharply. 'Is the patient stable? What's his level of consciousness? Does the ECG show ST segment elevation or depression? How long has it been since his pain started? What's his baseline like? What does his blood gas look like?' Rachael felt her heart rate escalate and she struggled to hear the community service doctor's questions above the flurried beating in her ears. Something in her throat started closing up and breathing became difficult. She had had anxiety attacks before, usually during exam time, and she knew that this was the start of one. They had never been bad enough to require medication, but they usually left her incapacitated for a couple of minutes. Right now she didn't have a couple of minutes to spare. Or more accurately, her patient didn't have a couple of minutes to spare. She forced herself to breathe deeply and slowly, trying to decrease her pulse rate and stop herself from hyperventilating (a technique that both her psychologist and yoga instructor had independently assured her would work to terminate the panic attacks, but that never previously had).

'Hello? Are you still there?' The voice was impatient now, almost aggressive.

'Yes.' Rachael forced herself to speak between deep drawn-out breaths. 'Yes,' she repeated. She knew that she had to say something other than yes, quickly, before the senior doctor on the other end of the line put the phone down on her. He probably already thought that she was a blithering idiot or a deep-breathing pervert. 'He's stable and fully conscious,' she said at last. Once the first words were out, the rest seemed to follow a little more easily. 'His blood pressure is one hundred and ten over sixty. He's on oxygen and I've given him morphine. His ECG shows marked ST segment elevation.' She knew that she hadn't answered the questions in the correct order or as comprehensively as she probably should have, but at least she had been able to get something other than exhaled air out of her mouth. And remarkably, the panic attack seemed to have abated.

'The protocol for STEMIs is on the wall of the doctors' office.' The voice was almost devoid of emotion now, brisk and businesslike. 'I'm about to go into theatre with a gunshot abdomen. I can't come and help you, not with a stable patient.'

It took Rachael's overwhelmed brain a few seconds to remember that STEMI stood for ST elevation myocardial infarction. She walked quickly back to the doctors' office, trying to hold herself together. She had been banking on the assistance of a senior doctor. She had not for one moment believed that she would have to manage the patient entirely on her own. The more she thought about the situation, the more she wanted to collapse onto the floor and weep (she might actually have done so, had the floor not been disgustingly filthy). She found the protocol where the community service doctor had said it would be and quickly copied it onto a piece of paper. She would need to give her patient a Streptokinase infusion. The benefit of the drug would be to break down the blood vessel clot that was preventing oxygen from reaching the patient's heart muscle. The effects of the drug, both immediate and long term, were frequently fatal, making the medication risky to administer.

When Rachael returned to the cubicle, the sister was busy increasing the percentage of oxygen running through the patient's oxygen mask. His skin looked greyer than before and Rachael noticed that his blood pressure had started to drop. She briefly explained to him what she was about to do, mentioning the risks of the medication.

'Isn't the senior doctor coming?' the patient interrupted her. 'You said you were going to call a more experienced doctor.' His eyes were wary, and worried.

Rachael tried to answer with as much confidence as she could muster. 'The senior doctor's busy in theatre so he can't help out here. He's explained to me exactly what I need to do. You're going to have to trust me.'

'Have you done this before?'

Rachael shook her head. She decided against elaborating further, against telling the patient that she hadn't actually done any of this before – that he was her very first patient since she had qualified as a doctor.

'I think I'll wait for the other doctor,' the patient said weakly, instinctively picking up Rachael's insecurities. 'I'll wait till he's finished in theatre.'

Rachael could empathise with his request. She, too, would not want to be treated by a self-confessed novice, especially one as bumbling and uncertain and deep-breathing as she. But the patient didn't have the luxury of choice: he was running out of time. Rachael made her voice as authoritative as possible, hoping it would both disguise her nervousness and reassure her patient. 'I've done lots of very similar procedures,' she lied, 'and I'm confident there won't be a problem. If we wait for the other doctor, we risk having you die and that's a chance I'm not prepared to take. As your doctor, I strongly advise that we start giving you this drug as soon as possible.' The patient appeared momentarily taken aback by her tone but then quietly acquiesced in her continuing management.

Rachael cautiously drew up the Streptokinase and connected it to the intravenous line. As the first few millilitres of the infusion started running in, she watched carefully for any signs of allergy or anaphylaxis. That was the immediate risk of using the drug. She checked her patient for a skin rash; swelling of his lips, face or throat; difficulty breathing or the presence of a wheeze; a drop in blood pressure. Once it seemed apparent that he was tolerating the drug, she relaxed a little and went to stand at the end of the bed to write up the prescription chart and nursing care instructions. The patient would need to be monitored vigilantly for the next few hours to ensure that he did not start bleeding from anywhere. Because Streptokinase stopped blood from clotting, it could also cause massive, uncontrolled haemorrhage.

'As soon as there's a bed available, he can go up to the ward,' she told the sister, 'but you'll need to make sure they've got enough staff to monitor him properly overnight. If the wards are short-staffed, it's probably better to keep him here.'

'Must he stay on oxygen?' the sister asked.

Rachael nodded. She was about to walk out of the cubicle when the sister stopped her.

'We didn't get a chance to meet properly before. My name's Sister Miriam,' she said, extending her hand to Rachael. Rachael grinned at the acknowledgement. It was almost as though she had passed a test, although she had no idea what the test had comprised or what passing it implied. She couldn't help wondering why a nursing sister's approval meant so much to her. She checked over her patient one last time before moving on. His condition was already improving: his chest pain had resolved almost completely and his blood pressure seemed to have stabilised. He even managed to smile at her as she told him, this time a little more confidently, that everything was going to be okay.

Although she was not particularly religious (her family was more concerned with Jewish culture than with the faith), as she walked to the pile of folders to call in her next patient, Rachael said a silent prayer of thanks.

Rachael only noticed the time (it was seven o'clock, the time her shift should have started had she not had to cover for the elusive Dr Zamla) because Sister Miriam came to say goodbye to her. In twelve hours she had seen only nine patients, a rate that she knew was dismally slow. Dr Singh, who had seen twenty-one patients, left without saying a word to her and Rachael wondered if it was because she felt that Rachael had been slacking. Rachael didn't know how she could possibly have worked any faster. Thus far, the past twelve hours had been the busiest and most stressful she had ever experienced. She hadn't had a single minute free to eat or drink anything – or even to pee, she realised, noticing for the first time a vague pressure on her bladder. She found a toilet next to the doctors' office and checked that the cistern was full – obviously the hospital didn't run on borehole water – before sitting down. Her back ached, her head ached and the blisters on her feet ached (how stupid she had been to wear new shoes, no matter how cute they were, for a twenty-four-hour shift!). There was no doubt in

Rachael's mind that this was the most tired, both physically and emotionally, that she had ever been and she still had to get through another twelve hours.

She shuffled through casualty, then down the corridor to the reception area, where she had noticed a vending machine earlier in the day. In her hurry to get ready for work that morning, she had forgotten to pack anything to eat or drink, and clearly the hospital didn't supply the doctors with their choice of food and beverage while on duty. She hadn't felt hungry or thirsty earlier, while she had been rushing around trying to sort out patients and subjugate anxiety attacks, but now that she had stopped for a moment's break, she noticed that her stomach was rumbling and her mouth felt like Velcro. Rachael scanned the vending machine, conjuring up in her mind the image of an ice-cold Liqui-Fruit, a packet of chips and a chocolate bar. Unfortunately, in reality the only item in stock was cream soda, which Rachael had hated as a child and had not tasted since. She put her coins into the slot and waited for the tin to fall into the receiving compartment. Nothing happened. She checked the change slot to make sure that her coins had not passed straight through the machine, but it was empty. She shook the vending machine, gently at first and then more aggressively, but the can seemed stuck. Reluctantly she fished more money out of her purse and deposited it into the slot. Again the machine swallowed her money but refused to relinquish its grip on the cream soda. One more try, she thought, third time lucky. She emptied the last of her change into the machine and waited. And waited. She was damned if she was giving up that cream soda, whether she liked the drink or not. She kicked the side of the machine, twice, hard. The pain in her big toe – already sore because of the pinch of her pink polka-dot pump – was worth it when she heard the metallic clatter of three tins of cream soda falling into the receiving compartment. She downed one of the sodas on her way back to casualty (she couldn't imagine why she had deprived herself of cream soda since childhood: nothing had ever tasted so good) and then another while she was counting the number of folders of patients still to be seen. There were twenty patients' folders in the pile. The new doctor on call with her, a short, stocky man from Bloemfontein, who looked a little like a Staffordshire terrier, had already taken a patient into a cubicle. Rachael handed the top folder to the sister, who called her next patient in for her. She made her way to an open examination cubicle and readied herself for another twelve hours of misery.

By seven o'clock on the morning of the second of January, Rachael had seen a total of twenty-three patients. Although it was officially the end of her shift, she had to wait until after the handover round before leaving. She had spent most of the previous twenty-four hours dreading the round because she knew that she would be expected to present her patients to the other doctors, but now that the handover round was about to begin, she was almost too tired to be nervous. Her current concerns were the most basic in Maslow's hierarchy: she needed food and sleep. She collapsed down into one of the chairs in the doctors' office and massaged her right shoulder with her left hand. Mark Conradie, the doctor that had been on call with her overnight, came into the office and switched on the kettle.

'Can I make you a coffee?' he asked. Rachael nodded, trying not to look too desperate. She usually avoided coffee, choosing healthier rooibos or green tea instead, but right now a cup of sweet, milky coffee sounded delicious. Mark pulled a thick ham sandwich from a lunchbox in his bag and settled down in one of the chairs with a copy of the previous day's newspaper. Rachael knew that if she tried to read anything she would be asleep within seconds. She gulped her coffee down, then glanced surreptitiously at her watch: it was five past seven and there was still no sign of any of the other doctors. It didn't appear that punctuality was all that important at Prince Xoliswe Hospital.

'I'm just going to the bathroom quickly,' Rachael said to Mark, getting up from the chair. She needed to do something to wake herself up before the handover round. The weak coffee had only seemed to make her sleepier. She closed the toilet door behind her and splashed her face with cold water. There was a tarnished mirror above the basin and Rachael looked at her reflection as she neatened her ponytail. She was unused to seeing her face bare of make-up and pale from twenty-four hours without sleep, but in an inexplicable way she was proud of her unadorned face, proud of the fact that it had carried her successfully through her first shift, proud that it was the face of a doctor. As she dried her skin with a wad of toilet paper and shaped her damp eyebrows with her fingers, she realised that she couldn't remember having looked at her face without criticising some aspect of it. For the first time, she was satisfied with the way she looked.

Seema

3

Seema was awake well before her alarm went off at six o'clock. Satesh was still sleeping deeply. He moved only slightly with the bleep of the alarm, pulling the sheet covering him closer to his face. Seema thought that he looked handsomer asleep than awake. His mouth seemed softer somehow, less cruel. She got up from the bed slowly, careful not to disturb her dormant husband, and padded her way barefoot to the bedroom cupboard. Although it was still early in the morning, it was already too hot to wear her towelling dressing gown. The air alone, thick and oppressive, seemed to stifle her movements more than any garment would. She covered her thin nightdress with a loose cotton robe that belonged to Satesh before heading to the bathroom to shower.

One of the advantages of being married was that she and Satesh qualified to stay in the married quarters. The accommodation for the doctors working at Prince Xoliswe Hospital consisted of a dark-red face-brick block of apartments, comprising the married quarters and the community service doctors' flats, and a chain of linked prefabs, which were delegated to the unmarried interns. Seema had heard that the prefabs relied on pumped borehole water (the married quarters' apartments had piped water), and it amused her to imagine what Satesh's reaction would have been had she told him that they were moving to a house without running water. As it was, he had made her feel unreasonably guilty about his having to follow her to Tugela Bridge. When Satesh eventually agreed to accompany her for the duration of her internship, she had had no illusion that she was the sole reason behind his decision; she suspected that it was rather the promise of a year-long holiday that had prompted his choice. Satesh had given her an ultimatum: he had supported her financially the previous year while she was completing her final stint at medical school, so if she wanted him to follow her, she would have to spend her intern year supporting him. He had rationalised his unfair proposal by claiming that there was no chance that he would find work (he had previously been working as a systems analyst for a large private bank) in a one-horse town like Tugela Bridge. Seema had refrained from mentioning the obvious to him: that Satesh didn't plan to spend the year studying furiously to further his career, as she had done while he had supported her the year before. She also hadn't bothered to remind him that his financial load hadn't been so heavy since they had been living rent-free on her parents' property and eating most of their meals with her parents. But she had agreed to the ultimatum because she had had no other choice. She had known that their fragile relationship would not survive a year apart and then, as now, she would have made any sacrifice to preserve her marriage.

After waiting for ten minutes for the water running from the hot tap to warm up, Seema realised that she was probably wasting her time. Although the married quarters had running water, the geyser seemed to be faulty and Seema had had numerous icy showers during the week that she had already spent at Tugela Bridge. She stepped under the cold stream and felt goosebumps rise on her skin. After the initial shock of the cold water had worn off, the sensation was not unpleasant. At least it took away the feeling of stickiness that seemed to have clung to her since moving to Tugela Bridge. She had grown up in Durban, so she should have been used to the December heat and humidity, but this summer felt hotter than usual. Perhaps it was because here she was three hours closer to the equator than she usually was. She stepped out of the shower and pulled the towel from the hook on the back of the bathroom door. It was a white hospital-issue towel, with PXH printed in blue on one corner, that she had found in the cupboard when they moved into the apartment a week before. The fabric was rough against her skin as she dried herself and for a moment she imagined herself a patient. She smiled sardonically to herself: the only ward in the hospital that she was fit for was the psychiatric one.

Seema wrapped the towel around her body and stood in front of the cracked enamel basin. Her face, still damp from the shower, stared back at her from the mirror screwed onto the wall above the basin. She opened her make-up bag, which was balanced on the side of the small basin, and applied her foundation and a red *kumkum sindoor* to the centre parting in her hair. Next, she touched her cheekbones with a bronze highlighter and shaded her eyelids with a creamy gold eyeshadow. She took care putting on her make-up. Satesh hated it when she looked less than perfectly groomed. She left her long hair loose. It was still straight from an hour with the straightening iron the previous day. She had taken out her clothes the night before and left them folded neatly on the toilet seat, so that she would not disturb Satesh while getting dressed. She unfolded them now and slipped on the blue satin blouse and tailored black trousers. Even though her outfit was not the most practical for the hospital, she enjoyed wearing it because she knew that Satesh liked her in it. She would put on her white coat, which was hanging ready next to the front door, just before leaving. At least that would protect her clothes from any bloodstains.

After dressing she went through to the lounge-cum-dining-room to the table that, in lieu of a prayer room, she had made her shrine. It was nothing fancy and consisted simply of a small gold statue of the Lord Krishna surrounded by a wreath of flowers and a few incense sticks. She lit a stick of sandalwood incense and offered the Lord Krishna water, milk and a piece of fruit. She rubbed some pure sandalwood oil on his body and then started her quiet chanting. The whole devotion took only twenty minutes, but the sense of peace and comfort that it gave her lasted throughout the day. When they were first married, Satesh had performed *puja* with her every morning, but over the last few months he had slacked and she could not remember when last they had said their prayers together. She had spoken to him about it, because it was something that was important to her and that she considered an integral part of family life, but he had simply snapped at her, telling her to mind her own business and to stop nagging him. It worried her that Satesh, who appeared to be such a strong devotee when they were courting, had so quickly seemed to forsake all the religious rituals that were of such importance to her. She had seen a similar degeneration in other aspects of his behaviour: she had noticed that he had stopped observing any fasts and that he seldom went to the temple with her and her family any more. She had expected that her parents would have at least commented on this, but they seemed determined to ignore the disintegration of his spirituality in much the same way as they seemed to ignore everything else. When she had brought it up with her parents, her mother simply observed that religion is an individual path.

Seema got to the hospital just after seven. She hated being late – the thought that she might have to walk into a room full of doctors and be the centre of their attention filled her with dread – and she cursed the time she had spent perfecting her make-up. But when she arrived at the doctors' office, there were only two other doctors waiting. One was a man she didn't know and the other was Rachael Lipawski, the doctor with whom she had worked the day before. Rachael was leaning on the desk, with her head tilted forward to rest on one fist. Her eyes were closed. Remembering how tired she had been the evening before, after working for only twelve hours during the day, Seema could imagine how exhausted Rachael must be. She walked to the chair nearest to her and started sitting down but then abruptly pulled herself up again, suddenly worried that perhaps the chairs were reserved and she was sitting in the place of a senior doctor. She glanced around the room for a clue as to whether certain chairs were kept aside for specific doctors, but she couldn't find any labels or signs. She hovered above the seat for a moment longer, trying to decide whether it would look stupider for her to get up again or to sit down. Eventually she decided on the latter, purely because her thighs had begun to wobble. The room was starting to fill up with people and she looked down at her feet in order to avoid making eye contact with any of them. She always felt awkward in the company of strangers, especially when in a group. She never knew what protocol was expected of her – whether she should greet the people coming into the room or wait for them to greet her first, or whether a nod was an acceptable form of introduction or if a handshake was required or, even worse, a hug. It was easier to appear busy so she fished a pocket-sized textbook from her bag and pretended to look something up. In the circumstances, reading a medical textbook before a ward round could hardly be construed as being impolite.

From over the top of her book, Seema noticed that Rachael had opened her eyes and lifted her head and was introducing herself to the other doctors as they walked into the room. Seema envied her self-confidence. She made it look so easy and natural, the handshakes and the relaxed smiles. Seema knew that if she did the same thing, she would blush and stammer and probably appear to be trying far too hard (which would, in fact, be true). She looked down at the pages of her book but was too nervous to read: her eyes could make out the individual words but together they made no sense to her. In a few minutes she would be expected to present to all fifteen doctors in the room the patients that she had admitted the day before, and Seema knew that her capabilities as a doctor would largely be determined by what they thought of her presentation. She hoped that she wouldn't stutter, that she would speak loudly enough and her presentations would make sense, and that her patient management would prove correct.

'Right, let's get started.' A gruff voice cut into the din of chatter that filled the doctors' office. 'It's getting late and we all have lots to do, I'm sure.' The man who stood up to speak was tall, with a halo of blond curls and a scruffy, straw-coloured beard. He reminded Seema of pictures of Jesus that, as a child, she had seen in her cousins' illicit Sunday School books. Unlike her own family, who were Hindu, her mother's sister's children had been brought up believing equally in the Church and the fact that their cousins were damned to hell. It was, indirectly, because of Jesus that Seema's visits to her cousin had been surreptitious.

'We usually do a handover round of all the newly admitted patients here,' the Jesus lookalike continued, indicating the doctors' office, 'before we start for the day. It's just a paper round, so we don't actually see the patients themselves. Whoever takes the patient over needs to see and admit the patient properly after the round. I was also asked to remind the new interns that there's an introductory meeting this morning in the seminar room on the second floor at nine bells, so you can go there straight after we finish here. Any questions, anyone?'

Seema saw Rachael raise her arm to catch Jesus' attention. 'I know this is a bit off the point, but can you tell us how the coffee system works? How much do we each need to contribute? Do we pay at the end of every month, or what's the procedure?'

Seema could not believe that Rachael had the audacity to ask about coffee in the middle of a medical meeting in front of a group of doctors that she barely knew. She would never have had the courage (or the stupidity – she didn't know which it was) to ask something so trivial immediately before the start of a ward round. She wondered whether Rachael cared at all about what sort of impression she made. Was she so self-confident that she didn't bother about what the other doctors thought of her? Jesus' response to Rachael was not nearly as angry or critical as Seema expected. He laughed and said that Rachael probably needed a cup of coffee more than anyone else, then told the interns that they would each have to make a monthly thirty-rand contribution to the coffee kitty if they wanted to help themselves to coffee. 'Don't think you get anything free in this hospital,' he laughed, 'except perhaps TB.' He glanced at the call roster stuck to the wall above the doctors' desk. 'Dr Singh,' he said, squinting slightly as he read the name, 'you can start with the patients you admitted yesterday.'

There was a subtle shift in the atmosphere in the room, from light-hearted to crisply business-like. Seema took a piece of paper from her bag, unfolded it and looked down at the list of names of patients that she had admitted the previous day. She had rewritten the list twice the evening before, summarising the salient points relating to each patient in neat handwriting next to the patient's name. She had gone over her presentation so many times that the list had become largely superfluous, something to give her confidence rather than information. She gripped the piece of paper and started talking. 'Mrs Cindi is a fifty-year-old lady with a background of hypertension and diabetes. She presented to casualty in florid congestive cardiac failure.' Out of the corner of her eye she saw one of the other doctors nodding in understanding. Reassured, she continued, 'I treated her with intravenous nitrates and a diuretic and she seemed to stabilise. Her ECG showed significant left ventricular enlargement. I've sent away bloods and requested a chest X-ray.'

A female community service doctor with short, peroxided hair and purple-rimmed spectacles interrupted her. 'Which ward did you admit her to?'

'Medical, G1,' Seema said, glancing down at her piece of paper.

'Okay, I'll take Mrs Cindi over,' the doctor said, writing the patient's name in a file.

Seema had presented her first patient successfully; none of the doctors in the room had criticised or questioned either her diagnosis or management. She felt more confident moving on to her second patient. Although she was shy and dreaded having to talk in front of a group of people, she actually liked the orderliness and logic of presenting cases. She wished that all aspects of her life were as neat and rational as medicine. It would make things so easy if she were able to sum up her marriage as elegantly as she summed up a case history. How would she start? Seema Maharaj, a young and innocent twenty-one-year-old girl, met her future husband, thirty-year-old Satesh Singh, through a business associate of her father's. After a whirlwind romance, during which the dashing Satesh charmed Seema with chocolates, roses and jewellery and her parents with family connections and pretences of devotion, they were married. Of course, had Seema come from a less conservative family, and had her parents been slightly less obsessed with preventing their daughter from losing her virginity before marriage, Seema and Satesh might not have been forced so quickly into marriage, thus circumventing the tearing apart and eventual collapse of Seema's heart. But Seema's parents believed in protecting the family honour at all costs (including that of their daughter's happiness), and so Satesh and Seema were united in a glittering red-and-gold ceremony at the Shree Siva Subramanium Alayam Temple in front of eight hundred and fifty people and sixty pots of vegetable pilau. The beginning of the changes in Satesh could probably be traced back to the wedding night, on which he failed to consummate the marriage because he got too attached to the ample-busted croupier at the blackjack table of the casino in their honeymoon hotel.

Seema struggled to go on from there because that was the point at which all the logic in her life seemed to have started unravelling. Behaviour that seemed to please her husband on one day caused him to throw plates across the kitchen on another. Clothes that he bought her for a certain occasion he would shred to pieces on another. Her parents, who had protected her so vigilantly for her whole life, seemed suddenly blind to her swollen lips and new clumsiness. The biggest difference, though, between Seema's life and the case histories that she presented was that, no matter how puzzling and illogical the medical cases were, Seema always had an idea of how they would eventually turn out. How hers would end was still a complete mystery.

The name 'seminar room', Seema realised as she sat down for the intern introductory meeting, was misleadingly optimistic. In fact, the room in which she and the other interns had gathered could not easily be summed up in only two words. It should probably be classified somewhere between infrequently used classroom (because of the old desks and the smell of chalk and the cracked overhead projector), storeroom (because of the stack of rusty bedpans and the pile of outdated patient files) and theme-park ghost house (because of the spider webs and the layers of dust and the chipped model skull acting as a pen holder on the front table). Apparently this was the room in which all the hospital meetings – the morbidity and mortality meetings, the radiology meetings, the combined surgical disciplines meetings and the internal medicine meetings – were held. Seema chose to sit down on a chair in the middle of the third row of seats, because she didn't want to seem too keen by sitting in the front or too nonchalant by sitting at the back. The middle was a good compromise and Seema had learnt to become good at compromising. It was the way she handled most decisions.

Seema saw Rachael sit down in the front row and immediately strike up a conversation with the intern sitting next to her. Again, she marvelled at Rachael's self-confidence. Seema was too shy even to look at the doctors that had taken the seats on either side of her (all she knew about them was that the one on her right was wearing blue jeans and the one on her left smelt of onion). Instead, she pretended to study the forms that she had been handed as she walked into the seminar room.

'Good morning, everybody, and welcome,' a female voice said, forcing Seema to look up. The woman standing in the front of the room appeared to be about forty. She was slight and had short black hair cropped close to her head. Her voice, even though it was gentle, carried enough authority to silence the room immediately. 'I'm Dr Chetty,' she introduced herself, 'and along with Dr Ribbentrop,' she pointed to a large, square-jawed man, 'and Dr Zamla, who isn't here today, am a senior medical officer. We'll work alongside you and provide you with any assistance you may require during the year. I'm confident that you'll also learn a lot from the community service doctors and medical officers who will be your colleagues for the next year.'

'Prince Xoliswe Hospital is a two-hundred-and-twenty-bed hospital,' she continued, 'and is understaffed, like most of the hospitals in our country. The key to your enjoying your intern year is teamwork. There's no single doctor who can take the place of the staff that the hospital can't afford to employ, but if we all pull our weight, we can lighten the load for everyone.' She went on to give them a rundown of how the hospital functioned, who was in charge of what and what was expected of them as interns. 'I hope you have a productive year and that you all leave here better doctors. I'm not going to lie to you: it will be a difficult year and there will be many times that you feel like giving up, but if you put the effort in and grab at every opportunity to learn, you'll leave here as competent and experienced doctors able to work with the best in the world.'

Dr Chetty's words left Seema feeling inspired. It was not just that Dr Chetty was, like her, an Indian woman. Behind Dr Chetty's words, Seema sensed a passion for medicine that matched her own. She realised that she was stupid to be drawing this conclusion, because she had only heard Dr Chetty speak for ten minutes, but somehow she felt as though she had met a kindred spirit. She knew, immediately, that she would be happy if she were in Dr Chetty's place in fifteen years. It was almost as though she had been allowed a glimpse, a visual snapshot, of her destiny. The only problem was that she knew that her becoming a senior doctor in some rural hospital didn't feature even momentarily in Satesh's plans for the future.

Dr Chetty had resumed speaking and Seema brought her attention back to the present. 'I was expecting the superintendent to come and talk to you,' she said, 'but she doesn't seem to have been able to make it …' Her words were interrupted by the opportunely timed entrance of a short, heavyset woman. She was wearing a bright green dress and had on matching green plastic triangle earrings. The rims of her spectacles were bedecked with rows of artificial diamonds. She wiped a drop of sweat from her brow with a green checked handkerchief as she took Dr Chetty's place.

'Hello, everybody, welcome, welcome!' she shouted, nodding at the seated interns. 'I am Mrs Hlope, superintendent of this hospital. I would just like to say what a privilege you have to be here this year. We expect only two things of you: to work hard and to be on time. Lateness and laziness are the devil's tools. Please, if you have any problems you are not to bother me directly. You are to contact my secretary and she will help you. I am a very busy lady, running this hospital, and I do not have time to deal with the problems of junior doctors.'

Mrs Hlope continued talking for half an hour, expounding the virtues of the hospital and the Department of Health. If Seema had not suspected differently, she would have been heartened to hear that the hospital was running on a full staff complement and that HIV and TB were not significant problems in the area and that the Department of Health was confident that first-class healthcare was now accessible to all. Earlier, Seema had overheard one of the other interns saying that the superintendent had previously been a typist at the hospital and that she had got the job of superintendent because of a family connection. At the time Seema had thought that was probably just a rumour, but the more she listened to the woman speak, the more she could believe that there was some truth behind the claim. Seema found it odd that the superintendent of the hospital was neither a doctor nor a nursing sister. It didn't make sense that the person who made all the major decisions regarding the running of the hospital didn't actually have any clinical experience.

4

Satesh was playing games on his laptop on the bed when Seema arrived home from the hospital. He didn't look up from the computer as she put her bag down and then walked across the bedroom to greet him. The room was dim, the curtains still drawn, and the light emitted from the laptop screen cast a flickering blue reflection on his face that emphasised the sharp angularity of his bone structure. Seema bent over him and kissed the top of his head softly.

'You're in a good mood,' he said without taking his eyes from the red racing car that was whizzing around the screen. Watching it made Seema feel nauseous. She turned away from the computer and her vertigo subsided. She *was* in a good mood. Earlier in the day, she had found out that she had been placed in the medical ward for the first half of the year, a placement she had prayed for because she was considering specialising in internal medicine once she completed her community service. The community service doctor with whom she was working – Eliza Engelbrecht, the wife of the Jesus lookalike – seemed like a kind person and was certainly knowledgeable. Seema was grateful that she would be working under someone from whom she could learn. Already Eliza had taken the time to show Seema how to place a chest drain properly.

Seema walked across the bedroom to the window. It was past five o'clock, but the curtains looked as though they had not yet been opened and Seema wondered whether Satesh had spent the entire day lounging on the bed in front of his laptop playing computer games. Even though it was already dusk, the time at which curtains are usually drawn, she flung hers open. The last few rays of sunlight filtered through the dusty glass panes, unsettling the stale lethargy of the room. Seema pushed open the window and took a deep breath. The air smelt of afternoon thunderstorm and damp earth. She took another breath and another, until she was light-headed. She hadn't known of the existence of Tugela Bridge before she had received her internship call-up, so it perplexed her that she felt the same kind of relief and contentment being there that one feels on arriving home after a long and difficult journey. Perhaps it had more to do with the job than with the place. Perhaps her vocation was her home.

'So, are you going to tell me why you're in such a good mood or must I drag it out of you?' Satesh demanded, interrupting her reverie. Usually Seema would not have bothered to try to explain to her husband why she was in a particular mood (she had learnt that he didn't actually care what she said, and that usually he had already formulated his own theories as to the cause of her state of being), but perhaps the after-storm electricity in the air had unwired her thinking: she told him about her day.

'Are you sick or something?' he asked her after she described to him how Eliza had shown her the correct method of placing a chest drain. 'How can something like that put you in a good mood? It's disgusting. No normal person would find that exciting. Either you're some kind of sick pervert or there's something else that put you in a good mood that you're not telling me about.'

Seema opened her mouth to protest but then shut it again without saying anything. Arguing with Satesh would be certain to cause a further deterioration in her already rapidly dampening good mood. She left the room, using the excuse that she was thirsty, and went to the kitchen to make a cup of tea. She would try to eke out her remaining happiness for five minutes more before starting supper. The kettle had just finished boiling when Satesh walked into the kitchen, startling Seema. His computer was still on and, deafened by the droning of racing cars and the roar of the kettle boiling, Seema hadn't heard him come into the room.

'So, aren't you going to ask me how my day was?' he asked. 'Or is my day not important because I'm not a doctor?' Seema concentrated on keeping the hand that was pouring hot water into her cup steady. She recognised the passive-aggressive tone of his voice, knew all too well the direction that the conversation was taking.

'Of course your day is important,' she said, trying to keep her voice light, as though she was discussing the weather with him or commenting on how quickly the year had passed, as though she had missed the tension and bitterness that underlay his question. 'What did you do?'

'Do you actually care what I did? It's not like I put in any fancy drains.'

'Satesh, of course I care about what you did today. You know that. Anyway, I'm sure your day was far more interesting than mine. Please tell me what you did,' she begged. She felt as though she was trying to placate a petulant child. The only difference was that if she were talking to a child, she wouldn't be constantly worrying about whether or not she was saying the wrong thing, about whether or not the next word from her mouth would be the spark that would create an explosion.

'Well, it's not like there's a lot to do in this shit hole. I'm not exactly spoilt for choice.'

'I'm sorry,' Seema said. 'I know it's my fault you're here and I'm really, really sorry. I am. If I could have chosen where to do my internship, I would never have chosen Tugela Bridge. I know it's incredibly difficult and I'm eternally grateful that you agreed to come here with me. I don't think you know how appreciative I am.' She hoped that her words would pacify him, that her apparent guilt would compensate for her earlier happiness.

'You'd better not forget how much I've sacrificed for you by coming to this place,' he grumbled. But her ploy seemed to have worked. He walked back to his laptop muttering under his breath. Seema breathed a silent sigh of relief and started taking out the ingredients for the spinach and lentil curry she planned on cooking for dinner. She couldn't drink her tea now. It, like her happiness, had become bitter and spoilt.

Seema was mistaken in thinking that Satesh had forgotten their earlier conversation. He brought it up again later, when they went to bed that evening.

'Well, at least one of us has job satisfaction,' he said. Seema tried to point out to him that since she had only been working for a couple of days, her good mood could hardly qualify as job satisfaction.

'Do you have any idea how boring it is sitting in this crappy flat all day long?' Satesh responded. Seema didn't answer, although she could have. She could think of a long list of things that she would have liked to say to Satesh: firstly, it had been his choice to come with her and nobody had forced him into the decision; secondly, she was supporting him completely financially, so he hardly had reason to complain; thirdly, he had never, since she had met him, had job satisfaction; and fourthly, it was hardly mature behaviour to be spiteful to her simply because she found her job fulfilling. But instead of saying these things, Seema kept silent. A year ago, she would probably have answered Satesh back, but she no longer had the energy to fight with him. She switched off her bedside light and curled up into the foetal position before falling asleep.

As Seema entered the hospital the following morning, a chorus of beautiful, haunting voices floated past her and escaped through the partially open sliding doors into the already warm morning air. She followed the sound down the corridor, interested to find its origin. She didn't usually associate hospitals with chanting, but that was what the music sounded like: a myriad of voices raised in praise. As she got closer to casualty, the singing got louder and soon she was able to pick out individual voices that leapt out from the harmony of the group. The sound echoed through the dirty hospital corridor, bouncing off the drab, peeling walls and bloodstained floors, and seemed, for a moment, to transform them into something a little less sordid. It was as though a spirit was rushing past her, moving her, filling her with something bigger than herself. She didn't want the music to end but it did, just as she entered casualty. She wasn't too late to see who had been singing, though. Gathered in the centre of the casualty unit, between beds holding broken bodies, was a group of about sixty people comprising staff nurses, sisters, porters and cleaning staff. As Seema watched, the assembly began to break up. Sisters collected their handbags and waved goodbyes, a staff nurse handed a porter a tin of instant coffee, a man in bloodstained overalls picked up a mop and squeezed it into a bucket of filthy water.

'They sing at every shift changeover,' a voice said from behind her. Seema turned around to face one of the medical officers. He was a short, squat man with a bald head. He spoke with a French accent and Seema wondered which of the ex-colonial African countries he was from.

'It's beautiful,' she said.

The doctor opposite her shrugged his shoulders noncommittally in response. 'Sometimes it's a waste of time,' he muttered. 'Just wait and see when you have an emergency that you need to have some help with and these sisters refuse to help you until they have finished singing their little hymns. You see when your patient dies, then you see how beautiful it is.'

Seema wanted to argue with him. She wanted to describe to him how, for a moment as she was walking in, the music had transformed the hospital. She wanted to convince him that it must be good for patients on some level, that even if it didn't change their physical conditions it must uplift them emotionally and that must have some benefit. But he had already turned away and was walking briskly to the doctors' office and she was too shy to follow him and offer her opinion.

Seema struggled to concentrate during the handover round. Usually she was good at pushing aside the intricacies of her personal life in order to concentrate on work, but today she was unable to rid her mind of the image of Satesh sitting in front of his laptop in the stuffy, half-lit bedroom chasing a red racing car around the screen. She felt guilty that she was so happy (so excessively, maniacally happy) at work while he sat around bored in a poky doctors' quarters apartment. As much as she tried to rationalise it and make excuses for the situation, it was her fault that he was stuck in a small rural town with nothing to do all day. The logical side to her knew that Satesh needn't be doing nothing – he could be studying something or working from home (he was on the computer all day anyway) – but her heart knew that this would be unreasonable to expect from Satesh. He didn't have that type of motivation, had never pretended to, and she knew that. She felt a sudden pain in her chest, an aching, inconsolable tearing that spread up her throat and threatened to choke her. Where had everything gone so wrong, she wondered? How much of it was due to her selfishness, her absolute obsession with medicine? She hoped that it wasn't too late to change things. Seema had grown up with a mother that righted all the injustices in the world with food, so she decided to spoil Satesh in the way that she knew best: she would make him his favourite curry for dinner, a proper lamb curry made the way her mother and her grandmother made curries. She knew that it would not atone for everything, but at least it would remind Satesh that she did actually care about him.

Seema was so intent on planning the curry for Satesh that she only realised that the handover round had finished when the other doctors started standing up and heading towards the door. She picked up her bag, berating herself for her lapse in concentration. Doctors dealt with people's lives, she reminded herself; wives didn't. As important as her marriage was, she refused to let it make her any less of a doctor. She caught up with Eliza Engelbrecht and walked behind her to the medical ward.

Eliza quickly divided the new admissions that had to be seen between herself and Seema. 'Give me a shout if you need any help or have any questions or anything,' Eliza said to Seema as she walked off. Seema thanked her and went to the bedside of her first patient. Again, she rebuked herself for not having concentrated during the handover round. Had she been listening, she would have known what her patient, Mr Ferreira, had been admitted with and what his history was, but because she hadn't, she would now have to ask him all those questions herself and it would take twice as long to see him.

She introduced herself as Dr Singh and asked Mr Ferreira why he had come to hospital. Mr Ferreira told her that he had gone to his GP for a general check-up, the first in many years (twelve years, to be exact; he was proud of the figure), and the GP had suggested some routine blood tests. Mr Ferreira had got a call from his doctor the following day and was told that there had been some abnormalities in his blood results and that he should see a specialist as soon as possible. He had come to Prince Xoliswe Hospital because he had no medical aid and couldn't afford to see a specialist privately.

Seema looked through the patient's file as he spoke, in search of a copy of the offending blood results. She had to stop herself from gasping out loud when she found them. Mr Ferreira's white cell count was seventy-eight thousand. The upper limit of normal was usually around ten thousand. Seema had never seen such a high white cell count and she wondered whether there had been a mistake in the analysis or a printing error in the report. She looked at the admitting doctor's notes to double-check the finding. There had been no mistake. The count was correct; the patient had a suspected leukaemia. He was fifty-one years old.

'And how are you feeling today?' Seema asked the patient. She didn't really know what else to say because she had no idea whether Mr Ferreira knew what his diagnosis was.

'I'm feeling great, Doc. Never felt better. You gonna let me go home this morning?' he chirped.

Seema's heart sank. Quite obviously nobody had told him his diagnosis yet. She looked down at the blood results again, stalling for time, trying to figure out how to break the news to him. She wished Mr Ferreira felt sicker because that, at least, would have given him some idea of his prognosis. She decided to examine him before telling him what was wrong. It would give her a little more time to decide what to say. They had had lectures at medical school on how to give a patient bad news. They had even been tested on it in one of their family medicine exams. In one of the testing stations in a clinical evaluation exam, a sister had pretended to be a patient with HIV. They had been marked on how delicately they informed the 'patient' of her diagnosis. Seema had passed with flying colours, but she had known that the patient was really a nursing sister who was getting paid a hundred rand to act as a patient for the day. And she had known exactly what the examiners wanted to hear. This was different. The patient was real, with a potentially fatal disease. There were no examiners listening behind a two-way mirror. Nobody would give her flying colours for the information she would impart today.

Seema washed her hands and started a general exam on Mr Ferreira. She looked at the whites of his eyes to see if he was jaundiced, at his conjunctiva to see if he was pale. She felt his neck for lymph nodes. There was a large one just above his clavicle. It had the consistency of a shelled hard-boiled egg. She looked at Mr Ferreira's hands and nails, searching for signs of chronic disease or kidney failure. She pushed her index finger onto the front of his shin bone to feel for swelling of his ankles and legs.

Next, she examined his heart and chest. Both his cardiovascular and respiratory systems were normal. She felt his abdomen, gently palpating it with the tips of her fingers. He had a massively enlarged spleen and liver. Her expression must have revealed her concern over her findings because, as she withdrew her hands from Mr Ferreira's abdomen, he asked her if everything was okay.

'Not really,' she answered. 'Your spleen and liver are a lot bigger than they should be.'

'Oh dear,' he laughed. 'My wife always told me whisky would kill me. Liver damage is from alcohol, isn't it? I have a tot or two every evening before dinner.' He smiled at Seema. 'I'll have to tell her she's right, again. You know, we've been married thirty years, and with each year that passes she seems to know more.' He chuckled, more to himself than to Seema. 'I should have learnt to listen to her years ago. Would have saved me a whole lot of trouble.'

Seema couldn't help wondering whether Satesh spoke as fondly about her when she wasn't around. Would he tell people, after thirty years together, that Seema always knew best? She doubted it. Perhaps fondness was something that grew with familiarity, something they would acquire in years to come.

'So, what's up with my liver, Doc?' Mr Ferreira asked, bringing her thoughts back to the present. She had to tell him.

'Your liver isn't really the cause of your problems,' she explained softly. 'The real problem is with your blood. Your body is making too many blood cells. The reason your liver and spleen are enlarged is that the cells are getting caught up there.' She chose her words carefully. It felt as though she were walking on the edge of a precipice: one wrong word and she would tumble irrevocably downwards, dragging Mr Ferreira with her. 'The white blood cells that your body is producing are abnormal,' she continued. 'They concern me because they can be produced in certain malignancies.'

'You have to speak English or Afrikaans, Doc,' Mr Ferreira said. 'I'm fully bilingual but I don't understand all those fancy medical words.'

'Of course, sorry,' Seema said. She knew that she had been hiding behind the distance that the medical jargon provided. It was conveniently impersonal, a useful façade. But she realised that she would have to drop it. 'I'm worried you might have a type of blood cancer.' She laid the words bare on the bed between them, dealt with apology, like an unexpected hand of cards.

'Cancer?' Mr Ferreira asked, avoiding Seema's eyes. 'There must be a mistake. You must have made a mistake. Maybe they mixed up the blood tests. I feel fine. Don't people have to feel sick with cancer?'

Seema explained that it was unlikely that the blood results were incorrect and that her clinical exam had confirmed the findings. She told him that the next step would be a bone marrow biopsy.

'A bone what-a-what?' he asked her.

She explained that they would need to drill into one of his bones to take a sample of the marrow in order to diagnose what type of blood cancer he had. She told him that they would send him to a hospital in Durban to do the procedure, because he would need to be started on chemotherapy as soon as possible and they didn't give chemo at Prince Xoliswe.

'So you're that sure it's a cancer then?' he asked softly. 'You wouldn't do that if you weren't sure, would you?' He folded his hands on the bedcover. It was an act of resignation, piteous in its finality. 'I'll have to let my wife know,' Mr Ferreira said, retrieving a cellphone from the drawer next to his bed. 'Would you mind telling her? I don't know what to say.' He handed the phone to Seema. And so Seema broke bad news for the second time that day. Unlike other things, it didn't seem to get easier with repetition.

Seema left the hospital at five o'clock, after finishing her ward work, and drove directly to the supermarket to get the ingredients she needed for the curry. She thought about Mr Ferreira the whole way to the shop. It was almost incomprehensible to her that, three days before, he had been happy in the certainty that he was healthy. His life paradigm hadn't included hospital admissions or cancer or chemotherapy. Three days before, Mrs Ferreira had probably taken her husband's existence for granted. The realisation made Seema glad that she had decided to make Satesh a special curry. She parked her black hatchback beneath the shade of a large avocado tree (even though it was already late afternoon, the sun was still vicious) and walked to the entrance of the supermarket.

Seema loosened a basket from the top of the stack next to the door and went into the shop. She had only shopped there once since moving to Tugela Bridge and the aisles were still unfamiliar. She looked for the meat section and selected a pack of lamb knuckles. Seema was vegetarian but Satesh wasn't, so she had learnt to cook meat after they got married. Even so, choosing a cut of meat still felt foreign to her and she had no idea if the quality of the meat she had selected was good or poor. Next she made her way to the fruit and vegetable section and picked two ripe tomatoes and a bunch of fresh dhania. The scent of the coriander leaves, crushed against the red plastic side of the basket, transported her immediately back to her mother's kitchen. All at once she missed home. It was not a simple longing for a place, but a yearning for a different time in her life: a time that had been safe and sheltered and predictable. She turned her attention back to her shopping. It was futile thinking of the past. She added a bunch of bananas and an onion to the basket and then walked down the next aisle in search of a tub of plain yoghurt. She picked out a few other staples to last her and Satesh through the remainder of the week and then, before going to the check-out counter, made her way to the sweets section and chose the darkest slab of chocolate she could find. It was a secret that her mother had taught her, to add four pieces of dark chocolate to a curry right at the end. 'It will make your curry irresistible,' her mother had assured her, 'and no man can resist a woman who makes an irresistible curry.' Seema hoped that her mother was right.

Satesh was not at home when Seema arrived back from the supermarket, which was good. At least he had not spent the whole day cooped up in a stuffy room again. She didn't bother to change out of her work clothes but went straight to the kitchen to start cooking. The sooner she could get the curry made, the longer the flavours would have to infuse before she served it. She put some oil in a frying pan and then opened the *masala dabba* that her mother had given her as one of her wedding gifts. The scent of coriander and fennel seeds, of curry and lime leaves, of cardamom and cinnamon, of whole black peppercorns and turmeric, escaped from the stainless steel tin as she lifted the lid. It was a comfortingly familiar smell; a smell integral to her very first memories; a smell that was imprinted permanently on her limbic system. She used a miniature pewter teaspoon to transfer a portion of the spices to a porcelain pestle and then crushed and blended them with the mortar.

Once the oil in the pan had heated up, she added the chopped onion, some crushed garlic and then the wet *masala* paste and the mixed spices. The lamb knuckles wept slightly as she removed the film of plastic cling-wrap that covered them, leaving a trail of diluted blood on her fingers. She quickly tipped the pieces of meat into the sizzling oil and washed her hands. She knew that she should have trimmed some of the fat off the knuckles before browning them, but she couldn't bear working with uncooked flesh: she hated its slightly springy touch, as though some part of it was still alive, and its raw, bloody smell made her nauseous. The oil spluttered and hissed as she turned the knuckles over in the saucepan. She wiped her eyes, which had started to water, and turned the pieces of meat over again. Soon the kitchen was murky with an astringent, chilli-infused smoke. Seema opened a window and went back to the meat, trying not to inhale too deeply.

Once the meat had browned, she added the other ingredients: the skinless, pulped fresh tomatoes, the caramelised onion, the yoghurt and, lastly, the chocolate. Then she left the curry to simmer on a low heat until the smell of it filled the small doctors' quarters flat and wafted out through the open window into the heavy, humid, early evening air.

Satesh was still not home and Seema had begun to worry about where he was. There wasn't much to do in Tugela Bridge – there was no cinema so he couldn't be watching movies and she and Satesh had no family or friends to visit – so it was unusual that Satesh was out so late. She was on the verge of phoning him when she remembered that he had mentioned wanting to join the soccer club. He was probably playing soccer, in which case he wouldn't answer his phone anyway. She decided to wait another half an hour before trying to call him; Satesh got irritated with her whenever she phoned to find out where he was.

She went to the bedroom to get changed into clean clothes. A while ago she had bought herself a lacy black lingerie set, which she had not yet worn because she hadn't had the right opportunity, but she decided to put it on now. Compared with the soft cotton of the underwear that she usually wore, the lace felt rough against her skin and the bra, which was padded, pushed her small breasts up and made them unfamiliarly full. The underwear was hardly comfortable but she thought that Satesh would like it. She knew from the adult magazines that he read (when they first got married he had tried to keep them hidden from her, but with time he had become careless and now he read them unashamedly in front of her) that he liked big, bouncy-breasted women. Seema wished she could see what she looked like, if her breasts compared with the silicone ones, but the only mirror in the flat was the small, square one on the bathroom wall. It would have to do. She looked at the upper half of her body first (her unusually perky breasts filled the mirror), and then climbed onto the basin to see what the lower half of her body looked like. It was difficult to assemble the images, but she imagined that she looked like Satesh's fantasies. She put on some jeans and a T-shirt, and the underwear was at once hidden, a secret wrapped around her almost as closely as her skin. She smiled to herself as she went to the dining room to set the table: she couldn't wait to see Satesh's reaction when she took the jeans and shirt off.

She had just finished laying the table when she heard her husband's step outside the door. Quickly she lit the two candles that she had placed in the centre of the table. Seema didn't need to see Satesh's face to know that he was in a foul mood when he entered the flat. She had learnt to become hyperaware of the nuances of his temperament; so much depended on them. He threw his keys down as he came inside and then went straight to the bedroom without a word of greeting to her. After a few minutes she heard the cupboard door slamming and she presumed that he must be changing. Eventually, after what seemed like an age to Seema, waiting between wilting candles, he came into the lounge, sat down on a beanbag in front of the television set and turned it on without saying a word to her. He couldn't not have smelt the curry, not have seen the table, so carefully set, alight with desperate romance.

Fifteen minutes passed – a slow, too-quiet fifteen minutes that niggled at Seema until she could bear it no longer. The studied silence was worse than any shouting.

'How was your day?' she asked Satesh eventually, sitting down on the floor next to the beanbag. The forced nonchalance of her tone made her voice sound false. What she hated most was the inconsistency, that she had no idea whether Satesh would scream at her, ignore her or answer her quite politely and carry on as though everything was normal. She thought that she could almost handle the screaming and shouting if only he did it consistently.

'Where were you this afternoon?' Satesh asked, not taking his eyes off the television screen.

'At work,' Seema replied, surprised. Satesh knew that she had been at the hospital.

'Interesting, because when I called the medical ward at five the nursing sister said you had already left.'

Seema felt her hands clench into fists. It was an almost involuntary action, as though her body had become so habituated to suppressing frustration and anger that she didn't even feel the emotions any more. They simply manifested themselves in a physical way, in the clenching of her jaw and the scrunching up of her fingers, in red nail imprints on the soft inner surface of her palms. She had believed, stupidly, when Satesh first started checking up on her that, with time, his trust would increase and the interrogations and sly pursuits would diminish. Instead the opposite had happened.

'I left the hospital at five and went straight to the supermarket to get some groceries. I hope I'm allowed to do that, or would you rather do your own grocery shopping?' Seema asked acerbically. On the table behind them the candles were melting down from elegant pillars to deformed lumps. Satesh ignored her question and changed television channels. Seema picked at a thread that was unravelling from the seam in the beanbag. She held her tongue because she didn't want to end up fighting with Satesh. She had put so much effort into the evening: she so wanted things to go right for once. Eventually Satesh spoke again.

'What's for dinner?' he asked.

'I made you a lamb curry. That's one of the reasons I had to go to the supermarket,' Seema answered quietly.

'Well, make yourself useful for a change and dish me up a bowl,' Satesh ordered. 'I'm starving.'

'I thought that maybe we could sit at the dinner table. I thought it might be nice to spend some proper time together,' Seema suggested. Satesh glanced at the table. Suddenly it appeared sad to Seema: sorry, wilted and pathetic. The candles moped in their flickering light. The hospital-issue crockery looked cheap and dirty, and the folded linen serviettes, so carefully ironed, gave the appearance of trying far too hard. 'Don't worry,' she said quickly, before Satesh could respond. 'We can eat here, in front of the TV, like we usually do.' She went through to the kitchen and dished up a bowl of curry and basmati rice for Satesh. Earlier, she had filled ramekins with sliced banana and desiccated coconut and chopped dhania, but they looked stupid and over-the-top for a television meal so she left them behind in the kitchen. She dished a bowl of plain rice for herself and went back to the lounge.

Satesh ate just three spoonfuls of his curry before throwing the bowl down. The thick porcelain cracked into two pieces; curry seeped onto the green linoleum floor.

'God!' Satesh said, getting up. His face was contorted with disgust and Seema couldn't help feeling that it was directed at her and not the curry. 'Didn't your mother teach you how to cook a curry? And you call yourself a wife!' He picked up his keys and stormed out of the flat, slamming the door shut behind him. Seema sat completely still. The crack of the smashing china had frozen her. The bones that had been spilt, which lay shuddering in pools of thick, oily grease, were her bones. She sat until the candles had burnt down completely and the room was left in darkness.

Satesh arrived home again an hour later. From the bed, where she was lying awake in her nightdress (she had carefully refolded the lacy underwear and hidden it at the back of her cupboard), Seema heard him come in and turn on the television. The next morning she found the packaging of the chicken takeaway that he had had for dinner, scrunched up next to the beanbag. He hadn't bothered to throw it away.

Nomsa

5

Nomsa carefully drew in neat kohl arches where she had waxed off her naturally thick eyebrows. She brushed the apples of her cheeks with rose-pink rouge and glided a frosted mocha gloss over her lips. She leant closer to the mirror to check the joins of her hair extensions, where the beautifully straight artificial nylon of the extensions was attached to the short roots of her own curly hair. She wished that she had a better mirror than the one hanging on the toilet wall of her prefab; this one was so stained and tarnished that she could hardly distinguish what was blemish on the mirror and what belonged to her reflection. She had had the extensions done only a week before, so she presumed, even though she couldn't visualise them properly, that they were still fine. She imagined that the rest of her looked good (she couldn't see below her neck in the small square mirror). She was wearing tight Levi jeans, a red leather jacket and high, shiny red peep-toe shoes. She twisted around and glanced one last time at her blotchy reflection as she walked out of the bathroom. A little girl winked back at her, a girl dusty with the red soil of Aliwal North, wearing oversized second-hand clothes and with hair braided too tightly into green ribbons. Nomsa quickly turned away, cursing. Tonight was an important night. She wanted to be self-assured, to ooze confidence and class, not to look like a charity case from the Eastern Cape. She clenched her fists in frustration. Every time she thought she had risen above her past, it appeared in some unexpected corner, taunting her, bringing an unwelcome reminder of who she really was. It was as though her ancestors were mocking her: *You will never be able to get rid of us, as hard as you might try to deny our existence,* the voices said. Well, she would show them that they were wrong. As though to prove her point, she turned back defiantly to the mirror, challenging the spirit of her past to appear again. It didn't and she smiled. But it was a hollow smile, a smile of self-reassurance rather than of victory.

Nomsa picked up her car keys from the small bedside table and walked outside. Because she had managed to get through most of medical school on scholarships and Mrs Watson's generosity, a large proportion of her student loan had remained unused. At the end of her final year, she decided to buy herself a car with the remaining money because the interest rate on the student loan was significantly lower than that on a motor plan. She knew that buying an expensive car was probably not the most intelligent investment option she could have made, but she had bought it anyway. And she didn't regret it, not for one minute. When she was sitting behind the wheel of her metallic grey BMW, she was untouchable. Her car symbolised the realisation of so many dreams, her reward for hours and hours of hard work and planning. It reminded her that she would never go back, that she would never land up like her mother, living hand-to-mouth in a squalid hut on the outskirts of a small Eastern Cape town, eking out a survival on mealies, beans and sorghum, her only assets an emaciated goat and a couple of scrawny chickens.

Nomsa started the engine and made her way to the Clay Oven. Since it was the only restaurant in Tugela Bridge, it was hardly difficult to find. One of the community service doctors had organised a social at the restaurant to welcome the new interns and Nomsa couldn't help wondering which of the other doctors would be there. As she pulled up outside the restaurant to park, she was glad to see Rachael sitting at one of the wooden trestle tables on the outside deck. Rachael lived in the prefab adjacent to Nomsa and they had chatted to each other a few times. Nomsa usually trusted her instinct when she formed an opinion of strangers and her first impression of Rachael had been positive. She seemed to be a warm, friendly person and she obviously came from a well-off family: almost every item of clothing she wore displayed a significantly insignificant designer label. As Nomsa got out of her car, Rachael beckoned to her and slid along the bench on which she was sitting to make a place for Nomsa next to her.

'Hi, I'm so glad you decided to come,' Rachael said as Nomsa sat down. She leant over and hugged Nomsa, as though they were already friends. 'I thought you were going to let me down and leave me alone with this bunch of hooligans.'

Rachael's welcome immediately made Nomsa feel less self-conscious. That Rachael identified herself with Nomsa in front of the other doctors, that she showed such public acceptance of her, meant a lot to Nomsa. Rachael was sipping on a pink cocktail and Nomsa ordered herself a whisky-and-Appletiser as she sat down. She took a deep sip of the honey-coloured drink, hoping the ambrosia would magically make her insecurities disappear.

The Clay Oven was a simple, rustic restaurant. The walls were painted an earthy orange, so that it looked almost as if they had been smeared with Natal mud, and the floor was made of slatted wood. An Italian flag had been pinned up above the outside bar and a miniature rubber model of a naked man sitting on a toilet graced the bar counter. Intermittently and, as far as Nomsa could make out, randomly, it would light up and belch forth an Italian folk song. And every time the song ended, everyone in the restaurant would stop whatever he or she was doing and clap three times and then lift his or her glass while shouting cheers. It made no sense to Nomsa but, after the third time the song played, she found herself doing the same. Inside the restaurant, there were proper tables decked with red-checked tablecloths, but on the outside deck the seating consisted of wooden trestles and benches. The menu was handwritten on a large, wall-mounted chalkboard above the bar. Condiments – salt, pepper, bright red tomato sauce and a darker red chilli sauce – were packed into wire baskets placed at the centre of each trestle table.

Of the doctors sitting round the table, Nomsa knew Nathan and Eliza Engelbrecht, Shane Pillay (the community service doctor under whom she would be working in surgery for the next six months), Andries Hendricks (another of the interns doing surgery, who also came from Cape Town) and Rachael. Some of the other faces were familiar, if not identifiable, to her, and others were completely unfamiliar. She noticed that the doctors sitting round the table – excluding the interns – seemed to have a very close bond. They shared private jokes, trod upon each other's personal lives and blurted out secrets almost in the way that the members of a large family would. Nomsa wondered if that intimacy came from working so closely together, often under very adverse circumstances. She had once read a newspaper article explaining why initiation rites, although they had been officially banned, still took place secretly at many schools and universities. The explanation had been that, in forcing a group of strangers to undergo hardship together, they not only derived a sense of common purpose but also formed an identity as a group.

Nomsa's feelings around initiation rites were mixed. She remembered the ceremonies from her childhood; they had formed a pivotal part of community life. They had defined men from boys, created order and social structure. *Khwetha* had been accepted and awaited in the same way that summer or winter had been expected. She had memories of the boys of her childhood disappearing for months, of goats being slaughtered on their departure and again on their return, of celebrations overflowing with beer and meat and dancing that had marked the young men's transition from boyhood to manhood. But they remained exactly that: childhood memories. She had left Aliwal North at the age of twelve, to attend a semi-private boarding school in Cape Town, and throughout high school she had returned home only during the annual December holidays. Unlike her younger sister, Noluthando, who had grown up in Aliwal North, she had never undergone *intonjane*. Her sister had told her a little bit about the initiation and what it entailed: that she had been taken to stay with her mother's aunt, who had been chosen to teach her the role of a woman; that she had been secluded in a hut for seven days and, on the seventh day, after she had been advised by all the elders on the significance of the custom, there had been the slaughtering of a sheep and the sweepings from her hut had been burnt. But Noluthando had been evasive when Nomsa asked her further questions. She had avoided going into any real detail

58

and Nomsa knew that it was because she was wary of divulging too much information about the sacred ritual to one who had not been initiated.

Initially, when Nomsa was a teenager going back to Aliwal North for the brief Christmas breaks, she had felt deprived in some way, as though she had lost out on an experience that would have cemented her place in her homestead's community of women. Perhaps that was why she never felt comfortable when she returned to the place of her birth, why she never felt as though she really belonged. Later, at medical school, she had learnt how dangerous the Xhosa initiation ceremonies were, how the use of communal knives for the circumcisions spread HIV and STDs and how every year boys died from sepsis following surgery by poorly trained sangomas. And although she had feigned the appropriate shock and horror that such things still occurred in the modern world, she secretly thought back to the excitement she had felt as a child during the feasting and drinking and dancing at the pre-initiation ceremonies and the collective pride that she had, by proxy, experienced on the return of the new young men after their initiation. So she didn't belong fully to her adopted home either. That was the problem with living in two worlds, one black and one white: she would always be a shade of grey. Would Prince Xoliswe Hospital form her initiation, she wondered? Did the experiences in the hospital serve as a type of initiation rite? If that was the case, perhaps at last she would find a place in which she belonged.

'So, what's the deal with Dr Zamla?' Rachael asked the table, interrupting Nomsa's thoughts. 'I'm still trying to recover from the call that I had to do for him. I haven't seen him yet at the hospital or at any of the meetings. Does he actually exist?'

'Oh, yes,' Nathan replied. 'You won't be able to miss him when he's around.' A few of the other doctors sniggered (obviously another private joke, Nomsa thought). 'He runs a cash practice in Nandi,' Nathan continued, referring to a township on the outskirts of Tugela Bridge. 'Charges eighty rands a patient and sees a hundred patients a day, and none of the money he makes is declared since his practice is run on a strictly cash basis.'

'I don't understand,' Rachael said. 'How can he work at the hospital and run a practice? Where does he get the time? And surely it's illegal?'

'It's all overlooked, probably because he's a cousin of Mrs Hlope. Or maybe he's paying off the right people in the Health Professions Council. We've tried to report him but nothing ever happens,' Nathan answered.

'How's this for irony?' Eliza interrupted. 'I had a patient the other day, a woman with an ectopic pregnancy, who was referred to the hospital for surgery by Dr Zamla from his private practice. I ended up seeing the patient in casualty while I was covering the call that Dr Zamla was supposed to be doing.'

'Let me get this straight,' Rachael said. 'Dr Zamla is never at the hospital but he still gets paid for working at the hospital and nobody can do anything about it because he's related to the hospital superintendent and bribes people?' She raised her eyebrows incredulously. 'Why bother to put his name on the call list, though? Surely it would be simpler just to leave his name off? That way people wouldn't get confused.'

Nathan shrugged. 'I suppose it's in case anyone checks up. Makes it look like he's working. When we tried to remove his name from the list, Mrs Hlope insisted that we put it back on. Now we just have the unofficial rule that whoever works with Dr Zamla does a twenty-four-hour shift. Over the year it ends up being pretty fair. So don't worry,' he said, looking at Rachael, 'we'll all get our turn.'

'It just seems crazy,' Rachael said. 'I can't get my mind around the fact that there's nothing anyone can do about it.'

'Well, if half of our cabinet ministers are corrupt, we can hardly expect lesser government officials not to follow their example. If corruption isn't punished high up, why would anyone expect it to be punished lower down in the government hierarchy?' Nomsa asked bluntly. Her question was followed by a moment's silence. It was a pause of contradictions: hardly a second long but lasting hours; quiet but filled with a thousand gasps. Nomsa knew that she was not expected to make that sort of comment. She was, after all, black. She had noticed that when she was in the company of non-blacks, she was automatically presumed to have certain beliefs and loyalties and capabilities. It always befuddled her that whites and Indians and coloureds were allowed socially to have many different and conflicting views and opinions, but blacks were all categorised together. Generally she liked the awkwardness and embarrassment that her comments caused. She liked the fact that they brought people face to face with their prejudices and made them rethink their paradigms. But occasionally it tired her to have to keep on proving herself an intelligent, thinking individual. As a black female, she knew that she was envied by many non-blacks, that she was supposedly at the top of the affirmative action ladder, that she was no longer previously disadvantaged but now very advantaged. But in fact it was a position she seldom relished. She wished that for once she could go into a post and immediately be recognised as having deserved the position. Instead, in her new intern job, as had happened so many times before at medical school, and at school before that, she knew that she would have to prove herself capable. She would have to do everything twice as well as everyone else, because she was a woman and she was black, and prejudices were still very much alive.

The abscess list was done twice weekly by the surgery intern on duty that day. The morning after the welcoming social at the Clay Oven, that intern happened to be Nomsa. Had she known the night before that she would be doing the abscess list the following day, she would have drunk fewer whisky-and-Appletisers. She planned to specialise in surgery one day and doing her very first list with a partial hangover was not an auspicious start to the rest of her career. She downed two Cokes in succession (Rachael, giving them to Nomsa that morning, had called them red ambulances, and Nomsa had replied that she hoped that they were private and not state ambulances) and then made her way to the theatre. The abscess list, she had been told, was done in a special theatre designated for particularly unsterile procedures. Nomsa, who had scarcely had a pimple in her life, never mind an abscess, found it hard to believe that there were enough abscesses to warrant both a special list and an isolated theatre. But apparently there were. When Nomsa arrived at the theatre, the list was full and two extra cases were being prepped just in case she finished early.

She put on her theatre mask and cap and then scrubbed up. Her first patient was already asleep on the table when Nomsa entered the theatre. One of the more senior doctors was covering as the anaesthetist and he greeted Nomsa with a nod as she came in. He was a short, squat man with a scorpion tattooed on the bulging muscles of his upper arm. Nomsa could see it peeping out from beneath the sleeve of his theatre greens as he put down his newspaper. He asked Nomsa whether she had done an abscess list before. Nomsa shook her head.

'You must at least know how to drain an abscess? That's hardly rocket science,' he said, an unmistakable note of sarcasm in his voice. Nomsa had seen abscesses being drained before, but she had never actually done an incision and drainage herself. It had looked simple enough: make an x-shaped incision, drain the pus out, irrigate the wound with saline and then pack it with iodine-soaked gauze. The last thing she wanted was for the anaesthetist to think her incapable, which he would certainly do if she admitted that she was unsure how to drain an abscess. His tone of voice had made that clear enough. She hesitated for a moment, unsure whether to admit ignorance or to lie. Eventually she decided on the latter.

'Of course,' she answered abruptly. She hoped that if she sounded impatient, as though the question was superfluous, it would disguise her nervousness. Her guile must have been convincing: the anaesthetist nodded and picked up his newspaper again.

The patient's abscess was underneath her right arm. Nomsa cleaned the skin carefully and then draped sterile green cloth around the area. She didn't know if what she was doing was right, but she hoped that if she acted confident the anaesthetist would not suspect she was doing this for the first time. The theatre sister didn't look surprised at Nomsa's actions, so Nomsa figured she couldn't be doing too much out of the ordinary. Beneath her own theatre gown she could feel her clothes growing damp and clammy with sweat. She picked the scalpel up from the tray, concentrating on keeping her nervous hand steady, and leant over the abscess. The skin was taut and shiny, ready to burst open. Nomsa touched it lightly with the scalpel. The stream of pus that exploded from the abscess would probably have made it to the ceiling if her face had not been in the way. She gagged, trying to keep down the two Cokes that she had drunk earlier. Were it not for the stink and the specks of pus, wet on her face, she would have believed she was caught in one of her nightmares. This wasn't the type of thing that happened in the real world. From the head of the bed, she heard the anaesthetist burst out laughing. He turned to the floor sister.

'Thank you, hand it over,' he said to her. 'I told you this one would be a winner.' The sister grimaced and gave the doctor a ten-rand note and Nomsa realised (a horrible, stomach-wrenching, blush-inducing realisation) that they must have taken a bet on whether she would get pus in her face or not. She felt humiliated. Humiliated and nauseous and disgusting, and she still had to finish the procedure before she could wipe the pus from her face. She concentrated on what she was doing to try to stop herself from crying. She should have told the anaesthetist that she had never drained an abscess. She felt more foolish now than she would have felt if she had just had the guts to admit her ignorance earlier. The anaesthetist was still chuckling to himself when Nomsa finished the case. She went to the basin and splashed her face with water. Luckily, most of the pus had landed on her plastic protective glasses and the theatre mask.

'Don't worry,' she heard the anaesthetist say, 'you aren't the first intern that this has happened to and you definitely won't be the last. Take a look at the ceiling.'

Nomsa looked up. The need for a special abscess theatre immediately became apparent. The ceiling was brown and yellow with the stains of previously lanced abscesses. It made her feel only slightly better that the same thing had happened to other doctors (although at least in their cases the pus had hit the ceiling and not their faces). She decided that she would rather appear ignorant in future than risk having pus landing on her face. It was too graphic a lesson to have to learn a second time around.

Rachael

6

Unlike the rest of Prince Xoliswe Hospital, which had no respite over the festive season, the outpatient department closed from the middle of December to the middle of January each year. It made little sense that this was the case, since the outpatient clinics had, on average, six-month-long waiting lists, but apparently it had something to do with the working hours of the sisters running the clinics. Rachael's first outpatient clinic, to which she was on her way, was scheduled for the twenty-third of January. Although she was three weeks into her stint at Prince Xoliswe, she still had no idea of what to expect from the outpatient clinics. Every time she had asked one of the senior doctors about outpatients, she had been answered with a groan or a 'Good luck, you'll need it', so it was with some trepidation that she walked from the ward, after completing her ward work, to the outpatient department.

On arriving and seeing fifty patients waiting on the wooden benches outside the examination cubicles, she thought that she would be working with other doctors. She simply presumed that she would not have to run the clinic single-handedly for the afternoon, and so she sat down in one of the examination cubicles and waited for another, more experienced doctor to arrive and tell her what to do. After half an hour of waiting she made her way to the sisters' desk. The clinic nurse was sitting at the desk drinking a cup of coffee and reading a gossip magazine. She looked up as Rachael approached and Rachael asked her what time the other doctors usually arrived.

'Aren't you the doctor?' the sister questioned.

Rachael nodded. She waited for the sister to continue, but the sister simply showed her a pile of patient folders. 'Those are the patients you need to see. You'd better get started. It's late already.'

'Aren't any other doctors coming to help?' Rachael asked. She could feel herself starting to panic and she tried to take a deep breath to calm herself down. Now was not an appropriate moment for a panic attack. 'Surely I'm not supposed to see all these patients on my own!'

The sister looked confused. 'We normally only have one doctor,' she said. 'I don't think they've changed things but I'll go and check for you if you like.'

'Please,' Rachael begged. She was trying to work out how she could possibly see in one afternoon all the patients that were waiting outside. The maths was confusing her. Usually, if she worked really quickly, she could manage to see one patient every half an hour. Which would mean she would finish seeing patients at approximately two o'clock the following afternoon, assuming she took no breaks to eat or drink or sleep or go to the toilet. Somewhere, she was missing a whole lot of time. The sister came back and confirmed Rachael's fears: she was working alone.

'What if I don't finish seeing everyone?' Rachael asked. The sister laughed loudly as though Rachael had made a hilarious joke, and Rachael didn't have the strength to correct her. She walked back miserably to the examination cubicle in which she had left her bag and sat down on the examination bed. She would have to see a patient approximately every seven minutes if she wanted to finish by five o'clock, which was when outpatients was supposed to close. She didn't know how she was supposed to make a diagnosis in seven minutes. It took her longer to put her make-up on in the mornings. She looked at her watch: her current episode of hysteria had brought the average patient consultation down to six and a half minutes. If she didn't get moving, her patients would end up getting two-minute consults. She walked quickly to the pile of folders and called in the first patient. The woman who responded was an elderly Indian woman who had recently been diagnosed with diabetes. She had been seen once before in outpatients and had come for a follow-up visit. The doctor who had seen her the first time had made hardly any notes in the patient's folder:

Dx: Type 2 diabetes – HGT 16

P: Metformin Review 1/12

Rachael translated the shorthand. The patient had been diagnosed with type two diabetes. Her sugar had been high, at sixteen, and the doctor had started the patient on oral treatment for the diabetes (Metformin). He had scheduled a follow-up visit for one month later, which was the current visit. Judging from the brevity of the notes, Rachael was hardly impressed with the doctor who had previously seen the patient. She wondered what kind of training he had had. She could not imagine writing such sparse and poorly detailed notes: it was, in her opinion, simply bad medicine. She sat the patient down, examined her thoroughly and then started speaking to her as she wrote:

Presenting complaint: Uncontrolled diabetes. Patient does not have glucose monitor at home to check sugar levels. Patient has not been properly educated about diabetes or a diabetic diet.

Current glucose measurement: 10

Patient currently has no symptoms.

Family history: Mother and father both had diabetes and hypertension. Father died of heart attack aged 55.

Past medical history: High cholesterol.

Past surgical history: Appendicectomy at age 11, Caesar x 2.

Allergies: None.

Social history: Non-drinker, non-smoker.

On examination: Overweight patient. Abdominal circumference: 108 cm, weight 97 kg.

Fundoscopy not done – ophthalmoscope not available.

Cardiovascular system: Blood pressure: 150/87; pulse 78, regular; normal heart sounds.

Chest: Clear with good breath sounds bilaterally.

Abdomen: Soft, non-tender, no masses or organomegaly.

Assessment: Uncontrolled diabetes.

Plan: Continue Metformin, educate patient, monitor blood pressure and consider anti-hypertensive in future.

Rachael explained to the patient that she needed to come back again in another month's time for her next check-up and gave her a script for a further month's supply of medication. She smiled to herself: now *that* was seeing a patient properly! She picked up the patient's file to take it back to the sister's desk and glanced at her watch, sure that she had taken just a little over seven minutes. In fact, she was eighteen minutes over seven. In dismay, she checked that her watch was working properly, which, unfortunately, it was. She had taken twenty-five minutes to see one patient. She understood now that the previous doctor had probably not been poorly trained; he simply had a far better sense of time management than she did. The next patient took her twelve minutes to see, and by the time she reached patient number thirty she had got her consultation time down to five and a half minutes.

As she was seeing patients (while keeping a close eye on her watch), rushing them in and then out of her consultation room with barely more than a blood-pressure check, Rachael couldn't help wondering whether this was what she had studied for so many years to do. She wasn't practising medicine; she was engaged in damage control. All she was really doing was making sure that patients weren't about to die; and if they were, she admitted them for somebody else to do further damage control. She wasn't telling her diabetics about the importance of losing weight and of exercising; she wasn't educating her hypertensive patients about the risks of smoking and the importance of complying with their medication; she hadn't had time to explain to her epileptic patient why and how he should stop drinking alcohol. All the patients that she had seen during the afternoon would be back again the next month, probably even sicker. She wasn't just not healing people; she wasn't even really helping to prevent them from getting more unwell. This certainly wasn't the medicine that she had envisaged practising.

Rachael called in her last patient, Mr Mtshali, at seven o'clock. The sister had left two hours before, exactly as the hands of the clock on the outpatients' clinic wall reached five. She had stuck her head into the examination cubicle in which Rachael was working and told Rachael that she couldn't wait any longer because she would miss the last taxi if she did, and that Rachael should lock the staff toilet door before leaving and hide the key in the drawer of the sisters' desk.

Mr Mtshali was thin, almost emaciated, with hollows above his temples and between the chest bones exposed by the open V-neck of his T-shirt. He walked into the examination cubicle painstakingly, as an old man would, but his file claimed that he was only twenty-one. Rachael gave a cursory glance through the folder in her hands as Mr Mtshali slowly lowered his body onto the examination bed. He had been seen once before at the clinic, for chest pain and weakness. At that visit, the doctor who had seen him had suspected that he was HIV-positive and had done a blood test to confirm it. Rachael saw the results tucked into the folder: the patient was positive. She wondered why the patient had been told to come back for his follow-up visit a month after that initial appointment. She knew that HIV results were usually available the next day, so it made sense that he should have had an appointment scheduled for the following day. Instead, he had been given an appointment a month later. It was obvious clinically that Mr Mtshali had stage four HIV, or AIDS, and that he needed to be started on anti-retroviral drugs as soon as possible. So why had he been forced to wait a whole month? Time is not absolute; it's relative, she thought to herself. In the same way that a month is a long time in a child's life, Rachael knew that it was a long time when death was as close as it was to Mr Mtshali. She sighed and pushed the folder away from her. She didn't know how she was going to manage to work under these conditions for a whole year. She was willing to bet that nobody had even told Mr Mtshali the result of his HIV test yet. She turned towards him, expecting the worst.

'Do you know the result of the blood test that you had?' she asked. He stared at her, raising his eyebrows slightly in confusion. Rachael hadn't expected the worst to be this bad.

'Do you speak English?' Rachael asked.

'Little bit.'

'Blood test?' she asked, pointing to the inside of her arm, from where she presumed he would have been bled. 'Result?'

'Yes,' he nodded.

Did that mean yes, he knew the result; or yes, he had had the test; or even yes, he would have another test? There was nobody around to translate for Rachael, so there was absolutely no way she could know what he meant. 'Why did you come here, to the clinic?' she asked, changing tactics.

'For my chest pain,' he answered, 'and because I have no power. My legs, he have no power, and my arms, he have no power.'

'Last time you came to the clinic,' she turned to the folder and checked the date of the patient's last visit, 'on the sixteenth of December, do you remember that you had a blood test?' she asked. Mr Mtshali nodded. 'Do you know what the test was for?' she asked.

'For the chest pain and the no power,' he replied.

How was this possible? Rachael wondered, close to tears. It was ethically unacceptable that the patient had not been counselled about HIV before having the test. Rachael didn't even know if he had given consent for the test. This simply could not be happening to her: it was half past seven in the evening, she hadn't eaten or drunk anything since breakfast, she had already seen forty-four patients and now she had to try to counsel someone about HIV, and give him his result, in a language that she couldn't speak. It would be far easier, she realised, just to draw blood for a CD4 count and explain everything to the patient at his next visit, in another month's time, if he was still alive. But that was probably exactly what had happened at his last visit.

'Do you know what HIV is?' she asked.

He nodded, suddenly wary of her. She couldn't do this. She didn't know where to start. She had to explain to him what HIV was, what caused it, what the symptoms were, how it was managed, what treatment options were available, that it became AIDS and that he might die from it. She had to make sure that he understood how it was transmitted and that he should talk to his wife or girlfriend about the result and that, from now on, he needed to use protection every time he had intercourse. And her entire Zulu vocabulary consisted of two words: *sawubona* and *siyabonga*, 'hello' and 'thank you'. It was impossible.

'Can you come back tomorrow?' she asked him, suddenly seeing a way out. If he came back tomorrow, she could find someone to translate for her. She could spend more time with him and answer all his questions. It would all make so much more sense in the morning. But he shook his head. He explained to Rachael, in broken, minimal English, that he lived far away and that it had cost him fifty rand to get to the hospital for the appointment and it would cost him another fifty to get home, and that he didn't have money to come again the next day. Also, he had to work the next day or he would lose his job. It was a new job and he had already been shouted at for coming to this appointment. He also told Rachael that he had missed the last taxi home (it had left at six), so he would have to stay somewhere (he didn't know where yet) for the night and leave very early the next morning, and that he hadn't eaten since three o'clock that morning, just before he had walked the five kilometres from his village to the taxi collection point. He spoke matter-of-factly, almost without emotion. He wasn't telling this to Rachael in an attempt to get sympathy or for some material gain; he was telling her because she had asked him if he could come back again the next day. He was explaining to her why he couldn't.

Rachael was disgusted: disgusted with herself because she had been complaining about her day and disgusted with a social system that somehow allowed this. And obviously this man was not an isolated case. She realised that she had spent most of her life wrapped up in a cocoon of ignorance and self-virtue. She had thought that she had been doing a *mitzvah* every time she gave her domestic worker her old clothes and that she was being charitable when she tipped a car guard or petrol attendant well. What a *schmoe* she had been! She looked at Mr Mtshali. He was waiting for an answer from her and she didn't know what she should do. There was only one possibility she could think of and she knew that it was the wrong thing to do because there were already too few beds available in the hospital and Mr Mtshali was not acutely ill (he was dying, but slowly, so his case was not a priority) and therefore did not officially qualify for one of the remaining open beds. But it was her only option. She phoned through to casualty and told them that she was

70

sending a patient down for admission. She would admit him to the medical ward and then she would be able to spend as much time with him as she wanted the next day. Satisfied that she had done the right thing, she explained to Mr Mtshali that he would need to stay at the hospital for a few days.

'No, no, Doctor. I can't,' he said, shaking his head vigorously. 'I must work tomorrow.'

'I'll give you a doctor's note to say you were sick.'

'No, if I don't work tomorrow, the boss, she will give my job away.'

Rachael tried to reason with him, to tell him that it was illegal and that he couldn't lose his job because he had a medical reason for missing work, but he was adamant that he would not be admitted. Eventually, out of desperation, Rachael told him that he was at risk of dying if he didn't stay in hospital and get treatment.

'No, I need this job. I can't lose this job. I waited long time for it,' he said, getting up.

Rachael knew from his tone of voice that he had made his decision and that there was nothing that she could do to change his mind. She wanted to tell him that the job wasn't nearly as important as getting onto anti-retrovirals, that the job wouldn't be of much use in a couple of weeks' time when he would be too weak to get out of bed, but she didn't have the vocabulary. She wished that she could force him to be admitted, that she could fall back on some sort of restraining order and call a security guard in to haul Mr Mtshali to the ward, but there wasn't any law and the security guards had left for home long before. So she did the only thing that she could think of doing: as Mr Mtshali got up to leave she tipped the contents of her wallet into his hand. She felt so helpless, so pathetic, as she watched him walk slowly down the corridor and out of outpatients. He wouldn't make his next appointment; he would be dead before then. And in a way, because she was part of the system, she would be partly to blame.

Rachael's prefab didn't look quite so bad to her that evening. She almost managed to convince herself that she didn't need the furniture from her previous flat in Cape Town, which was due to arrive in three days' time, on the following Saturday. It felt shallow and crass worrying about a microwave and television when there were people who lived like Mr Mtshali did. She took a container of ready-made lasagne out of the luminous orange freezer and put it in the oven. As the grill started to warm up, it released the odour of countless dinners cooked (some burnt) before. Ordinarily the smell would have disgusted Rachael, but this evening it didn't. This evening it seemed trivial. She was still worrying about Mr Mtshali, wondering if she could have done things differently. The way that he had been managed was so wrong. He should not have had to travel fifty kilometres just to get tested for HIV, and he should have been counselled properly before having the test, in his own language, and he should have given consent to having the test, and he should have been told the result the next day and had a CD4 count done at the same time, and then he should have been counselled again. He should have been started on anti-retrovirals three weeks ago. What frustrated Rachael more than anything else was that it wasn't so complicated or difficult to get it right. It was all potentially possible, but there seemed to be a prevailing attitude of apathy. It was almost as though as soon as a diagnosis of HIV was made or suspected, everybody (not only the caregivers but the patients too) just gave up. It seemed such a sad, sad waste of life.

7

A not altogether welcome surprise arrived with the furniture removal van on Saturday morning. Initially Rachael had thought that the smart silver hired car that pulled up behind the van belonged, for some reason not immediately obvious to her, to the removal company. She was abruptly disillusioned when the passenger door was flung open and she heard her mother's voice erupting from inside the car. Gloria-Jean's voice was distinctive: when she was very, very excited, it climbed its way up the octave until it was of such a high frequency that it was almost inaudible to the human ear.

Dogs whimpered when Gloria-Jean was excited. The rest of Gloria-Jean was as remarkable as her voice. She had huge black hair, a pout that made her resemble a very expensive blowfish, and breasts so artificially large that they continually threatened to topple her not insubstantial frame. Rachael's father, Norman, was the perfect antithesis to Gloria-Jean. He was a small, balding man who wore thick, unfashionable black-rimmed glasses, spoke in a soft, nasal tone and never left home without a handkerchief.

It seemed odd to Rachael that, as she stood watching her parents park the car and the delivery men offload her furniture, she was not ecstatic. She knew that she should be; she had wished for the arrival of her parents and her furniture innumerable times in the past month, but now that both had come (the one on schedule, the other unexpectedly) it felt almost like an anticlimax. It wasn't so much that she had enjoyed 'roughing it', but that she was proud of the fact that she was managing to cope on her own. By coming, albeit with the best intentions for their daughter, her parents had once again reaffirmed Rachael's – and their – belief that she was somehow incapable. Her mother, with her keen maternal instinct, picked up immediately that something was wrong.

'My darling, darling *bobeleh*,' Gloria-Jean said, standing on her tiptoes and smacking Rachael's cheek with cherry-red kisses, 'you look absolutely awful. What's happened? Are you eating enough?'

'Yes, Mom, I'm eating fine,' Rachael said. 'I probably look awful because I don't have any make-up on. I don't have a decent mirror in this place.' It had been some time since Rachael had felt the need to excuse her appearance.

'What? You don't have a mirror?' Gloria-Jean screeched, obviously horrified. 'I thought they said your accommodation was furnished.'

'Mom, I don't have water unless I pay someone to pump it from the borehole for me, or pump it myself, so a mirror is hardly high up on my list of priorities right now.' Rachael realised from her mother's expression that she had probably responded too harshly. 'Come, let me show you around. It's not too bad,' she said softly. With her parents in tow, Rachael wove around the men who were

73

offloading boxes and furniture and made her way to the front door.

'*Oy vey!*' Rachael heard Gloria-Jean exhale sharply as she entered the prefab. 'You can't stay here. This is dreadful. It's a real dump.'

'Mom, it's fine. It'll look better when my furniture is all in place and I've unpacked the boxes. It looks a mess now because everything's all over the place.' Rachael couldn't believe the words that were coming out of her mouth: she was actually defending her little hovel.

'No, it's not fine. I'm not having you stay in this … this … dilapidated shack!' Gloria-Jean was shrieking now. She turned towards her husband. 'You can't let this go on. You can't let our daughter stay here. We need to have a proper family discussion about this. This is just not on.' She walked over to Rachael and put her arms around her. 'My poor, poor child,' she said. 'I'm so sorry that you've had to spend two weeks in this place. If only I'd known, I would have sorted things out ages ago.'

'Mom,' Rachael interrupted, 'please calm down. I don't need you to sort things out for me. This place is fine. I'm actually quite happy here. Please, just relax.' Rachael noticed that the men unloading boxes were staring at her mother. She realised, with embarrassment, that her prefab was probably more comfortable and better equipped than many of their homes. She had to stop her mother from making more of a scene. 'I know it's a bit of a schlep, but won't you help me start unpacking some boxes?' she asked, changing the subject abruptly. She didn't actually want her mother to help unpack; she wanted to decide herself where she was going to put everything, but she knew that she had to distract her mother.

Her ploy worked. Gloria-Jean, by nature an organiser of others' lives, jumped at the opportunity to unpack boxes. She lifted shiny kitchen appliances from the first box she opened and placed them on the short sideboard next to the oven. They looked incongruous in the old prefab, like outsiders. Actually, everything looked out of place: the piles of boxes stacked on the floor, the leather couch, the glass coffee table, the plasma-screen television. Rachael had become used to the sparseness of the prefab and in a way she relished it.

She lingered around the boxes, unwilling to start opening them. She wished she could just leave the boxes taped up and dispose of them, which was strange because just a few days before she would have given anything for the relative luxury of their contents. She leant back against the wall and watched her mother. Gloria-Jean was unpacking at remarkable speed. She shared none of Rachael's hesitancies. Her red nails ripped through boxes and whizzed things into corners and cupboards. She had roped Rachael's father into unpacking and he scuttled around after her like a dog ... no, a dog implied a willing loyalty. He was more like an old donkey that had long ago been beaten into submission. Suddenly Rachael felt sick. She wanted her parents out of her house; they didn't belong there. This was her bit of life, the first bit of life that she had created on her own, and they were running all over it, trying to change it and make it theirs.

'Mom, Pops,' she interrupted the flurry of activity. 'Where have you booked to stay tonight?' Her question was impolite, a slight. It hardly left her parents the option of staying with her. Rachael saw a moment's confusion in her mother's eyes, quickly covered up by a brave smile.

'Don't worry, we won't stay with you,' Gloria-Jean said. 'We saw the sign for a bed-and-breakfast on the way into town. We thought we could stay there.'

Rachael knew that her mother was lying and that her parents had just assumed that they would stay with her. She also knew that she should invite them, but she didn't want to. For the first time in her life, she didn't want them in her space, organising everything for her.

The offloading of furniture and boxes took well into the afternoon and, once the removal van had left, Rachael suggested to her parents that they go to the Clay Oven for a late lunch.

'I'm sure you're wondering what we're doing here,' Gloria-Jean said to Rachael as they sat down at the restaurant table. Rachael nodded. 'Well, we came to visit you for two reasons. The one was to see you all settled in, obviously, and the other one was to discuss something with you.' As she said this, Gloria-Jean looked at her husband, as though for affirmation. 'Do you remember the Greenblatts?' she asked Rachael.

The Greenblatts had been their next-door neighbours until Rachael was twelve. It was improbable that she would ever forget them: she had had an all-consuming crush on the eldest Greenblatt boy and had cried continuously for three days when they emigrated to the UK.

'Well, I contacted Donny Greenblatt – you remember he's a doctor,' Gloria-Jean continued, cutting short Rachael's treasured memories, 'and he said that he's sure he could organise work for you at the hospital he's working at. Apparently he's on quite good terms with the HR lady that organises locums. She could organise you locum work until you get a foundation-year post. I told him that you would be there by the beginning of March.'

The beginning of March. That was six weeks away. Gloria-Jean continued talking without giving Rachael any space to object.

'I told him that you're already registered with the General Medical Council so it would just be a matter of getting a highly skilled visa for you, which I'm sure would be easy enough. I've heard that they take a couple of days if you have all your documents in order. Your father's booked you a ticket for the twenty-seventh of Feb ...'

'What?' Rachael interrupted, incensed. 'How could you buy a ticket for me without speaking to me first? What if I don't want to go?'

'Of course you want to go,' her mother assured her. 'You can't stay here. There's no future for you in this country. I mean, just look at the place they expect you to live in.' Gloria-Jean stopped talking briefly to acknowledge the arrival of the pizzas. 'We've spoken so often about you emigrating. I knew you wouldn't want to give up this opportunity. Plus Donny's been so helpful and he's had to pull so many strings to organise you a place in the hospital. You wouldn't want to let him down, would you?'

'You'd be a fool to let this slip, my girl,' Rachael's father interjected. 'It's a once-in-a-lifetime opportunity.'

Rachael took a bite of her pizza. She had ordered a Mexicana with extra chilli and the peppery heat made her nose run. She dabbed at it with a tissue. She was so tired of her parents planning her life for her like this, so sick of them just presuming that they knew what was best for her. They hadn't even bothered to ask her what she wanted to do.

'I suppose you'll have to give them some notice here,' Gloria-Jean continued, 'and you'll need to organise for your furniture to come back. Seems such a pity we bothered to start unpacking!' she laughed. 'Don't worry, Daddy has said he'll pay for you to have it moved back. I thought you could reasonably be home by the end of the month.'

'Mom, slow down!' Rachael said loudly. 'There's nothing reasonable about what you've been saying. You haven't even asked me if I want to go.'

'Of course you want to go. Why on earth would you want to stay? You don't even have decent water in that little hole you're living in.'

Rachael wanted to tell her mother that the state of the water in her accommodation was hardly a rational criterion on which to base a decision that would affect the rest of her life. She wanted to explain to her mother that there was so much she could learn at Prince Xoliswe Hospital that she would be unlikely ever to learn at a British hospital and that, for the first time in her life, she had started to see that she could make a difference. She wanted to tell her mother how happy she had been for the last two weeks, even despite, or perhaps because of, all the challenges she had faced. But she knew that her mother would never understand, so she just told her parents that she would think about it and that they should probably cancel the ticket because it wasn't a sure thing.

'Well, I think you're crazy,' Gloria-Jean said. 'Absolutely crazy. And I'm sure once you've thought about it properly you'll change your mind.'

Rachael did think about her mother's statement, later that evening when she was alone in bed, surrounded by stacks of half-emptied cardboard boxes and reams of crumpled-up packing tape. Perhaps her mother was right; perhaps she *was* crazy. She could think of a whole list of reasons to leave South Africa and take up the offered post in the UK, not least of which was the chance that she might bump into Daniel Greenblatt, but she knew with an instinctive certainty that she did not want to run away from Tugela Bridge (because as much as she could try to disguise the fact in well-justified excuses, it would still be running away). Running away would constitute a failure that would leave her not only forever dependent on her parents, but also completely bereft of self-belief.

Rachael was on call in casualty on the Sunday after her parents had unexpectedly arrived and, because they seemed in a hurry to leave anyway, she said goodbye to them at half past six, before she left for the hospital.

'I'm not going to say a long goodbye because I'm sure we'll see you at the end of the month,' Gloria-Jean said, kissing Rachael first on one cheek and then on the other. 'Let us know if you need any money and Daddy will do an EFT. If the worst comes to the worst, just pack a bag and spend the rest of the month at the B&B that we stayed at last night. It's really very pleasant. Quite civilised, actually.'

'Thanks, Mom,' Rachael said awkwardly. She hadn't changed her mind about her decision to stay at Tugela Bridge, but she didn't want to argue about it with her mother then, just as her parents were about to leave.

'Oh, I almost forgot, we popped into the supermarket on the way here yesterday and got you some goodies,' Gloria-Jean said, running back to the car. She retrieved two packets from the boot and handed them to Rachael. The bags were filled with tins and boxes of food.

'Mom, I can manage my own shopping,' Rachael snapped, irritated that her mother, yet again, was showing such a blatant lack of faith in her capabilities.

'I know,' Gloria-Jean said, unusually softly. 'I just thought you might like some treats to fill up your fridge and cupboards.' She put the packets down at Rachael's feet and walked slowly back to the car. As her mother walked away from her, Rachael noticed that Gloria-Jean's shoulders were slightly hunched. It made her look vulnerable, almost frail, and Rachael all at once felt guilty that she had shouted at her mother. She knew that the bags of food that her mother had pressed on her were not really an indication of her parents' lack of faith in her. The circumstances had caused her to overreact. In spurning her mother's bags of groceries, she had spurned a far greater gift than some shopping, but she couldn't bring herself to call out to her mother and apologise. Something – perhaps pride, perhaps a fear of dependency – stopped her. She stashed the shopping bags inside the prefab and then slung her bag over her shoulder and made her way briskly to the hospital, relieved that her upcoming shift would take her mind off her parents.

Rachael was on call with Dr Ribbentrop, one of the senior medical officers. She hadn't worked with him before and had only met him once, at the interns' introductory meeting. He was head of trauma and casualty and she was nervous about working with him, both because he had a reputation among the doctors as a stern taskmaster and because she was worried about how slowly she worked. She had managed to speed up the time it took her to see patients, but her average consultation was still a good ten minutes longer than most of the other doctors'. Rachael arrived in casualty just as the nurses finished singing. She went to the doctors' office to put her bag down and was surprised to see Dr Ribbentrop already there, sitting on one of the chairs reading a newspaper. His solid legs, clad in theatre greens, protruded from below the lower edge of the paper. Rachael greeted him and he grunted a response without moving the newspaper. She commented on how unusually quiet casualty was and he answered with a gruff 'Humph'. Her offer of a cup of coffee was met with a snort which, after some consideration and deciphering of body language, Rachael decided she would interpret as being in the negative. After a few more minutes of awkward unilateral conversation, Rachael decided to go through to casualty to see if any patients had arrived: it was infinitely preferable to trying to talk to a non-committal newspaper.

There was one folder in the tray waiting for her when she got to the sisters' desk. She called in the patient – a man who had cut his hand with an angle grinder – and led him to an examination cubicle. She checked that no tendons, major blood vessels or nerves were injured, sutured the wound and then discharged the patient. The tray on the sisters' desk was still empty. Rachael wandered around casualty fiddling with instruments and memorising where everything was. Time dragged. She repacked some bandages in a drawer, organising them according to size, and then neatened the stationery on the doctors' desk. Another patient came in, a woman with diarrhoea and vomiting, to whom she gave some intravenous fluid before discharging. She braved going back to the doctors' office to make herself a cup of coffee. The newspaper had been replaced with a novel (the cover suggested a political thriller). The substitution of book for newspaper afforded her a view of crew-cut blond hair and a square forehead. She drank her cup of coffee as quickly as was possible without burning her mouth and then made her way back to the sisters' desk. Even if the sister on duty was deaf, blind and mute and had the personality of a cupboard, Rachael reasoned, she could not possibly be worse company than Dr Ribbentrop. When she got to the sisters' desk, the tray for patient folders was still empty. It was uncanny, almost unnerving, how quiet the shift was compared with the previous three calls that Rachael had done. The sister on duty, who looked about Rachael's age, was reading a gossip magazine. She put it aside when Rachael introduced herself.

'Sister Naidoo,' the sister said, extending a hand to Rachael in greeting. 'Pleased to meet you.'

'It's strange how quiet it is today, isn't it?' Rachael said.

Sister Naidoo shook her head. 'Not really,' she said. 'It's because Dr Ribbentrop's on. It's usually quiet when he works.'

'Why?' Rachael asked. She wondered whether he had some magic charm that kept patients at bay. She glimpsed the potential to make a lot of money.

'Patients are scared of him,' Sister Naidoo explained. 'They see his motorbike parked outside the entrance and they decide their problems can wait a few hours. Only really sick patients come in when he's on call. Or people who are new to Tugela Bridge and don't know about him yet.'

'Why are they scared of him?'

'He doesn't exactly have the best bedside manner. Actually, I don't think he's got any bedside manner.'

'So I noticed,' Rachael said. 'I tried to make conversation with him earlier and he pretty much ignored me.'

'He's not too talkative,' Sister Naidoo agreed, 'but he's a good man and a good doctor.'

Rachael knew that the two didn't necessarily go together. She was about to ask Sister Naidoo what she meant when Dr Ribbentrop walked into casualty.

'Dr Lipawski,' he stated, staring at Rachael with deep-set blue eyes. 'You're from ...?' He raised his unruly blond eyebrows.

'Cape Town. I studied at UCT,' Rachael answered quickly.

'Ah, an Ikey. And how are you finding it here, so far away from the Atlantic and the mountain?' His tone was slightly mocking, as though he hardly expected a Capetonian to survive Tugela Bridge.

'So far so good,' Rachael lied. She wasn't about to give him the satisfaction of finding out just how challenging the past few weeks had been for her.

'Good,' he nodded. Sister Naidoo came in with a patient file and Dr Ribbentrop's attention was immediately diverted. He took the folder from the sister and called the patient in. A teenage girl responded to his call and Rachael watched her follow him into a cubicle. She could hear their voices float up over the curtains.

Dr R: So, what's wrong?

Patient: My head pains and I feel like I want to vomit all the time.

Dr R: For how long?

Patient: What?

Dr R (*harshly*): How long have you had a headache and felt sick for?

Patient: A long time.

Dr R: What's a long time?

Patient: One month. Maybe two months.

Dr R: So why have you come here? Why haven't you gone to

the clinic for this problem? This is an emergency unit. EM-ER-GEN-CY! Do you understand what the word emergency means? One month, maybe two months, does not constitute an emergency.

Silence from the patient.

Dr R (*finally*): Are you pregnant?

Patient: I don't know.

Dr R: When was your last period?

Patient: I don't know.

Dr R (*sarcastically*): Do you know your name?

Patient: Yes.

Dr R: So, were you using contraception? Pill or injection or condoms?

Silence, presumably while patient shakes her head.

Dr R: Why not? How old are you? Sixteen? And you want a child? What on earth were you thinking? No wait, let me guess, you don't know.

(Dr Ribbentrop was almost shouting and Rachael was beginning to understand why the motorbike was a deterrent.)

Dr R: Go and wee for me, in the bottle.

Rachael saw the girl scuttle from the cubicle and collect a urine sample bottle from Sister Naidoo. She returned a few minutes later, urine sample in hand.

Dr R: You're pregnant, that's why you're feeling sick. Who's the father?

Patient: I don't know.

Dr R: How can you not know? Who did you sleep with? It can't be that difficult.

Patient: My boyfriend.

Dr R: How old is he?

Patient: Sixteen also.

Dr R: And did you think about this before you had sex? Did you think about how you – a girl who is still at school – would bring up a child? Did you think about what it costs to bring up a child? Can you afford to buy food and clothes and nappies for the baby?

Patient (*tearfully*): No.

Dr R (*tone suddenly much gentler*): Well, it's a bit late to suddenly start thinking about these things now. You need to go to outpatients next Thursday afternoon for an ultrasound scan to see how far you are. I'll write you a letter to take with you. In the meantime, you need to think about whether you're going to keep this child or not. Sister will give you a multivitamin tablet on your way out.

Exit patient.

Dr Ribbentrop followed behind the patient and made his way to the doctors' office. Rachael wondered what had motivated him to become a doctor. He didn't seem to care very much. Perhaps he hadn't started off like that; perhaps that was what happened when one worked at a state hospital for too long.

Rachael called in her next patient, a young man dressed in overalls who walked into casualty with a limp. He told her that he had been bitten by a snake.

'A snake? Did you say a snake?' Rachael asked, hoping that she had heard incorrectly. She had never had to treat a snake bite before. She had never even seen a snake bite before. In fact, the only snakes that she had ever had any contact with had been safely behind glass at the reptile park. 'Where did it bite you?' she asked.

'In the garden. I was busy gardening.'

'No, I meant where on your body did it bite you?'

The man lifted his trouser leg to reveal a swollen, red lower leg. The puncture mark was visible at the centre of the swelling. Rachael looked around casualty for Dr Ribbentrop; her knowledge was far too limited to manage a snake bite on her own. She caught sight of him leading an extended Indian family into one of the free cubicles. 'I'm just going to speak to one of the other doctors quickly,' she explained to the patient.

As she was walking away she vaguely remembered learning that one should always ask snake-bite victims what kind of snake had bitten them, or at least what it had looked like. She went back and asked the patient, glad that she had remembered to do so before she spoke to Dr Ribbentrop so that she would be able to give him an answer when he asked her. Engrossed in self-congratulation, she was only partially aware of the patient opening an old cooler box in response to her question. The slate–grey snake inside, obviously desperate for freedom, flung itself from the cooler box as soon as the lid had been lifted and headed straight in Rachael's direction. Rachael screamed. It was a scream so primal that it was partially out of her mouth before she actually registered why she was screaming. She jumped backwards onto the examination bed, a feat that she would never have been able to perform without the presence of a hissing reptile to incite her, and continued her screaming from the relative safety of one metre above ground. Sister Naidoo was also screaming now, and started running in the opposite direction to the snake, and the large Indian family that Dr Ribbentrop had been on the verge of seeing had spread itself out in various panic-stricken directions. Only Dr Ribbentrop seemed calm. Rachael watched the snake slither over the grey linoleum floor, on which she had been standing a few seconds earlier, and make its way beneath one of the casualty cupboards.

'Right, could we please have some calm in here!' Dr Ribbentrop shouted. 'It's only a bloody snake.'

Startled anew by his voice, Rachael abruptly closed her mouth and clamped off her screaming. The casualty unit was in chaos. Rachael's patient had tried to jump up onto the examination bed next to her but, because of his lame leg, had fallen and was now lying on the floor below Rachael, trying to drag himself in the direction of the exit. Sister Naidoo was standing on the sisters' desk with a fork in one hand and a letter opener in the other (Rachael couldn't imagine that either would be particularly effective against a snake, since both were rather close-proximity weapons). The sick child who belonged to the extended family, and whom Dr Ribbentrop had been about to put onto a nebuliser for asthma, had pulled the nebuliser from the wall when his mother grabbed him to escape. The child was clinging desperately to the disconnected mask, inhaling ineffectively through it, while oxygen was escaping into the room. The asthmatic child's father had managed to pull himself up into one of the large stainless steel sinks at the back of casualty. Unfortunately, the sink already contained a bloodied delivery set that had been used for a birth earlier in the day, and the placenta from the same birth.

'My God, my shattered nerves,' he wailed, realising what he was standing in. He extricated himself from the bloody mess, shaking pieces of placenta from his trousers. 'My shattered nerves,' he reiterated. 'I think I'm going to have a heart attack. I can feel the poking starting in my chest. I need something to calm me down.' He reached into the breast pocket of his shirt with shaking hands and pulled out a single cigarette and a lighter.

The next few seconds seemed to Rachael to unfold in slow motion. She heard Dr Ribbentrop screaming something at the man. She heard his shout a split second later, just before the very loud bang. The explosion, as the leaking oxygen combusted, was almighty. Luckily, the gas had been on a very low flow rate. Sister Naidoo sprang from the desk, dropped her fork and letter opener and, with extraordinary presence of mind, grabbed the fire extinguisher from the wall behind her. Remarkably, it was still working. The fire was quickly put out, but by the time Sister Naidoo had gained control of the fire extinguisher the room was covered in a thick layer of white foam. The mother, now resembling a bedraggled snowman, grabbed her asthmatic child and ran from casualty. The father followed, leaving behind him a trail of placenta-specked froth. The snake was nowhere to be seen.

It took Rachael and Sister Naidoo and Dr Ribbentrop and one of the porters and the hospital cleaner two hours to create some sort of order from the mess.

'It was a Mozambican spitting cobra, an *m'fezi*,' Dr Ribbentrop said to Rachael matter-of-factly afterwards. 'I've sent your patient through to the snake-bite unit.'

'Oh, fantastic,' Rachael said, relieved that she no longer had to manage the patient. She should have known that snake bites would be sent to a special unit. It was probably somewhere in Durban; perhaps the patient had even been airlifted there.

'Down the corridor and to the left,' Dr Ribbentrop continued. 'You can go see your patient there.'

Rachael's heart didn't just sink, it plummeted. She still had no clue how to treat the snake bite and she was far too embarrassed to ask Dr Ribbentrop now. From the way he had looked at her while he was wiping fire-extinguisher foam from the casualty floor, she got the distinct impression that he blamed her entirely for the huge casualty fiasco. She would have to hope that there was a sister in the snake-bite unit who could give her some advice. She turned around and was about to walk away when she remembered the snake. It had disappeared beneath the cupboard but had not subsequently reappeared.

'What about the snake?' she asked Dr Ribbentrop, momentarily too concerned about being bitten to worry about what he thought of her. 'Will you get someone in to remove it?'

'The *m'fezi* is a shy snake; it won't attack unless it's cornered,' he answered impatiently. He was still wiping foam from his hair. 'They can spit, though,' he continued, a small smile starting to flicker at the corner of his mouth. 'According to some records they can spit from a distance of up to two metres with incredible accuracy. They usually hide in rock crevices ... or any other dark place,' he said, looking pointedly at the bottom of the cupboard. Rachael made her way as quickly as possible from casualty to the snake-bite unit.

The *Handbook of Trauma* (proudly published in the United States of America) informed Rachael that she should administer antivenom as soon as possible in order to treat the bite. When she asked the sister in the unit for antivenom, the sister looked at her as though she had asked for cocaine.

'For that bite?' the sister asked. Rachael nodded hesitantly. 'We'll have to order some from Pretoria,' the sister continued doubtfully.

'Don't you usually treat with antivenom?' Rachael asked, beginning to doubt her trauma handbook. The sister shook her head. Obviously, they did things differently in America. Since she didn't possess a South African trauma book (she made a mental note to buy one as soon as possible), Rachael had no option but to swallow her pride and go ask Dr Ribbentrop for help. She walked back to casualty, carefully avoiding the cupboard, and asked Dr Ribbentrop if he could help her manage the patient. Contrary to what she had expected, he wasn't at all irritated with her. While they walked back to the snake-bite unit together, he gave her a quick tutorial on the management of snake bites.

'Ninety-eight per cent of snake bites aren't fatal,' he reassured her. 'Giving antivenom is usually more dangerous than the bite itself.'

By the time Rachael got back to casualty after treating her snakebite victim, Seema, the rather aloof Indian intern, had arrived and was getting ready to take over from her. Rachael handed over her patients to Seema and then lingered in the unit for a while, listening to the sisters and staff singing. It amazed her that they managed to harmonise together, without an instrument to guide them. It also amazed her how much energy they seemed to be able to muster for their singing after working a full twelve-hour shift. She was so exhausted she was sure that if she tried to sing all that would emerge would be a tired whimper. She felt something wet her ankle and bent down to wipe it off. As she did so, she felt another squirt, this time on the back of her neck. She was looking up at the ceiling to see where the water was dripping from when she realised that what she had felt had not been a drip. It had been a distinct spray. Dr Ribbentrop's words played through her mind like something from a horror movie: spitting cobras could aim from two metres. She screamed and clambered onto the nearest examination bed, something she was by now getting good at. The singing stopped abruptly and Rachael waited for the sisters to start running out of casualty, or at least to climb to places of safety, but they remained where they were – and started laughing. Something was not right. Rachael slowly turned to look behind her. One of the community service doctors was standing with a dental syringe and needle in his hand, laughing.

'I'm sorry,' he spluttered. 'Dr Ribbentrop told me what happened and I couldn't let the opportunity slip. I'm really sorry.' He exploded into a fresh bout of guffaws, which rather threw in doubt the sincerity of his apology. Rachael didn't know whether to laugh or cry or shout at the doctor. Before she could make up her mind, he extended his hand in greeting.

'Shane Pillay,' he said.

He has nice eyes, Rachael noticed. Under different circumstances, she probably would have thought him quite good-looking. She decided to join in the laughter.

Seema

8

Seema had Saturday free and so, when Satesh suggested that they drive to Durban for the day, she jumped at the opportunity. It had been a long time since she and Satesh had done anything special together. Actually, it had been a long time since they had done anything together. Although they stayed in the same house and greeted each other every day, they seemed to live parallel lives whose paths hardly ever intersected: Satesh on his computer and Seema in the hospital. Perhaps he too was excited at the prospect of spending some time with her because he was in an inexplicably good mood (or perhaps it was only the idea of an outing that had prompted his joviality). As they drove out of the hospital parking lot, he turned up the volume of the CD player in his car. Even with the speakers blasting forth tunes, the roar of the modified engine was audible above the music. Satesh had adapted his 1.3 litre hatchback, lowering the suspension and putting in a free-flow exhaust to make the car faster. Seema panicked whenever she was in the car with him because he drove so fast and so aggressively. She would think of patients she had seen in the trauma unit, the victims of car accidents, and then superimpose her and Satesh's faces on the injured bodies. She didn't tell him to slow down, though, because she knew that would just prompt him to drive faster. Instead, she looked out of the window at the sugar-cane plantations, trying not to imagine what the speedometer was reading.

'So, what do you want to do today?' Satesh asked her, interrupting her thoughts.

'I don't know,' she responded. 'Whatever you want to do.' It was enough for her just to be spending time with her husband.

'I thought maybe we could catch a movie,' Satesh said.

'That would be nice,' she agreed.

They arrived at the shopping mall in time to watch the midday screening. Standing in line to buy the tickets, Seema felt a strange bubbling of nervousness and excitement wriggle across her stomach. She hadn't felt like this for years; it was almost as though she was a young girl again, going to watch her first movie. Satesh wanted to see a horror film, and even though she hated the genre Seema agreed to see it because she didn't want to ruin the perfection of the moment. She would rather sit through spooky dolls eating little children than put up with the sulkiness that she knew would follow if she suggested watching something else. Her treat was not the choice of movie; it was that her husband wanted to watch a movie with her. Seema could still clearly remember the first time they had gone to the movies together as a couple. Her mother had sent an elderly aunt along with them as a chaperone. Satesh had bought a box of popcorn for her aunt and one for her and then asked if he could share her box with her. She remembered the brief moments of contact that their fingers had made behind the printed cardboard of the popcorn box – illicit, electric, salty skin-on-skin moments. He had slipped his hand surreptitiously onto her leg and she had touched it hesitantly in the darkness. It had been the first time she had been so close to a male who was not a relative; the first time she had smelt the musky scent of lust poorly disguised by aftershave; the first time she had felt the warmth of desire deep within her pelvis. Later, she had seen their intertwined fingers illuminated by the flickering blue-white light of a midnight axe-murderer and had wished she would one day marry the man whose hand was inseparable from hers.

After the movie, she and Satesh went to a seafood restaurant for fish and chips. Satesh behaved like a perfect gentleman, like the man who had courted her for eight months and with whom she had fallen so desperately in love. He paid attention to what she was saying and nodded in agreement with her opinions; he pulled her chair out for her and offered to carry her bag; he looked at her as though she was the only woman in the room, as though he adored her, as though she, and only she, could fulfil him. After lunch, they wandered arm in arm around the shopping centre looking through shop windows. Seema pointed out an evening dress that she thought was lovely. Satesh escorted her into the shop and urged her to try it on.

'No, it's much too expensive. We can't afford to spend this on a dress right now,' she protested, showing Satesh the price tag.

'Go try it on anyway,' Satesh said, forcing the dress into her hands. 'Let's just see what it looks like.'

She put the dress on and then called Satesh to the fitting cubicle so that she could show him what it looked like. She knew that it flattered her, that she looked good in it, and she wanted Satesh to see it on her even if she wasn't going to buy it. He reacted just as she had hoped: he grabbed her by the arm and swirled her around and told her she looked like a princess, a model, the most beautiful girl in the world. And then, when she was changing back into her clothes, she heard Satesh whisper theatrically to the twittering sales assistant that he would buy the dress as a surprise gift for his wife. It dampened Seema's joy only slightly knowing that it was in fact she who was paying for the dress and that they actually could not afford it.

Two years previously, before they were married, Seema would have believed this to be reality. Now, she didn't. Now, she knew that what felt like perfection was tenuous. The smallest inconvenience, one misplaced word spilt from her lips, a laugh too loud or a glance too bold, could bring it all tumbling down. And so she kept quiet and tried to hold on to the present, capture it and make it last. She listened to Satesh telling her about a new car that he wanted to buy and she tried to pretend that this time Satesh had changed for sure, that this time it would last.

Satesh was still in a good mood the next morning when Seema left for the hospital. It was the first time since she had started working at Prince Xoliswe that she wasn't desperate to get to work simply to escape Satesh's company. He gave her a kiss as she left, not a quick peck on the lips, but a deep, wet kiss that lingered in the most secret recesses of her mouth, and she didn't want to leave him. It was pathetic, she thought as she walked to the hospital, the taste of her husband still with her, that her esteem, her sense of self-worth, her whole outlook on life, was so dependent on Satesh's labile mood. Nevertheless, she walked through the doors of casualty feeling like a princess.

Seema was on call with Dr Ribbentrop. He was reading the newspaper when she walked into the doctors' office, but he threw it angrily onto the desk before she had even put her bag down.

'Stupid bloody papers, always out for sensationalism,' he said, stabbing at an article with his stubby index finger. Seema could read the headline: *Meningitis Outbreak in KwaZulu-Natal*. It was the first that Seema had heard of it and it was a huge disaster if it was true. Bacterial meningitis was highly contagious and could kill within hours. She didn't understand what Dr Ribbentrop was so angry about. Surely it was preferable that people were aware of the meningitis outbreak so that they could go straight to hospital if they displayed any symptoms? Her face must have reflected her surprise.

'Look at this bullshit,' Dr Ribbentrop continued, still jabbing at the offending article with his finger. The newspaper was beginning to crinkle under his anger. Seema noticed that red blotches had appeared on the apples of his cheeks. 'Some GP diagnosed a few patients with headaches as having meningitis and this stupid bloody reporter has turned it into a full-scale bacterial meningitis outbreak. We'll probably end up seeing every cold and flu and hangover in Tugela Bridge today just because every idiot with a headache will think he's got meningitis.'

As though on cue, a sister put her head round the door and told Dr Ribbentrop and Seema that there were sixteen patients waiting to be seen.

'What, already?' Dr Ribbentrop roared. 'And you thought I was ranting on for no reason,' he said, raising one eyebrow in Seema's direction. She felt her face get hot in embarrassment. She had been thinking that he was overreacting. But she had also been thinking that she would rather see a hundred patients than risk missing one case of meningitis. She couldn't help feeling that Dr Ribbentrop was not very professional.

By the time Seema walked over to the pile of folders, there were twenty-four patients waiting to be seen. She called in her first patient. A twenty-year-old woman limped in, leaning on the arm of a young man who introduced himself to Seema as the patient's brother. By the manner in which the patient had walked into casualty, Seema suspected that she had an ankle or leg injury, so she was surprised when the woman held her hands to her head and started moaning about a headache. Seema examined the patient thoroughly and found nothing wrong apart from a mild sinusitis, which would account for the headache (but not the limping). Seema prescribed some Paracetamol and an antihistamine and told the patient that she could go. The patient held her hands to her eyes and told Seema that the light hurt her head and she was sure that she was far too sick to go home. Seema reassured her again that there was really very little wrong and that she could go.

'But don't you think that I've got the meningitis?' the woman asked, almost panting in her effort to appear ill.

Seema didn't know whether the patient had a serious problem that she had missed, or whether she was merely a drama queen prompted into action by the newspaper article. Suddenly unsure of herself, she re-examined the patient and confirmed what she had found before: the patient had none of the clinical signs of meningitis; she didn't even have a fever. She sent the woman out and called in her next patient.

A portly forty-year-old man followed Seema into the cubicle and asked her how long it was likely that he would need to be admitted for. Seema explained to the patient that she would first need to examine him to see if admission was necessary.

'But Doctor, I could die in my condition,' the man objected.

Confused, because the man looked far from terminally ill, Seema asked the man what his condition was.

'Meningitis,' the man stated morbidly. 'My aunt is a receptionist for a doctor and she knows all the signs of meningitis and she told me that I have it. Look at this: I can't even turn my head to the side.'

Knowing that the neck stiffness of meningitis affected only neck flexion, not movement to the sides, Seema was beginning to understand why Dr Ribbentrop had been so irritated by the newspaper article. She silently added her curses to his and examined the patient. Even though she thought it very unlikely, she still had to confirm that the patient did not have meningitis. As she was discharging the patient (much against his will – he was still convinced that he was in the throes of a meningitis attack), she heard Dr Ribbentrop storm out of casualty shouting something about sorting the problem out. Unable to contain her curiosity, Seema followed the direction of his voice. She found him standing outside casualty, in front of the rows of chairs that the patients waiting to be seen were sitting in.

'Right!' he shouted. 'Put your hand up if you have a headache and think you have meningitis.' Twenty-three of the twenty-four waiting patients raised their hands. 'Okay, all of you with your hands up, look down and put your chins against your chests.' The patients stared at him as though he was crazy. 'Come on,' he commanded, 'like this.' He flexed his neck so that his chin was jammed into his chest. The patients imitated him nervously. 'Now, all of you, get up and go home,' he said, waving his hand in the direction of the exit. 'If you can do that, you don't have meningitis.' The patients stood up and quickly filed out. 'No, not you,' Dr Ribbentrop said, grabbing the man at the end of the queue of departing patients and pulling him back onto his chair. Seema couldn't help noticing the knife sticking out of the wound on the back of his skull.

Seema's next patient was a fourteen-month-old infant that had been brought to the hospital by its aunt. The baby was dressed in a dirty blue T-shirt and stained leggings. Seema noticed immediately that there was something wrong with the child, although she could not identify exactly what it was. More than a specific medical sign, it was something about the resigned way that the infant lay in the aunt's arms and the child's lack of response to being brought into the examination room that worried Seema. It was usual for children to show some hesitancy or curiosity on being brought to see her, and even to cry, but to show nothing was decidedly abnormal.

· 'How can I help you?' Seema asked, interested to find out what was wrong with the child.

'His mother said he fell into the bath and burnt himself,' the aunt replied. She avoided making eye contact with Seema as she spoke.

'Where about is the burn?' Seema asked. She was already suspicious of the story, both because the aunt had refused to look her in the eye when she answered her and because fourteen-month-old babies do not fall into baths often or easily.

The aunt pulled the child's leggings down and undid the soiled nappy in response to Seema's question. She pointed to the infant's bottom. Seema saw that the skin on the child's bottom was raw but was able to make out little else. She took the infant from the aunt (still concerned by the baby's lack of complaint) and laid him down on the examination bed, then lifted his legs into the air to examine the wound properly. The burn was circular in shape and extended across the genitalia and both buttocks cheeks. The scalded area was excoriated, raw and blistered. A film of pus covered the burn, presumably as a result of coming into contact with faeces and urine in the nappy. Seema couldn't help glancing at the dirty nappy that the aunt had just removed. How could the infant's caregivers have been so negligent as to have left a soiled nappy on an open wound? The injury looked at least three or four days old, and she wondered why the child was only being brought in now.

Seema had seen a burn like this before. It had been neatly projected from a PowerPoint presentation onto the white screen at the front of her forensic medicine lecture theatre. The pattern of the wound was typical because the mechanism of injury was well recognised: as the child was dipped into scalding water, it lifted its legs in a desperate attempt to escape, leaving burn marks in an almost perfect circle on the buttocks and genitalia. The feet were always spared. Seema flinched at the thought of the pain that the child must have endured, must still be enduring, and it worried her that the infant was not crying. What other horrors had it suffered that it didn't cry for this? Or, even worse, was the baby too frightened to cry? She looked over the child carefully, searching for any other evidence of abuse. One of the infant's hands was swollen and badly bruised, and Seema asked the aunt what had happened to the hand, even though she already suspected what had occurred. The aunt looked down and shrugged her shoulders in response to the question; she was just visiting, she said, she didn't live with the child. Seema wondered whose foot it was that had stamped on those plump, dimpled little fingers.

'We need to admit him,' Seema said to the aunt. She didn't know what to do, what the protocol was regarding non-accidental injuries, but she knew that to send the child home would be tantamount to being an accomplice to murder.

'I think it's better to keep him here for a while,' the aunt agreed, looking directly at Seema for the first time. Seema wondered whether she should ask the aunt about the abuse or whether that would be impolite. She would hate the aunt to think that she was accusing her of abusing the child. It was an awkward situation and she felt completely out of her depth. She knew what to do to treat the burn and the fractured hand – that was easy – but she didn't know where to begin to try to sort out the social problems. She decided that her best option would be to ask Dr Ribbentrop for some advice.

'I've got a suspected non-accidental injury,' she told him, catching him between patients. 'I don't really know what the protocol for management is in a case like this. Do we get a social worker involved only on a suspicion or do we have to prove the abuse first? I'd really appreciate it if you would take a look at the child and make sure that my assessment of the situation is correct.'

Dr Ribbentrop walked with her to the cubicle where the aunt and infant were waiting. The baby was still quiet; not one cry or moan had passed his lips since Seema had started seeing him. Seema showed Dr Ribbentrop the burn and the hand injury.

'That's not a suspected NAI,' he said gruffly. 'That's a textbook example of child abuse. Who's hurting the baby?' he asked, turning to the aunt. Seema cringed at his brashness. The aunt looked down, avoiding Dr Ribbentrop's piercing stare. 'Is it you?' he asked sternly.

'No, no, no, never,' the woman cried. 'I would never hurt a child like this. He's only a baby. You need to help him, please.' Seema noticed that tears were rolling down her cheeks.

'Who is it, then?' he asked, more gently this time. 'You need to tell me. That's the only way we'll be able to help the child.'

'It's the mother's boyfriend. He does this to the baby when he gets drunk. I think he's jealous of the attention that my sister gives to the baby.' Now that she had started talking, she couldn't stop. And the more that she spoke, the more she cried, until the words were almost indistinguishable from the tears. 'He supports the whole family. Without him we would be living on the street. My sister has forbidden me to bring the child to the doctor, but I couldn't handle it any longer. I can't see him suffer like this. She doesn't know that I've brought him. She'll kill me when she finds out. She'll be so mad. She'll probably kick me out the house. And I don't even want to think what Diederick will do. Oh God, this is such a mess,' she wailed.

'Sister!' Dr Ribbentrop called loudly. One of the nurses peeked nervously around the curtain of the examination cubicle. 'Please take this lady and give her a cup of tea with some sugar. See if you can get hold of a counsellor for her to talk to.' He turned to the aunt. 'You did the right thing by bringing the child in,' he reassured her. 'You've probably saved his life.'

The aunt left with the sister and Dr Ribbentrop turned his attention to the child. He touched its forehead softly and Seema was surprised at how gentle his touch was. He smiled at the baby and the infant looked back at him, its eyes briefly clear. It didn't smile or gurgle at him, but it reached out with its undamaged hand and grabbed Dr Ribbentrop's finger. He sat for a few minutes with the child, allowing it to hold the finger of one hand while he stroked its head with the other. Seema would never have imagined that such a stern giant of a man could be so tender.

'You should probably do a full radiological skeletal survey,' he said eventually, looking up at Seema. 'Do X-rays of the whole body. We need to make sure there's no other damage. Have you examined him?'

Seema nodded and told Dr Ribbentrop what she had found on examination.

'Did you check the abdomen?' he asked.

'Yes,' she said. 'It was soft and undistended. There was no evidence of blunt trauma to the liver or spleen.'

Dr Ribbentrop opened his mouth as if to say something but then shut it again. He handed the child gently to Seema. 'I think it's best you call the radiographer in even though it's a Sunday. We need those X-rays done as soon as possible,' he said, walking towards the cubicle curtain. 'Oh, and well done for picking this up, Dr Singh, and for the way in which you managed it.' He nodded once at her and then disappeared to see his next patient.

Seema took the child up to the paediatric ward herself and explained the situation to the sister. On Dr Ribbentrop's advice, she directed the sister not to let any visitors in to see the baby. 'Call me once the X-rays have been done,' she said, writing up some analgesia on the child's prescription chart. As she walked back to casualty, she tried to clear her mind. She knew that if she didn't, she wouldn't be able to concentrate on seeing other patients. The child had been so fragile and helpless in her arms as she had carried it, and it had been so trusting in the way in which it had clung to her. She couldn't begin to understand what would drive someone to hurt such a tiny being, to wilfully inflict pain on it. Such behaviour was inhumane and contrary to every human instinct. The worst thing, though, the niggling worry that concerned her most and that she didn't even allow to rise properly from her subconscious, but that she was also unable to ignore, was that she was not sure that Satesh was incapable of such behaviour.

Seema was called back to the ward three hours later to review the X-rays. She slipped them from the large brown envelope in which they had arrived from radiology and placed them one by one on the light box. As directed, the radiographer had done a full skeletal survey, taking images of every bone in the child's body.

Seema was looking for evidence both of current and past fractures. She started with the feet and legs, comparing the left side to the right to make sure that she missed nothing. The feet appeared normal but the legs showed evidence of two old fractures. Large calluses of new bone were visible where the breaks were healing and Seema guessed that the fractures were at least six weeks old. She checked that the pelvic bones were intact, paying special attention to the ischial bones, which are often fractured in cases of sodomy or rape. Thank God there was no evidence of that, Seema thought, taking the plates of the lower limbs off the light box. She put up another small X-ray, this time of the infant's chest. The rosary was immediately visible. Rosary: the line of partially healed fractures visible along consecutive ribs when a child's chest is forcibly compressed. Prayer beads. The irony of the name gave Seema pause. She checked that the lungs had not been punctured by fragments of rib, then put up the next plates. The arms showed evidence of only one fracture, at the end of the right humerus. It was a typical fracture, resulting from a pulling force on one arm.

Seema felt her stomach turn and quickly leant forward over the basin in the ward. She concentrated on the mould growing on the edges of the plug hole; on the rust-stained water that had pooled around the base of the tap; on the empty soap dispenser. She concentrated on anything other than the image of a delicate little body being shaken and trodden on and picked up by one arm and thrown to the floor. She still needed to check the cervical spine for neck fractures and the skull for injuries. She had to do it, had to pull herself together and finish doing her job. She turned on the tap and ran her hands under the cold water. It was a trick that she had learned from her father when he had been trying to give up smoking. The sensation of the cold liquid trickling between her fingers and sliding over the backs of her hands helped to calm her.

She turned off the tap and put the last three X-ray plates on the viewing box. Fortunately, she could make out no further fractures. She put the X-rays away and took the brown envelope to the foot of the child's bed, then made some notes in the folder. The sister was busy putting a dressing on the burn wound. It looked worse than it had before and Seema asked the sister to take a swab and then start the antibiotics immediately. She was about to go when she noticed that the baby was making a strange jerking movement. Seema panicked for a moment, worried that the child was having a seizure. Had she missed a head injury on her examination? Seema checked the infant's pupils and level of consciousness. He wasn't having a fit. It took her a while to realise that there were tears rolling down the baby's cheeks. The silence of the child's crying filled the whole ward.

Seema was exhausted when she got home from the hospital at a quarter past seven that evening. She fantasised about what she would do if she didn't have to cook dinner for Satesh and put in a load of washing and finish the ironing and write up her patients for the following day's handover round: she would run herself a deep, hot bath (it really was a fantasy – there were no baths in the doctors' quarters, only showers) and soak away all the traumas of the day and then she would go to bed, to her own bed, alone, and sleep until the sun woke her. But that was not to be. Satesh started complaining about how hungry he was the moment she walked into the flat. Obviously his good mood had not survived the day without her. Seema didn't have the energy to make a full meal, so she quickly kneaded some salted dough with water and rolled out thin rounds, which she fried for a second on each side in a hot pan. She took a bowl of left-over curry from the fridge and wrapped servings of the curry in the rotis. Satesh would have to make do with convenience food tonight: she still had to do the ironing and clean the house.

'Dinner's ready,' she called to Satesh.

'About bloody time too,' he moaned, taking a roti from her. She waited for him to complain about the meal, but surprisingly he didn't. He went to eat in front of the television and she went back to the bedroom to finish folding the clean laundry.

'So, am I not good enough for you to eat with?' Satesh shouted to her from the lounge. 'I suppose my company's too boring since I'm not a doctor.'

Seema didn't have the energy for this argument, one they had had a thousand times before. After what she had been through at the hospital, she didn't have the emotional reserves to sit and reassure him for half an hour that it didn't make any difference to her that he was not a doctor. She took the laundry basket to the lounge and started folding one of Satesh's shirts, hoping her presence in the lounge would avert an argument.

'Aren't you eating?' he asked her, his eyes fixed on the television screen.

'I'm too tired to eat,' she replied softly. 'I want to get the laundry done and clean the house as quickly as possible and then go to bed.'

Satesh took a bite from the roti and then suddenly spat it out. Seema wasn't surprised. Satesh seldom ate a meal that she made without at least one derogatory comment. She wondered whether the food didn't have enough salt in it or whether it had too much, or whether it was too hot or if this time it was too cold.

'Are you trying to poison me?' Satesh asked, grabbing his throat dramatically.

'I'm sorry,' Seema said, still under the impression that Satesh didn't like the way that she had cooked the meal. 'What did I do wrong?'

'You tell me,' he said, his voice cold and hard. 'Are you trying to poison me? Have you put poison in my food?'

The question was so bizarre that were it not for the tone of Satesh's voice, Seema would probably have started giggling. She didn't know how to respond to such a ridiculous question.

'Well?' Satesh demanded. Obviously he was expecting a response to his ludicrous suggestion.

'No, of course not,' Seema replied, picking up another shirt from the laundry basket.

'Then why aren't you eating?'

'I told you why. I'm too tired.'

'Bullshit. It's because you're trying to poison me, you stupid bitch. Did you actually think I would fall for it? I bet there's some doctor you're trying to fuck and I'm getting in the way.'

Seema flinched at his words. She wanted to run away. She wanted to escape through the door and take the steps two at a time and sprint back to the hospital, where she would be safe. But her legs would not move.

'Answer me!' Satesh shouted.

'I haven't put anything in your food, I promise. I swear it. I've never thought of poisoning you.' Her voice was a whimper now. Any thoughts she had had of giggling had fled.

'Then eat the food,' Satesh said, handing her the plate.

'Sorry?'

'I said, eat the food. If it isn't poisoned, then eat it.'

Seema took the roti from him and took a bite. Her nervousness made the food stick in her throat. She took another mouthful, forcing it down.

'Finish it,' Satesh said. He was standing up now, watching her.

'Satesh, I'm not hungry,' she protested. 'Surely the fact that I've taken two bites is enough evidence that I haven't poisoned your food.'

'Finish it,' Satesh said. His voice was steely. Seema knew better than to argue further. She forced mouthfuls of roti down her throat, struggling to quell her nausea. Her hands were shaking as she lifted the food to her mouth. Satesh watched her without saying a word. It felt to Seema that it had never taken her so long to finish a simple roti.

'Are you happy now?' she asked Satesh, after swallowing the last mouthful.

'Yes,' he smiled. 'In future you eat with me.' He sat back down in front of the television and continued watching his programme, picking up a second roti and biting into it as though nothing had interrupted his meal. Seema was too afraid to leave the lounge until he had finished, too afraid even to carry on folding the laundry. She sat quietly next to him and pretended to watch television, waiting for him to finish eating. As soon as his plate was clean she took it to the kitchen, then ran to the bathroom and leant over the toilet. She felt her body shudder and saw her shame splattered on the toilet bowl.

Nomsa

9

Shane Pillay was asking Nomsa about Rachael as they scrubbed up.

'She seems really nice,' Shane commented.

Nomsa knew that what Shane really meant was that Rachael was beautiful, glamorous, and had a figure that made an hourglass look rectangular. Guys didn't ask about girls they thought were nice. 'She seems friendly enough,' she agreed, playing along. She touched the wall-mounted soap dispenser with one elbow and caught the soap that dripped from the nozzle in her other hand. She rubbed her hands together until they were frothy with brown, iodine-stained suds, then worked the foam up her arms to the level of her elbows. She could see from the corner of her eye that Shane was watching her and she wondered if he was checking up on her scrubbing technique. She knew that no matter how hard he looked, he would find no fault with it. Deliberately she picked up a sterile nailbrush and scrubbed the brown foam beneath her fingernails. The iodine would kill off any germs lurking there. Shane finished scrubbing up and went to dry his hands with sterile paper towelling.

'So, do you know each other well, you and Rachael?' Shane asked Nomsa, reverting to their previous topic of conversation.

Nomsa knew what he was fishing for: he wanted to find out whether Rachael had a boyfriend, but she decided to keep him hanging a little longer. It wasn't as though his line of questioning was entirely appropriate anyway.

'I only met her at the beginning of the year,' Nomsa said, trying not to smile, 'so I don't really know her that well.' She picked up the paper towel from the top of the sterile pack that the sister had opened onto a trolley for her and dried her hands and elbows. Once

103

she had finished, she threw the paper towel away, careful not to let her now sterile hands touch anything in the process. She shook out the green theatre gown that was folded on top of the sterile pack and slipped her arms into the sleeves, then asked the sister to tie the bow at the back of her neck. Lastly, she put on the sterile gloves.

'Do you know if she's married or has a boyfriend or anything?' Shane asked eventually. His tone was deliberately nonchalant, obviously meant to imply that he was just asking because he had nothing else to ask and that he really didn't care what the answer was.

'I presume she's not married since she's living in the single quarters,' Nomsa said rather sarcastically. She knew that Shane had seen where Rachael stayed. His flat in the community service doctors' block was almost directly opposite Rachael's prefab. 'But I don't know if she has a boyfriend or anything. Sorry.' Rachael had never mentioned a boyfriend to Nomsa, so she presumed that she didn't have one, but she didn't feel like explaining this to Shane. He could ask Rachael himself if he was interested.

Shane turned his attention to the patient. He adjusted the sterile green cloth draping the patient's right leg and pointed out a pen mark below the patient's knee to Nomsa. It encircled the knee in a shape resembling a fish mouth.

'That's the line we're going to follow to cut,' Shane told her. 'Have you seen an above-knee amputation before?'

Nomsa shook her head.

'I'll explain to you what I'm doing as I go along and then you can do the next one,' Shane said.

She was glad that she didn't have to do this amputation: she was trembling so much with excitement she would hardly have been able to hold a blade. At last she felt like a real doctor. This was what she had studied for so many years to be able to do. She wanted to shout out and raise her fist to the sky in a triumphant punch, but she knew that she had to contain her excitement. This wasn't the place or time for a show of emotion. Besides, it would make her appear sadly desperate.

'The reason we cut in the shape of a fish mouth extending below

104

the actual joint', Shane was explaining to her, 'is that we need the excess skin to close up over the stump. It makes fitting a prosthesis easier and gives a better result cosmetically.'

Nomsa wondered whether the person who had done her amputation had thought of such niceties. It was unlikely, considering the scarring she had been left with. She didn't remember much of the procedure, just the snippets that had been imprinted on the receptive mind of a three-year-old. She hadn't had the top joint of her little finger amputated at birth, as some of the other children had. However, when she had been sick with vomiting and diarrhoea and then developed a heavy chest and become weak and thin, her grandmother decided to have *ingqiti* done to ensure that her granddaughter's health would improve. It was strange, Nomsa thought, that she didn't remember the pain. The only memories she had were of the darkness and sour smokiness of the stranger's hut to which she had been taken during the night, and the feeling of wet, warm cow dung afterwards, and the shouting of her mother when she had come back from Cape Town and seen her daughter's hand wrapped in a bandage. Nomsa shook her left hand slightly, as though trying to brush off the memories. 'Why is the man having an above-knee amputation?' she asked, trying to distract herself.

'Snake bite,' Shane replied. 'Puff adder. The tissue necrosis was too bad for us to save the limb.' He picked a scalpel from the instrument tray and sliced cleanly into the flesh along the pen markings that he had made earlier. Beneath the blade, the flesh seemed to offer itself up willingly. Far more willingly than the man must be offering up his lower leg, Nomsa thought.

Shane was a good teacher. He talked Nomsa through the operation and, once they had sawed through the bone of the lower femur, he allowed Nomsa to help him close the wound. Nomsa had spent hours and hours practising her suturing on thawed-out frozen chickens that she bought in bulk from the hypermarket while she had been studying. She had become used to picking bits of stitch from between her teeth when she ate the chicken. She worked quickly, her hands leaving a neat trail of sutures behind them.

'You stitch well,' Shane commented. 'Are you planning on

105

specialising in surgery when you finish your training one day?'

Nomsa nodded.

'There aren't many female surgeons around. You're rather brave.'

'Brave or stupid, I haven't decided which yet.' Nomsa wondered why she could never just choose the easy path. Never in her life had she taken the easy option. When her mother had relayed to her Mrs Watson's offer to pay for her schooling, Nomsa had jumped at the opportunity, even though it meant leaving all she knew to go to a distant Cape Town boarding school. Two months before she was due to begin at her new school, she had left her grandmother and younger sister in Aliwal North and had gone to stay with her mother in the small back room of Mrs Watson's Cape Town house. She had stayed up late at night watching English programmes on the box-like black and white television in her mother's room and reading English magazines until she had mastered the language. Before she left for the boarding school, her mother had explained to her that she would be one of the very few black children in the boarding house and had asked her once again if she was sure she wanted to leave. She had told her mother that she had never been surer of anything in her life. Perhaps that was the moment in which she had made her choice.

She had worked hard at school, hard enough to win a bursary to do a BSc, because she had known that her mother would never be able to afford to send her to university and she had not expected Mrs Watson, who was by then an invalid, to pay for her university tuition. And then, two years later, she had been awarded another bursary, this time to study what she had always dreamed of studying: medicine. This time, Mrs Watson had helped to pay for her studies. Now, once again, she was choosing the difficult path. Most female doctors specialised in disciplines that would one day afford them flexible working hours and little overtime, disciplines such as dermatology or rheumatology. Surgery, however, was a male-dominated specialty with plenty of after-hours work. Because of affirmative action, she knew that she was likely to get a registrar post in any specialty she wished, so it was crazy for her to choose

106

one of the most demanding. And yet she could think of doing nothing else. It was almost as though she needed to prove a point, to prove to everyone else that she was as good as she knew she was.

The next patient wheeled into theatre was a much more complicated case than a simple amputation, and Shane paged Dr Ribbentrop just before he started cutting to make sure that he would be available should he need him. Shane explained the procedure briefly to Nomsa while they were scrubbing up and she listened carefully, making a mental note of the steps that he would follow intra-operatively. The sister had already draped the patient with sterile green cloth by the time they got to him. The only exposed flesh was a large rectangle stretching the length of the patient's abdomen. Shane made a vertical incision down the abdomen, then gave Nomsa the electric cautery probe to cauterise small bleeding vessels as he worked. It was not a job she enjoyed: she didn't like either the hiss of the probe touching the flesh or the smoke and the smell of burnt hair that followed, and she was glad when Shane entered the abdomen and she could take a break. He gave her a large metal retractor to pull open the abdominal cavity while he worked. Nomsa carefully watched everything he did, trying to commit his technique to memory. Twice he called for the sister to hold up an anatomy textbook for him so that he could double-check the anatomical relations of various structures. It was a relief to Nomsa that Shane was able to show that he didn't know everything and that the sisters and other doctors didn't seem to think any less of him because of it.

'Great, that's the worst part over,' Shane said, once he had finished the major surgery. He turned to Nomsa. 'Would you like to close up?' Before Nomsa was able to answer, Shane tilted his head slightly to one side. 'Can anyone hear that noise?' he asked.

Initially Nomsa couldn't hear anything, but after a few seconds she made out the sound that Shane was referring to. It seemed to be coming from the ceiling, and it sounded like someone, or something, scratching.

'It's a rat in the ceiling,' one of the floor nurses said. 'They like the warmth.'

'But there are two floors above us,' another sister argued.

'So, there's still a gap between the ceiling here and the floor above us. I'm telling you, it's rats. I've seen them before,' the first sister said. They were still arguing when the ceiling emitted a loud groan, followed by a clang.

'Shit!' Shane exclaimed. Particles of dust, plaster and paint were raining down from above, making the previously sterile field now far from aseptic. An ear-piercing screech filled the room and Nomsa looked up, half expecting a dead body or an alien to fall from the ceiling. Instead, she saw the cover for the air-conditioner duct hanging down by some loose wires, and then a mangy cat falling from the open duct – directly onto the operating table. Without thinking twice, Nomsa flung the green drapes over the patient's still-open abdomen. The cat landed on the cloth, sunk slightly into the wound, shook some plaster off its coat and then jumped off the theatre table and ran from the room. A moment of stunned silence, broken only by the deep ventilated breathing of the anaesthetised patient, followed its departure.

'Holy shit!' Shane exclaimed, eventually. 'Why the hell was there a cat in the ceiling? I can't believe this just happened.' He shook his head in bewilderment. 'I've got to hand it to you,' he said to Nomsa, 'that was really quick thinking. Well done.'

'Thanks,' Nomsa said, nodding her head in acknowledgement. With the movement, a piece of plaster that had been balancing on her theatre mask fell onto her gown. 'We're going to have to scrub up again,' she said, flicking another piece of plaster off her arm.

Shane and Nomsa took off their soiled theatre gowns and scrubbed up again while the sister got fresh sterile drapes. They irrigated the abdomen with saline to try to remove the pieces of plaster and paint that had fallen into the wound. Once they were certain (or as certain as they could be in the circumstances) that they had removed all the foreign matter from the patient's stomach, Shane left Nomsa to close up the abdomen. She finished the suturing, then went to write some notes in the patient's file while the anaesthetist woke the patient up. As he was wheeling the patient from the theatre, the patient caught sight of Nomsa.

'Doctor,' the patient said, still slightly drowsy, 'Doctor, did my operation go well? Am I going to be all right?'

Nomsa nodded. 'Fine,' she lied. 'Everything went fine.' She tried to ignore Shane in the background, singing under his breath. *It's raining cats*, he sang softly, *hallelujah, it's raining cats ...*

10

Nomsa had two hours free between finishing work and starting her evening call and she decided to spend them having a shower, some dinner and, if there was time, a short nap. She rushed back across the hospital grounds to her prefab, anxious not to waste a precious second of her short break. When she got inside, she took off her trousers and shirt and folded them neatly on her bed, then went to pour herself a glass of chocolate milk. She had had a good day, but an exhausting one. Her brain felt overwhelmed by all the new information it had received. Not only had she learnt how to do an above-knee amputation (which she would be expected to be able to do on her own from now on), but she had also been taught how to do an appendicectomy and had assisted with six other cases. Plus there had been the whole drama with the cat. Her feet ached from standing up all day and her lower back was sore from bending over the theatre table. She massaged it with one hand, wondering if she would ever get used to the exhaustion. What she needed now was a long, hot shower and a large cup of very sweet coffee. She hoped that would give her enough of a lift to get her through the call.

She turned on the tap and the plumbing emitted a deep burp. A sluggish brown trickle dripped from the shower head. Great, she thought, this is just what I need. Obviously the water in the tank had run dry. She debated skipping the shower but knew she would regret it halfway into the call if she did; she was already sticky and imagined she could smell her sweat beneath the astringent scent of iodine that the theatre soap had left on the skin of her arms and hands. It was a smell unlikely to improve with time. She quickly pulled on a tracksuit, dug a twenty-rand note from her bag and went off in search of the dope-smoking borehole attendant.

Nomsa had only ever seen the man leaning against the low wall next to the pump, so she simply assumed he would be there. When she got there and he was nowhere in sight, she didn't have a clue where she should begin to look for him. She didn't even know if he stayed on the hospital premises. She sniffed, hoping to catch a whiff of dagga to give her some direction to follow, but the only scent in the air was of dry earth. Her shower was becoming more and more elusive. As she was about to give up hope and leave, Nathan ran past her. He was dressed in poly shorts and a vest and Nomsa wondered how he had the energy at the end of the day to exercise voluntarily. She waved a greeting at him and he slowed down.

'You looking for Sipho?' he asked.

Nomsa nodded.

'He's probably doing some gardening. Check behind the laundry,' Nathan said, accelerating again.

Nomsa shouted a thank you to his retreating back.

The doctors' laundry was a squat face-brick building that housed three coupon-driven top loaders and tumble dryers, all of which looked like they had given good and long service and were ready to retire. It was permanently shrouded in a humid mist of washing powder and fabric softener. Nomsa walked behind the building and found herself staring at a well-maintained, carefully cultivated plot of prime marijuana. Obviously Sipho had an occupation other than borehole attendant, and it was probably a much more lucrative one. He was standing on the far side of the plot, watering the plants. After catching sight of Nomsa, he turned off the hose and made his way across to her. She handed him the twenty-rand note.

'Keep the change,' she said, 'but please get going now. I need to shower in the next half an hour.'

'Sure. Sharp, sharp,' Sipho said, smiling. He blinked his bloodshot eyes and Nomsa wondered whether time had any meaning whatsoever for him. Her shower was, once again, looking unlikely. As she walked back to her prefab, she wondered whether Nathan knew what Sipho was growing in his 'garden' and how much extra money Sipho made selling dagga to doctors.

The water came through at six thirty. Just as she had given up all hope of having a shower, the pipes let off a gurgling sound and Nomsa sprang off her bed in joy. She turned on the tap and waited for the water to warm up. As she stepped into the shower, she heard her phone ring. She hesitated, tempted to leave it, but she knew that she wouldn't enjoy her shower if she didn't check who it was. She turned the tap off again and picked up her phone. Her mother's name was flashing on the screen. She rejected the call and then phoned her back, aware that her mother was on pay-as-you-go and that airtime was expensive for her.

Nomsa spoke to her mother once a week, more out of a sense of duty than anything else. She had felt for a long time that she and her mother no longer had anything in common and she struggled to find things to talk to her about. Their calls, punctuated with awkward silences, were seldom easy or pleasant. But there was more to it than simple awkwardness or drifting apart: Nomsa's telephone conversations with her mother were an unavoidable reminder to her of where she had come from. Once a week, as her mother's voice showered her with Xhosa through the cellphone speaker, Nomsa felt as though she was slipping backwards into the dark backwater from which she was working so hard to emerge.

'Ma,' Nomsa said, as her mother answered the telephone. '*Kunjane*? How are you?'

Her mother replied that she was sick and Nomsa thankfully shifted gear from daughter to doctor. This was a realm she was far more comfortable in. She asked her mother to explain her symptoms.

'I've got a cough, all the time, that is making me weak. It's stealing all my strength,' her mother said. 'And I'm getting very thin, so that now I am like a shadow, and I'm sweating at night until it looks like I have been walking in the rain.'

Nomsa's heart sank as she heard her mother's words. The symptoms her mother had just described were typical of pulmonary tuberculosis. Nomsa told her mother that she needed to go to the clinic urgently.

'I walked to the clinic the week before last week,' her mother replied. 'The nurse there gave me some pills. Let me fetch them.'

Nomsa could hear background noises as her mother searched for the tablets. There was the crescendo and decrescendo of a male voice on the radio (she could picture the antiquated portable radio perched on an upturned crate); intermittently there was the clang of metal on metal and Nomsa knew it was her aunt, head wrapped in a scarf and arms encircled with beaded bangles, cooking supper on the paraffin stove; there was the cry of a young baby and then a soft voice singing and she realised that it must be that of her younger sister singing to her child: the niece Nomsa had never met because she hadn't been back to her mother's house in three years. The sounds evoked an unexpected response in her, almost a longing. Her mother started speaking again and she pushed the thoughts of homesickness from her mind.

'I don't know how to say the words that are written on the packets,' Nomsa's mother said.

Nomsa was not surprised: her mother had only a standard two education. She asked her mother to spell the names out to her. The clinic sister had prescribed an antibiotic and an anti-inflammatory. Obviously they weren't working.

'You need to go back to the clinic and tell them to check for TB,' Nomsa told her mother, speaking quickly. She had to get off the phone soon or she wouldn't make it to the hospital in time. Her mother asked her about some cough mixture but Nomsa brushed the question aside. Cough mixture wouldn't help.

'I've got to go,' she told her mother. 'I've got to get to work. I'll speak to you later in the week. Go to the clinic and ask them to check for TB; they'll help you.'

Nomsa put the telephone down before her mother had a chance to reply. But it was not only because she was running late that Nomsa had been so keen to end the call. The feeling of longing, of familiarity, that she had felt while waiting for her mother to find the tablets had unsettled her. She wondered what had precipitated it, whether it was being alone in a new place. She couldn't remember when last she had thought of her mother's house in a positive light. She hated the place. It symbolised all that she wanted to move away from. She put her clothes from the day back on and tied her hair extensions up in a hairband. She would have to run to the hospital to make it there by seven o'clock.

She succeeded in getting to the hospital in time but not in pushing the thoughts of Aliwal North from her mind. It was as though the sounds of the radio and the pots clanging and the baby crying had acted as stimuli, triggering a tumbling avalanche of memories. Memories that she had long thought forgotten. Happy memories: the late afternoon sun filtering through the open door and warming the bare skin of her legs; the heaviness of red clay soil beneath her nails and between her fingers; the smell of her grandmother, of talcum powder, starch and tobacco. The memories were uncalled for, unwanted, and she pushed them away. She picked up a folder and called in her first patient, determined to rid her mind of the past.

Nomsa had hoped that her call would be busy, in order to distract her from thoughts of her mother, but she hadn't wanted it to be quite as busy as it was proving to be. Three hours into the shift and fifteen folders down the line, the flow of patients was showing no sign of ebbing.

'It's full moon tonight,' Dr Chetty, who was on call with her, told her as they met briefly at the pile of patient folders. 'We're always busy on full moon.'

Nomsa found that hard to believe. It sounded a little too much like witchcraft, like something her mother would say, but she couldn't think of any other, logical reason for it to be so busy on a Thursday night in the middle of the month. If the nightmare ever ended she would ask Dr Chetty about the significance of the moon's role, but for now she was too busy to contemplate lunar cycles any more deeply.

She was about to call in another patient when one of the sisters said something to her in Zulu. She could understand the odd word of Zulu, because there were some similarities with Xhosa, but she couldn't understand whole sentences. It irritated her that the sisters spoke to her in Zulu, that they just presumed that she would

113

understand them or should understand them. They would never speak to the white or Indian doctors in Zulu.

'Speak to me in English, please,' she requested curtly. She knew that the sisters didn't particularly like her, but it didn't bother her much. She wasn't at the hospital to make friends with the nursing staff. She definitely wasn't going to pander to them the way she had heard Rachael doing.

'The hospital's full,' the sister said sulkily.

Nomsa didn't know what to make of the statement. There were still about twenty patients waiting to be seen. Did this mean that she would have to send them elsewhere? The next closest hospital was a hundred and seventy kilometres away. She looked at the folder in her hand that she had picked up a moment before, unsure whether to call the patient in. The sister was still within earshot, but she was definitely not going to humiliate herself by asking her what the protocol was when the hospital was full. She went off to find Dr Chetty.

Dr Chetty was busy putting up an intravenous line on a patient when Nomsa found her. The other casualty nurse was with her, inserting a urinary catheter into the patient. This surprised Nomsa because when she had asked the same nurse earlier in the evening to put a catheter in for her, she had refused, saying it was not part of her job description. Nomsa had to restrain herself from making a comment. It seemed that the nursing staff's job description changed according to who was asking. In that case, Nomsa thought, she should get really good at putting in urinary catheters. She waited until Dr Chetty had finished inserting the IV line and then asked her what the protocol was when the hospital was full. Nomsa was desperately hoping that Dr Chetty would say that they closed Prince Xoliswe and sent all the patients to another hospital. She was exhausted and starving and the thought, the possibility, of getting to sit in the doctors' office for a few hours and do nothing except shovel chips and coffee into her mouth was blissful. Unfortunately, the thought did not seem to occur to Dr Chetty.

'Thanks,' she said in response to Nomsa's question. 'I'll call the ambulance service and let them know that we can only accept emergencies.' But wasn't that what they usually did anyway? Nomsa waited for Dr Chetty to say something more, but she had turned once again to her patient and was filling in a prescription chart. Nomsa slowly walked back to the pile of patient folders, which had miraculously managed to grow since she had left. The situation made no sense to her. If the hospital was full, surely they couldn't see any more patients? Where were they going to put all the patients that needed to be admitted? And what happened if a resuscitation came in? The intensive care unit was full and all the ventilators were in use. It wasn't as though the situation was about to change anytime soon, either. They could hardly discharge patients in the middle of the night, and it was unlikely that more than two patients would die overnight, so that eventuality wasn't going to free up many beds.

For the rest of the shift, Nomsa was ruthless. Any patient that was not likely to die overnight unless admitted, she sent home. She sent home a woman with pneumonia and told the daughter to bring her back when she became more short of breath. She knew that she would see the woman again in a few hours and she hoped that by then a bed would be free. She saw a teenage boy with a substance-induced psychosis who had become violent. She sedated him so that he passed out and told the family to take him home, hoping that the drug-induced mania would have lapsed by the time he woke up. She sent home a child with diarrhoea and prayed that the mother would be able to get the same amount of fluid down the child's throat as it was shitting out. And that the water that the mother made the rehydration fluid with would be clean.

But she couldn't send home the woman who had set herself alight. She had been brought in by ambulance and, because there were no beds, the paramedics had deposited her onto one of the metal gurneys that lined the corridor leading to casualty. Nomsa could smell the paraffin on her before she reached her. The woman was wearing the remains of a sari, once turquoise but now grey with soot, the edges black and charred. According to the paramedics, she had set herself on fire because her husband had left her. Nomsa sited an IV line on the woman's foot, because she had no skin left

115

on her hands or arms (her shoes had not been as flammable as the polyester-silk blend of the sari), and started running fluid into her, trying to replace the fluid that was leaking from her skinless body. She managed to find some Burnshield at the bottom of a cupboard. It had expired but she used it anyway, wrapping the woman's hands and arms and disfigured breasts in its cool mintiness. The morphine that Nomsa gave the patient didn't stop her screams; it merely reduced them to whimpers. Nomsa wondered how a man could have driven this woman to hurt herself in this way. No man she had ever met was worth setting oneself alight over. She discussed the patient later with Dr Chetty, who explained that it didn't happen infrequently. In certain conservative Indian families, the shame of a husband leaving his wife was so great that suicide was the only honourable option that remained to the wife. So it had not been only a man who had driven the woman to set herself on fire; it had been a whole community.

By the time Nomsa finished stabilising her burns patient, the passage had become a makeshift ward. Gurneys lined both sides of the corridor, making passage down it difficult. The air was thick with moans. Nomsa walked past a man who had been stabbed in the abdomen. The ambulance had dropped him off, but in the mayhem he had somehow not been brought to the attention of either her or Dr Chetty. Blood had pooled on the gurney and was slowly dripping onto the floor. The man's abdomen was tense and distended and his skin was clammy. Nomsa checked his blood pressure: it was seventy over forty, far too low. The man needed to be taken to theatre urgently. She ran to find Dr Chetty, who took one look at the patient and phoned Dr Ribbentrop.

'We're going to have to open a second theatre,' Nomsa heard her say. 'I know you worked last night but we're desperate. It's chaos here.'

Nomsa wondered how often the senior medical officers got woken up from their sleep to come and help with an emergency. Did they ever really have any time off? But there wasn't time for her to ponder that now. She ran to the still-growing pile of patient folders and called in the next patient. Nomsa didn't even have to examine the patient to know that she needed to be admitted. She was shivering and delirious with fever. Her chest caved in and out and her nostrils flared with the effort of each breath. AIDS and TB, Nomsa guessed. The stabbed abdomen had gone to theatre, so Nomsa wiped the blood from the gurney and put the new patient in the stabbed abdomen's place. The sister managed to find a portable oxygen cylinder to put at the patient's bedside. That would have to do for the moment. Nomsa ran back to the pile of folders and called in her next patient.

Twelve hours passed quickly, so quickly that Nomsa was startled by the sound of singing at seven o'clock. She had no idea what the time was; she couldn't even remember when last she had looked at her watch. She finished stitching up the panga wound that she had been suturing and stumbled her way to the doctors' office. There were patients everywhere: on gurneys lining both sides of the corridors, lying on the benches in the waiting area, sitting between beds. Often relatives stood next to the patients, holding up their bags of intravenous fluids in lieu of drip stands. Nomsa thought she would be glad if she never had to experience another night like this. She put the kettle on and sat down. Her feet were throbbing, the muscles of her legs ached, her clothes were filthy and her brain felt numb, as though her head had been stuffed with cotton wool. The kettle turned itself off with an audible click, but she didn't have the energy to get up to make herself a cup of coffee. She heard Dr Chetty come into the office.

'Oh good, the kettle's boiled,' Dr Chetty said, taking her stethoscope from around her neck and placing it on the desk. 'Can I make you a cup of coffee?'

Nomsa nodded. 'Please,' she said. She knew that, as the junior, she should offer to make Dr Chetty a cup of coffee, but she couldn't even think about moving from the chair. She didn't know how Dr Chetty managed to look so perky and bright, especially since she had probably seen double the number of patients during the night that Nomsa had. Nomsa had a horrible thought that perhaps the previous calls she had done had been unusually quiet, aberrations, and that the night that had just passed was what calls were normally like. No, it simply was not possible. There could not be so many sick and wounded people.

'Thanks for all the hard work,' Dr Chetty said, interrupting Nomsa's thoughts. She handed Nomsa a warm cup of coffee. 'It was a busy night and you handled it really well.'

Nomsa gave a quiet prayer of thanks. At least Dr Chetty also qualified it as a busy night. Even in her exhausted and befuddled state, she couldn't help feeling a little bit proud at Dr Chetty's praise. Dr Chetty didn't seem like the kind of woman who handed out compliments without good reason.

'I know it's difficult when we run out of beds,' Dr Chetty continued. 'Things tend to get a bit disorganised.'

A bit disorganised? Nomsa thought this had to be the understatement of the year. Perhaps the way to survive at Prince Xoliswe Hospital was to live on euphemisms.

Dr Chetty took a sip of her black coffee and sighed deeply. 'You know, it's awful for the poor patients, having to lie on those horrible metal gurneys. They're unbelievably uncomfortable. But that's how it goes. We do our best.'

Nomsa thought back on the evening – to the running around and the exhaustion; to the blood splatters, the cries for help and the hopeless faces; to the patients that she had been able to help and to those she had sent away. She might not always have worked quickly enough and she might have made a small mistake here or missed something there, but yes, she had done her best.

Rachael

11

Rachael had been avoiding answering her mother's telephone calls for the past week, but she knew that the situation was unsustainable. Gloria-Jean had obviously figured out that her daughter was ignoring her calls and had become more and more persistent in her efforts to contact her, eventually phoning every hour. Rachael finally decided to call her mother back, more because she was worried that her mother would phone the hospital and get switchboard to page her, and she would have to have the conversation within earshot of her colleagues, than because she actually wanted to.

Gloria-Jean didn't even greet Rachael when she answered her phone. She just asked her bluntly why she had been ignoring her calls. Rachael vacillated between making up a story about having been too busy to get to the phone and telling the truth. After a moment's hesitation, she decided on the latter. Her mother would be able to sniff out a lie, even from two thousand kilometres away. She told her mother that she had been avoiding answering her telephone because she had decided to stay at Prince Xoliswe Hospital and she knew that her parents would not be happy with her decision.

'Wouldn't be happy?' her mother exploded. 'Wouldn't be happy? How could we be happy when our precious *bobeleh*, for whom we've sacrificed so much, is making the mistake of her life? We've given you everything, Daddy and I, done everything possible for you and now you treat us like this. Do you know what a schlep it was for Daddy to organise this post for you in the UK? Have you thought of that? Or are you just thinking of yourself, as usual?'

Rachael opened her mouth to argue with her mother, but

Gloria-Jean was far from finished. 'You're throwing away a golden opportunity. A golden opportunity that we are serving to you on a platter. I bet most young doctors would give their eye teeth for a chance like this. You must be crazy, mad in the head, *meshugga*. Or you've met someone. Have you gone and fallen in love with someone?' Gloria-Jean demanded.

How like her mother, Rachael thought, to presume that the only reason for her staying was a man. 'No, I haven't fallen in love with anyone recently,' Rachael answered sarcastically. She was about to continue in the same tone and then realised that sarcasm was unlikely to help the situation. The best way to get through to her mother was to talk calmly and logically, without getting caught up on the wave of emotion that her mother continually rode. 'I've decided to stay here because I think it's better for me to finish my internship and community service in South Africa. I can always go to the UK once I've finished and that way, if I want to come back here one day, I'll be able to work here. If I don't do my internship and community service now, I'll just have to do it at a later stage. And who knows, perhaps then I'll already have a husband and children. I'd hate to have to come to a place like this with children.' Rachael threw the last bit in because the possibility of grandchildren was Gloria-Jean's greatest weakness.

'I suppose you have a point,' her mother conceded, 'but I still think you're wrong. I don't see you having a future in South Africa anyway. Why would you want to come back here? This country is going to the dogs and now we've got a criminal for a president. It's not going to be long before they chase us whites out of South Africa, just like in Zimbabwe.'

'Mom,' Rachael interrupted, knowing that if her mother started talking about the state of the country they would never get back to the more important topic: Rachael's future. 'Please will you tell Pops I've decided to stay? You're so much better at telling him things than I am.'

'I suppose I have no choice,' Gloria-Jean mumbled. 'I warn you, he's not going to be happy about this. Not happy at all.'

On the whole (presuming her parents didn't pitch up at

Tugela Bridge in the next few days to forcibly remove her), the conversation had not gone as badly as Rachael had anticipated. She had done rather well, she thought, considering she still wasn't sure herself about her reasons for deciding to stay. The reason she had given her mother was valid, but there was something more than that. For the first time Rachael felt like she was living. It was almost as though her life before she came to Tugela Bridge, with its neat conveniences, its expensive accessories, its electric fences and panic buttons, had been part of a fantasy childhood play and that she had only recently removed her dress-up clothes and stepped off the stage. She couldn't turn back, either. Her worries from the past now seemed so petty: whether she had gained an extra kilogram; if the food she was eating was organic or not; how she could fit her Pilates lesson in before rushing to the book club. Obviously, she still thought about those things (although, unfortunately, there was no book club and definitely no Pilates at Tugela Bridge), but they were no longer the issues upon which her state of being hinged. It was strangely liberating. She had, in a very short time, become addicted to the high of being able to make a difference in other people's lives.

Rachael had three very good reasons not to feel like being on call: firstly, she hadn't slept well the night before and was tired; secondly, the other doctors were all meeting for dinner at the Clay Oven and she would much rather be attending the social than spending her evening at the hospital; and thirdly, she was yet again substituting for the absent Dr Zamla and so was working a twenty-four-hour shift. She put her bag down in the doctors' office and switched on the kettle. She was already five minutes late, but she hadn't been able to make coffee at home because the water had run out. She was not about to do a twenty-four-hour shift caffeine-free. The patients would simply have to wait an extra five minutes, she thought, pouring water into a cup.

'Ah, good morning, Dr Zamla,' a voice said behind her. 'Can I bother you for a cup of coffee too?'

She turned around, eager to see Dr Zamla both because she would be let off the hook for twelve hours and because she was dying to see what the elusive man looked like. Instead, she saw only Shane Pillay. It took her a few seconds to realise that Shane was teasing her. *She* was Dr Zamla. 'If that's an attempt at a joke,' she said, 'it's cruel. So, no, you cannot have any coffee. Make your own.'

'Hey, I did his last shift,' Shane said, 'and that was only four days ago.'

He had a point; besides, he was too good-looking for her to stay cross with him for long. She poured him a cup of coffee. She hadn't expected to be on call with Shane. Suddenly her day was looking a whole lot better. In fact, she was momentarily even rather grateful to Dr Zamla.

'So,' Shane said, sitting down and taking a sip of coffee, 'tell me about yourself.'

Rachael didn't know where to start. What did Shane want to know? 'I'm from Cape Town, Camps Bay to be exact,' she said. 'I studied at UCT. I'm Jewish. I'm an only child. What else do you want to know?'

'Do you have a boyfriend, a good Jewish husband lined up for you?' Shane asked, smiling.

Rachael felt herself blush. She hadn't expected him to be so direct, but then she wasn't sure if he was joking or not. 'My mother would be very, very happy if I did, but sadly, no, I don't,' she said.

'Well, I'm happy that you don't,' Shane said. 'Makes my chances better.' He looked at his watch. 'I suppose we'd better do some work,' he said, putting down his coffee mug.

Rachael nodded and got up. She was somewhat taken aback by Shane's self-confidence. She had never met a guy who had the courage to ask her directly whether she had a boyfriend. Usually it took at least half an hour of chit-chat before the men flirting with her got to the point, and even then they would ask the question in some roundabout way. *So, did you and your boyfriend see the movie?* they might ask, hoping, waiting, for Rachael to correct them. Shane not only just jumped right in but also presumed that he stood a chance with her. She found his arrogance refreshingly sexy, although she didn't know if she was up to going out, even for one date, with an Indian guy. She had only ever dated Jewish men before but, judging by the outcomes of all her previous relationships, a change might not be a bad thing. She hurried from the doctors' office, determined to abort the line of thinking that her mind seemed insistent on following. She told herself that Shane had probably just been teasing her anyway.

Rachael picked up a folder from the pile and called the patient in. It amazed her how quickly she had become used to the procedure. She remembered her first call, how nervous she had been and how foreign everything had felt. It had taken such a short time for it all to become routine. A woman, dressed in an assortment of dirty clothes, responded to Rachael's call and followed her into the cubicle. She smelt of alcohol and urine and had pieces of grass and twigs stuck in her hair. Rachael presumed that she must be homeless. She had a grubby bandage wrapped around her lower leg and Rachael wondered if that was why she was at casualty. The woman said something to Rachael. Her English, already poor, was made incomprehensible by the effects of too much alcohol. Rachael asked her to repeat herself. This time, when the woman spoke she held a bandaged finger in front of Rachael, and Rachael eventually realised that the woman needed to have some stitches removed. Rachael couldn't face touching the filthy, stinking bandage, so she told the woman to unravel it herself. As the woman unwound the last bit of dirty bandage, something fell to the floor. Rachael ignored it, presuming it to be a piece of dirt. But then something else fell down, and another thing appeared to jump from the finger. Rachael looked at her feet in horror. Three fat white maggots wriggled around on the floor. The woman, apparently unperturbed by the creatures that had been gnawing on her wound, shook out the end of the bandage and three more maggots hit Rachael's foot. She shook her leg and ran screaming from the cubicle – into Shane.

'Is everything okay?' he asked, obviously concerned.

'No, no,' Rachael hyperventilated. 'There's, there's …' She couldn't bring herself to say the words but instead pointed to the cubicle. Shane pulled open the curtain. The woman was standing patiently waiting with her bandage in her hand. Shane looked at Rachael in confusion, then followed her gaze to the floor.

'Bloody hell!' he exclaimed. He looked at the patient. 'Pick them up and take them outside and then you can have your stitches out,' he said sternly.

Completely unruffled, the woman bent down and picked up the maggots one by one, then walked out with them. Rachael shuddered to imagine what would emerge if she removed the larger bandage on her leg.

'You can take the stitches out when she gets back,' Shane said to her.

'You're joking, right?'

'No, she'll throw the maggots outside. I doubt there are more.'

Rachael gulped. The thought of being near the woman made her stomach turn. She didn't want to be anywhere within fifty kilometres of the patient.

'Remember, maggots usually clean the wound really well,' Shane said.

Rachael got the feeling he was mocking her. 'It's not the maggots I'm concerned about,' she said grumpily. 'It's what other creatures the woman might be harbouring.'

Shane laughed and patted Rachael good-naturedly on the back, then walked away. Rachael waited for the woman to return but, luckily, after ten minutes there was still no sign of her. Obviously she had become distracted on her way back or decided that the removal of her stitches was unimportant. Rachael wasn't about to send out a search party to look for her: someone else could remove the stitches.

Rachael was irritated with herself that she had made a fuss about the maggots in front of Shane. He had been laughing at her. No doubt he thought her ridiculous. He probably didn't expect her to last very long at Prince Xoliswe and, quite frankly, she didn't want to. She wished that she could take back what she had said to her mother the day before, change her mind about her decision to stay. She didn't want to work in a hospital where maggots jumped out of wounds. She was sure that didn't happen in the UK. No reasonable person could be expected to stand calmly in the face of maggots. She supposed it wasn't too late to change her decision. Her parents would be happy, at least. But that didn't help her now; she still needed to get through the remainder of this shift.

The next patient Rachael saw was an eleven-month-old infant that had been brought in to hospital by its mother. She held the limp child in one hand and a blanket and bottle of clear fluid in the other. She told Rachael, as she placed the child on the examination bed, that the child had had bad diarrhoea for the past two days, as well as some vomiting. The mother's English was good and she was able to tell Rachael about the child's other symptoms and the relevant issues in the child's history. She took a piece of paper from her pocket and showed it to Rachael. She had written down all the fluid the child had consumed in the past twelve hours and how many times the child had had a wet or dirty nappy. Rachael was impressed with the mother: it was not often that a mother gave such a good history or seemed to take such good care of her child. Rachael started examining the little boy. She could see that his baseline was good. He was well fed and appeared to be the correct weight and height for his age. However, he was badly dehydrated. Far more dehydrated clinically than the piece of paper that the mother had shown Rachael would suggest.

'How often has he vomited?' Rachael asked the mother, trying to figure out why there was such a discrepancy between what the mother had told her and what she was seeing.

'He vomits almost every time after I give him the rehydration fluid,' the mother said. 'But it's not a proper vomit. It's more like a choke. Not much comes up. He keeps most of it down. I made up some rehydration fluid like the clinic told me. I boiled the water before I made it.' The mother showed Rachael the bottle of clear fluid.

'Well done, that was the right thing to do,' Rachael said. She could see that the mother was proud of what she had done but also that she was worried that perhaps the fluid was making the child sick.

'You've done everything right, but unfortunately we need to admit your little boy,' Rachael told the mother. 'He's not well at all.'

The mother looked relieved and nodded. 'Good,' she said. 'I'm worried about him. He's normally such a busy child. He doesn't just lie still like this.'

Rachael put a drip up on the infant and took some blood samples to try to figure out what was going on. An hour later the lab paged her.

'I've got the urea and electrolyte results for baby Welcome,' the lab technician said to her. 'They're very abnormal. The sodium is extremely high.'

'He's quite badly dehydrated,' Rachael responded.

'I can see that,' the technician said, 'but the sodium is relatively much higher than the urea and creatinine.'

The pattern didn't fit with the child's history. The baby seemed to have simple gastro, but the blood results were implying something else. Rachael mentally reviewed the list of causes of high sodium, trying to figure out the reason for the infant's raised blood salt level. She didn't want to ask Shane for help, not after the maggot incident, but she knew that she had no choice. She couldn't let a child die because her pride got in the way. She told Shane the baby's history and showed him the blood results.

'I've seen a result like this before with almost exactly the same clinical picture,' Shane said. 'Ask the mother about the rehydration fluid. Ask her how she made it. I'll bet you get your answer.'

'How are you supposed to make it?' Rachael asked Shane.

He looked at her in disbelief. 'Don't you know?' he asked. He was about to say something else but Rachael saw him stop himself. She could feel her cheeks turning red. How was she supposed to know how to make oral rehydration fluid? The only rehydration fluid she had ever seen came in little square foil packets from the pharmacy.

'One litre of boiled water, one teaspoon of salt, eight teaspoons of sugar,' Shane said.

Rachael went back to the mother. The child was looking only slightly better. She asked the mother how she had made the fluid.

'I boiled one litre of water,' the mother said proudly, 'then mixed in one teaspoon of sugar and eight teaspoons of salt.'

No wonder the child had high sodium. No wonder it retched

after every feed of oral rehydration fluid the mother gave it. The stuff must taste foul. The child's mother was watching Rachael, waiting for a sign of approval. Rachael didn't know what to do. She didn't want to tell the mother that she had inadvertently poisoned her child because she could see that the mother was proud of what she had done and thought she had made the rehydration fluid exactly as she had been told to. Rachael knew, precisely because the mother cared so much, that finding out she had done the wrong thing and had made her child sicker would devastate her. But she had to tell her; otherwise it would happen again. She let the mother know, in the gentlest possible terms, what had happened. Tears streamed down the mother's face and Rachael hugged her.

'You did your best,' she said. 'Everything's going to be fine now. Your child will be okay, I promise.'

As she changed the bag of fluid running into the child's arm, it struck Rachael that the mother would never forget the correct way to make oral rehydration fluid. Neither would she.

Rachael called a man in his early thirties into the cubicle. He was wheeled in in a chair by a friend. He sat leaning forward in the wheelchair, pressing his hands into his thighs in an effort to breathe. Rachael could hear him wheezing without needing to use her stethoscope. She quickly shouted to the sister to set up a nebuliser for the patient while she inserted an intravenous line through which she could administer steroids. She worked quickly, but the man's condition seemed to deteriorate even more rapidly. By the time Rachael finished putting up the line the wheeze had stopped, not because she had treated it but because the man was no longer getting enough air moving into his lungs to create a wheeze. Rachael quickly pushed the steroids through the intravenous catheter and asked the sister to put the man on continuous nebulisation. Nothing seemed to be helping. Out of desperation she administered two other drugs through the intravenous line, but neither seemed to make any difference. The patient looked more distressed than he had before she started treating him. His lips were becoming blue and he was starting to lose consciousness.

'Can you put a sats monitor on him,' Rachael asked the sister, trying to make her voice sound calmer than she felt. The sister attached a clip connected to a monitor to the man's thumb: his oxygen saturation was seventy per cent. Normal was between ninety-five and a hundred.

'Quickly, get the resus trolley,' Rachael shouted to the sister. The sister ran off and Rachael tried to collect her thoughts. She searched her memory for any other treatment for asthma that she might have forgotten, but nothing came to mind. She was certain that she had done everything possible. The man had lost consciousness completely and Rachael called the other sister on duty to help her lift him onto the bed. The first sister arrived with the resuscitation trolley as they got him onto the bed. Rachael went to the top of the bed so that she was standing behind the patient's head, ready to intubate him. She needed to insert a pipe down his throat and into his lungs so that she could artificially ventilate him. She knew that there was a formula to work out what size pipe she should use, but she couldn't remember it. All she knew was that it had something to do with the angle of the jaw.

'Size eight tube?' the sister asked, handing her a tube. Rachael presumed that must be the size most commonly used and nodded. She took the tube and thanked the sister. She didn't have time to look up a formula now; her patient was dying. She opened the patient's mouth and inserted a laryngoscope, then pulled up the base of the patient's tongue to visualise the vocal cords. She had intubated before but electively, on anaesthetised patients who had been waiting to go to theatre. This was completely different. In theatre, the intubation was controlled. If one struggled to get the tube in, one could simply ventilate the patient with a bag and mask and then try again. The patient had normally been starved and there was no risk of him or her vomiting and choking on the vomit. In theatre there were other doctors around and help was always available. Here, in the emergency situation, none of those circumstances applied. The patient might recently have had a huge meal which could be regurgitated at any time, there were usually no other doctors around, and the patient was close to dying, so one couldn't take as long as one liked to intubate. Rachael lubricated the end of the tube and pushed it through the vocal cords into the patient's lungs. She was sure that the tube was positioned correctly, in the patient's lungs and not his oesophagus, but needed to confirm the placement by auscultation. She tried to attach the bag to the end of the tube but her palms were sweaty. It took her two attempts before she managed to secure the bag onto the protruding end of the tube. She asked the sister to compress the bag and placed her stethoscope over the patient's chest. She was hoping to hear the movement of air as the bag pushed oxygen down the tube and into the patient's lungs. But the chest was silent.

'Shit,' she cursed under her breath. She must have intubated the patient's oesophagus instead of his lungs. She didn't know how she had made the mistake, but she had to do something to rectify it quickly: the patient's oxygen saturation had dropped to sixty per cent. She quickly removed the tube and attached the bag and oxygen to a face mask. She compressed the bag, trying to push oxygen into the patient's lungs, but the bag hardly compressed. It was almost as though there was something blocking the flow of air into the patient's chest. She removed the mask and checked that everything was working properly. It was. She repositioned the mask and tried again. The patient's saturation dropped to forty per cent.

'Quickly, call Dr Pillay. I need some help,' she shouted to the sister. She was getting desperate. Her patient was dying in front of her and she couldn't even bag him. She grabbed the laryngoscope and tube and tried once again to intubate the patient. Again, she visualised the vocal cords easily. She watched the tube slip through them as Shane arrived. There was absolutely no way that she had intubated the oesophagus this time.

'Holy shit!' Shane exclaimed as he came into the cubicle. 'What's wrong with the patient?'

'Asthma,' Rachael replied.

Shane quickly put his stethoscope to the patient's chest and Rachael tried to compress the bag. Again there seemed to be some resistance.

'No, it's not in,' Shane said, almost harshly. 'I'm going to take

129

over. This man's dying.' He almost pushed Rachael over in his haste to take her place. He pulled the tube out and put the face mask and bag over the man's mouth and nose and tried to compress the bag. The patient's saturation dropped to twenty per cent.

'Fuck, what's going on here?' he cursed again. He did exactly what Rachael had done earlier: checked that the bag was in working order and then repositioned the mask and tried to bag the patient again.

'I did all of that,' Rachael said helplessly. 'Nothing made a difference.'

Shane nodded. 'Pass me the tube,' he said, picking up the laryngoscope. He quickly and confidently intubated the patient. 'I'm sure it's in,' he said. 'I saw it pass through the vocal cords, but you'd better listen just to make sure.'

Rachael put her stethoscope to the patient's chest. Nothing.

'What the fuck's going on?' Shane mumbled. Rachael could see sweat beads forming on his brow. The patient's saturation dropped to ten per cent. 'Percuss the chest and make sure that the man hasn't got a tension pneumothorax,' he ordered Rachael.

Rachael tapped her fingers against the patient's chest, listening for the hollow sound that would imply that the lung had collapsed and was being kept deflated by surrounding air pressure, but the percussion sounded normal.

'I can't pick up a pneumothorax on either side,' she said to Shane.

The man's heart had stopped beating and Rachael started doing chest compressions on him. In desperation, Shane pulled the tube out and tried to intubate once again. Nothing changed. Shane ordered the sister to give adrenaline, but it had little effect. After fifteen minutes, Shane terminated the resuscitation. The man was dead. Shane went to tell the patient's friend the news and the sister went to collect the paperwork that needed to be completed. The patient would need a post-mortem. Rachael sat down next to the man's dead body. She had watched him die and she had been unable to do anything. She had failed. One of the main driving reasons she had had for studying medicine was that she hated being helpless and out of control of situations. Now, she had been both: she had panicked; she hadn't called Shane early enough; she had failed to get oxygen into the patient. A thirty-two-year-old man had died because of her inadequacy. She cupped her eyes with her hands and started sobbing. She wasn't supposed to be a doctor; she wasn't good enough.

'Hey,' Shane said, touching her shoulder gently. She hadn't heard him come back. 'Don't be upset. There's nothing else you could have done.'

'Yes there is. I could have been better. I could have … I could have … I don't know, done something. He shouldn't have died, he's so young. It's my fault. I should never have thought I could be a doctor,' she blubbered.

'You did everything correctly,' Shane said, handing her a tissue. 'I would have managed him exactly the same way. There was nothing that you forgot to do or did incorrectly.'

His voice was soothing and Rachael let it wash over her.

'I've just spoken to the patient's friend,' Shane continued. 'The one that brought him in. The patient was a known asthmatic. He'd been smoking mandrax just before he came in. It obviously caused irreversible airway bronchospasm. We couldn't get air through the tube because the airways had closed up so much. You did everything possible.'

'Do you really think so? You're not just saying that?' Rachael asked.

'Of course. We'll get a post-mortem on the patient anyway, so you can find out exactly what happened. The first time a patient dies on you is often the worst and it's normal to feel a failure, but don't. You're far from a failure.'

'Do you really think so?' Rachael repeated, dabbing at her tears with the crumpled tissue. She felt a failure. Not only had she screamed at the sight of maggots, but she had been unable to save a patient's life.

'Yes, of course. You handled a very difficult resus well. You stayed calm, you took control of the situation, you had the knowledge to make the right medical decisions and you had the sense to call me when you knew you weren't winning. If you stick to those principles, you can manage any resus.'

Perhaps what Shane was saying had some element of truth. At least she hadn't had a panic attack in the middle of the resuscitation. She had been nervous, obviously, but she hadn't frozen in terror as she would have a few months before. She hadn't even had time to think about her deep breathing. Perhaps she wasn't so useless after all.

'Now cheer up,' Shane said. 'If you stop crying, I'll take you out for dinner tomorrow night.'

Rachael didn't know if Shane was teasing her again, so she didn't say anything. But she managed to dam some of the tears.

'Great stuff,' Shane said, handing her a fresh tissue. 'I'll pick you up at seven.'

He hadn't been joking. Rachael smiled. 'Okay,' she said.

12

By default, Shane and Rachael's dinner date was at the Clay Oven, the only restaurant in Tugela Bridge. When they arrived, Rachael glanced surreptitiously around to see whether she recognised any of the patrons. She wasn't sure she wanted the news of her and Shane's date broadcast around the hospital. Luckily, it appeared as though none of the other doctors at Prince Xoliswe had decided to eat out that night. Although Rachael had been on innumerable dates before – always with Jewish men – going out with an Indian guy, albeit just for dinner, contained a very pronounced element of the risqué for her. She suspected it was partly because of this that she was looking so forward to the dinner. She felt similar to the way she had as a teenager, when she had disobeyed her mother and had her belly button pierced on the sly. She had walked around for weeks harbouring her secret, cultivating it, giving it surreptitious glances of attention when she was sure she was out of sight of the watchful eye of her mother. And the secret had made her stronger and had conferred on her a completely foreign ability to stand up to her mother that had lasted until her mother had walked in on her getting dressed. It was not only because she found Shane attractive that she was looking forward to the date; it was because she knew that, in going out with him, she was asserting, even if it was only to herself, her independence. Dinner with Shane symbolised her new life in Tugela Bridge; it represented a breaking away from her parents and from all of the cultural bonds that had restricted her in Cape Town. It was another secret.

'I've ordered us both a vodka and Red Bull,' Shane said, interrupting her thoughts. 'I know I sure as hell need it and I suspect you need it even more, since you worked twelve more hours than me.'

Rachael thanked him. Strangely, she didn't feel so exhausted. Perhaps it was the excitement of going on a date again that was keeping her awake. She wasn't going to take the chance of falling asleep halfway through dinner, though: she downed the drink as soon as it arrived and ordered herself another.

Rachael had been worried that, outside the hospital setting, she and Shane would have nothing to talk about. That afternoon, while ironing the strappy cream dress for her date, she had felt briefly unnerved by the thought that they would spend a rushed dinner discussing the weather, maggots in finger wounds and mandrax smoking before beating hasty retreats home. But her fears proved groundless. She and Shane got on well – in fact, remarkably, refreshingly well. Naturally, since it was the one obvious thing they had in common, they spent the earlier part of the evening talking about the hospital. Shane appeared to be a wealth of gossip and hearsay. He told Rachael about the hospital superintendent's five-thousand-rand telephone bill, which one of the community service doctors had accidentally seen lying on her desk.

'But we have to pay for our personal calls anyway,' Rachael interrupted, not really seeing the problem in a five-thousand-rand telephone bill, provided the superintendent paid it herself. Each intern had been given an access pin code to use when dialling numbers outside the hospital's speed-dial system. At the end of the month, they received a bill for the telephone calls.

'That's the funny part,' Shane said. 'When the pin codes were introduced, Mrs Hlope said that the admin staff would be excluded from paying for outside calls because they formed part of the job. Of course, she falls under admin staff.'

'She seems a real peach,' Rachael commented.

'That's one way to put it. You know that Dr Zamla is her mother's cousin or something, which is why he gets away with all his shit?'

Rachael nodded. She had heard the rumours from Nathan that first night out at the Clay Oven.

'It really pisses me off because everyone else works so hard, especially Dr Chetty and Dr Ribbentrop,' Shane said. 'They've been here for years. I don't know how they do it.'

'Speaking of which,' Rachael said, 'what do you think of Dr Ribbentrop? I can't figure him out.'

Shane's face softened very slightly. 'You have to be a bit odd to stay on here,' he said.

Rachael understood what Shane meant. The working hours and conditions pretty much precluded any social life and the work was so emotionally draining that she imagined that anyone who stayed at Tugela Bridge for longer than a year would need to be on major antidepressants permanently.

'He's not the most friendly guy,' Shane said, referring back to Dr Ribbentrop, 'but he's a brilliant doctor and beneath his rough exterior he has a heart of gold.'

This was not the first time Rachael had heard this about Dr Ribbentrop. The sister with whom she had discussed him had said something in a similar vein.

'You should see him with children,' Shane continued. 'He really cares. I think most of us just care superficially; we care as long as it doesn't impact on our comfort or security or inconvenience us at all. He cares properly. He does the things we all think we can't do.' Shane told Rachael how Dr Ribbentrop had driven one hundred kilometres, at his own expense and in his free time, to a rural village to fetch the mother of a little girl who had been admitted and was dying. The mother had been unable to get transport to the hospital. The girl did die, but at least the mother got to spend her child's last night with her. He also told Rachael how Dr Ribbentrop had managed to get NGO funding for two hundred patients to be started on anti-retrovirals before the official government roll-out for HIV treatment began.

'He got into huge trouble for it,' Shane explained. 'He was suspended for ages without pay and ended up being subjected to more than one disciplinary hearing. Anyone else would have left, or at least given up on the project. He didn't, and a hundred and sixty of the patients are still alive. You'll probably see some of them at the clinic.'

Rachael wondered whether she cared so much. Would she have the courage to go against the rules to save the life of a stranger, to risk losing her job and her future? Would she stick it out or would she just give up and leave the country, as she had thought so often of doing? Shane asked her what she was thinking about and she told him. 'Would you stay?' she asked.

Shane hesitated for a moment before answering. 'It's probably not the right answer to impress you, but I don't think I would be able to. I don't think I'm made of saint material. I probably like my luxuries a bit too much,' he said, pointing to his latest-model cellphone. 'And luxuries require a decent salary.'

Rachael nodded at him and smiled. 'Honesty impresses me,' she said. 'Besides, I'm probably the same.' Since coming to Tugela Bridge she had changed her lifestyle completely. She had given up her weekly manicure and pedicure and her bimonthly spa facial. She had not been able to go out and buy a new handbag or pair of designer shoes each time she felt upset or depressed. She hadn't met friends for coffee and cake since she had left Cape Town or had a private Pilates or yoga class. She didn't really miss very much any of the things she had given up, but she wondered if that was because she was being kept occupied with all the new things she was experiencing. She suspected that once the novelty of Tugela Bridge had worn off, she might hanker after the manner in which she had previously been accustomed to living. She also had enough insight to realise that it was easy to make the changes she had made in the isolation of Tugela Bridge; it would be far more difficult to sustain them in Cape Town, where she already had a persona with accepted friends and habits. Still, she hoped that she might be able to maintain some of the changes she had made. She liked who she was in Tugela Bridge.

The pizzas arrived and Rachael took a bite of the tikka chicken that she had ordered. 'Delicious,' she said, offering Shane a piece.

'No, thanks,' he declined. 'My mom only ever feeds me spicy food, so when I'm away from home I try to avoid it. It ends up giving me stomach ulcers.'

Shane's mentioning his mother opened up the conversation, extending it beyond the boundaries of the hospital. It allowed Rachael to ask him, quite easily, about his family. He told her he had grown up in Durban with his mother and older sister. His father had died of a heart attack at the age of forty, when Shane was only ten.

'I missed growing up with a father,' Shane said reflectively. 'I was always the kid on the sports field who didn't have anyone watching his hockey or soccer. And my mom is very sickly, so she never made it to any of my games. I got cross with him when I was older, when I was able to understand how preventable his death actually was. If he had just lost weight and stopped smoking, listened to his doctor and taken his medication, he could still be alive. I suppose, indirectly, he was part of the reason I studied medicine.'

'And the other part?'

'My mother. As I mentioned she's never been very healthy and she's entirely dependent on me. My sister is married and has her own life. She lives with her in-laws, so my mom essentially has no one except me. And my dad didn't exactly leave her rolling in cash when he died. Medicine seemed like a compromise: a job I could enjoy but that would also make me enough money to support her. Anyway, enough about me. What's your family like?'

'Jewish, and rich, I suppose. Very protective: I'm an only child. My mom's biggest aim in life is to get me married to a nice, wealthy Jewish boy and start producing grandchildren for her. She would probably be on the next flight to Durban to drag me back to Cape

Town if she knew I was having dinner with an Indian guy.'

It was out in the open, the race issue. Somehow it strengthened their bond, made them accomplices. They were complicit in something tempting and delicious, something that seemed to lure them away from the light and the business of the Clay Oven to the secretiveness of darkness. It teased them all the way to the shadows of the back step of Rachael's prefab. The step was narrow so they sat pushed together, the skin of their thighs touching. The air was still humid and warm, the last lingering sigh of a too-hot summer, and Rachael could feel the moistness of sweat where Shane's arm rested on the back of her neck and shoulders. It was as though her skin was hyperaesthetic, sensitive almost to the point of pain where his skin touched hers. She was burning up. Her nostrils filled with an unfamiliar night scent and she inhaled deeply. Shane did too.

'Someone's smoking dope,' he said, rather unromantically.

'Oh, is that what the smell is?' Rachael said, inhaling again. She was suddenly embarrassed that she had reached her mid-twenties and didn't even know what marijuana smelt like. The air had become thick and grey, as though filled with smoke. Rachael had a surreal thought that the smoke was an externalisation of what she was feeling, that the lust burning inside her had somehow become manifest. It made her want to giggle.

Shane stood up. 'I thought so,' he muttered.

'What?' Rachael stood too. Sitting down on the step, she had been unable to see beyond the slight rise in the ground behind the prefabs. Standing, she could see the flames coming from the far boundary of the hospital grounds, behind the laundry. '*Oy vey*,' she exclaimed. 'There's a fire. Quick, call the fire brigade!' she shouted at Shane.

Shane laughed. 'Don't worry,' he said. 'The fire won't reach us.'

'But maybe it will. Maybe it will burn down all these dreadful prefabs.' The thought amused her.

Shane laughed again. 'No, it won't,' he said. 'It's a controlled fire. Sipho grows dagga behind the laundry. Every few months the police come and burn the patch. Everyone will probably be down there: they all go and watch, for obvious reasons.'

'Do you want to go and watch?' Rachael asked.

'No,' Shane said, putting his arms around her. 'I want to take you inside.'

Rachael woke up with a hangover far worse than she thought she deserved, and with Shane in bed next to her. She was glad that she had woken up first; it gave her time to gather her thoughts. She slipped quietly out of bed, careful not to wake Shane, and went to the lounge. She supposed she should feel disgusted, or ashamed, or at least concerned (she didn't usually leap into bed with a man after one dinner date), but she felt none of these emotions. Instead, she felt an unexpected freedom. It made her want to shake off all her inhibitions, throw her head back and laugh and laugh and laugh. She wondered whether the effect of the burning dagga from the night before was still lingering in the air. She could smell the scent of Shane's aftershave on her skin and she liked it. She sniffed her wrist, her forearm, her shoulder. A ray of sun streamed through the window and she moved closer to the pane of glass to feel its warmth on her skin. Behind her, she heard Shane walk into the room and she turned around to smile at him. He looked at her tentatively, obviously trying to judge her mood.

'You okay?' he asked.

'Oh, yes.'

Shane smiled, relieved, and came across to the window. He slipped his arms around Rachael's bare body. He smelt like sweat, like sex and like sleep. It was luscious and provocative and made Rachael want to drag him back to bed.

'Look,' Shane said, pointing at the distant black patch of burnt ground.

'Oh, so there *was* a fire,' Rachael said. 'I thought I'd imagined it.'

'No, you didn't make it up,' Shane said, smiling. 'Although women often say that sort of thing to me the next morning. You could be excused for thinking you imagined a fire.'

'Ha, ha,' Rachael said sarcastically. 'I'd better be careful. I was always taught it's dangerous to play with fire.'

'But that's exactly why you're playing with me, isn't it?' Shane asked.

The question was light-hearted, a continuation of their earlier banter, but Rachael knew that what he had said was partially true. She thought Shane realised it too.

He bent down and kissed the nape of her neck. 'We'd better get ready for work,' he said softly.

Nomsa

13

It was directly as a result of Sipho's breaking of the law and the subsequent lack of water that Nomsa saw Rachael and Shane together. Because she had no water to make her mandatory morning drink, Nomsa decided to go to the hospital early and have a cup of coffee in the doctors' office before the start of the ward round. As she walked past Rachael's prefab, far earlier than usual, she caught sight of Rachael at the window. Rachael was naked, so Nomsa quickly averted her eyes in embarrassment, but not before noticing the figure of Shane Pillay standing behind her. Nomsa had known that Shane was interested in Rachael, but things had really moved fast if they had already reached the stage of spending the night together. Nomsa wasn't particularly conservative, but she couldn't help judging Rachael: it was, she thought, a bit slutty to sleep with someone on the first date and it was definitely not the type of behaviour she had expected from Rachael. There was a stone in her path and she kicked angrily at it. Apart from the moral dilemma that the situation presented, the professional ethics of the liaison were also highly questionable. Nomsa would never even consider having a relationship with a doctor working at the same hospital: it was simply unprofessional.

Seema Singh was the only other doctor in the doctors' office when Nomsa arrived. Nomsa wondered if she too had come early to use hospital water to make a cup of coffee but then remembered that Seema stayed in the married quarters and so would have had water. So what was she doing in so early? She hadn't been on call the night before.

'You're in early,' Nomsa commented, hoping to get an

explanation from Seema. She needed a conversation to distract her thoughts from Shane and Rachael, but Seema kept her reply short and closed. She had come in early to do some work, she said. Nomsa made herself a cup of coffee and sat down. The naked images of Shane and Rachael sat down next to her. She slurped at her coffee loudly, hoping to irritate them enough to chase them away. Rudely, they ignored her and started kissing. She wondered why she was so affected by their relationship. It was hardly reasonable. Would she have reacted in the same way if she had seen another doctor, say Seema, with Shane? She tried to imagine Seema and Shane together but then realised she had chosen a bad example. Seema seemed too shy to be the type to indulge in an affair and was far too conservative for Shane ever to show interest in her. For a horrifying moment Nomsa wondered whether she might subconsciously be attracted to Shane: perhaps her anger at Rachael stemmed from jealousy. Was she upset because Shane had ostensibly chosen Rachael over her? She thought back to the times that she had worked with him and reassured herself that she had absolutely no romantic interest in Shane Pillay. She didn't even find him good-looking. So why was she so perturbed?

Nathan and Eliza walked into the doctors' office and Eliza put a bag of chocolate-chip muffins down next to the kettle.

'Please, help yourselves,' she said to Nomsa and Seema. 'I thought these would go down well today.' Nomsa thanked Eliza and cut herself half a muffin, but Seema just looked up from her textbook, smiled nervously and then went back to her reading.

'Shane spent the night with Rachael last night,' Nomsa said, cursing herself mentally before she had even finished the sentence. She hadn't meant to gossip, but the news seemed to bubble out of her, almost as though it had grown too large and volatile to be restrained. She should have held her tongue. She quickly took a bite of muffin to prevent herself from saying anything else.

Nathan laughed triumphantly. 'Told you,' he said to Eliza. 'You owe me a back massage.' He wriggled his shoulders in anticipation, then turned to Nomsa. 'Let me enlighten you,' he said. 'We saw them sitting side by side on Rachael's step last night and took a bet on whether they would spend the night together. Quite obviously, I won.'

'Shane's a nice guy,' Eliza said, 'but he's a bit of a Don Juan. He likes women, especially beautiful women. I just hope Rachael knows what she's letting herself in for. I didn't think she'd fall for his charm so easily.'

All at once, Nomsa's anger at Shane and Rachael's liaison made sense. Eliza had summed it up. Nomsa wasn't disappointed in Shane or by his lack of attention to her; she was disappointed in Rachael. Since meeting Rachael, Nomsa had idolised her. She had believed that Rachael encompassed everything she herself desired to be. Rachael had the natural self-confidence of someone who had grown up effortlessly and for whom everything had always simply fallen into place. Rachael was at ease with money and labels and pretences in a way that immediately identified her as having reached adulthood with too much of everything. She was the physical manifestation of all of Nomsa's desires. And now, with one action, Rachael had shattered Nomsa's illusion. It wasn't so much that Rachael had slept with someone on the first date; it was that Rachael had slept with Shane. Had she had a romantic fling with a handsome visiting consultant or specialist rather than a lowly medical officer, Nomsa wouldn't have minded. In fact, she probably would have approved but Nomsa could not imagine what possible advantage or allure there was in having a fling with Shane. Rachael had behaved in a way that didn't fit in with Nomsa's ideal of her, and the illusion that Nomsa had nurtured so carefully had collapsed in on itself. It had been exposed for the untruth that it was, leaving Nomsa with the bitter, undesired realisation that none of her dreams were untouchable.

Nomsa was in theatre with Dr Ribbentrop for the day's list, which was a relief to her. She would have felt uncomfortable having to work with Shane for the whole day. As it was, she hadn't been able to make eye contact with him for the duration of the ward round, which had been awkward since the ward round had consisted of only her and Shane. Soon after scrubbing up, though, she realised that her relief at working with Dr Ribbentrop was premature. She walked into theatre in time to see him throw a tray of sterile instruments across the room. The scissors, artery forceps, toothed forceps and needle holders skidded onto the floor in a cacophony of angry metallic clangs. Nomsa hesitated at the door, too shocked to move.

'Well, are you going to deign to assist me or not?' Dr Ribbentrop demanded grumpily.

It took Nomsa a second or two to realise that he was talking to her.

'Yes, sorry,' she apologised, walking swiftly to the patient's side. She didn't want to antagonise Dr Ribbentrop any further. She wasn't particularly keen to find out through personal experience what he would throw next or where it would be aimed.

'That's Zandile,' Dr Ribbentrop said, using a pair of scissors to point at the cleaner who was sulkily picking up the theatre instruments off the floor. 'She's worked here for two years. In two years she has been unable to grasp the simple concept of sterility. Today, as was the case three days ago, she touched the sterile instruments with the handle of her mop, thereby rendering them unsterile. I have spent the past two years explaining her mistakes to her politely and patiently. Since that tactic obviously wasn't working, I decided to try a fresh approach.'

Nomsa got the impression that this explanation was more for Zandile's benefit than for hers. Dr Ribbentrop calmly used a forceps to pick up an iodine-soaked piece of gauze and started cleaning the patient's abdomen. The theatre sister opened a new sterile tray and placed it next to Dr Ribbentrop. The operation that they were going to perform was a laparotomy. The patient had been shot in the stomach the night before, and Dr Ribbentrop would need to open the abdomen to see whether the bullet had penetrated and perforated any of the intra-abdominal organs.

He made a longitudinal incision on the patient's abdominal wall, then cauterised the small bleeding vessels. He cut through the layer of superficial abdominal wall fat and Nomsa was amazed, yet again, at how much adipose tissue even a relatively thin person

143

had between the skin and the abdominal muscles. She shuddered to think how much blobby, yellow fat would ooze from beneath her skin were she cut open. Once Dr Ribbentrop had parted the abdominal muscles, he slipped a metal retractor below the muscle and skin layers and asked Nomsa to pull on it, thereby opening up the abdominal cavity.

'So, I hear you think you're a surgeon in the making?' Dr Ribbentrop said to Nomsa.

Nomsa nodded. Shane must have told him.

'And what on this beautiful earth, containing so many other possibilities, would make you consider specialising in surgery?' Dr Ribbentrop asked, shaking his head in apparent dismay.

'I enjoy surgery,' Nomsa said nervously. It was such a pathetic answer, a childish, unsophisticated answer, but she couldn't think of anything more sensible to say. Dr Ribbentrop's tray throwing and his blunt questions and mocking tone had intimidated her so much that when he spoke to her it was almost as though he was speaking in a foreign language. She missed the easy camaraderie of working with Shane.

'Specialise in something like dermatology instead,' Dr Ribbentrop advised. 'The hours are far better, you can still have a social life and you can work half-days while you're raising your kids. Isn't that what all you girls want?'

Nomsa didn't know how to respond. She didn't know whether Dr Ribbentrop was goading her or being serious. What a chauvinist! She wanted to tell him that she wasn't afraid of hard work and long hours and that she hadn't put herself through medical school to stay at home and look after children, but she didn't have the courage. Instead she smiled stupidly and cursed herself silently for being so spineless. Dr Ribbentrop loosened a length of the small bowel and started examining it for perforations.

'So, Ms Poponi,' Dr Ribbentrop said. He was obviously teasing Nomsa, using the 'Ms' in the same way that 'Mr' was used to address surgeons overseas. 'What is the blood supply to this area?' he asked, referring to the section of intestine he was holding up. He seemed to be enjoying the discomfort that he was causing Nomsa.

'The superior mesenteric artery,' Nomsa responded confidently. She was thankful she had decided to revise her abdominal anatomy a few nights before. She got the feeling that Dr Ribbentrop was trying to catch her out.

'Good,' Dr Ribbentrop responded. 'And can you point out the inferior mesenteric artery?'

Nomsa pointed to another blood vessel. 'It's the inferior mesenteric until this point over here,' she said, following the course of the blood vessel with her finger, 'at which point it crosses over the common iliac artery. Once it's crossed the left common iliac artery, it becomes the superior rectal artery. The superior rectal artery then branches into the left colic artery and several sigmoid arteries.' She could see that Dr Ribbentrop was impressed. She had given far more detail than she knew he was expecting, far more than she thought he expected her to know. She didn't care that she was showing off; she would prove to Dr Ribbentrop that she would make a good surgeon.

Nomsa had always known that following a career path in surgery would be challenging, not only academically and because of the high trauma load, but also because surgery was a male–dominated field. The challenge didn't frighten her. In fact, it excited her. She was used to working hard to get what she wanted, and until this point in her life she had always succeeded. There was no reason why, with the right amount of work and dedication, things wouldn't continue that way.

The next case on the list was a cholecystectomy, but just as the porters were about to wheel the patient into theatre, one of the community service doctors on call ran into the side room in which Dr Ribbentrop was scrubbing up. He said something to Dr Ribbentrop and Nomsa heard him sigh.

'Change of plan,' he announced to the theatre staff. 'There's another gunshot abdomen that's come in. We'll have to do that one first. It looks like the bullet hit the liver. The gall bladder will have to wait.'

One of the theatre sisters let out a groan and Nomsa looked at her questioningly. A gunshot abdomen would always take precedence over the elective removal of a gall bladder, especially if the liver was injured. Surely the sister should know that?

'The gall bladder's been waiting for three days,' the sister explained, obviously in response to Nomsa's look. 'Every time she gets wheeled into theatre, a fresh trauma case comes in that needs to be treated as an emergency. The poor woman hasn't eaten in three days because she's been waiting for her operation to be done.'

It boggled Nomsa's mind to think there had been that quantity of trauma in three days, that the theatre staff had been unable to squeeze in a single non-emergency case in seventy-two hours. She wondered whether all the patients waiting for their elective cases were still in hospital, killing time until their turn eventually came up. It seemed like a huge waste of money if they were. Surely it would be cheaper just to open another theatre? And that would also free up more beds. But she didn't have time to try to solve the problem. The new gunshot abdomen had been wheeled in and Dr Ribbentrop was already draping the patient.

'Well, if doing surgery at Prince Xoliswe Hospital doesn't put you off surgery for life, nothing will,' he grumbled to Nomsa as she took her place opposite him.

'I suppose most of what you do is trauma,' Nomsa said. It was an almost redundant observation, one to which the answer was obvious, but she felt as though Dr Ribbentrop was expecting her to make some comment and she could think of nothing more intelligent to say. She wondered what it was about him that seemed to turn her into an imbecile.

'Ninety per cent. Ninety per cent of the cases we do are trauma. It's not sustainable. We've tried to motivate for another theatre to be opened, but the powers that be don't see the need. I can guarantee you they would see the need soon enough if it were one of their mothers waiting for her gall bladder to be removed, but of course they all have medical aid, so they don't have to worry about things like that. I think the only way to sort out the mess that the health system is in would be to force every government minister to receive treatment at a government hospital, anonymously.'

Dr Ribbentrop was ranting, letting out his frustrations, but

Nomsa couldn't help feeling pleased that he had stopped teasing her and was treating her more like an equal.

'I've learnt that it's pointless complaining,' he continued. 'I used to protest and make a big fuss about things, but all it got me was disciplinary hearings. The only way to tackle the problem is not to think about it. Just concentrate on the surgery in front of you.' He stopped speaking and made an incision down the abdomen. It was strange timing, almost as though his own words had goaded him into action. As he breached the abdominal wall, blood poured onto the table and floor. Nomsa grabbed the suction, trying to remove the blood to clear a visual field for Dr Ribbentrop, but it seemed to reappear as quickly as she suctioned it up.

'Lacerated liver,' Dr Ribbentrop shouted to the anaesthetist, a medical officer with a diploma in anaesthetics. He responded by running a pint of blood into the patient.

'Do you think there's going to be much more bleeding?' the anaesthetist asked Dr Ribbentrop.

'Probably. From what I can see, this is a large laceration.'

'Oh dear,' he muttered. 'We're into our emergency blood. We've only got three pints left in the hospital.'

'What?' Nomsa exclaimed, without thinking. It was incomprehensible to her that a hospital could physically run out of blood. 'What will you do if we run out of blood?' Blood was life-saving. Without it, the patient on the table could easily haemorrhage to death. She suctioned more vigorously, as though by getting rid of the blood she could somehow preserve it.

'We'll change to a colloid,' the anaesthetist replied, referring to a protein-based resuscitation fluid, 'until some more blood gets flown in. It depends on how much the blood bank has in stock.'

Nomsa still could not fathom how a hospital could operate without blood. What if another patient came in that needed blood? Would it just be really rotten luck for that patient? Sorry, she imagined having to tell a patient, if you'd started coughing up litres of blood a few hours ago, I could have helped you, but unfortunately you were a bit late and so now we'll have to leave you to bleed out. Enjoy the last few minutes of your life.

Dr Ribbentrop was working swiftly, trying to curb the bleeding as quickly as possible. Nomsa watched him, impressed. Throughout the previous case he had questioned her on her anatomy, but now he worked silently, only raising his voice when requesting an instrument. Nomsa concentrated on what Dr Ribbentrop was doing, trying to pre-empt the requests he made of her as his assistant. His hands moved swiftly and surely and Nomsa hoped that one day her hands would be as deft.

After two and a half hours Dr Ribbentrop had managed to repair the bowel and contain the bleeding from the liver. The patient had lost two-thirds of his liver and easily the same fraction of his blood volume. Dr Ribbentrop repacked the organs into the abdominal cavity and asked Nomsa if she would like to close up. The request surprised Nomsa, not only because he had closed up the previous patient himself, but because this would be a tricky abdomen to close. The abdominal organs had been exposed for so long that they had become oedematous and swollen, and closing the abdomen over their increased bulk would be difficult. Nomsa would have to strike a balance between stretching the skin over the organs and not suturing too tightly, which would cause tissue necrosis. She accepted the request, however, eager to prove her capability to Dr Ribbentrop.

She picked up the needle holder and loaded it with a suture. With her other hand she picked up a toothed forceps. Carefully, she pierced the edge of the wound with the curved blade of the needle and pulled the stitch through. She worked slowly and carefully and Dr Ribbentrop came to look over the wound when she had almost finished closing it.

'Neatly done,' he said. 'And thanks. You did a good job assisting in a complicated case.' It was a small compliment, but it made Nomsa feel as proud as if she had just performed a heart transplant single-handedly.

By the time Nomsa got home, she had assisted with three laparotomies, a wound debridement, an appendicectomy (for an appendix that had eventually ruptured after the case had been delayed for two days because of more urgent trauma cases) and eventually the removal of the gall bladder. And after all that, she had had to do a ward round. She collapsed onto her bed and decided that she wasn't going to move until morning. Unfortunately her plans were scuppered by the ringing of her phone. She had left her phone on the table in the lounge-cum-kitchen and hauled herself up to fetch it. She saw her mother's number on her screen and phoned her back once the ringing had stopped. Her sister, not her mother, answered the call. Nomsa exchanged greetings with her sister and asked after the health of her niece before moving on to the reason for the phone call.

'Ma's in hospital,' Noluthando, her younger sister, said. 'She's very, very sick.'

Nomsa questioned her sister on her mother's admission, trying to discern if her mother's condition was serious or not, but Noluthando knew little. From what Nomsa could gather, her mother had been admitted for tuberculosis. Nomsa thought back guiltily to the last telephone conversation she had had with her mother. She should have taken it more seriously.

'Let me know what the doctors say,' Nomsa told Noluthando before putting the phone down. She was exhausted; she couldn't deal with this right now. Anyway, she suspected that her mother wasn't so ill. She was strong and young, only fifty-three. She would easily be able to fight TB with the correct treatment.

Since she was up anyway, Nomsa decided to make herself a cup of tea. She put some milk in a pot on the stove, added a teabag and waited for the liquid to boil. Once the milky mixture was the colour of golden syrup, she stirred in four teaspoons of sugar, then decanted some of the tea into a cup. She sipped the tea slowly, thinking of her mother.

Nomsa had last seen her mother three years ago, when she went home to Aliwal North for Christmas. She had spent a week there, a week that seemed to drag on forever. She had been living in Cape Town for the past twelve years and had become used to the luxuries of city living – large shopping malls, takeaway joints, restaurants, gyms and coffee shops – and she had struggled to adjust to the rustic way of life in the small town. It was more than that, though. Her mother had irritated her. A few hours after she had arrived in Aliwal North, when all she felt like was being left alone to recover from the drive, a string of visitors started arriving at her mother's house. Her mother had told Nomsa proudly that she had organised a welcoming home party for her firstborn. The guests had milled around, drinking from the large pot of *umqombothi* that her mother had brewed and chewing on the fire-roasted mealies that her mother had prepared. She had fluttered next to Nomsa, proud as a peacock.

'Nomsa has come back, she is a doctor now,' her mother had exclaimed to the group. When Nomsa mumbled that she wasn't a doctor yet, her mother had laughed at her protests and reassured her that it was only a matter of time until she was. Pawing hands had patted her and gawking men had stared at her over half-empty mugs of beer and she had wanted to run away and hide. That night she had a nightmare. She dreamt that dogs were barking at her, chasing her with teeth bared, and she had tried to ignore the meaning of the dream: that the dogs were her ancestors, reprimanding her for the way in which she was rejecting her mother and her family.

For the week that Nomsa spent in Aliwal North, her mother had spoilt her. She had insisted that Nomsa sleep in her bed – the only bed in the house. She had plied Nomsa with food – greasy, fatty food dripping with oil and calories. She had buzzed around Nomsa like a bee around honey, waiting to fulfil her daughter's every desire. She had faffed and petted and giggled, and yet all she had succeeded in doing was to irritate Nomsa and drive her away.

As Nomsa sat and sipped her sweet, milky tea, she felt ashamed at how badly she had treated her mother, at how mean she had been to her. She realised now, with the insight afforded by time and distance, that her mother had also found the reunion awkward and that her fussing had been her way of covering up her nervousness. It wouldn't have killed Nomsa to eat greasy food for a week, or to smile at her aunts and uncles and indulge their pats and probes, or to thank her mother for the use of her bed and invite her to sleep in it with her. It wouldn't have hurt her to make small talk with her, to tell her mother all those details of her life away from home

150

which she knew her mother was craving to hear and which she had so spitefully withheld.

The sun had set outside and the half-light of dusk filled the prefab with shadows. The window was open and Nomsa could hear the buzz of mosquitoes close to her, but she didn't have the energy to close the window or to cover herself in mosquito repellent. She was not only physically exhausted from the day, but emotionally worn out from the memories that her sister's telephone call had triggered. She felt tears trickle down her cheeks and for the first time in very many years she didn't try to stop them from falling. She missed her mother now, with an aching that seemed to penetrate even her bones. She had mistaken selfishness and rigidity for strength. No, it was her mother who was the strong one: her mother who had cried and who had held one-sided conversations with her, who had persisted in phoning her and who had never complained about the way Nomsa treated her.

Nomsa eventually managed to pull herself up. She wiped her eyes with a piece of toilet paper and took her empty mug to the sink. A thick, brown scum had formed over the leftover tea in the pot. She poured it down the drain. Tomorrow, when she had more energy and when her mind was not befuddled by memories, she would call the doctors looking after her mother and find out what was wrong with her and how they were treating her. Perhaps she would even think about putting in for some leave to go visit her.

Seema

14

Seema woke up at fifty-eight minutes past five, two minutes before her alarm was set to go off. She leant over the edge of the bed, reached for her phone and switched off the wake-up call before it started bleeping. Furtively she lifted the cover sheet from her body and painstakingly wriggled her way out of bed, making as little noise or disturbance as possible. She wanted to leave the house before Satesh woke up; she didn't have the energy for a confrontation before work.

She tiptoed across the room and edged the cupboard door open. It squeaked slightly but Satesh just sighed in his sleep and changed position. Seema couldn't help wondering how Satesh, with so much guilt on his conscience, could sleep so soundly and she, who had nothing to hide, would be woken by even the tiniest noise. It didn't seem fair. Perhaps Satesh didn't have a conscience, which would explain why it could not be burdened, but that would imply he was a psychopath and Seema didn't know if she was ready to classify him as such. She reached in the cupboard for a blouse and skirt and carried her clothes to the small bathroom to get dressed. Once she was clothed and had performed a quick, and quiet, *puja*, she took an apple from the fruit bowl in the kitchen and then made her way stealthily to the front door. She was hungry, far too hungry for one green apple. What she would really like to do would be to scoop up mouthfuls of cold curry from the night before in a warm *naan* bread, but she was afraid that the noise of making a proper breakfast would wake Satesh. She quietly unlocked the front door, stepped outside and closed the door gently behind her.

Seema breathed a sigh of relief. She knew it was ridiculous

that she had to creep around her own house as though she were a thief, but the discord in her and Satesh's relationship had definitely escalated since the move to Tugela Bridge. A year ago she would not have been so afraid of waking him, not unless they had recently had a fight. Now she was arriving at the hospital half an hour early every morning simply to avoid interacting with him, and she was the first to offer to cover a call if one of the other doctors was on leave or ill. At least when she was busy at the hospital, she could forget about the mind games and the taunts and the beatings; she could, for a few hours at least, pretend that her life was normal. At the hospital, as a doctor, she was capable and equal and respected. She was treated as a human being.

She walked slowly between the married quarters and the interns' accommodation. There was no reason for her to rush. The lights were on in some of the prefabs and she imagined the other doctors getting ready for work. She walked past Rachael's house and the floral scent of shower gel or shampoo wafted from the half-open window on a wisp of steam. She envied Rachael the luxury of being able to get dressed on her own. What freedom it must be, she thought, to sleep right up until the moment that one's alarm went off; to stretch and yawn out of sleep with abandon; to sing in the shower; to clatter the kettle for a morning cup of tea. The next prefab that she passed belonged to Nomsa. She imagined that Nomsa had been up early to get ready: she always looked so stylish and perfectly groomed. Perhaps she was putting on her make-up now or leisurely choosing which clothes to wear for the day. The prefab on the other side of Nomsa's was empty and Seema wondered, if she were not married, whether she would be staying there. And if she were, would things be different? Would she meet up with Nomsa and Rachael in the mornings, as she had seen them do on occasion, and walk to the hospital with them? Would she come home with them late at night, from the Clay Oven or some party, giggling and stumbling and searching bags to find keys? Would she hug and whisper and raise eyebrows and share nail files?

A movement from behind the prefabs caught her eye and interrupted her chain of thought. She didn't have her glasses on and it took a while for her to realise that the rhythmic movement was a figure bending repeatedly up and down, and it took her a few more seconds to register that Sipho must have returned to the hospital. He lifted his head and waved at her. Embarrassed, she looked down, pretending not to have seen him, and started walking more briskly to the hospital. She was stupid, she thought, to have imagined herself friends with Rachael and Nomsa: she was too shy even to greet the man who pumped water from the borehole.

Seema had one new admission and one readmission to see in the medical ward.

'You can see the new patient, Mr Khumalo,' Eliza had told her after the handover round, 'and you've seen Mr Ferreira before, so you might as well readmit him. You know him much better than I do.'

Seema wondered why Mr Ferreira was back at Prince Xoliswe and not at Inkosi Albert Luthuli Hospital undergoing chemotherapy, but before she could see him she needed to admit the new patient. She had scribbled down a few details about Mr Khumalo from that morning's handover: thirty-four-year-old man; HIV-positive on anti-retrovirals; now presenting with pneumonia; has previously received treatment for TB twice. Seema walked along the ward to find Mr Khumalo. The hospital had reached maximum capacity and four extra beds had been squeezed into the already full ward to make space for more patients. The beds were now so close together that their sides touched. Occasionally, patients shared one dirty sheet between two adjoining beds because there was a shortage of linen. The curtains that were supposed to separate the beds in the ward had long ago been stolen, and a man with bilateral below-knee amputations sat on his bedpan, defecating in full view of his neighbours.

Seema found Mr Khumalo at the back of the ward, between a man shaking with malaria and one retching into a stainless-steel kidney dish. Mr Khumalo was too short of breath to lie flat and was sitting propped up at a forty-five-degree angle. He was pale and his skin was covered in a thin film of sweat. One side of his face

154

was badly disfigured by scarring, most likely secondary to a severe shingles exacerbation. Seema glanced at the chart at the foot of Mr Khumalo's bed to check his vital signs. The nurse had recorded a blood pressure of one hundred over sixty, a pulse rate of one hundred and fourteen and a temperature of thirty-nine degrees. All were abnormal and probably indicated a severe infection. Seema introduced herself to the patient and started taking a history from him. She had been told at the handover round that Mr Khumalo was on anti-retrovirals, but when she asked the patient what medication he was taking he failed to mention them. She asked him about the treatment directly, presuming that he had not told her about the anti-retrovirals because he was ashamed to mention his HIV status, but he told her instead that he had stopped taking them.

'Why?' she asked, horrified. Without anti-retrovirals he would be dead within the next few months. That he had stopped taking the medication explained why he was so ill.

Mr Khumalo shrugged his shoulders in response to her question.

She asked him again, just in case he had not understood or heard what she asked. 'Why did you stop taking the medication that we gave you to treat the HIV?' she asked, making her question more clear.

'I took a treatment that cured the HIV, so I didn't need to carry on taking your drugs,' he said.

Seema's heart sank. There was no medication that could cure AIDS. She asked him what he had taken that had cured him and he pulled a plastic bag from the scuffed backpack underneath his bed. Inside the plastic bag were two medicine bottles and a bank envelope filled with small yellow tablets. The one bottle, its contents gone, was labelled 'HIV CURE. DRINK ALL AT ONCE FOR 100% CURE'. The other bottle contained about twenty millilitres of a green, foul-smelling liquid and was labelled 'Dr R's Vitamin Tonic. Take one teaspoon daily'. The bank envelope had 'GARLIC EXTRACT AND GINGER ... FOR GREATER STRENGTH' scrawled in permanent marker across its front. Seema balked. The medications were obviously fraudulent. She felt angry at the patient for having chosen some quack's cures above clinically trialled drugs, but her anger at the patient was eclipsed by an even greater fury at the charlatan who was selling the drugs. She wanted to take Mr Khumalo to the false doctor and show him or her the effects of Mr Khumalo's having stopped the anti-retrovirals for some untrialled *muti*. Mr Khumalo, like so many other people afflicted with HIV, was not educated or literate, and he was desperate. It was natural that he would have stopped a treatment that merely prolonged his life for a medicine that promised to cure him forever with no adverse effects. He clearly didn't know any better and Seema thought that if she were in his situation she would have acted in the same way. The greedy quack who had posed as a doctor and sold Mr Khumalo the fake medicine deserved to be put on trial for murder.

'How much did you pay for this?' she asked Mr Khumalo.

'It was eight hundred rand,' he replied. 'I saved for a long time to buy it.'

Eight hundred rand. Eight hundred rand was a lot of money to save, especially for someone who was not earning a regular income, for someone who lived below the breadline. Mr Khumalo had bought his death expensively.

Seema knew she should feel like crying but all she felt was anger, an immense, roaring, all-consuming anger. She had never felt anger like this before, not even when Satesh had raped and beaten her. It was as though she had a beast caged within her chest that was trying to fight its way out. It was somehow a wonderfully empowering feeling but now was not the time to let it loose. She still had to examine and treat her patient. She lifted Mr Khumalo's hospital gown and placed her stethoscope against his chest. His breath sounds were harsh and over one area made a hollow whistle as though his breath was blowing over the top of a glass bottle. It was a sound highly suggestive of an open cavity in the lung. She remembered the second piece of information she had been given during the handover round.

'You've had TB twice before?' she asked the patient.

Mr Khumalo nodded.

'Did you get treatment for the TB? Both times?'

The patient explained that he had to stop his TB treatment early the first time because he had to go back to the Drakensberg to rebuild his house there, and that he had stopped the second time because the injections had not been working. Seema tried to digest the information: he hadn't completed his treatment initially, which meant that the second time he had contracted TB he probably already had some resistance, and he hadn't finished that course of treatment either. Seema put her hand in front of her mouth and nose. It was an instinctive action, a natural response to the realisation that she was probably dealing with a patient with multi-drug-resistant tuberculosis. The patient needed to be in an isolated room. At the moment he was breathing drug-resistant TB bacteria into a room full of immunocompromised patients. It was like throwing a match into a tank of petrol. Seema ran off to try to organise a single room for the patient. When she asked the ward sister about it, the sister laughed.

'You want a single room?' she snorted mockingly. 'Let me show you the single rooms.' She led Seema back through the ward and across the corridor to the two single rooms that were supposed to house infectious or severely immunocompromised patients. The first single room had been turned into an isolation room. The patient inside was from the DRC and had suspected Ebola fever, a generally fatal viral disease.

'I don't think you want your patient to share with this man,' the sister commented sarcastically.

The second single room was no longer a single room. It contained one bed and two metal gurneys, on which patients lay. It had, in effect, been turned into a mini ward.

'What am I supposed to do?' Seema asked in desperation. She was close to tears. The sister must have realised that Seema could not handle any further sarcasm because her tone of voice changed.

'Why don't you go up to theatre and get a mask for the patient?' she suggested gently. 'At least that will trap some of the TB bacteria.'

Seema nodded. 'Thanks. I suppose that's better than nothing.'

'All we do here is try to do better than nothing,' the sister said. 'You'll get used to it if you stay here long enough. But you won't, will you? All you young doctors go overseas now. I would too, if I were in your shoes.'

The sister walked away slowly, as though the conversation had used the last of her energy, and Seema made her way up to theatre to get a mask. One of the community service doctors, Shane Pillay, was busy writing notes outside theatre. Seema hesitated for a moment, too shy to ask him where the theatre masks were. He looked up and caught sight of her.

'Hi,' he said. 'Can I help?'

Seema felt her cheeks begin to burn. 'I … I … I'm looking for a theatre mask,' she stuttered. Shane pointed to the mask dispenser and Seema quickly pulled one out, then disappeared as quickly as she could. She knew that it would be embarrassing for her patient to wear a mask in the ward, but she would have to explain to him how important it was. And she would tell the sisters to make sure that he wore his mask at all times when he wasn't attached to oxygen.

Mr Ferreira was in the same ward as Mr Khumalo. This was unfortunate for Seema, because she would have to spend more time in the ward and increase her risk of contracting drug-resistant TB, and unfortunate for Mr Ferreira, because the cancer and chemotherapy had killed off all his white blood cells, leaving him without any immune system. The TB bacteria would have a field day when they found him. Both of her patients should be in isolation rooms for different reasons, Seema thought grimly. In order to minimise the time she physically spent in the ward, Seema took Mr Ferreira's file to the corridor and read the notes from Inkosi Albert Luthuli Hospital there. The oncologist had sent back a report stating that the cancer was too advanced for curative chemotherapy and so they had given Mr Ferreira what palliative radiotherapy they were able to and had then discharged him back to Prince Xoliswe for further management.

Seema was shocked when she reached Mr Ferreira's bedside. He had aged ten years since she had seen him last, just one month ago. His face had become gaunt and his parchment-like skin hung loosely from his bones. He looked frail now and Seema couldn't help staring at his shaking hand as he raised it to greet her. She knew it was unprofessional to gape and she quickly averted her eyes, but Mr Ferreira had noticed that she had seen the trembling.

'I'm like an old man now, all skin and bones,' he said to her. 'I've lost so much weight my wife hardly recognises me. I tell you, if I could market this cancer for weight loss, I would die a rich man.'

Seema was amazed that he was still able to make jokes: although his body looked broken by it, his demeanour seemed unaffected by the cancer.

'How are you feeling?' Seema asked.

'I've felt better. But I suppose it could be worse, so I mustn't complain.'

Seema wondered how it could possibly be worse. Mr Ferreira had end-stage cancer, his chemotherapy had failed and now he was stuck in a crowded, filthy ward with drug-resistant tuberculosis bacilli floating around.

'At least back here I'm closer to my wife. I missed her in Durban. Without her, I'm like half a man.' He started chuckling and Seema wondered whether the cancer was affecting his brain.

'Don't you get it?' he asked her.

'No.' Seema shook her head, wondering what it was she was not getting.

'Half a man. All the weight I've lost …' Mr Ferreira was waiting for Seema to laugh, but she found the joke more sad than funny. Eventually she forced something that vaguely resembled a laugh from her mouth, then quickly started explaining to Mr Ferreira what palliative treatment she would be able to offer him so that he didn't take offence at her poor response to his humour. He interrupted her almost as soon as she started speaking.

'What I just don't understand, Doc, is how it all happened so quickly.' His tone had become serious and he looked down at his trembling hands as he spoke. 'One minute I was fit as a fiddle, going to my house doctor for a general check-up because the wife was nagging me, and the next minute I look like I'm eighty in the shade.'

Seema stood awkwardly at the end of the bed. She didn't know what to say because she didn't have an explanation.

'You know what the funny thing is, Doc?' Mr Ferreira asked. But he didn't expect a reply. Seema got the feeling that he was talking regardless of and not because of her presence. 'I was fine until I found out I had the cancer. Things just seemed to go downhill from there. I can't help wondering if I would still be healthy today if I had never found out about the cancer. You know, mind over matter and all that.'

Seema shook her head. She wanted to reassure Mr Ferreira that the leukaemia would have progressed regardless of his awareness of it, but he continued talking before she had a chance to say anything.

'Can I go home, Doc? I know there's nothing more you can do for me. I'd like to be with my wife for the last little bit.'

Seema told him that she would discharge him immediately and prescribed some morphine syrup for him to take home. There was no reason for him to stay in hospital unless he needed a morphine drip for pain relief.

'If the pain is ever too much, make sure you come back and we'll sort something out for you,' she said. She was happier with him at home, anyway. At least there he would be far away from people coughing up TB bacteria and Ebola virus.

'Thanks, Doc. I will.' He grabbed Seema's hand and cupped it between his two frail hands. 'You're a good doctor,' he said. 'You care. Not many doctors really care.' He squeezed her hand gently. 'Carry on caring, even when you're a busy, big-shot doctor.'

Seema nodded but he seemed to be expecting more. 'I will,' she whispered. He smiled and released her hand.

She walked slowly from the bed, thinking about what Mr Ferreira had said. She wondered whether she did really care. She knew that she cared about her patients on a medical level: she was proud of her ability to diagnose correctly, her clinical skills were better than good and she knew that her treatment was excellent, but she didn't know whether she cared for them on a personal level, on the level that Mr Ferreira implied. She thought back to the call that she had done with Dr Ribbentrop, to the gentle way that he had handled the abused child. He cared. Dr Chetty cared too. Every time Seema worked with her, she surprised Seema with her dedication. She worked longer hours than her calls required; she made the effort to talk to patients and to their families; she spent time, precious time, organising transport for a patient or a visit from a social worker or a Babygro for a newborn to go home in. Seema felt a tiny flicker of excitement tickle her chest. She would start caring; from this moment on, she would really care. She knew she could make as good a doctor as both Dr Ribbentrop and Dr Chetty. She thought that perhaps Mr Ferreira was some sort of demigod, cleverly disguised as a sick man, sent to enlighten her. His words had been a revelation: they had laid bare, without any obscurity or doubt, her destiny. And it was a shining, golden path that she couldn't wait to start travelling.

Rachael

15

Since the community service doctor who was supposed to be working in paediatrics with her was on leave, Rachael was doing the ward round on her own. Luckily the paediatric unit was quiet and she had to see only twenty-three children. She started in the 'A' room. Four metal cots lined either side of the wall. Above one of the cots someone had painted a picture of Winnie-the-Pooh, but the paint had faded and flaked off and all that was left of Pooh was a square of his red shirt and one yellow paw.

Rachael examined the child in the first bed – a four-year-old girl who had been admitted with pneumonia – and made some notes in the patient's folder. Even though she had managed to pare her notes down to the barest minimum, they still seemed to be triple the length of any of the other doctors' notes. She knew it was largely because of her lengthy documentation that she took far longer than anyone else to complete her ward rounds. The problem was that every time she tried to leave out some detail in order to make her notes briefer, she spent the rest of the day imagining a lawsuit against her and then had to go back and fill in the information to prevent herself from spending the rest of the day in a panic. After having wasted many hours walking backwards and forwards between different wards to insert details she had purposefully omitted in an attempt to keep her notes succinct, she realised that it took less effort and time to include all the information in the first place.

The second child that Rachael examined had also been admitted with pneumonia but was much sicker than the first child. She had a cannula running beneath her nose from which oxygen was flowing and a nasogastric tube protruding from her mouth, presumably because she was eating poorly. The nasogastric tube had been taped to her cheek but it must have been irritating the child because she kept scratching at the plaster in an attempt to remove the tube. Rachael didn't need to read the patient notes to know that the child was HIV-positive; she had seen enough children with AIDS at Prince Xoliswe to be able to recognise the signs immediately. She examined the child, made some changes to the prescription chart and scribbled a note in the patient's folder questioning why the child wasn't on anti-retrovirals, then made her way to her next patient.

A three-year-old boy smiled at her as she got to his bedside. She quickly read his notes: he had been admitted with diarrhoea secondary to HIV, but the gastroenteritis had largely resolved and the child was almost ready for discharge. Rachael knew that the boy should be being treated in a separate room because of the infectious nature of gastroenteritis, but the isolation rooms were all occupied by equally worthy candidates. Rachael pulled on a pair of latex gloves before examining the child, hoping that this paltry attempt at infection control would be enough to prevent her from passing the diarrhoea on to the next patient that she saw. She greeted the boy as she reached over to feel his abdomen and he answered her back in English. It was a pleasant change for Rachael: she had become used to trying to communicate with her patients in a blend of rudimentary Zulu and hand signals, which seldom made for very successful or satisfying interactions. She had ordered herself a 'teach-yourself isiZulu' book and CD online, which had arrived over a month ago, but she was finding the language, with its unrecognisable vocabulary and unusual pronunciation, difficult to learn and, because of her awkward articulation, when she attempted speaking to people in Zulu, they inevitably just stared back at her uncomprehendingly.

Although the boy was still mildly dehydrated, he seemed quite cheerful and chattered to Rachael continuously as she examined him. Rachael was satisfied that he had improved enough to be discharged and asked the boy if he wanted to go home. He lurched into a violent coughing fit in response to her question. Initially, Rachael

163

thought that he was feigning the cough to avoid being discharged. Before coming to Tugela Bridge, Rachael would have thought it unimaginable for a child to prefer hospital to home, but after a few weeks at Prince Xoliswe she realised that some homes were, almost impossibly, worse than hospital. But the boy's coughing got worse, until he was gasping and gagging between bouts of debilitating barks, and Rachael realised that the situation was far more serious than she had originally imagined. It almost looked as if the boy was choking on something. Without hesitating further, she picked the child up, put him over her knee and started whacking him on the back. He vomited on the floor and the coughing stopped.

'Are you all right?' Rachael asked breathlessly. The exertion of lifting the child, combined with her panic, had left her momentarily short of breath.

The child, however, seemed unperturbed by his near-death experience.

'Yes, I want go home,' he said, obviously in response to Rachael's earlier question.

'Okay,' Rachael said. 'How about tomorrow?' She was somewhat hesitant now to discharge the child immediately. She took a step over the vomit to return the boy to his bed and noticed that it appeared to be moving. She looked at the vomit more closely. What she had presumed to be vomit was, in fact, a mass of seething worms. She managed to stop the scream before it left her mouth. She had been in close proximity to maggots and a spitting cobra; worms should not bother her one iota. Neither should the fact that they had just been regurgitated from a child's body. She looked at the little boy. He was watching the creatures, fascinated. The worms were long and flat with segmented bodies. Rachael thought they looked a little like the pictures of tapeworms that she remembered from the parasite section of one of her fifth-year textbooks. The major difference was that in the textbook picture the worms had been nicely laid out with labelled body parts, not scrabbling over each other in a hysterical, wriggling heap. She wondered how long the creatures would survive outside the child's body.

'Snake,' the child said, pointing at the mass of worms that was now resolving into individuals dispersing across the floor in search of new hosts.

'No,' Rachael said, 'they're only worms.' She wondered what the boy thought about the fact that they had appeared from his mouth. 'Better that they're all out now, don't you think?' she said to the child, trying to reassure him that everything was fine.

As Rachael went off to find a cleaner to get rid of the floor-borne parasites, she couldn't help marvelling at how much she had matured in the time she had been at Tugela Bridge. A few months ago, she would have run from the room screaming at the sight of the worms (which would probably have frightened the poor boy more than the appearance of worms from his mouth had seemed to). Now she took a pile of regurgitated worms in her stride. She had every right, she decided, to be proud of herself. She thought of phoning her mom to tell her how pleased with herself she was, but then realised that her mother wouldn't understand either the worms or Rachael's response. And Rachael would probably be subjected to a half-hour rant about how this sort of thing could only happen in Africa. Mentally she ran through her list of friends, trying to find someone with whom to share her joy, but eventually she realised that none of them would be able to comprehend her pride. They would all just be disgusted. She scrolled down the contact list on her phone. Of everybody she knew, there was only one person she could find who would appreciate her story: Shane. She dialled his number.

'Can you talk?' she asked.

'Quickly – I'm about to scrub up for a lap.'

Rachael rushed through the story and waited for his words of approval. They didn't come.

'Check the boy out properly,' Shane said instead. 'The worms often know when the child's about to die. They try to get out before that happens. If the kid dies, they die along with it. Obviously there are other causes for the worms looking for a new host, but make sure you haven't missed anything.'

Rachael could almost hear the sad little hiss of her ego deflating. She had been so sure that this time she had done the right thing.

She wondered if she would ever be more than simply adequate. Perhaps she wasn't good enough to cut it as a doctor outside the comfort of a tertiary academic hospital. Even worse, perhaps she wasn't good enough to be a doctor at all. She walked slowly back to the ward and re-examined the child, trying to figure out what she could have missed. She still couldn't find anything terribly wrong with the little boy, but she definitely wouldn't be discharging him in the near future. She told him that he wouldn't be able to go home the next day and he started crying. Now she wasn't only a substandard doctor, but a horrible one too. Rachael picked the little boy up and hugged him.

'I'm sorry,' she said. 'I promise you can go as soon as you're better.' The comfort of the hug was as much for her as it was for the child.

'I better,' he said, smiling convincingly through his tears.

'Almost better,' Rachael countered. She hoped that there wasn't anything seriously wrong with the child that she was missing and that these particular worms had just decided it was time to move house.

By the time Rachael reached the last child in the ward, she had counted sixteen of the twenty-three children as being HIV-positive. That was almost seventy per cent. She found it hard to comprehend that the majority of the children she had seen that morning were dying. The only real difference between them was the length of time it would take them to die. Since medical school she had known that HIV was far more prevalent than the general population believed it to be or than government figures suggested, but she had not realised that the incidence was this high. And she was seeing only the children. For each child that she saw, there was at least one, probably two, HIV-positive adults. She knew that it was impossible that the hospital had been half empty all the time before HIV became so widespread and she wondered where those children were now who would previously have been occupying sixteen of the twenty-three beds. Had HIV raised the entrance criteria for hospital admission, she wondered, and who was looking after those who were not yet close enough to death to warrant a bed?

Rachael read the file of the last child that she had to see. She was a sixteen-month-old girl admitted a week before with what appeared to be kidney failure. She was HIV-positive but had not yet been started on anti-retrovirals because the hospital had run out of stock of the paediatric syrups. Rachael walked over to the cot to examine the little girl. She had ribbons braided into her hair and a cute, button nose, and she smiled at Rachael as she approached. Rachael put her stethoscope to her ears and the little girl lifted up her pink T-shirt. The implications of the gesture tore through Rachael. It made her put her stethoscope down and pick the child up and hold her swollen body tightly and kiss the top of her little head. It was wrong, so very, very wrong, that a sixteen-month-old child should have spent so much time in hospital that she knew exactly what a stethoscope was for. Rachael couldn't help wondering if the child would know as easily what to do if she was handed a teddy bear or a xylophone.

Rachael left the hospital at four o'clock that afternoon, immediately after finishing her ward work. Usually she would go to the doctors' office and have a cup of coffee and a chat with whoever happened to be around before heading back to her prefab, but this afternoon she was supposed to be driving to Durban and she wanted to leave before it got dark. Besides, she knew she wasn't exactly good company; the day's events had put her in a melancholy mood. Had her mother and father not been expecting her, she probably would have given up the trip and instead curled up in bed with a very large chocolate and a magazine. Unfortunately, she had already committed to meeting her parents. Her mother had called her earlier in the week.

'Guess what?' she shouted at Rachael as she answered.

Gloria-Jean loved surprises and Rachael had long before given up even attempting to guess what they were because they were so completely variable. Her mother shouted the same high-pitched 'Guess what?' when telling Rachael that she had bought a new bra as she did when passing on the news that someone in the family had decided to emigrate to Israel.

'What?' Rachael had asked, determined not to be provoked into a guessing game.

'No, guess,' her mother had said coercively.

'I'm not guessing,' Rachael had said matter-of-factly.

'Then I'm not telling you,' her mother had responded, slightly sulkily.

'Fine,' Rachael had replied calmly. She had had little curiosity about her mother's secret, both because she had learnt that her mother's surprises seldom involved her at all and because she had little doubt that her mother would be unable to keep the secret for very long. She had been right.

'Your daddy and I are coming to visit you!' Gloria-Jean had blurted out after less than three seconds.

'What, here?' Rachael had asked, trying to keep the horror from her voice. Images of a naked Shane stumbling out of her bed and bumping into a pyjama-clad Gloria-Jean flickered through Rachael's mind. It couldn't happen. Luckily, her mother had no intention of voluntarily returning to Tugela Bridge. She had booked an apartment at an exclusive beachside eco-estate half an hour north of Durban. Rachael was to meet her parents there.

Although it was only late afternoon when Rachael left Tugela Bridge, the roads were busy and the trip took longer than she had expected, so it was already dark when she arrived at the gates of the security estate. Her mother had texted to her an access code that she was required to give to the security guard in order to gain entry to the estate. The guard made her sign something, handed her a visitor's card and then gave her directions to the chalet into which she was booked for the night. Outside she could hear the chirp of crickets and the raucous chorus of hundreds of unseen frogs calling to each other. Her headlights picked out the reflection of a pair of eyes and behind them Rachael could just make out the dusky shape of a buck. On either side of the road were mansions, most of them mere silhouettes in the darkness. Lights shone in a few of them, momentarily revealing the promise of warmth and food and family. Rachael felt the tensions of the day ease from her body and disappear into the song of the frogs. This is paradise, she thought as she drove; this is how life is supposed to be.

Rachael's parents had booked two adjoining apartments in the so-called forest estate, one for themselves and one for Rachael. Her parents had already gone to dinner, so Rachael immediately opened the door of her chalet and went in to put her bag down. The bed was piled high with down pillows and plump cushions. At the foot of the bed a towel had been laid out, on top of which were strewn a welcoming yellow rose and an expensive Belgian chocolate. In front of the window, covered now by plush curtains, was a fashionably upholstered chaise lounge. When Rachael reclined in it, she could see her reflection in the wooden-framed mirror on the opposite wall. The en-suite bathroom was almost the size of the bedroom, with both a shower and a large Victorian-style bath next to which miniature bottles of shampoo, conditioner, shower gel and body lotion had been neatly lined up. Rachael walked across the bathroom to the bath and her feet seemed to melt into the heated floor tiles. She undressed, dropping her clothes on the floor, and then turned on the tap: clean water gushed, steaming hot, from the faucet. Deciding she would bath after dinner, when she would be able to spend as much time as she wanted to in the tub, she turned off the tap and stepped into the shower. She stood under the spray and let the hot water pound the skin of her back. Compared to the dribble that came out of her shower at home, this felt like a massage. She turned her face up to the ceiling and let the water fall onto it. Slowly she spun around, making sure that every inch of her skin was drenched. She stepped out of the shower feeling cleaner and more relaxed than she had since her move to Tugela Bridge. She found it difficult to imagine that once this had been what she had done every day, that she had taken luxury like this for granted.

The lodge, which was where she was meeting her parents for dinner, was decorated in an expensive colonial style, with heavy wooden furniture, dark paintings depicting hunt scenes or botanical specimens, and animal skins strewn tastefully on the floor. The muted strains of a violin concerto filled the dining room. Occasionally, the call of the frogs, floating in through the open windows, overwhelmed the strings. A waiter dressed smartly in a

169

suit and bowtie took Rachael to her parents' table and poured her a glass of red wine from the bottle that her father had ordered.

'My *bobeleh*,' Gloria-Jean said, getting up to hug Rachael. 'It was getting so late I was about to get Daddy to call you to find out if you'd got lost walking from the chalet to the lodge.' Rachael explained to her mother that she had taken her time in the shower and apologised for holding up their dinner.

'Of course you haven't held us up,' Gloria-Jean said, squeezing Rachael's hand. 'It's worth waiting however long to see you. I feel like I haven't seen you in absolutely ages. I've been missing you terribly, you know.'

Rachael wished she could say the same to her mother, that she had been missing her, but she couldn't get the words out of her mouth. She knew they would sound like what they were, false. She had hardly missed her parents at all since moving to Tugela Bridge, not only because she had been too busy to miss anyone, but also because she had been enjoying the freedom that being away from her family allowed her. It wasn't so much a physical freedom (she had, after all, been living away from her parents' house for the past six years) but an independence on a different level. It was the freedom to think and to act in a way that defied the cultural boundaries that had defined her life until now. In Tugela Bridge, nobody had preconceived ideas about who Rachael Lipawski was and so nobody had any expectations of her.

Gloria-Jean raised a finger into the air and a waiter materialised at the side of the table to take their order. Rachael was glad that the food didn't take too long to come after that, because she was struggling to talk to her parents without the conversation turning into an argument, and she didn't want to ruin the evening with fighting. She wondered whether there had always been so many issues about which she disagreed with her parents. Had she changed so much or had she before subconsciously suppressed her views in order to comply with her parents' expectations?

Rachael excused herself almost immediately after dinner, using the excuse that she was tired from the trip, and went back to the solitude of her chalet. She ran herself a deep bath and lowered her body into the scented, steaming water. She could feel her muscles relax as the heat and expensive aromatherapy oils penetrated them, but her mind would not quieten. She felt as though she was being torn between two different lives, as though her personality was split into two personas that were at war with each other. She didn't know which Rachael was the real Rachael, the person she had been before moving to Tugela Bridge or the person she was now, and she didn't know if the two could coexist or if they were mutually exclusive. She went to bed, not relaxed as she should have been, but muddled and confused.

A knocking at the chalet door woke Rachael the next morning. She put on her dressing gown and stumbled to the door. She hadn't slept well and her head felt thick and dull. Gloria-Jean was standing outside, dressed in a hip tracksuit and wearing sunglasses that covered half her face.

'Come on,' Gloria-Jean said brightly. 'Time to burn off that dinner we had last night.'

Rachael sighed. The last thing she felt like doing was going power-walking with her mother. What she really wanted to do was to go straight back to the huge, springy double bed and snuggle under the Egyptian cotton sheets and the plump down duvet, but she knew that her mother wouldn't let her get away with being lazy. She sleepily put on a shirt and shorts, pulled her hair into a ponytail and joined her mother outside.

'Surely you're not going out like that?' Gloria-Jean asked, eyeing Rachael up and down. Rachael was wearing a pair of red board shorts (something she had never owned before moving to Natal) and a T-shirt that had been given to her by a medical rep.

'Mom, we're exercising,' Rachael protested.

'Yes, but you never know who we could bump into. In this place, it could be your future husband. I can guarantee you it certainly won't be if you dress like that. Off you go and put some decent clothes on. And at least some lipstick. You look like death warmed up.'

'No, Mom, I'm going like this. If my future husband doesn't like me like this, then tough, and if you don't like it you can walk alone and I'll go back to bed.' Rachael wasn't going to get changed, both because her mother was being ridiculous and because she hadn't actually packed any other clothes in which to exercise. Gloria-Jean mumbled something that Rachael couldn't make out, but she seemed to accept the ultimatum.

The morning was still and clear and not yet too hot. An orchestra of bird calls floated from the trees on either side of the paved paths, and every now and then Rachael caught sight of a buck grazing in the undergrowth. They turned onto a wider road that was signposted as leading to the beach. In the daylight she could clearly make out the opulence of the mansions that lined both sides of the road. Most of them were huge pillared buildings with sweeping glass windows and turquoise swimming pools. Many of the homes appeared to be unoccupied.

'Are these all holiday houses?' Rachael asked.

Gloria-Jean nodded. 'Most of them are,' she confirmed. 'If you were going to stay in Natal for longer, I'd get Daddy to look into buying a place here. It really is divine!'

Rachael knew that, six months ago, she would have agreed with her mother, but now she had a shadow of doubt. She remembered the patient she had seen who hadn't had fifty rands to come back to hospital for life-saving drugs. It didn't seem fair that only a few hundred kilometres away people had ten-million-rand holiday houses that were unoccupied for most of the year. She tried to explain her thoughts to her mother.

'*Oy vey*! You're turning into a true communist,' Gloria-Jean snapped. 'What's that place doing to you? Are they indoctrinating you there? You've stopped putting on make-up and caring about what you wear. Next thing I know, you'll have stopped waxing your legs and underarms. I don't think I want to hear what'll come from your mouth next.'

So Rachael kept quiet. She definitely wasn't a communist, but she struggled to accept that such poverty could exist so easily alongside such wealth. Since her mother appeared to be ignoring her, she had time to think as they walked. She wondered whether the owners of the houses they were walking past had ever visited a state hospital or seen the inside of a rural government clinic. She wondered whether they lived in ignorance or if they were burdened by guilt. Had they ever looked into the eyes of a child so used to poverty that in comparison with its home a government hospital seemed like a hotel? She had, and she knew that she would never be able to return to the blissful state of oblivion in which she had existed before. The problem was where to draw the line: at which point did a need become a desire, and when did a necessity turn into a luxury? She wished that she had someone with whom she could discuss the issues that were bothering her, but she knew that all her friends would have the same reaction that her mother had. Even Shane didn't seem to feel the same way that she did.

Seema

16

Seema hurried home as soon as she had completed her end-of-day ward round. She was on call that evening and had an hour to spare before her shift started. She had had a busy day and so she wanted to shower and have some supper before facing the next twelve hours of mayhem. Satesh was in the dining room when she got home, sitting at the table playing games on his laptop. She shouted a greeting to him as she made her way through to the bedroom. She picked a fresh outfit from the cupboard and took the clothes with her to the bathroom. She quickly undressed and folded her dirty clothes into a pile on the floor, making a mental note that she would have to do some laundry the following day after returning from the hospital. She wound her hair into a tight bun and covered it with a plastic shower cap, then stepped into the shower.

Satesh caught her as she was getting out of the shower. She quickly grabbed the towel from the hook behind the door and covered herself with it as he came into the postage stamp-sized bathroom.

'Going somewhere?' he asked. Nothing in his expression or tone of voice gave his mood away and Seema knew that this was not by chance. She told him that she was on call that evening.

'But you've just come from work,' Satesh argued. Seema knew that Satesh was not an imbecile, that by now he knew how the call system worked and that once a week she did a night call during the week after having spent the day at the hospital. Which meant that he was questioning her only to be obtrusive. She pulled the towel closer around her body and answered him as calmly as she could, patiently explaining to him what she knew he already knew. She wished he would move away from the doorway. His presence, his lean, predator-like body filling the frame, made her feel caged in. She wanted to get out of the small bathroom, into a room with more air to breathe.

'Satesh, please move. I need to get dressed,' she begged.

'What's stopping you from getting dressed? Your clothes are right here. Feel free to get dressed,' Satesh said indifferently, pointing to the clothes she had brought with her to the bathroom.

She couldn't, not with Satesh watching her. Naked, she was too vulnerable.

'I'm starting to wonder about you,' Satesh continued. 'Too much of working all the time. It doesn't seem normal to me.'

'I'm a doctor,' she said quietly. 'You should understand that doctors work long hours. What I'm doing isn't abnormal.' She knew, as the words fell from her lips, that she had said the wrong thing. She had been careless, thoughtless. She should never have mentioned her qualification. She bit her lip, as though physically trying to prevent herself from saying anything else. Satesh was silent for a moment and the walls of the bathroom seemed to grow thicker, to close in on her.

'Don't you want to get dressed? Surely you're running out of time?' Satesh asked eventually. 'It's already six thirty. Don't you start at seven?' It was so easy to mistake the tone of his questions, so easy to mistake the taunting for caring. And Seema almost wanted to. She almost wanted to trick herself into believing that Satesh was asking the questions innocently and that he really was worried that she wouldn't make it to the hospital in time for her shift. But he didn't move from the doorway. As she gripped the towel more tightly around her body, she noticed that her hands had begun to shake. Nausea welled up from the pit of her stomach. She had to get out of the bathroom right now. There wasn't enough oxygen in the small room. She gasped, trying to stop herself from suffocating. She wanted to run, to push past Satesh and escape, but her legs were dead weights that she couldn't lift.

'Or is it that you're hiding something from me?' Satesh asked icily. 'Is that why you won't let go of your towel?'

'No,' Seema stammered. 'No, I'm not hiding anything. What would I be hiding?'

'I don't know. You tell me,' Satesh spat. All at once his tone had changed from taunting to angry. 'Maybe the evidence of your doctor boyfriends.' Tiny white droplets of spittle clung to the corners of his mouth.

'I'm married, Satesh,' Seema wailed. 'I don't have other boyfriends, I swear. You know I don't. Why would I have other boyfriends? You're my husband.' She was crying now, uncontrollable tears flooding down her cheeks. She knew that the conversation was irrelevant, that the situation was unsalvageable.

'I don't know anything. I don't know what you and your doctor friends get up to all that time you spend together. You expect me to believe that you all work those long hours?' he sneered. 'I won't be taken for a fool. I might not be a doctor but I'm not an idiot. You forget that, don't you? Just because I don't have a long list of letters behind my name doesn't mean I'm stupid. Now take the towel off. Let's see the marks your doctor boyfriends have left on your body.'

Seema hesitated. Again, she felt paralysed. She knew that she had no choice but to do as Satesh instructed, that to ignore his commands would make him even angrier, but she seemed unable to move her hands. The message was getting stuck somewhere between her brain and her limbs. Fear had blocked her nerve synapses as effectively as any spinal fracture would have.

Satesh leant forward and yanked at the towel. She felt it slip from her fingers and fall to the floor. Quickly she covered what she could of her breasts and her pubic mound with her shaking arms.

'Please, Satesh. Please stop,' she begged. Her voice was a pathetic whimper.

'Drop your arms to your sides. I want to see what you're covering up,' Satesh ordered harshly.

'No,' Seema sobbed. Her body quivered with the force of her misery. 'Please, no.'

'You're a doctor; you're supposed to be clever. If you were so clever you'd do what I tell you.' Satesh's tone was mocking again, but Seema knew that he was right. It was best not to put up any resistance, not to show any glimmer of spirit. That way, perhaps, Satesh would get done quicker and she would not be too late for her call. She slowly released her arms to her sides. She felt more than naked, as though she had been skinned. Satesh told her to turn around in a circle so that he could examine her. She followed his command robotically. Her mind had left now. It always did. It looked down on her slight body giving itself up for Satesh's scrutiny. It noticed Satesh's erection beneath his tracksuit pants. It watched as Satesh pushed her body onto the cramped bathroom floor and ordered her to open her legs.

'Let me see what disgusting things you've let your other boyfriends do to you,' Satesh said. His voice was harsh and cold. Seema saw that her legs were shaking, her knees knocking together. Her mind, numb, watched as Satesh pulled her knees apart. He ordered her to part the lips of her cunt and her fingers followed his command like obedient little schoolgirls. She was open, exposed to him. A piece of plump pink flesh. He pushed her over. The pain of her head hitting the toilet brought her mind abruptly back into her body. The smell of stale urine filled her nostrils. She fought, pushing her mind back. It couldn't stay in her body; the humiliation and the pain were too great. She wouldn't survive it. She repeated a meditation mantra over and over again, trying to force her mind to be distracted, to think about anything but what was happening. Satesh parted the cheeks of her buttocks and stuck his fingers into her anus. She felt the burning as he stretched her sphincter. She was losing control of her mind. She could feel it slipping back into her body, being drawn in by the pain. The mantra was erratic, distorted by Satesh's grunts. She clung onto it, like a falling man would cling to a parachute.

'You disgusting piece of shit,' Satesh spat and Seema knew that he was finished. He always finished like that. She felt him get off her and watched as he pulled up his tracksuit pants and walked out of the bathroom. Slowly, she let her mind re-enter her body. She curled into the foetal position and succumbed to the sobbing that racked her. She could feel the moistness of Satesh's semen dribbling down her bottom. After a while she slowly pulled herself

177

into a sitting position. The shower was still running. Strange that she hadn't noticed that before. She stepped into the stream of water and rubbed soap onto a nailbrush. And then she scrubbed and scrubbed, until there was no trace of Satesh left on her.

Dr Ribbentrop didn't comment when Seema walked into casualty fifteen minutes late. Seema was glad because she didn't know what excuse she would have given for her tardiness. She wasn't good at lying. Fortunately there were patients waiting to be seen and she could get to work immediately. She knew that the only way to steady her mind would be to concentrate on what lay in front of her. She hoped the patient she called in would be a complicated case that would require all her attention, that would leave no room for her mind to wander.

'Mr Ngombo,' she said, picking up a folder. Nobody responded to her call.

'Doctor must shout louder,' the sister said, taking the folder from Seema and screaming the patient's name. A man walked into casualty within seconds. His one hand was wrapped in a bloodied bandage and he was using the other to support it.

'What happened?' Seema asked, leading him into a cubicle.

'Panga,' the man replied.

Seema had seen many panga wounds as a student. The KwaZulu-Natal coast was heavily planted with sugar cane and each year, after the cane had been burnt, gangs of cane cutters would harvest the cane using pangas. Pangas sliced through limbs with almost the same ease with which they sliced through cane. Seema unravelled the bandage. It fell softly onto the floor in bloody folds. As the pressure of the bandage was released, the wound started bleeding, and by the time Seema had unwound the full length of the bandage, blood was spurting rhythmically from the laceration. The panga must have cut the radial artery, Seema realised. She hurriedly rifled through a suture tray and found two needle holders. They would have to substitute for artery forceps. She opened the wound, turning the man's arm away from her to prevent blood from spraying onto her face, and hunted in the bloody mess for the cut ends of the artery. It was difficult to see beyond the blood and she continually dabbed the wound with gauze to try to create some sort of visual field. Eventually she called one of the nursing staff to come and help her. The sister pressed gauze over the wound, then periodically lifted it for a second or two while Seema sorted through ligaments and tendons and nerves and blood vessels trying to find the lacerated artery.

After what felt like hours she managed to find the cut ends of the artery and pinched them closed with the needle holders. Hopefully that would maintain haemostasis until the patient was able to get to theatre, where the artery could be properly repaired. The patient started swaying and Seema grabbed him to stabilise him, then helped him to lie down on the bed on which he had been sitting. He looked pale and felt clammy, as though he was about to faint. Seema was hardly surprised. Apart from being in severe pain and having lost about a litre of blood, the patient was lying on a bed in the middle of a room that looked like it had been the scene of a mass slaughter. There was blood all over the patient. There was blood on the curtain and covering the bed and pooled on the floor. Seema looked down. There was blood on her toes too. She usually wore closed shoes when she was on call, but she had left home so upset this evening that she had put on the same open sandals that she had been wearing during the day. She grabbed an alcohol swab and started wiping the blood off her foot, checking for any cuts as she did so. Luckily, she could see none. She knew that there was a possibility that the man was HIV-positive. She felt anger build up inside her. This was all Satesh's fault. If it weren't for him, she would be wearing sneakers and she wouldn't have exposed herself to the risk of HIV. She wiped her toes one last time and threw the swab away. The anger now boiled inside her, warming her up. It was entirely disproportionate to the response that she should have had after having been splashed with blood: this was anger that had been brewing for a very long time. She didn't know why tonight was different from every other time Satesh had raped her, why tonight she felt fury where before she had only ever felt disgrace and humiliation. She wondered what had changed inside her, what it was that had allowed the anger to escape. But she couldn't dwell on her emotions for long. Her patient was waiting for her. She turned towards him.

'You're going to have to go to theatre,' she said. 'You need an operation to fix the injury. The panga cut a blood vessel.' She explained to him that she was going to organise the procedure with a surgeon and left the patient lying on the examination bed. The anger was still inside her and it seemed to be growing. She watched it tentatively, not quite knowing what it would become. It was like an untamed beast inside her but she was loath to control it. It made her, for the first time ever, strong. It turned her slouch into a stride, pulled back her shoulders, lifted her chin.

The next patient Seema called in was a woman in her thirties. She had shoulder-length blond hair scraped back into a low ponytail and was wearing jeans and a red halter-neck top speckled with splatters of dried blood. She walked in on the arm of a man who introduced himself as her husband. Seema noted that the woman was limping and had a small laceration on her forehead. Her one arm was poorly immobilised in a grubby home-made sling. Seema could smell the sour reek of alcohol on the breath of the patient and her husband as they introduced themselves. Seema asked the woman what had happened and she told Seema that she had fallen down the stairs.

'I'm so clumsy,' she said with a forced laugh. 'I just keep on tripping down those damn stairs.'

Seema knew without having to examine the woman that she hadn't fallen down the stairs. She was lying. Her husband had beaten her up. Seema didn't know how she knew, whether it was something in the woman's demeanour or the husband's, or perhaps their interaction, but she recognised it immediately. It was almost as familiar to her as the image she saw when looking into a mirror. She wondered, with horror, whether other people saw that in her; whether the doctors she worked with all suspected what went on behind the closed door of her flat. Did she carry around the same guilt and shame as this woman?

Seema examined the laceration on the woman's forehead. It was superficial and would require only a couple of stitches.

'It won't leave much of a scar,' she reassured the woman. The patient's leg injury was also minor, just a bruise, but her arm looked like it was broken. It was swollen and exquisitely tender when Seema tried to palpate it. The woman was unable to move her arm at all. Seema recognised the type of injury: it was called a defence fracture. It was usually sustained when the victim raised his or her arm in self-protection from a blow. Seema looked up at the patient's husband. He was a small, mean drunk. He wasn't worth broken bones. He wasn't even worth a bruise. She looked into his eyes, feeling her hatred brim over, and he shifted his gaze.

'She fell down the stairs. It's because she can't control her bloody drinking. She shouldn't have drunk so much,' he said forcefully, and Seema knew that he could see her wrath. He shuffled his feet and picked at one of his fingernails. Seema continued to stare at him, willing him to make eye contact, willing him to see her disgust. All she had felt at the hands of Satesh, all the humiliation and shame and degradation, was fuel for the rage burning within her. She wanted the man to look into her eyes and face her fury. But he refused to make eye contact.

'Your wife needs an X-ray of her arm. I think it's likely that it's broken. You can wait outside while she goes to radiology,' Seema said eventually.

'I'll go with her,' the man said. 'She might need some help.'

Ordinarily Seema would never have pushed the issue, but tonight was different. Her anger made it different.

'No, you can't go to X-rays with her. I'll send a porter to accompany her in case she needs any help. Besides, I need to ask her a few questions alone.'

'About what?' the man barked. 'What do you want to ask her about that I can't hear, hey? Is there something you want to say to me?' He had moved closer to Seema, too close, and she could feel the warmth of his rank breath as he spoke. He took a step closer, threatening her with his nearness. 'What are you trying to prove, girlie?'

Seema knew that she should back down. She should tell him that there was no problem whatsoever, that there was nothing important that she wanted to discuss with his wife privately and that he could go to radiology with his wife, but she didn't. She felt reckless, as though her rage had put her on a high. She almost wanted the man to hit her because it would unravel the curtain of lies behind which he was hiding. For the first time, he would be forced to face the consequences of his actions. Here, in casualty, there were no closed doors. She smiled at him and took a step closer, changing the balance of power. Let him hit me, she thought, let him give me his best shot. No smack or punch could come close to what she had already suffered that evening. How welcome the straightforward tangibility of the pain of a punch would be. Seema saw his eyes fill with hatred – she didn't know whether it was for her or for himself – and perhaps he would have struck out at her had Dr Ribbentrop not walked into the cubicle.

'Is there a problem here?' Dr Ribbentrop asked, looking directly at the patient's husband.

'No, no problem,' the man said, stepping back from Seema. In the presence of Dr Ribbentrop he shrank immediately. He was all at once a pathetic, drunk bully. Dr Ribbentrop waited, without saying a word. The man started fidgeting, playing with the worn leather strap of his watch, fiddling with his cigarette lighter.

'Come, let's go,' he said to his wife, grabbing her uninjured arm. 'We don't owe these arseholes anything.'

'You're free to go,' Dr Ribbentrop said, 'but your wife stays. She's injured. She needs treatment.'

The man hesitated. He looked from his wife, to Seema, to Dr Ribbentrop. Sweat darkened the underarms of his shirt. His fear smelt feral.

'It's okay,' the wife said eventually. 'I'll go with him. My arm's not so bad anyway. It's hardly even sore now. I don't know why I made such a fuss. It's typical, I always overreact. Sorry to have caused you inconvenience.'

The husband shot Seema a triumphant look, acknowledging that his wife's leaving was another victory for him, and walked out of the cubicle. His wife followed painfully behind him. As she passed Dr

Ribbentrop he touched her injured shoulder gently.

'You come back if it gets any worse,' he whispered softly to her. 'Come back tomorrow, if you need to.' She gave a slight nod, almost imperceptible, and scuttled from the cubicle after her husband.

Seema suddenly felt exhausted, drained of strength. Her anger had left her and without it she felt like an empty shell. In the woman, in her patient, she had faced herself. She had been forced to confront the possibility of her future. She wondered if she would ever have the courage to defy Satesh or if, like her patient, she would forever walk away, betraying herself. Would she spend the rest of her life pretending she had fallen down stairs? She felt her head start to spin and held on to the edge of the examination bed.

'Are you okay?' Dr Ribbentrop asked, grabbing hold of her arm to steady her.

Seema nodded. 'I'll be fine,' she said.

'I suppose you're wondering why I let her go, aren't you?' Dr Ribbentrop said. 'You think I made a mistake. You think, perhaps, that I should have apprehended the man and got the police involved? Or that I should have forced the woman to stay and convinced her to lay a charge against her husband?' Dr Ribbentrop didn't give Seema time to respond. 'Do you know what would have happened if I'd tried to make her stay? When she eventually went home, which she would have done, her husband would have beaten her up even worse. He would have punished her for our behaviour. Now, perhaps, he'll leave her be. She'll come back tomorrow, when he's calmed down or when he's out, and we can treat her then. She's not going to leave her husband. They never do. I've filled in hundreds of assault forms for women who've been abused and who swear it's the last time they're going to let it happen, but they never end up taking the case to court. I always have this tiny glimmer of hope that one day I'll receive a call from the state prosecutor requesting my presence at a trial, but it hasn't come yet, not in the fifteen years that I've been here. The women always forgive their husbands. Until it's too late. Until they end up in the morgue.'

Seema couldn't look at Dr Ribbentrop. She was too afraid that if she did, he would see the truth. It was almost as though he was talking directly to her, as if his words were meant as a warning to her. He seemed to think it was so easy to leave, that it was a straightforward decision, but she knew it wasn't. If it were easy, she would have left Satesh ages ago. Without looking up, she tried to explain that to him.

'It's not always that simple to leave,' she said. In an indirect way, she knew that she was trying to justify, to herself more than anyone else, her inability to leave Satesh. 'Maybe the women are too afraid to leave; maybe they can't leave because it would bring too much shame on their families; maybe they stay with their husbands because they consider marriage a sacred, binding rite. In our culture it's often thought to be better to be in an abusive marriage than to be divorced. There are few people who are shown more disrespect than divorced ladies.' Seema could hear the tremor in her voice. She knew that she had shifted the level of the conversation from the objective to the personal. She realised that she had laid herself bare, that Dr Ribbentrop would have to be a fool not to realise that she was speaking from experience. And of course he was no fool.

'Dr Singh,' he said, looking directly at her, 'none of those problems are insurmountable if the desire to overcome them is great enough. What's your value? What do you believe you're worth? Remember that life is a lot like medicine: at the end of the day, everything is a matter of choice, a balance of risk versus benefit, pro versus con.' He didn't wait for Seema to respond but turned and walked out of the cubicle. As he reached the curtain he looked back at her. 'And if you need any help on the practical side of things, let me know. I'll do everything I can to make your decision easier.'

By eleven o'clock Seema was starting to feel the effects of not having eaten anything since breakfast, sixteen hours before. Her hands had begun to tremble and the hunger pains in her stomach had turned to a constant, dull nausea. She knew that if she didn't have some glucose soon she would faint, but the number of patients waiting to be seen seemed to be growing, not diminishing, and she still felt guilty for having arrived late. She picked up the cuff of a blood pressure monitor and started inflating it.

'So, is my pressure okay?' the patient whose blood pressure she was taking asked her. She heard his voice but couldn't manage to answer him. It seemed as though he was talking from a great distance away, as though time had warped and elongated his words. 'Doctor, are you okay?' she heard him ask as she felt her legs collapse beneath her. Black dots jumped before her eyes, like busy ants or the screen of a television when the tuning goes.

'Dr Singh! Seema, can you hear me?' She heard Dr Ribbentrop's voice.

She opened her eyes to see his face looming over her. She was momentarily confused. She didn't know why she was lying on a hospital bed having her blood pressure measured by Dr Ribbentrop and her finger pricked by a nurse.

'Blood glucose is low,' she heard the sister say to Dr Ribbentrop.

Seema saw Dr Ribbentrop nod his head in acknowledgement. 'BP's also a bit on the low side,' he said. 'You're not on some ridiculous diet, are you?' he asked Seema. He turned to the sister. 'It makes me mad, these fad diets that you girls seem obsessed with. Think you can live on cottage cheese and celery sticks.' He took a cup of glucose water from the sister and handed it to Seema. 'Drink that quickly. It should make you feel a bit better,' he instructed.

'I'm not on a diet,' Seema said, after taking a sip of the sugar water. She didn't know why she was so disappointed by his assumption that she was or why she so desperately didn't want him to think that she was one of those pathetic girls. 'I ... I ... didn't have time to eat. I had some problems at home.'

Dr Ribbentrop seemed to accept her explanation. 'Well, go get something to eat now. And a Coke to drink. Did you bring some food with you?'

Seema shook her head. 'I'll get a packet of chips or a chocolate from the vending machine,' she said.

Dr Ribbentrop muttered something under his breath and walked away. Seema felt more devastated by his disappointment in her than by her hypoglycaemia. She had so desperately wanted his approval. She made her way slowly to the doctors' office and switched on the kettle. She would be fine after having a cup of sweet tea. She had lied about the vending machine: she hadn't brought any money with her, so she wouldn't be able to buy anything to eat. Dr Ribbentrop came into the office while she was busy pouring her tea and started scratching in his bag.

'Here,' he said, pulling an ice-cream container out of his satchel and handing it to her. 'Go on, open it. It won't bite, I promise.'

Seema lifted the lid of the container, wondering what he had given her. Inside was a large, chunky sandwich. 'No, I can't possibly take this,' Seema said. 'It's yours. Isn't this your supper?'

'Eat it!' Dr Ribbentrop commanded. 'The last thing I need is you passing out on me again. I don't have time to look after you as well as my patients.'

Seema acquiesced quietly. She was too embarrassed to protest any more. She unwrapped the sandwich from its greaseproof paper covering. The white bread was sliced thickly, into chunks rather than slices, and the filling consisted of slabs of cheese and quarters of tomato. Margarine oozed between the bread and cheese. Because Dr Ribbentrop was watching her, Seema forced herself to take a bite. It was surprisingly tasty. She took another bite and then another, and suddenly she was ravenous. She stuffed huge bites of sandwich into her mouth, hardly chewing between mouthfuls. It was the most delicious thing she had ever eaten. She had meant to leave half of the sandwich for Dr Ribbentrop's supper, but she seemed unable to stop herself from eating.

'When last did you eat?' Dr Ribbentrop asked as she stuffed the last bit of bread into her mouth.

'Breakfast,' she mumbled. 'Thanks so much for the food. I really appreciate you giving me your dinner and I'm so sorry I fainted. I feel one hundred per cent better already. I'll make sure this never happens again, I promise.'

'Well, I didn't particularly want another patient on my hands,' Dr Ribbentrop said gruffly. 'Besides, it was worth watching you eat. I've never seen anyone polish off a sandwich so quickly.' He smiled at Seema and got up to go back to casualty. 'Come through when you're ready,' he said. 'I should be able to cope without you for a few more minutes.' Seema had no doubt that he would. As she placed the empty ice-cream container back on top of his bag, she decided she would make him a curry to thank him. She'd bring it to work for him in an ice-cream container.

Nomsa

17

Nomsa was having a bad night, not solely because her precious cream patent-leather jacket had been stolen from the doctors' office earlier in the evening, or because she had given a dose of penicillin to a patient who was allergic to the drug and was now both very angry with her and covered in big red hives, or because the doctor who was supposed to be on call with her had phoned in sick half an hour before the shift was due to start, but also because she had stumbled upon a dead body. Literally.

She had been called up to the medical ward to reinsert an intravenous cannula on a demented patient who had pulled her drip out. According to the sister, the woman believed that one of the nurses was a witch trying to steal her soul through the intravenous line and this was the thirteenth time in two days that the cannula was being replaced. Nomsa arrived at the dimly lit ward to find the sister asleep at the nursing station. She tiptoed past the sister, aware that if she woke her the sister would be in a foul mood because of the untimely interruption of her nap, and made her way to the room in which the patient was supposed to be lying. According to the admission board, the patient was sleeping in the 'A' bed. The main lights were off in the room and, while Nomsa was stepping carefully around the sleeping patient to turn on the overhead light at the head of the bed, she tripped over something hard and cold protruding from beneath the bed. She landed not on the floor, as she had expected, but on a large, immobile object that felt disconcertingly body-shaped. She turned her head, in an attempt to ascertain what it was that she was lying on, and felt her lips make contact with a nose. A very cold and breathless nose. She screeched and jumped upwards and backwards, landing on the bed behind her and precipitating an equally vociferous response from the woman in the bed (who happened to be the patient for whom Nomsa had been looking). A strange woman jumping on her in the dark obviously added a new dimension to the woman's delusions of witchcraft. The chain reaction of screeching that dominoed through the room woke the sister, who stomped into the ward angrily.

'What's going on in here?' she shouted grumpily, flicking on the main light.

Nomsa squinted in the sudden harshness of the light. 'I think the patient in "A" bed – or who was in "A" bed – is dead,' she said hesitantly. She didn't have the courage to look down at the floor to see exactly who it was that she had kissed.

'No,' the sister said with absolute certainty. 'She can't be. She's better. She was ready for discharge. She could have left today but she said she didn't have transport. She was waiting for some other patient to be discharged so she could get a lift with him.'

'She's lying on the floor, she's not breathing, she's ice cold and has no pulse. And she didn't scream when I landed on her. She's either dead or very close to it.'

The sister pulled on a pair of gloves and strode to the bed. She gave the distinct impression of someone preparing to go into battle and, for a fraction of a second, before she had time to realise the implications of her thoughts, Nomsa prayed that she had actually landed on a dead body and had not imagined the whole scenario. The sister knelt down at the bedside and dragged the body into full view. Nomsa saw the expression on her face change from one of triumph (albeit premature) to one of confusion.

'This isn't the patient who was in this bed,' the sister said slowly. 'This is a man.'

Nomsa peered down at the ground and saw the body of an elderly man lying supine on the ground. He was wearing a hospital gown and blue slippers. His grey hair was neatly clipped and he wore a gold wedding ring on his left hand. Unfortunately, his most remarkable feature was a large erection over which the thin cotton of the blue hospital gown formed an obvious tent. He was unmistakably both male and dead.

'This is a female ward,' the sister added. As if on cue, a young woman walked into the room. She had obviously been smoking in one of the toilets. 'That's my patient,' the sister said, pointing to the young woman. The woman nodded in agreement.

'So who's that?' Nomsa asked, tilting her head in the direction of the corpse. This precipitated a fresh bout of screaming, instigated by the new arrival, who, until Nomsa's question, had been oblivious to the presence of a dead body next to her bed.

'Shiven, Shiven!' the young female patient wailed, falling to the floor next to the dead body. She leant over and stroked the mouth and nose that Nomsa had so recently found herself inadvertently kissing. 'Shiven, you can't be dead. My Mercedes,' she cried.

Nomsa thought the girl looked far too young to be the man's wife. Obviously the sister thought so too.

'Do you know this man?' the sister asked the young patient. 'Are you related?'

The patient just sniffed and let out another wail in response.

'Are you his wife?' the sister asked, more directly this time.

'No, he was going to leave that stupid whore after he was discharged, after he got better from his heart attack. He truly loved me. He was going to marry me. He promised. I was going to go live in his big house and he was going to give me a Mercedes-Benz to drive.'

'Well, he's not going to be giving you anything any more,' the sister said grimly.

And his wife certainly isn't either, Nomsa thought. She wondered what had been going on in the ward. Surely the couple had not been having an affair in hospital! It seemed that the extramarital activities of the elderly gentleman (possibly enhanced by the use of a certain little blue tablet) had put a bit too much strain on his heart. She decided that she was not going to wait around to find out the details.

'You'd better call security to get rid of the body, or maybe forensics,' she said to the sister over the wailing of the young patient. 'I suppose the man will need a post-mortem.' She picked up her bag and started heading hastily out of the ward. She had already had far more contact with the dead body than she was comfortable with; she didn't feel like spending any more time in its presence. The demented patient would have to wait for her drip to be changed – in any case, she surely had more entertaining things on her mind now than soul stealing.

With the unpleasant sensation of dead nose still on her lips, Nomsa made her way back down to casualty. She had five more hours of her call to get through; her only consolation was that it was unlikely to get any worse. She figured she had used up all her bad luck for one night.

Picking up a folder, Nomsa shouted a name down the corridor and started walking to an open cubicle. As she walked past the adjoining cubicle, she saw Seema's shoes from beneath the lower edge of the curtain. They were pacing up and down and Nomsa presumed that Seema must be examining a patient. After she got the phone call earlier in the evening from the doctor who had claimed to be too sick both to work and to find a replacement to work for her, Nomsa had paged Seema to ask if she could cover the shift. Seema agreed to do the cover immediately, as she always did when there was any emergency. Seema was the doctor everyone had got into the habit of calling first when they wanted to swap or change a shift. Nomsa wondered how it was possible that someone could enjoy being at the hospital so much. Seema's passion for medicine seemed almost to border on obsession. Nomsa often got the feeling that Seema would be happy to be permanently on call if she could be.

By the time Nomsa entered the examination cubicle, the patient had caught up with her. He was a thin, wiry man in his early forties with greasy black hair tied into a ponytail. He was wearing thick yellow overalls and black wellington boots. The stench of rotting fish hung over the patient and Nomsa felt herself involuntarily gasp as he drew close to her.

'Sorry, Doctor,' the man said, obviously noticing Nomsa's not-so-subtle reaction. 'I've just come off the boat, so I know I smell a bit. I don't notice it but my girlfriend always complains when I get home. Makes me shower before I come near her. You get used to the smell, you know, working with it all day.'

Nomsa didn't really know how to respond to the man's apology. She didn't think that she would ever get used to such a stink and she certainly couldn't imagine how the man's girlfriend tolerated it. So she ignored his apology and asked the man why he had come into hospital. He showed her his hand, into which a large fish hook was embedded. Nomsa winced instinctively at the sight of the metal protruding from the fisherman's palm.

'We'll have to take that out for you,' Nomsa said. And get you on some antibiotics as soon as possible, she thought. The fish hook was not particularly clean. She wondered why the man had not pulled the hook out himself. He didn't appear to be the queasy type (he couldn't be, to work in that smell all day) and surely removing the hook was preferable to walking around with it embedded in his hand. Without thinking about it further, she stabilised the patient's arm with her left hand and pulled at the hook with her right. The patient let out a scream and yanked his hand away from Nomsa.

'Are you crazy, Doctor?' he shouted.

'We've got to get this done,' Nomsa replied firmly, 'and the quicker we can do it, the less painful it will be. Just try not to think about what I'm doing.' She hadn't expected the man's reaction. He hadn't come across as the sensitive type. In fact, he looked like the type of man who would give himself injections if given a chance. Obviously, in this case, appearances were deceptive. She reached out to grab the man's hand and the patient backed away.

'Come on now,' she said, rather sharply (two o'clock in the morning was not the time to test her patience). 'Stop being a baby. We have to get that hook out, and the sooner we do it, the better.'

'I think I'll go to another doctor,' the patient said hesitantly. 'No disrespect, but can I see another doctor?'

Nomsa lost her already frayed temper. 'No,' she said loudly, 'you'll stay right where you are. I'm your doctor – just deal with it. Have you got a problem with me? Do you think I'm inadequate because I'm black? Or because I'm a female?'

The patient didn't flinch. 'No,' he said calmly, 'but I know that you can't just pull a fish hook out. If you could, I would have done it myself.'

'What?' Nomsa asked. It dawned on her that she couldn't remember having learnt how to remove a fish hook. She had simply presumed that it would be done in the same way in which one would remove any other hook but, as her patient had made clear, it obviously wasn't. She looked down to avoid the patient's eyes, self-doubt suddenly making her sheepish. 'Why not?' she asked softly.

'Because the hook's barbed,' the fisherman answered.

Nomsa felt her face heat up. She wished that she could retract her words, that she hadn't lost her temper, that she hadn't made the comments about her patient being sexist and racist. 'I'm sorry,' she apologised. 'I really had no idea, I'm so sorry.' There is nothing quite so immediately humbling as making a complete arse of oneself, Nomsa thought.

Briefly, the fisherman explained the mechanics of a fish hook to Nomsa. It made sense, retrospectively, that a hook used to catch a living thing would be designed to stay embedded in its prey. Nomsa explained to the patient that she was going to ask the advice of another doctor and slunk from the cubicle. She prayed that none of the sisters had heard her ranting. She didn't think she could tolerate any added humiliation. She caught Seema between patients and asked her if she knew how to remove fish hooks.

'I've only ever read about how to remove them – I haven't actually done it myself,' Seema said. 'From what I can remember you have to push the hook all the way through, then cut off the barb, and then retract it. Apparently that's the way it's done. Does that make sense?'

Nomsa nodded. It was so simple she was embarrassed that she hadn't thought to do it herself. 'Thanks,' she said to Seema. 'Do you think I must give a local?'

'There's no harm in anaesthetising it,' Seema said. 'I'm sure it must be painful pushing it through. Maybe ask your patient what he wants.'

As she walked back to her patient, Nomsa realised that that was the longest conversation she and Seema had had.

She explained to the fisherman what she was going to do and, contrary to her expectations, he smiled at her.

'Yes, that sounds about right,' he said. 'Don't bother to give me any anaesthetic or anything. I'd rather you just get it over and done with.'

Her question pre-empted, Nomsa took the patient's wrist in her hand to steady it and started pushing the hook through his palm. He winced but his hand didn't budge in hers. It was a horrible feeling, pushing the hook through the man's flesh, and Nomsa was glad when she saw the barb emerge from the cut. She picked up a pair of scissors from the suture tray. The scissors made an odd, scratchy sound against the metal of the fish hook, then started bending. She hadn't expected this; she'd just presumed that the metal scissors would cut through the metal of the hook. This was turning into a disaster. She felt like a first-year student and not an intern. And she was sure that her patient was regretting ever coming to hospital.

'You need a metal cutter,' the man pointed out.

Nomsa didn't have a clue what a metal cutter was but she wasn't going to argue with the patient again, so she trudged from the cubicle in search of a sister. In response to her request, the sister handed her an object that looked like a giant pair of pruning shears.

'Why do you keep this here?' Nomsa couldn't help blurting out. 'Is it just for removing fish hooks?'

The sister laughed. 'No,' she said, 'we usually use it for cutting off rings when patients' fingers have swollen too much to allow us to pull them off.'

The metal cutter sliced easily through the metal of the fish hook and Nomsa pulled the remaining portion of the hook out along the path through which it had entered the hand. As she threw the fish hook into the sharps container, she couldn't help wondering whether she would ever reach a point at which she knew enough to get by without asking for help, at which unusual injuries would cease to baffle her.

By six in the morning, Nomsa was exhausted and disgruntled. She had had busier calls, but she couldn't remember having had a worse call. She walked slowly to the pile of folders. She had already decided that if there were five or fewer folders on the pile, she would leave them for the doctor coming on call during the day to deal with. She could think of nothing better than going to sit in the doctors' office and closing her eyes for the remaining hour of her shift. Seema arrived at the pile of folders at the same time as Nomsa and took the top file off. It was the sixth folder. Nomsa smiled to herself, waited until Seema had taken her patient through to a cubicle, and then made her way to the doctors' office.

She had just kicked off her shoes and turned on the kettle when she heard a series of loud bangs coming from casualty. They sounded suspiciously like gunshots, but it made no sense that someone would be shooting in casualty. Her doubt lasted for at most a second: the length of time it took for the screaming to start. She had heard gunshots at such close proximity before, as a child. The shots had been accompanied by the same hysterical screams that she was hearing now.

She rushed from the doctors' office into a tornado of sisters, porters and cleaning staff running in the opposite direction of casualty. She knew that the logical step would be to join the sisters in their escape, but something drew her to casualty. It was as though her legs refused to listen to her mind. She tiptoed quietly down the corridor, unsure of what to expect. In the wake of the desperate screaming, the hospital was now eerily quiet. As she walked, she took her cellphone from her pocket and dialled the number of the flying squad. The casualty doors had swung closed, but Nomsa was able to see through the small square windows in their upper halves. Her stomach had tightened into a hard ball and her heart was beating like a trapped bird desperate to escape its cage. She knew that what she was doing was stupid, that the police could take hours to arrive and that she was likely to get shot herself, but she had an almost instinctive desire to make sense of what was going on. The last time she had heard gunshots a woman, the victim of crossfire in a taxi war, had fallen down in front of her. Nomsa remembered the body crashing at her feet, almost crushing her. She remembered the red scarf that the woman had been wearing, how it had spread out on the gravel like a dead bird. A bad omen, her mother had said later. She remembered that the woman's apron had flown up with her fall and had covered her chest and face. And she remembered the blood that had gushed from below the apron, collecting in a pool that had eventually grown so full it had drowned the bird-scarf. Nomsa was seven at the time and she had stood there frozen, a helpless child, unable even to join in the screaming around her. All she had wanted to do was to lift the woman's apron from her face. Only later, once her mother had taken her home, did she notice the blood that had stained her shoes.

Nomsa peeped through the square window. Her whole body was tense, ready to duck, to run instantly, should the assailants catch sight of her. But nobody moved in casualty. She could see no men with guns, no gangsters, no assassins. The beds, bar one, were empty. The occupied bed was red. A figure, distorted by the force of the gunshots, lay twisted and contorted on the bloodstained sheet. A movement caught Nomsa's eye and she withdrew her head quickly. She counted thirty slow seconds before peeping through the window again. As she did so, she realised the full danger of her position. She was standing at one of only two exits from casualty. If the killer, or killers, were still in casualty, they would probably pass her on their way out. Instinctively she withdrew from the door, but as she did so it swung open.

'Nomsa,' a voice sobbed. 'Thank God you're alive. I couldn't see you. I thought they'd hit you.'

It took Nomsa a second to register that it was Seema who had come through the doors, and that she was not about to be shot at. Seema was pale and trembling. Her clothes were splattered in blood. She started swaying and Nomsa grabbed her, steadying her.

'Are you okay?' Nomsa asked. 'Have you been shot?'

Seema shook her head and started crying. Tears cleaned a path through the blood on her cheeks. 'They just shot …,' she began, but Nomsa interrupted her.

'Are they still inside, the men who did this?' she asked Seema.

'No, they left,' Seema said.

Nomsa realised that they must have left before the cleaners and sisters, before the screaming had started. Nomsa felt Seema lean into her arms. 'I think … I think … I'm going to faint,' Seema whispered.

Nomsa half dragged, half pulled Seema to one of the empty beds in casualty. Seema was petite and Nomsa managed to lift her onto the bed. A movement caught her eye and she turned to see a patient emerge from beneath the bed next to her. Almost simultaneously a patient came out from beneath the bed onto which she had just placed Seema. Soon patients had appeared from beneath each of the empty beds. They had obviously dived under their beds as soon as the shooting started. The patient that had been occupying the bed that Seema was now lying on waited while Nomsa tried to revive her.

'She's lucky she didn't get shot too,' he commented.

'Why?' Nomsa asked, wrapping a blood pressure cuff around Seema's arm and inflating it.

'She tried to stop them from shooting her patient. I think maybe she didn't see they had guns. Lucky one of the *tsotsis* just kicked her out of the way. She fell down and they shot the man and then left.'

Only then did Nomsa notice the large bruise and laceration on Seema's temple. She was surprised at what the patient had told her: she hadn't expected Seema to be made of hero material. Nomsa was starting to worry that Seema had passed out from a head injury and not a simple faint when Seema opened her eyes.

'My patient's dead,' Seema said softly. 'I checked as soon as they left. He must have died immediately. They shot him ten times, I think. He came in with a stab in his back; I was busy putting in a chest drain when they came in. All I could think about was getting the drain in before they shot me. I kept thinking that the man would die if I didn't get his chest drain in before being killed.'

Nomsa couldn't help wondering whether she would have been as brave as Seema. Would she have tried to save the man or would she have dived under the bed, like the patients, or run out with the sisters? Although she did feel some guilt that when the shooting happened she had been in the doctors' office, and not in casualty as she should have been, she couldn't help also feeling relieved. It shamed her that her relief was not at having avoided danger, but at not having had to face the choice of whether to be a hero or a coward. She didn't know if she would have made the right decision.

18

Nomsa arrived back at her prefab at half past eleven in the morning. She was totally exhausted. The post-call handover round had taken longer than usual because there had been police wandering around casualty obstructing any form of work while trying to make a case out of the shooting. She had planned exactly what she was going to do: she would shower and then crawl into bed with a bowl of Coco Pops; then, once she had guzzled the chocolate-coated cereal, she would fall into a deep sleep and not wake up again until her bladder absolutely required her to. As she was about to settle into bed with her bowl of cereal, she got a message on her phone asking her to call her sister's number urgently. Her heart sank. Her sister probably wanted her to send some more money to Aliwal North for this or that to be fixed or replaced. Things were always breaking or disappearing in her mother's house and Nomsa sometimes felt as though her family was a large vacuum that constantly sucked her savings dry. She wanted to ignore the message, but she knew that if she did she wouldn't be able to sleep properly because she would be worrying about how much money her sister wanted. Reluctantly she dialled Noluthando's number. Her sister answered almost immediately.

'Ma is very sick,' Noluthando said, dispelling Nomsa's assumptions. She told Nomsa that their mother was still in hospital and she seemed to be getting worse, not better. 'The medicines that the doctors are giving her are making her too sick, they are taking away all her strength, they are killing her,' Noluthando said.

'Oh please, stop talking like that,' Nomsa snapped. She didn't have the energy to deal with her sister's melodramatics. 'She's hardly an invalid. I'm sure they're treating her fine and the medicines can't possibly be making her sicker.'

'They are,' Noluthando wailed. 'You have to help us, Nomsa, you are the first born from our mother. You need to speak to the doctors. You need to do this for our mother. She is getting too thin. Her flesh is falling off her bones, Nomsa.'

'Do you know what kind of night I've had? No, you have no idea! I haven't slept for the past thirty hours and I'm exhausted. I've had to deal with dead bodies, fish hooks sticking out of people's hands and almost being shot. I don't have the strength or patience to deal with this now. I'll phone the doctors in the morning, if it'll make you happy. I'm pretty sure Ma's condition is not about to deteriorate overnight.'

'No, Nomsa, you need to do it today. You must do it today. I visited *igqirha* and she read the bones. She said that if we leave our mother in the hospital for any days after today she will die.'

'Oh, so that's why you're phoning me!' Nomsa shouted in exasperation. 'Because you believe made-up lies whispered into your ear by a witch with white beads. I'm not going to disturb my sleep or bother the doctors looking after Ma just because of the stories told to you by a crazy person.'

'Shoo, don't talk like that, Nomsa. It's not good. You will bring bad luck onto our family.'

'I've listened to enough of this superstitious nonsense. Will you never see that it's rubbish, all of it? Next time you phone me, give me facts. I'm exhausted and I'm going to bed. If I get time I'll phone the hospital tomorrow.'

Nomsa turned her phone off and lay down on her bed, but she was unable to fall asleep. As unlikely as it was, she couldn't help wondering if her mother really was somehow close to death. She knew the *igqirha* that her sister had visited: she was a woman just a little older than Nomsa, from the same village, and they had occasionally played together as young children. She had been nicknamed 'Nomtobhoyi', the strange one, by all the children because of the dreams she had, and because she was able to see things and spirits that others were not able to see, and because she had preferred to sleep outside with the dogs than inside with her family, and because she had foretold prophecies. As a child, Nomsa believed that the girl had been chosen by the ancestors to become a diviner, but once she started medical school she had come to understand that the woman had untreated schizophrenia. While she accepted this diagnosis as true, Nomsa couldn't help wondering now whether her medical training had perhaps been misleading or somehow off base. She couldn't help thinking back to the time Nomtobhoyi had foreseen that the child of Winile was going to die from a giant worm in his stomach, or the time she had known that it was Siphiwe who had stolen the spade from the school and exactly where it was that he had hidden it. What if Nomtobhoyi wasn't just schizophrenic? What if she was able to foresee the future? What if her mother was near to death?

Nomsa switched her phone back on again and called directory services for the number of the hospital in Aliwal North to which her mother had been admitted. It took five minutes for the hospital switchboard to answer her call and five more minutes for her to be successfully transferred to admissions. As she was asking which ward her mother had been admitted to, she got cut off. Angrily, she dialled the number again. Fifteen minutes later, her call was answered by the sister in charge of the ward to which her mother had apparently been admitted. Nomsa introduced herself as Dr Poponi and asked to speak to the doctor looking after patient Poponi.

'Doctor has left,' the sister said unhelpfully.

'Do you have a cellphone number for the doctor?' Nomsa asked. She didn't expect the sister to give her the number – she herself didn't allow her number to be given out – but she thought it was worth asking for just in case.

'No,' the sister said.

'Do you know when the doctor will be back?'

'No.'

'Can I leave a message for the doctor?'

'No.'

'I'm sorry, but what did you say your name is?'

'All right, you can leave a message.'

'Thank you.' Nomsa left her cellphone number. She didn't have much hope that she would be called, but at least she had tried. She would try to phone again the following day.

Surprisingly, just over an hour after phoning the hospital Nomsa was woken by the ringing of her phone. It was the doctor looking after her mother. Nomsa introduced herself, thanked the doctor for getting back to her and asked about her mother's condition.

'Not good, I'm afraid,' the doctor said. He spoke with a strong accent and Nomsa thought he might be Cuban. 'We need to get her on to ARVs but we're still waiting for the results of her TB workup. Her CD4 is 38.' He was explaining something about tuberculosis sensitivities, but Nomsa couldn't hear him. All she could hear was 'ARVs'. Anti-retrovirals. Anti-retrovirals were used only for HIV. HIV. AIDS. ARVs. The acronyms played over and over in her head. They were words she used in relation to her patients, not to her mother. The doctor must have made a mistake.

'Are you sure you're talking about patient Poponi? You haven't confused her with someone else?' Nomsa asked.

'No, of course not. I know my patients,' the doctor responded. He sounded justifiably offended.

'Thanks.' Nomsa forced the word out of her mouth. She wasn't thankful at all. She knew she ought to say something else, but her brain was unable to work out what it should be. 'Please call me if she gets any worse,' she eventually managed to request.

The doctor to whom she had been speaking put the telephone down and Nomsa's phone emitted a long engaged tone. What the doctor had said made no sense to Nomsa. Her mother could not have HIV. She didn't have a boyfriend – hadn't had one since the birth of her fourth child fifteen years ago. How could she have AIDS? Perhaps she had come into contact with someone else's blood or pricked herself with a dirty needle or had a blood transfusion of which Nomsa was unaware. The cellphone dropped from Nomsa's hand and the clatter of it hitting the floor shocked her into action. She knew that the possibilities she had imagined were unlikely, a form of denial. She picked up her phone and punched her sister's number into the keypad.

'Did our mother have a boyfriend?' she asked immediately.

There was a moment of silence before Noluthando answered. It was less than a couple of seconds long, but it revealed more information than could have been traded in hours: Noluthando knew that their mother had HIV and she knew from whom she had contracted it; their mother knew that she was HIV-positive; Noluthando and their mother had purposely excluded Nomsa from the knowledge – they had kept it a secret from her.

'You've spoken to the doctor. He has told you,' Noluthando said eventually.

'Why didn't you tell me?' Nomsa wailed. 'Why? Why didn't you tell me?' She felt like an outsider, an intruder into the privacy of her family. How dare they keep this information from her? What else were they hiding? What other secrets was she not privy to? 'Who is he? Do I know him?' she demanded angrily.

She heard Noluthando sigh. 'No,' she said. 'He worked at the prison here. He was transferred from Joburg two years ago. He was a prison warder.'

'Was?' Nomsa screeched. 'Was?' She felt as though she was losing control, as though her sanity was slipping from her grasp. She was unable to manage the emotions raging inside her.

'He died three months ago,' Noluthando said matter-of-factly. 'The doctors said it was a chest infection but he was the same like our mother is now.' There was a tone of resignation in her voice that prompted Nomsa to keep on questioning. She could hear that Noluthando had become weary of being a keeper of secrets.

'Why didn't you tell me earlier?' Nomsa shouted. Her frustration had grown huge inside her; it was overwhelming her, dwarfing her other emotions. It spread beyond her own body: to her mother for her stupidity, to her sister for withholding the information from her, to the prison warder for killing her mother. 'How could she have been so stupid? She's not a teenager; she shouldn't have been sleeping around with whatever man crossed her path. She should have known better. What kind of mother behaves like this? Does she have no self-respect?'

Noluthando was silent on the other side of the telephone.

'Have you got nothing to say? What's wrong with you?' Nomsa

shouted. Implied in the 'you' was not only her sister but also her mother, her aunt, the prison warder who had given her mother the HIV, Nomtobhoyi. Everyone.

'Why do you care anyway?' Noluthando asked Nomsa. 'You have turned away from the family a long time ago. Do you wonder why we do not tell you things? You speak about respect, but where is your respect?'

Nomsa threw her phone to the floor. She had nothing further to say to her sister. She collapsed onto her bed and started sobbing, burying her face in her pillow to mute her cries. She had had a night from hell; she should be fast asleep right now, not trying to come to terms with her mother's HIV status. It wasn't fair that she had to handle this now, on top of everything else that she had been through in the past thirty hours. She was sure that Rachael didn't have family problems like this to deal with. After her calls, Rachael probably slept as soundly as a baby. Seema too.

Nomsa got up and started pacing the floor of her prefab. Fury gnawed inside her, drove away her tears, made her body feel too large for the small, cramped room. How could her mother have made yet another wrong decision? Was she incapable of learning? Her mother's life had been a series of poor decisions and silly mistakes: dropping out of school before even reaching high school; pregnant at sixteen, unmarried; then pregnant again at twenty-two, and at twenty-five and at twenty-eight; choosing first a boyfriend who drank and philandered and then one who abused her; deciding to go back to Aliwal North, to a worn-out shack and small patch of barren land, after Mrs Watson's accident, instead of looking for another job in Cape Town; allowing her second-born daughter to keep a baby at twenty-one. And now choosing a boyfriend who gave her the sole gift of a fatal virus. She could have forgiven her mother many things, but not stupidity.

The walls of her prefab seemed to be closing in on her. Claustrophobia tempered her anger with anxiety. She needed to get out, to escape. She flung an old tracksuit on over her pyjamas, picked up her car keys and hurried to her car. She turned up the volume on her CD player and sped out of the hospital grounds. She wanted to drive forever, to drive until she fell asleep at the steering wheel and woke up to find everything back to normal.

Nomsa hadn't made a conscious decision to go to the beach, but she found herself travelling along the coastal road towards the sea. By the time she reached the beach parking lot, her anger had shrunk and shrivelled up into a tiny, hard seed inside her. She got out of her car and stepped on to the coarse sand. In front of her, waves rhythmically pounded the shoreline: the soundtrack to her fluctuant emotion. She slowly walked down to where the sand became wet, to where the strength of the waves dissipated into gentle white froth. Her sister's words arose in her mind, an echo of their telephone conversation: *You have turned away from the family a long time ago. Do you wonder why we do not tell you things? You speak about respect, but where is your respect?* Her sister was right. She had rejected her family and their traditional way of life, shunned them, so much so that she had been too ashamed of her mother to invite her to her graduation from medical school, the most important event of her life. She had cast off the beliefs that she had been brought up with and had swapped them for the hard logic, rationality and materialism of a culture that she pretended was perfect. She had no right to expect her mother and sister to tell her their secrets: she had stopped telling them hers long ago. She leant down and scooped salt water in her hands and brought it to her mouth. She drank handful after handful of salty seawater until her stomach rebelled and pushed it out of her. She vomited on the sand until she had nothing left inside her stomach. The emptiness that she felt in the pit of her abdomen was nothing compared with the emptiness that she felt in her heart.

Rachael

19

The paediatric ward was dilapidated and dreary, Rachael thought as she looked around her. Apart from the faded, peeling painting of Winnie-the-Pooh, the only decorations were the greasy dirt marks above the beds where grubby hands and feet had pawed and kicked the grey walls. The windowpanes were almost opaque with dust, the steel frames rusted and the net curtains stained and torn. It was definitely not the type of environment conducive to healing and health, and Rachael was hardly surprised that the children in the ward were so miserable. But it would take so little to change the entire atmosphere of the place: a good cleaning, a fresh coating of paint, a few stencils on the walls and perhaps some brightly coloured curtains, and yet the hospital administration claimed they didn't have the money or the manpower to make the changes (which was strange, Rachael thought, since they had recently found enough money to redecorate the boardroom in the administration building with leather couches, expensively framed prints and a state-of-the-art coffee machine). Thinking about the nonchalant and uninterested response she had got from the hospital superintendent when she enquired three weeks before about the possibility of upgrading the paediatric ward made her angry. She took a deep breath to curtail the emotion. Her yoga teacher had spent many hours and had earned a lot of money teaching Rachael that anger was a negative emotion that ultimately brought pain only to the person experiencing it. Besides that, anger wasn't particularly constructive in this instance, since there was absolutely nothing she could do about the budget choices that the hospital superintendent made. She turned to the child she was supposed to be examining and put her stethoscope on the girl's chest.

Thandeka, the seven-year-old lying in the bed in front of her, had been admitted after having been repeatedly raped by her uncle. She had not only suffered extensive local trauma – her vagina had been torn and her uterus ruptured – that had required surgery, but the girl had also contracted every sexually transmitted disease that her exemplary uncle had harboured. She was on prophylactic anti-retrovirals as well as a cocktail of intravenous antibiotics. When Thandeka initially came in, she had been completely withdrawn. It had taken her three days merely to acknowledge Rachael's presence and she still had not made eye contact with or spoken a word to Rachael. Rachael had tried to organise for a psychologist or social worker to see the child, but the psychologist was on sick leave and the social worker had recently been admitted to hospital herself for refractory depression. So Rachael had been trying, very inadequately, to counsel the little girl herself. It hadn't helped her efforts that the girl's uncle, who had inexplicably already been released from prison on bail, had come to visit the child with the child's mother. Had the visit not occurred after hours, when Rachael was not at the hospital, Rachael thought she would probably be in jail herself for murder or attempted murder (or out on bail). As it was, after finding out about the visit she had lost her temper and screamed at both the sister and security for letting the uncle into the hospital. Later that day she had typed out an official-looking letter on a hospital letterhead using complex, legal-sounding language, prohibiting any contact between the child and her uncle, and had stuck it above the girl's bed. She had simply signed it 'By order' and had then scribbled an illegible signature beneath that. Thus far it seemed to work: to her knowledge, the uncle had not been back. It was amazing, Rachael thought, what a little chutzpah could do.

She let Thandeka touch her stethoscope, to reassure her that it wouldn't cause her any pain, and then listened to the child's chest. She monitored the girl's temperature and felt her abdomen. She was just about to give the child a sweet (she had got into the habit of buying sweets in bulk to dish out to the children after examining them) when Thandeka pointed out her drip to Rachael. Rachael felt her heart sink at the sight of the intravenous line. Blood had clotted in the administration set, blocking it. The child required three more days of intravenous antibiotics. Rachael would have to resite the line, which would mean even more pain for the child. She knew the little girl didn't understand English, so using broken Zulu and hand gestures, she tried to explain to her what she was about to do. She pulled the blocked drip from the girl's hand and put a plaster over the area, then started searching for a fresh vein to cannulate. Unfortunately, the drip had already been replaced numerous times since the girl had been admitted and all the best veins had been destroyed. Rachael eventually found a small vein on the side of the girl's foot. She cleaned the area and slowly inserted a cannula. She attached the line and used a plaster to secure it.

When she had finished, she stroked Thandeka's cheek. 'What a brave, beautiful girl you are,' she said to her, fishing in the pocket of her white coat for a sweet. She made her way out of the ward to the corridor, where she leant against the wall to gather her thoughts. While she watched one of the cleaners half-heartedly washing the windowsill, the idea came to her that she could try to raise the manpower and money herself to give the paediatric ward a makeover. She had thought earlier that it would not take much to make a difference in the ward. Surely, since the hospital administrators were unable to raise the 'not much', she could at least try to get it together herself? She knew she was good at organising. She had organised every single social event and function that her class had held over six years of medical school. A simple ward redecoration would be a breeze to arrange compared with what she had done in the past and she didn't expect that the administrators would object to her idea. On the contrary, she was sure they would welcome an upgrade to the hospital at no cost to their budget. She could feel herself beginning to get excited. She started planning the changes she would make: she thought she might decorate the ward in an underwater theme, paint little clown fish and octopuses and lobsters on the walls – and maybe a mermaid or two. She left the ward singing under her breath, imagining herself the star of a television reality show: *Healing Your Hospital with Rachael*.

Two nights later, Rachael had worked out a complete plan for the ward makeover. She had calculated how much money was required to buy the paint and curtaining and stencils and cleaning equipment, and had drawn up a list of the jobs that needed to be done. Armed with a folder of paperwork, she made her way to the Clay Oven. Her timing had been carefully planned: Wednesday night was buy-two-get-one-free pizza night at the restaurant and Rachael knew that few doctors ever missed the special. This was a perfect opportunity for her to do some canvassing.

When Rachael arrived, Shane, Nomsa, Nathan and Eliza Engelbrecht, and two other interns were already sitting at a table drinking. Rachael squeezed in next to Shane and kissed him on the lips. She and Shane had long ago realised that it was futile trying to keep their relationship hidden: Tugela Bridge was too small for secrets. Within half an hour, almost all the doctors from the hospital were at the Clay Oven. The only doctors missing were Dr Zamla, Dr Ribbentrop, Dr Chetty, the two doctors who were on call and Seema Singh. Rachael had guessed that Seema wouldn't be at the Clay Oven and had spoken to her about the ward makeover earlier in the day, after she finished her ward round. It hadn't taken much convincing to get a promise of help from Seema. In fact, she had seemed slightly too keen, almost as though she was trying to avoid something else, but Rachael couldn't imagine what that could be.

Two rounds of drinks later, when most of the doctors at the table were pleasantly tipsy, Rachael broached the subject of the paediatric ward makeover. She threw the idea on the table like a surprise present she couldn't wait to open and share with everyone. She explained, with smiles and giggles and surreptitious flirty glances, that all that would be expected of everyone would be a small donation (less than the cost of a few beers) and one measly Saturday of their time. She explained that all that would do all the rest herself: buy the paint and stencils and brushes, get the curtains made, organise the logistics of moving the children out of the ward while they redecorated. She exuded enough enthusiasm to ensure that anyone who refused her request would appear reptilian in their cold-heartedness. By the end of the evening she had collected two thousand rands and extracted promises of help from almost all the doctors.

'You scared me this evening,' Shane said to her later that night as they lay in bed together.

'Why?'

'Because you managed to convince a group of doctors to part with money and time, two things in very short supply in the medical profession. And you made it look easy.'

'So why did that scare you?'

'It makes me shudder to think what power you have over me … and what you could make me do if you put your mind to it.'

'Lots, I think,' Rachael whispered, tracing her fingers up the inside of his naked thigh. She flung her leg over him and rolled on top of him, then pinned his arms down with her hands. 'Let me show you just how much power I have,' she said, pressing her mouth against his. But as she teased Shane, she knew that their conversation was nothing more than banter. She had no illusions about their relationship: it was a passionate, lusty fling, not the material of which marriages are made.

The drunken promises made at the Clay Oven were kept. All the doctors who had given their word that they would help redecorate the ward, including Seema, arrived at the paediatric ward at eight o'clock on Saturday morning. Even Dr Chetty and Dr Ribbentrop turned up, and Rachael wondered how they had found out about her project. She hadn't had the nerve to ask them to come and help paint walls and scrub floors. Only later, when she mentioned their appearance to Shane and he winked at her, did she realise that he must have roped them in.

Rachael had organised for all the stable children to be moved to an unused ward for the day so that the redecorating could proceed unhindered. She had been at the hospital since seven that morning, helping the nursing staff ready the children for the move. She had thought that the sisters and nurses would object to her ward makeover because of the extra effort and work it would mean for them, but they had responded surprisingly positively when she told them of her plans. It probably helped that she had brought them a couple of packets of chips and a few bottles of Coke to help ease the strain of the renovations.

In a characteristic move that explained exactly why she had been social organiser of her medical class for six years, Rachael had drawn up a work roster for all the volunteers, and as the doctors arrived she handed them painting or cleaning equipment and assigned them to their designated jobs. Initially it felt odd telling the more senior doctors, especially Dr Ribbentrop and Dr Chetty, what to do, but as the day progressed, paint and dust and dirt and glue started obliterating individual identities and rank became unimportant. Of all the doctors, Seema appeared to be the most enthusiastic, the most willing to get her hands dirty, to do the boring or painstaking jobs that nobody else volunteered to do. Rachael couldn't help wondering, as she watched Seema pass paint up a ladder to Dr Ribbentrop, why she never joined in any of the usual social events. This was the first time Rachael could remember ever seeing Seema looking relaxed.

By five o'clock that evening, two hours before handover to the night staff, the ward had been transformed. Rachael looked around her, happy at the changes. The doctors, all filthy and covered in green and blue and orange paint, sat in a circle on the floor around the cooler box that Rachael had filled with beers. Even Seema had joined them and was laughing at somebody's joke, although Rachael noticed that she hadn't taken a drink. Only the curtains still needed to be hung. Rachael had bought some fabric from a factory shop and had paid one of the sisters to sew the curtains for her. They were blue and green striped, and fitted in with the underwater theme of the new ward. Rachael pulled a chair to the window, stood up on it and started hanging the curtains. She felt a hand tickling the back of her leg and looked down to see Shane.

'I have to admit that I didn't think you'd pull this off, but somehow you did. The ward looks awesome. Well done,' he said.

Rachael leant down and kissed him on the nose, carefully avoiding a splotch of blue paint that was smudged across his cheek.

'Thanks for helping, and thanks for the vote of confidence,' she teased. 'What do you mean you didn't think I would pull this off?' But she knew what Shane had meant: it wasn't a lack of confidence in her abilities that he was expressing, but rather a recognition of the difficulty of what she had set out to accomplish.

Rachael felt inordinately happy, as though she had achieved something far greater than just the makeover of a ward. She jumped off the chair and went to fetch herself a beer from the cooler box. She was about to sit down with the other doctors when she noticed a movement at the entrance of the ward. An Indian man was standing at the door watching the goings-on. Rachael was about to ask him what he wanted when she recognised him. He was Seema's husband. Although she had never been formally introduced to him, she had occasionally seen him around the doctors' quarters with Seema. Seema was deep in discussion with Dr Ribbentrop, but she looked up briefly and Rachael managed to catch her attention with a slight wave. She indicated Seema's husband at the door and Seema immediately got up. Although it was a very subtle change, Rachael couldn't help noticing that Seema's expression, which had been open and receptive the whole day, became at once closed and guarded at the sight of her husband. It made little sense, but Rachael thought she could see fear in Seema's eyes.

'Do you want to join us for a drink?' Rachael impulsively called out to the man at the door. Something about Seema's expression had made Rachael want to know more about their relationship, and about the man who stood at the door. Seema's husband shook his head brusquely and, without a word, started walking away from the ward.

'I'd better go,' Seema said to Rachael as she left to follow him. Her voice was even quieter than it usually was. 'So silly of me, I forgot that we have to be somewhere.' But Rachael knew that Seema was lying. And Seema knew that Rachael knew, because she shot Rachael a glance as she departed through the door. It was an odd glance, filled with pleading, but Rachael could not decipher whether Seema was asking for her silence or for her help. The whole incident had occurred without anyone else noticing, except perhaps Dr Ribbentrop.

Later that evening, once Rachael had finished helping the nursing staff return the children to the revamped ward, and she was back at her prefab sitting on her leather couch eating a warmed-up ready-made lasagne, she reflected on the day. Overall she thought it had been a success. The ward looked like a ward from a different hospital, a hospital that actually cared. Most of the children had shrieked and jabbered in delight when they were moved back to their beds, pointing out a starfish or a whale or a sea horse, and Rachael had found herself unconsciously smiling at their joy. Only Thandeka, the seven-year-old rape victim, had been unmoved, not even seeming to notice the changes that had been made to the ward. Although the girl had shown no outward emotion, Rachael hoped that somewhere deep inside her psyche the improvements in her surroundings had sparked a small note of joy. If, indeed, there was any joy left in her.

Rachael picked up her phone and called Shane. She wanted to hear from someone else that the day had been a success. She knew it was probably pure vanity on her part to seek out further congratulation, but after all the effort she had put into the day she felt she deserved some complimenting. Shane didn't disappoint her.

'Of course the ward looks fantastic,' he gushed. 'You did a great job. I don't know anyone else who could have pulled it off. I'd love being in there if I was a sick child. Now you just have to get the rest of the hospital sorted out,' he joked.

Rachael laughed at his comment, but a part of her couldn't help thinking, why not? She tried to dismiss the thought; it was impractical and she knew she could not expect the doctors in the hospital to give up all their spare money and every free Saturday. But perhaps she could organise it differently, get funding from some big business, organise other volunteers to help? She tried to push the thoughts from her mind. She knew that they were probably part of the post-success glow she was revelling in and that in the morning they would reveal themselves for what they were, unrealistic and fanciful, but they refused to leave her mind completely. Much against her will, she kept remembering a phrase her mother had drilled into her: *You've been given gifts by God. Don't scorn Him by hiding them!* Of course, her mother had been referring to Rachael's looks. The phrase had usually come up when Rachael hadn't bothered to dress properly for an occasion or had forgotten to put on make-up and style her hair and her mother had been berating her. Although most of her mother's claims were nonsense, there was a small ring of truth to some of them. Rachael knew she was exceptionally good at organising events and persuading people to do things, and she loved it, almost thrived on it. It made sense that she should find a way to use her talent and to combine it with her other love, medicine. She had wished before that she could be as good a doctor as Dr Ribbentrop and Dr Chetty, that she could give the kind of care and dedication that they did. She saw now that it was possible. She would show her dedication in a different way but she could make just as much difference. Now she was sure that she would apply to do her community service the next year at Tugela Bridge, and that once she had finished that year, she would stay on at Prince Xoliswe for as long as it took her to realise all within her potential. The knowledge was accompanied by a strange exhilaration, the type of joy bred out of a sudden removal of choice, an absolute certainty. She knew this was the path that would fulfil her, not going overseas or moving back to Cape Town to work at a tertiary or private hospital. This, she thought, is exactly what I am meant to do.

Seema

20

Seema was too embarrassed to give the vegetable curry she had made for Dr Ribbentrop directly to him, so she decided to leave it on top of his bag in the doctors' office after the handover ward round. She had stuck a short thank-you note to the lid of the container. She waited until everyone had left for their wards and she was alone before taking out the curry. As she lifted the container from her bag, the aroma of coriander and cardamom and cumin infused the cold, sterile air of the doctors' office. The scent, so different from the clinical smells of the hospital, made Seema worry for a moment that she was doing the wrong thing. Perhaps she was acting inappropriately by giving a curry to Dr Ribbentrop. Perhaps he didn't even like curry. She should have brought him a slab of chocolate or a cake, something far more conventional. That would have been much safer. She was just about to capitulate to her self-doubt and take the container back when Dr Ribbentrop returned to the doctors' office. He had obviously forgotten something. Seema felt herself blush: she was still leaning over Dr Ribbentrop's bag. She thought she had better say something quickly, before he got the impression that she had been rummaging through his belongings.

'I ... I ... wanted to leave this for you, to say thank you,' she stuttered, pointing at the container of curry. 'I didn't expect you to come back. I was just going to leave it for you. I'm sorry, I didn't even check whether you eat curry or not.'

'Good heavens, why on earth are you sorry?' Dr Ribbentrop thundered, picking up the container and lifting the lid slightly. He sniffed at the contents and his face broke into a rare smile. 'I live in Natal; it would be a travesty if I didn't like curry. Thanks very much for this. It wasn't necessary at all, but I appreciate it. I don't think any bachelor is ever ungrateful for a home-cooked meal, whatever it is,' he joked.

Seema relaxed slightly. He appeared to be happy with her gift, and if he wasn't, he was at least bothering to put on a good act. She wished that Satesh would occasionally show the same gratitude for the meals she prepared for him. It would be nice, she thought wistfully, to cook for someone as uncomplicated and unfussy as Dr Ribbentrop. She smiled shyly at him. 'I'm glad you like it,' she said. 'And I promise I won't make the same mistake again. I'll make sure that in future I eat something before coming on call.'

'You'd better,' Dr Ribbentrop growled playfully. 'Having said that, though, I'd swap a cheese-and-tomato sandwich for a curry anytime.' He took some sheets of paper out of his bag and excused himself, thanking Seema once again before leaving.

Seema had a long ward round to get through, for which she was already late, so she picked up her bag, ready to follow Dr Ribbentrop out of the doctors' office. As she made her way to the door, the edge of her bag knocked a pile of papers off the desk. They fanned out over the floor and Seema bent down to pick them up. She was glad that the doctors' office was empty and that no one had been present to witness her clumsiness. She collected the sheets of paper into a pile and was about to place them back on the desk when the heading on the top page caught her attention. It appeared that the paper was an application form for a scholarship to study postgraduate medicine at Harvard University. Seema scanned the form with interest. The scholarship seemed to cover everything, from tuition to accommodation. Seema looked at the next page, which listed the scholarship requirements. She knew that even considering a scholarship was pointless. She could think of a whole list of reasons why she would never be able to take up an opportunity such as this one even if she was accepted: Satesh would never allow it; she was petrified at the thought of going overseas; she would be too far away from her family; it would be completely impractical; Satesh wanted to start a family in the next two years and the scholarship was for four years; they couldn't afford it. It would never work. Nevertheless, she found herself wanting to see what the requirements for the scholarship were, just for interest's sake. Just to see whether she would be eligible.

Seema was amazed to see that she could fulfil all the requirements. It was almost as though the scholarship had been tailored specifically for her. Studying medicine at one of the best medical schools in the world was a dream that Seema had never allowed herself to imagine for longer than a second or two. It was, simultaneously, the thing she desired most in the world and the thing she was least likely ever to have. It was the wish that had the potential to destroy her more than any other dream she had. She looked at the form again, wondering whose it was. The thought entered her mind that perhaps she should apply for the scholarship, just to see if she could get it, to see if she was good enough. It was a niggly, irritating thought that, once considered, refused to give her a moment's peace. It wouldn't do any harm to apply, she reasoned, and anyway the chances were incredibly slim that she would get the scholarship (Harvard must receive hundreds of applications from all over the world). Still, she had nothing to lose by sending in the application, except the possibility of shattering a dream that she had been too afraid before to voice. Nobody else need even know that she had considered the scholarship.

All at once it seemed of incredible importance to Seema to find out whether she would meet the criteria, whether she was good enough for the scholarship. Against her better judgement, she took the form to admissions and asked the receptionist there to make a copy for her. The woman charged Seema six rands for using the hospital copier, which she pocketed, then gave Seema the photocopied pages. Six rands was a small price to pay, Seema thought, for something that could change her life. No, she mustn't think like that. She shook her head, as though to dislodge the thoughts from her head. She didn't really stand much chance of being accepted and, even if she was, she would never be able to take up the scholarship. She knew that she shouldn't fill in the form, that she should throw it away immediately, before it started exposing more impossible dreams.

She could hear her mother's voice in her head, scolding her: *They'll bring you nothing but unhappiness. What's the point in hankering after something you'll never have?*

She shut the voice out of her mind. This time, she would ignore her mother. She sat at the doctors' desk and filled the form in immediately, before she could change her mind, and then paid the receptionist to post it for her. She knew that if she waited until the afternoon she would lose the courage to follow through with her idea. She kissed the back of the letter as she handed it to the receptionist, as she had once done with the love letters she had written to Satesh. For good luck.

Satesh had injured his ankle playing soccer. He had twisted it and the ankle had swollen slightly and turned deep purple in places. After examining his foot, Seema reassured him that it wasn't broken and suggested that he rest it, use an ice pack and take some anti-inflammatories, but Satesh managed to convince himself that he had done serious damage to his leg and that he required X-rays, at the very least. Reluctantly Seema agreed to organise X-rays for him. She slipped the woman working at the radiology reception desk a hundred-rand note and the woman promised to phone Satesh to come in for the X-ray as soon as she could create a gap.

The next day Satesh limped into the flat with the X-ray in his hand. He took it out of the brown envelope and held it up in front of Seema.

'Let's see how good you are, Doctor,' Satesh taunted. 'Can you tell me what's wrong with my foot?'

Seema had not thought there was a fracture clinically, but she realised that she must have made a mistake, as otherwise there was no reason for Satesh to be holding the X-ray up in front of her. Had she been right, he would probably not even have mentioned to her that he had had the X-ray done. She took the X-ray and carefully examined the image of the ankle and the bones of the hind foot, but she was unable to see evidence of even the tiniest hairline fracture.

'Show me again where your ankle's most sore,' she said to Satesh. He grinned and pointed to the inside of his ankle. Seema looked at the corresponding medial malleolus on the radiograph but still couldn't find any pathology.

'I can't see any fracture,' she eventually admitted.

'Well, look harder,' Satesh said. 'You say you're such a good doctor. If you are, you should be able to pick up my problem.'

Seema stared at the radiograph of Satesh's ankle, trying to figure out what it was that she was missing. She even checked that she was looking at the correct ankle. 'I'm not a radiologist,' she said, finally giving up. 'I can't see anything wrong with the ankle joint. I don't see any fractures.'

Satesh laughed cruelly and took the X-ray away from her. 'Well then, you'll never know,' he said.

'Come on, Satesh,' Seema pleaded. 'Please show me what's wrong. I need to know what I'm missing in case I miss it on a patient.'

'No,' he said petulantly. 'If you're too stupid to see it, then I'm not showing you.'

Satesh was behaving like a child, and Seema knew that the more she begged him to show her the pathology the more he would enjoy withholding the information from her. The surest way to get him to show her what was wrong was to feign lack of interest.

'Fine,' she said. 'Don't show me then.' She walked away and started making dinner.

It took Satesh an hour to capitulate. He walked into the kitchen with the X-ray in his hand.

'So, do you want to see what's wrong?' he asked.

She shrugged her shoulders as though she didn't really care and tipped a tin of puréed tomatoes into the pot on the stove. Satesh held the X-ray up in front of her, forcing her to turn away from her cooking, and pointed at the bones of his big toe.

'The radiologist told me I've got a congenital abnormality,' he stated, bizarrely proud of his defect. 'I've got three of those small bones in my big toe instead of two. Most people only have two. You didn't see that, did you? Looks like I should have studied medicine, not you.'

'But Satesh,' Seema protested, 'I wasn't even looking at your toes. I was looking at your ankle, where you were injured. And I was looking for a fracture, not a congenital abnormality.'

'Don't try to make excuses,' Satesh gloated. 'You didn't even see it and you think you're such a hotshot doctor. That's a laugh. Maybe you need to go back to medical school for a little revision.'

'Satesh, I didn't even look at your toes. How could I see it if I didn't look at your toes? I probably would have seen your abnormality if you'd injured your toes and not your ankle.'

'Bullshit. You just can't admit you're not as good as you think you are.'

Seema realised she would be wasting energy trying to argue with Satesh, so she said nothing more but turned back to the biryani she was making. She knew that Satesh's argument was ridiculous and that she should just disregard it, but she couldn't ignore the flicker of self-doubt that had crept into her mind. Perhaps she wasn't so good a doctor after all. The reality was that she hadn't picked up the congenital abnormality. One of the golden rules of looking at X-rays was to examine everything, not just the part of the anatomy pertaining to the pathology. She had forgotten to do that. She had been arrogant to think she would ever get that overseas scholarship. There were probably far better candidates that had applied, candidates that would have picked up the congenital abnormality. It was just as well she hadn't mentioned to anyone that she had bothered to apply.

It was September, the time of sweet flat-crown blossoms and wind, and there was almost exactly a month to go until Diwali. Seema had put in for leave to go home for the duration of the festival and, as soon as her leave had been approved, she phoned her mother to inform her that she and Satesh would be visiting for the five days in October. Diwali had always been a special time in her family's home. Some of Seema's earliest, most precious memories were of the Diwali preparations: of staying up into the early hours of the morning helping to bake sweet *karanji* and peppery, oily *malpua*; of throwing up after stealing one too many pieces of the sickeningly sweet *barfi* that her mother made (and thought she had carefully

219

hidden from her children); of the excitement of wrapping presents and copying Diwali cards; of the anticipation of the fireworks, their luminescence and colour and whizzing and popping and flinty, metallic scent. Diwali was a happy time, a time of light and joy and family togetherness. Diwali was a time of hope.

As Seema had expected, her mother was thrilled that she and Satesh would be coming to visit.

'The house is too empty without you here,' she said to Seema. 'Do you want me to order you a new sari from Prevani? I saw her stock last week. She's brought new stuff over from Delhi – very, very fashionable. It really is too beautiful. I think a silver one will be nice for you. You haven't got a silver sari. Prevani's running a special: fifteen per cent off if you buy two. I'm getting a sari for myself, so we can make use of the discount if we get one for you too.' Her mother spoke more quickly than usual, her words fighting each other to get out.

'Thanks, I need a new sari anyway. I didn't get one last year. And silver would be nice; Satesh likes silver,' Seema said. She could feel her mother's excitement, the excitement of Diwali, starting to rub off on her.

'And I'll get you some shoes to go with. I saw some beautiful silver beaded ones at the trade fair last week. Did I tell you your cousin Varsha is coming over from Bhopal? You haven't seen her since you were three.'

Her mother's words made Seema realise how much she missed her family. Before they moved to Tugela Bridge, she and Satesh had stayed on her parents' property, in a small outhouse that her father had built for them. This year was the first time she had stayed away from her parents' home for an extended period. It was only now, talking to her mother, that Seema realised how much she missed the comfort and familiarity of home. When her children were grown up one day, if she ever had children, would they remember their home with the same affection? Seema doubted it, unless Satesh changed dramatically.

'Mother, how are you and father so happy?' she asked impulsively. She was breaking unspoken protocol: her family's conversations rarely ventured into the realm of the intimate. Once the question was out, though, once the boundary had been breached, Seema seemed unable to stop. 'You had an arranged marriage but you're so happy together. Far happier than Satesh and I are. Please tell me how you do it. What am I doing wrong?'

'Ah, my daughter, happiness in the family is only created when the wife surrenders to her husband. You need to put his desires above your own; then you will achieve happiness for your family. That is the key to happiness.'

'But what if the husband is wrong?' Seema protested. 'It's easy for you, because you have a husband who knows right from wrong, who respects *vivah sanskara*, the sanctity of marriage.'

'The husband is never wrong, and the sooner you learn that the happier you'll be,' her mother said. And it seemed to Seema that, for the first time, she detected a hint of sadness in her mother's voice. 'When you think that your husband is doing something wrong, look closely at what you are doing yourself. Look what it is that you are doing that is making him behave that way.'

'Thanks for the advice,' Seema said. When she put down the telephone, she realised she was torn between her instinct, which told her that Satesh's behaviour was pathological, and what her mother had told her. Perhaps her mother was right. Perhaps Satesh treated her in the way he did because he felt emasculated around her, because she was cleverer and more educated. Perhaps she needed to be more subservient to him, make him feel more important than her. It was worth a try. Anything was worth a try.

Nomsa

21

Nomsa was on the verge of calling in her next patient when the paramedics rushed into casualty with a young boy on a stretcher. Nomsa put down the folder she had picked up and ran over to the stretcher. The boy looked ten or eleven. He had short, tousled brown hair and blue eyes. His bare feet were stained orange with played-in mud. He had been intubated and one paramedic was manually ventilating him while another was doing chest compressions.

'Electric shock,' the paramedic who had been ventilating the boy said to Nomsa as they transferred him to a bed. 'He was bouncing a metal Slinky off the side of a bridge and the Slinky connected with the overhead railway lines beneath the bridge. Obviously it acted as a brilliant conductor. When we arrived he was unresponsive and had no pulse, but we did pick up some disorganised electrical activity on the defibrillator.'

Nomsa glanced at the screen of the defibrillator, which was monitoring the young boy's heart rhythm. The green line indicating the heart tracing was erratic and polymorphic. It was not a rhythm she could immediately identify.

'So far we've only given adrenaline,' the paramedic said. 'We didn't know what else to give.'

'Thanks,' Nomsa replied, dismissing the paramedics with a nod of her head. She pulled on some gloves and started feeling for a pulse but couldn't find anything.

'I'll continue with chest compressions; there's no palpable pulse,' Nomsa said to the nurses who were waiting at the bedside for her instructions. She leant over the boy's chest and pressed down forcefully, then told one of the sisters to get another milligram of adrenaline ready for administration. As she spoke she continued pressing down on and then releasing the boy's chest, trying to create an artificial heartbeat to move oxygenated blood to the brain. She asked another nurse to connect the patient to an ECG machine. Once the electrodes had been applied, a wobbly green tracing appeared on the monitor screen. Nomsa stared at it in confusion. She still couldn't identify what rhythm it was, which complicated further management of the patient. Whether she should shock the patient or continue to give drugs and chest compressions was dependent on the type of rhythm. She continued chest compressions while trying to figure out what to do. After another minute and another milligram of adrenaline, she stopped compressions to check the rhythm again. At last it was recognisable. But her relief at being able to decipher the rhythm was dampened almost immediately when she realised what the implications of the rhythm were: the patient was in PEA, pulseless electrical activity, which was almost uniformly fatal. It was useless trying to defibrillate a patient in PEA; all she could do was continue to give adrenaline and chest compressions and wait until she had attempted resuscitation for a reasonable enough length of time.

She handed over the job of doing chest compressions to another of the nursing staff and went to draw a sample of blood for a blood-gas analysis. At least if the child had any major electrolyte abnormalities she could correct them. She glanced at the clock: she would give the resuscitation another ten minutes before giving up. She checked the boy's rhythm again, hoping that it had become a shockable rhythm, but the monitor screen still showed PEA.

Nomsa took the blood sample to the blood-gas machine and fed it into the thin, proboscis-like capillary tube. After about a minute the machine spat out a small piece of paper, the size of the receipt for a parking ticket. She read the values printed on the slip. There were a few electrolyte and acid–base imbalances, but Nomsa suspected they were the result of the prolonged resuscitation rather than from the initial electric shock. She corrected what she was able to and went to draw a repeat sample from the patient's other wrist.

As she turned the boy's wrist flexor-surface up, she noticed the burn wound on his hand. It was, more precisely, on his palm: a circular, brown-and-grey blemish on his fair skin, about the size of a five-rand coin – so misleadingly innocuous. He must have been holding the Slinky in that hand. An image flashed into Nomsa's mind: the boy standing on a bridge, looking down at the silver flashes as the spring extended and recoiled, smiling, laughing, oblivious to the danger he was in. She pushed the image from her mind forcefully. She didn't have time for sentimentality now. She had to try to save the child's life. She deliberately looked at the entrance burn wound again, trying to see it as nothing more than the site at which the voltage had entered the child's body. There would be an exit burn somewhere else, probably on one of his feet, Nomsa thought.

Just before the allowed ten minutes was up, Nomsa checked the rhythm on the monitor again. It still showed PEA. Nomsa knew that there was nothing more she could do, that she needed to terminate the resuscitation, but she didn't know how to stop it. A part of her recognised that the child was dead, had been dead since he was wheeled into casualty, but another part of her clung to the hope that somehow he could be saved. Modern medicine enabled miracles to happen, after all. That was one of the reasons she loved the science so much.

A thought entered Nomsa's mind: perhaps she had missed something. It was a strong possibility because she wasn't very experienced at resuscitations, especially those following electrocution. Ironically, it was also a reassuring thought, because if she had forgotten or missed something there could potentially still be a way to save the child – a way that she didn't know about or hadn't thought of. 'Please will someone call Dr Chetty,' she said urgently. She was excited now, hopeful that the child still had a chance. None of the sisters responded immediately to her request. 'I'll take over ventilating,' she said to the sister bagging the patient. 'You go call Dr Chetty.'

A few minutes later Dr Chetty ran into casualty, followed by the sister that Nomsa had sent to call her. Nomsa briefly described to Dr Chetty what had happened and what her management had been until then. 'He came in with such a strange rhythm I thought maybe I missed something,' she explained to Dr Chetty. 'I didn't want to stop the resus until I was sure I'd done everything possible.'

Although Dr Chetty's expression didn't obviously change, Nomsa noticed that her eyes clouded over slightly as she examined the boy. Initially Nomsa thought Dr Chetty was angry. Had Nomsa missed something obvious? Had she done something wrong? Somehow killed the child? But she soon realised it wasn't anger she was seeing in the implacable Dr Chetty's eyes; it was grief. 'The strange rhythm that you picked up on the ECG was probably residual activity from the electrical current that shocked the child,' Dr Chetty said slowly. 'You've done everything possible, Nomsa. It's time to terminate the resuscitation.'

Terminate the resuscitation. Terminate a life, a life that had hardly begun. Nomsa couldn't do it. The sister next to her had discontinued chest compressions as soon as Dr Chetty had spoken. Another of the nurses was shutting off the intravenous infusion. They were starting to pack away but Nomsa couldn't stop pumping the bag that was ventilating the child.

'Nomsa,' Dr Chetty said softly as she came over to her side, 'you need to stop now. There's nothing more you can do.' She gently but firmly pressed on Nomsa's arm, stopping her from inflating the bag again.

It was over, just like that. A few hours ago, the child had been playing on a bridge, full of life. Perhaps it had been a beautiful evening, still and warm. Perhaps his laughter had rung out into the dusk. Perhaps he had been looking forward to supper time. Had the Slinky been new? A gift? A toy he had saved up his pocket money to buy? Nomsa knew that she had to end her imaginings. She couldn't break down now, not in front of Dr Chetty and the nursing staff. Doctors were not expected to show too much emotion; a clouding over of the eyes was enough. She picked up the boy's file and sat down to write notes on the resuscitation, hoping that occupying her mind would stop her imagination from running amok. She concentrated on what she was writing, on the details of the resuscitation, the doses of the drugs she had administered

– anything to stop her from thinking about the bouncing silver Slinky. She had just finished writing when one of the sisters came to call her.

'The boy's parents are outside,' she said to Nomsa. 'They want to know what's happening.'

'Has ... has ... nobody told them?' Nomsa asked. 'Don't they know?'

The sister shook her head.

Nomsa stood up reluctantly. She didn't know what she was going to tell the parents, how she was going to tell the parents. Were they under the impression that their son was still alive?

'They followed the ambulance to the hospital,' the sister volunteered, 'so they must have known their boy was in a critical condition.'

A tiny breath of relief tempered Nomsa's anxiety. If the parents had seen the on-scene resuscitation, they must surely have had an inkling that the situation was serious.

She walked out into the waiting room and called the boy's parents into one of the examination cubicles. The child's mother was short and petite, with curly ginger hair. Her eyes were puffy and red-rimmed from crying. The boy's father had the same brown hair and blue eyes as his son. He kept touching his wife's hand, reassuring her that everything would be okay.

'Ah, here's the doctor,' he said as Nomsa led them into the cubicle. 'She's going to tell us what's going on. You can stop worrying now, honey. I promise you, Keegan's going to be fine.'

Nomsa wanted to turn around and run out of the examination cubicle. She had no idea of what she was going to say. The boy's parents still thought he was alive; how was she going to tell them that he had died? They were staring at her expectantly, waiting for her to tell them their son was going to be fine. She knew she had to say something but she had no idea what words to use.

'Is Keegan going to be okay, Doctor?' the dead child's father asked, more urgently now. Nomsa could see from the expression on his face that, for the first time since arriving at hospital, the possibility that all might not be right with his son was dawning.

'No, no,' Nomsa said. 'Not really.' She wanted to smack herself. What kind of answer was that? Not really. It made absolutely no sense. Being dead could hardly classify as not really being okay.

'Oh dear, is it serious, Doctor? Is he going to need to go to ICU?' the boy's mother asked. Tears were pooling in her eyes, spilling over their edges and down her cheeks.

Nomsa knew that she had to tell them. She couldn't delay it any longer. She had to find the words. 'The electric shock that your son got, that Keegan got, was a very high-voltage shock. I'm sorry, but it killed him almost instantly. We tried to resuscitate him, but the electrical current had caused too much damage to his heart.'

For the briefest of moments, both parents simply stared at her. It was as though they hadn't heard what she said. Then suddenly, the meaning of her words hit them with a force that was almost physical, that made them recoil. The child's mother sat down on one of the cubicle chairs and held her hand to her forehead, a gesture almost of confusion. The dead boy's father moaned, a deep, primitive cry that shuddered through his body.

'I'm so sorry,' Nomsa repeated, 'so, so sorry.' She felt helpless. She knew there was nothing she could do to make the situation any better for the parents. And being helpless, she felt superfluous – an unwelcome aspect of the parents' grief, perhaps even the cause of it. 'I'll be in casualty,' she said. 'You can stay here as long as you need to. Please call me if you need any help or if you have any other questions.' She slipped out of the cubicle as quickly as she could.

The image of the dead boy would not leave Nomsa. It haunted her, followed her around the ward and worried her while she was trying to see patients. It made her drop instruments while she was suturing lacerations and write up incorrect medications on prescription cards. It danced in front of her eyes, waving a silver Slinky. She couldn't make sense of the evening. She spoke sternly to herself, in an attempt to banish the spirit.

'Stop this nonsense,' she scolded as she splashed her face with cold water in the small staff lavatory. 'You're a doctor. Doctors deal with shit like this. You can't let your patients affect you so much. If you don't stop, you're going to make a mistake and harm somebody else. You have to learn to control your emotions. You can't let your heart rule; your brain must be in control all the time.' She rolled some gloss over her lips, loosened her braids from the band that was holding them into a ponytail and emerged from the bathroom feeling slightly better. The spectre of the little boy had temporarily left her.

Dr Chetty passed her in the corridor as she was walking back to casualty.

'Are you okay?' Dr Chetty asked, stopping her. 'I know a child's death is always difficult to cope with. It's the worst for me, when a child doesn't make it.'

'I'm fine,' Nomsa said quickly, and probably too forcefully. She didn't want to talk about the little boy's death. She had just managed to empty her mind of him but she knew that talking about it would summon his spirit back.

'Are you sure?' Dr Chetty asked.

'Yes,' Nomsa said. 'Obviously I would have preferred to have been able to save the child, but you don't always get what you want. He was dead when he arrived anyway. I've got other patients that need my attention now.' Nomsa knew that she was being rude, that Dr Chetty was trying to offer her some form of rudimentary counselling and that her abrupt answers were shunning those efforts, but she was trying desperately hard to stay in control. She would rather Dr Chetty think her rude and insensitive than an emotional wreck.

Dr Chetty nodded. 'I suppose that's a sensible approach,' she said, 'but if you find you aren't coping, let me know. We can talk through it. Sometimes that helps.'

'Thanks,' Nomsa said, but she knew she wouldn't talk about it again. The boy had died and she would have to make sure she got over it. And the best way to get over it would be to concentrate on work.

She walked briskly to the pile of patient folders and called in her next patient. A tall, middle-aged man with a bandage over his right cheek followed her into the cubicle. Nomsa was just about to

228

ask him what was wrong when she felt her cellphone vibrate in her pocket. She glanced at her watch as she reached for her phone. It was one o'clock in the morning: an odd time for anyone to be calling her. She presumed it was someone who had dialled an incorrect number, but she stepped outside the cubicle and answered anyway.

'Dr Poponi?' the voice on the other end of the telephone enquired.

'Yes,' Nomsa answered. Obviously not a wrong number. She thought perhaps it was another doctor looking for her, someone co-managing one of her patients.

'Please hold on for Dr October,' the voice said. Nomsa's curiosity was satisfied. It must be a doctor from another hospital calling her about a patient. Switchboard must have given out her cell number. She decided that she would speak to the operators in the morning and remind them that she didn't want her cell number handed out to just anyone without her permission.

'Hello,' a new voice said. 'It's Dr October speaking. Is this Dr Poponi on the line?'

'Yes,' Nomsa replied. 'Can I help you?' There was silence for a moment and she thought that perhaps the call had been cut off.

'I'm calling about your mother,' the voice said eventually.

'Yes?' Nomsa asked, slightly irritated now. She didn't have time to deal with her mother's issues in the middle of a shift, especially one that had been as traumatic as this. Surely her mother's problems could wait until morning?

'I'm sorry to have to tell you this, but your mother has passed away,' the voice said.

Nomsa heard the words, but they made no sense to her. What did the doctor mean? Her mother could not possibly be dead. Nomsa didn't know how to ask the doctor what he was talking about without sounding stupid. Was there another meaning for the euphemism 'passing away' that she was unaware of? Perhaps it meant that her mother had left the ward against the doctor's orders, or that she had been discharged. Maybe the doctor had the wrong patient.

'Mrs Poponi?' Nomsa said. 'Are you sure it's Mrs Poponi, Mrs

Agnes Poponi, that you're talking about?'

'Yes,' the doctor confirmed. 'You know she had multi-drug-resistant tuberculosis. We were struggling to get it under control before starting her on anti-retrovirals. Unfortunately she went into respiratory failure which then progressed to multi-organ failure two days ago. We were unable to reverse it.'

'How could this have happened without me knowing?' Nomsa demanded. 'Why wasn't I told? I didn't even know she had MDR TB. Was she admitted to ICU?' Nomsa kept her phone to her ear and made her way to the doctors' office, where she would be able to talk in relative privacy.

'I'm sorry.' The doctor sounded uncomfortable. 'It's policy at our hospital that we don't admit patients who aren't on anti-retrovirals to ICU. We just don't have enough space. You work in a government hospital; you know how it is.'

Nomsa didn't say anything. She didn't know how it was, not when her mother was the patient being excluded from ICU.

'I'm so sorry,' the doctor continued, and Nomsa couldn't help remembering earlier on in the evening when she had used the same phrase so ineffectually. 'We did try to call you about her condition two days ago, when it deteriorated. My colleague left a message on your phone.'

Nomsa thought back guiltily to the phone call she had avoided answering because she had been tired and had wanted to sleep and to the message that she had deleted from her voicemail before having heard it because it had been unclear and she hadn't thought to relate it to her mother. She had thought that someone had been calling her about a patient. She just hadn't realised that the patient had been her mother.

'I'm really sorry,' the doctor reiterated and, bizarrely, Nomsa felt empathy for him having to give her such bad news.

'It's okay,' she said. 'Thanks for letting me know.' She knew that he must be feeling very awkward and probably wanted to get off the phone as soon as possible. 'I'll call tomorrow if I have any other questions,' she said, making it easier for him.

She heard the click as he put the telephone down, but Nomsa

couldn't put her phone back into her pocket. She stared at it, as though willing it never to have rung. How was it possible that her mother had died? She couldn't be dead; Nomsa hadn't had a chance to say goodbye. She thought back to her last conversation with her mother, to how rushed and impersonal it had been, to how irritated she had been with her mother. Why hadn't she taken the time to speak to her mother properly? She wished she could have the telephone conversation over again, have the last three years over again. She would do things so differently. If only she had taken leave when she heard that her mother had been admitted to hospital. If only she had driven to Aliwal North to visit her, she might have realised how sick her mother was.

Nomsa made her way slowly back to casualty. She kept hoping that her phone would ring again and that it would be the doctor, calling to say that he was terribly sorry about the misunderstanding but he had confused her mother with another patient. There must have been a mistake made somewhere along the line. Although her brain realised the possibility existed that her mother was dead, her heart refused to believe it. Perhaps it was a form of denial, because her desire for her mother to still be alive was so strong. She had known since her previous conversation with her sister that her mother was HIV-positive, but she wasn't prepared for her mother's death. There were still too many things she needed to speak to her mother about, too many unresolved issues.

Nomsa walked back into the cubicle where her patient was waiting for her. He had removed the bandage from his cheek to reveal a laceration. Nomsa didn't ask him how he had sustained it; it didn't seem important. She picked up a suture pack and started suturing the wound on autopilot. She knew she should phone her sister but she didn't want to. As long as she did not speak to her sister, not confirm the doctor's news, there was still the possibility that the doctor had made a mistake. And at the moment her grasping on to that possibility felt like the only thing that was keeping her from falling apart.

She finished suturing the man's laceration and called in the next patient. It was a drunk man who had tried to commit suicide by overdosing on vitamin B tablets after his girlfriend broke up with him. All he had succeeded in doing was to push himself into a cycle of projectile vomiting. Nomsa was half-heartedly examining him when she felt her phone vibrate. She grabbed at it eagerly. Her mother's name was flashing on the screen. Nomsa smiled and then started laughing, almost hysterically. She knew there had been a mistake.

'Ma!' she answered. 'I knew they'd got something wrong. I knew you weren't dead.'

Instead of her mother's voice, Nomsa heard her sister wailing on the other end of the telephone. She could hear the grief in her sister's cry, the loss and the anguish. Noluthando did not need to say anything to confirm to Nomsa that their mother was dead. Nomsa felt her heart stop beating. It was as though a great big bird was choking her, clawing at her throat with its talons. She rushed from the cubicle, her patient immediately unimportant. She had to get out. Behind her, she heard her patient calling for her, but she ignored him. He would survive his drunken vitamin B overdose without her help.

Nomsa ran through casualty, past the benches of waiting patients, through the sliding doors and out into the stillness of midnight. She collapsed onto a low concrete block on the far side of the hospital parking lot and buried her face in her hands. She could feel her body shaking, hear her loud, uncontained sobs breaking the night-time silence. She lifted her face to the stars and called out her mother's name over and over again, but there was no reply except for the croaking of distant frogs. There would never again be any reply.

Time passed, but Nomsa didn't notice. She noticed nothing except the anguish consuming her. She didn't even notice Dr Chetty coming towards her, until she felt Dr Chetty's hand on her shoulder.

'Come inside with me. It's not safe out here alone,' Dr Chetty said softly.

Nomsa didn't have the capacity to argue. Dr Chetty took Nomsa's hand and led her back into the doctors' office. She sat her down on one of the chairs and handed her a box of tissues. She switched on the kettle and started making Nomsa a cup of tea, and all the time Nomsa could not stop the howls that rose up inside her chest and escaped through her mouth. The tea got cold. Nomsa was unable to drink it. She noticed Dr Chetty looking at her watch, obviously worried about the waiting patients, but she could not stop her keening to tell Dr Chetty to go back to casualty, that she would be fine on her own.

'You need to go home,' Dr Chetty said to Nomsa eventually. 'It's not that busy tonight; I'll cope on my own. I'm going to call security to escort you home. I don't want you walking back alone in this state.' She picked up the telephone and dialled the number of the hospital security guards and then requested that one of them come to the doctors' office.

'I'm going to go now,' she said to Nomsa, 'I need to get back to the patients. Are you going to be okay? There's a guard coming to walk you home.'

Nomsa nodded. What else could she do? She wanted to tell Dr Chetty that she wasn't going to be okay, that her entire world had collapsed, that she had a pain ripping through her chest that made her think she was having a heart attack, but she couldn't stop crying to say the words.

Dr Chetty leant over and hugged Nomsa. 'It's always difficult when a patient dies, especially when it's a child,' she said sympathetically, and Nomsa realised that she must think she was crying for the dead boy. Dr Chetty had no way of knowing that that evening Nomsa had been both the giver and the receiver of bad news. And Nomsa could not tell her now that she was not crying for the boy. She didn't want to utter the words out loud: *My mother has died.* That would make them too irreversible, too real, too final.

For three years she had pushed her mother away. No, for longer. She had rejected her mother for far longer than three years. She had been ashamed of her mother for almost as long as she could remember, embarrassed of her ways and her lack of education. She had spent half of her life wishing that she had a different mother, someone more suave and slick and Western, like the mothers of her classmates. She had spent fifteen years ignoring her mother, avoiding her telephone calls and making excuses for not visiting her. Now what she wanted more than anything else was to hear her mother's voice and bury her face into her mother's neck and inhale deep breaths of her mother's scent. Now it was too late.

Rachael

22

Rachael was fed up with insects and reptiles and parasites and fungi. In fact, she would be quite happy if the only creatures she ever came into contact with again had four legs and fur. The day before, she had had to wait outside her house for an hour because there had been a green snake sunning itself at her doorstep when she arrived home after work. One of the other interns had assured her that it was a harmless Natal bush snake, but she had been unwilling to take any chances, so she had sat staring at it from a safe distance of two metres until the snake had decided that it had had enough of her front door and moved out of her way. While waiting outside her prefab – hungry and desperate for a cup of coffee – how she had longed for domesticated, urban, reptile-free Cape Town! This morning, she had already had an unwelcome encounter with an amphibian (she had put her foot into her running shoe before work to find that a frog had made a temporary home in her shoe) and now … this. She stared down at the cauliflower in front of her in disgust.

Earlier she had led a diabetic patient – a short Indian woman who was as broad as she was tall – into the cubicle. The woman explained to Rachael that she came to the hospital once every two weeks for a doctor to check that an ulcer on her heel was healing adequately. Rachael had not been too surprised that this was the woman's sixteenth visit: diabetics, especially those with uncontrolled sugars, took far longer than non-diabetic people to heal. Rachael helped the patient onto the bed and, after slipping on a pair of gloves, began unravelling the bandage around the woman's foot. The removal of the bandage revealed not only the ulcer, which was healing well, but also what appeared to be a piece of rotting cauliflower attached to the woman's big toe. Rachael couldn't help staring at it. It was greyish-brown and about the size of a golf ball. She had absolutely no idea what it was. Was it a parasite? A large tumour? Or did the woman have a bizarre reason for smuggling rotting vegetables beneath her bandages? Whatever was attached to the woman's toe was completely foreign to Rachael. She touched it gingerly. It had a slightly spongy consistency, similar to a mushroom. Rachael didn't want to appear a complete ignoramus by asking the patient what was attached to her big toe, but she couldn't ignore the cauliflower either.

'How long has this been here?' she asked eventually. She thought that asking this question struck the right balance between probing for information and not disclosing the fact that she had no clue of what she was looking at.

'What?' the patient asked. 'The ulcer?'

'No, this … this on your toe,' Rachael said, unsure of what to call the growth.

'Oh, ages, I think,' the patient replied vaguely. Her answer was singularly unhelpful. It was quite obvious that if it was a cauliflower it had been there for a long time, but instinct told Rachael that the growth was unlikely to belong to the vegetable family.

'Has any other doctor seen it?' Rachael asked, grasping at straws.

The woman nodded and Rachael read through the patient's notes in an attempt to see what the other doctors had written about it. All she could find were comments on the ulcer. How was it possible that none of the other doctors who had seen the patient had thought it noteworthy to remark on the cauliflower? Rachael gave up guessing and went to find Seema, who was on call with her, to ask her what her opinion of the growth was.

Seema took one look at the rotting cauliflower and smiled slightly. 'It's only a fungal infection,' she told Rachael

'What?' Rachael asked in disbelief. This could not possibly just be a fungal infection; it was a giant, fungating mushroom protruding from the woman's toe.

'I suppose you don't see them this bad in Cape Town, where

there's no humidity,' Seema laughed. 'I have to admit that this one's particularly severe, though. Probably because of the diabetes and because it's been all wrapped up under the bandage for months. Agh, I wouldn't like that growing on my foot,' she whispered as she left the cubicle. Rachael could not agree more. Even though it was only a fungal infection, she couldn't understand how the woman could have been able to walk, or rather hobble around, with it for so long.

'How's the ulcer looking, Doctor? Is it any better?' the woman piped up, interrupting Rachael's contemplation.

'It's looking fine. It's actually healing quite well,' Rachael said.

'I can't see my feet, you know,' the woman said. 'It's my back. It's too stiff. It's the arthritis.'

Rachael knew it wasn't the patient's back. It was her very large abdomen that prevented her from seeing her feet. But at least it explained why she hadn't noticed the fungus.

Considering how her day had evolved until this point, and the range of amphibians and fungi she had been exposed to, Rachael should hardly have been surprised when her next patient came in complaining of bites on his back in which he could feel something moving. She should also probably have known better than to think that her patient was imagining things, but she had instructed her patient to remove his shirt confident in the knowledge that she would see nothing extraordinary. Things didn't move inside bites.

Her patient had unbuttoned his shirt and taken it off, then pointed to his back. 'The bites are here,' he said, turning around so that Rachael could see his back, 'and I can feel something moving inside them.'

Rachael wondered whether her patient had been taking drugs or if he was using some cultural metaphor to describe the bites. He was from Zimbabwe: perhaps she didn't understand what he was trying to tell her. All that Rachael could see on her patient's back were three large egg-shaped boils or abscesses.

'We'll have to cut these open to get the pus out,' Rachael explained to her patient.

The man nodded. 'Yes,' he said, 'and then you can get the

worms out at the same time.'

'I really don't know if there are any worms,' Rachael said. Then suddenly one of the boils wriggled. Rachael blinked. There was no other way to describe it: the lump had wriggled. The movement lasted for only a fraction of a second, but the lump had definitely moved. She stared at it in fascination. It wriggled again. Her patient had not been imagining things. There was something causing the boils to move.

'Seema!' Rachael called, poking her head round the curtain enclosing the cubicle. 'I need your help again.'

Seema appeared within seconds. 'What's wrong?' she asked, obviously expecting an emergency.

'Can you spare a minute?' Rachael asked.

Seema nodded. 'My patient's so drunk he probably won't even notice I'm not there,' she said. 'What's the problem?'

'I need help with these Natal creepy-crawlies again,' Rachael said, pointing to the man's back. 'I don't have a clue what these are.'

Seema looked at the man's back and then at Rachael. 'I think they're abscesses,' she said.

'No, look at them more closely,' Rachael said, praying the boils would wriggle again. If they didn't, she knew she would look like a real idiot.

Seema stared at the lumps. They behaved exactly as abscesses should behave: motionlessly.

'Sorry, but what exactly am I looking at?' she asked Rachael. 'Am I missing something obvious?'

Rachael was about to explain to Seema what to look for when one of the boils wriggled.

'Oh,' Seema exclaimed. 'What is that?'

Rachael couldn't help smiling triumphantly. At least she wasn't going crazy. She was also rather relieved that Seema didn't know what the moving lumps were. She walked out of the cubicle, motioning for Seems to follow her.

'It looks like something from the movie *Alien*. I half expect a monster to emerge from the man's back any second now,' Rachael whispered theatrically.

Seema giggled. 'Let's hope not,' she said. 'We'd probably be safe, though; I don't think any alien would survive this casualty ward. I'll go look it up if you want. I've got a dermatology textbook in my bag.'

'Thanks,' Rachael said, 'that would be great. I'm far too disorganised to remember to bring textbooks to the hospital.'

As Seema made her way to the doctors' office, Rachael couldn't help thinking how much Seema had relaxed in her company since they had spent the day redecorating the ward together. Rachael had thought that Seema was proud and arrogant, too proud and arrogant to bother to make conversation with her. Now she realised that it had merely been shyness. Seema hadn't built up friendships with any of the doctors, not because she thought she was superior to them or cleverer than them, but because she had been too timid. Seema must have had a lonely year until now, Rachael thought. She resolved to include her in social activities more often, assuming Seema's rather odd husband allowed it.

A few minutes later, Seema returned with an open book in her hands. 'It's something called myiasis,' she said. 'The tumbu fly lays its eggs on wet clothing that has been left in the sun to dry. Once the clothing makes contact with the skin, the larvae burrow into the skin.'

'No, no, no,' Rachael said. She was starting to feel squeamish. 'I can't actually believe it. Does your book say how we have to treat it? Are we supposed to cut them open? Do you think flies will fly out if we do?'

Seema started giggling. 'I don't know,' she said. She was giggling so hard now that she started snorting. Her laughter was infectious and Rachael found herself joining in.

'I haven't laughed so much in ages,' Seema said, holding her sides. 'I think I'm going to be stiff tomorrow.'

'I think I'm going to call in sick tomorrow if I see one more gross creature on this shift,' Rachael said.

'I suppose you want to know how to treat your patient?' Seema asked, opening her textbook again. Rachael saw her eyes skim down the rest of the page.

'It says you have to smear the lesion with a thick layer of petroleum jelly. That causes the larva to suffocate and forces it to the surface so that you can remove it.'

'You have got to be joking,' Rachael said, horrified.

'Sorry, that's what it says. I have to admit, I'm going back to my drunk patient far more gladly now than before. I think I'd rather deal with drunken belligerence than suffocating larvae.'

'Thanks for the support,' Rachael said.

Seema's expression changed from light-hearted to concerned. 'Do you want me to stay and help you?' she asked. 'I really don't mind.'

'No, it's okay,' Rachael said. 'I'm only joking. I need to learn how to deal with this type of thing if I intend staying here.'

'Are you planning on staying at Prince Xoliswe?' Seema asked. She sounded surprised.

Rachael nodded. 'I think there's a lot I can do here. I don't know, I have this stupid idea that I can make a difference if I stay on in Tugela Bridge. Maybe I'm deluding myself. And you? Where do you want to go next year?'

Seema hesitated before answering. 'I haven't decided yet,' she said. 'It depends on my husband … and some other things. I don't think I'll stay here, though. I don't think Satesh – that's my husband – can handle another year here.'

As Seema walked away, Rachael realised this was the first time she had voiced her intention to stay on at Prince Xoliswe the following year. Saying it out aloud, to someone else, made it far more of a reality than it had been when it existed solely in her mind. She knew that the more times she said it, the more people that she told, the more concrete the decision would become and the more irreversible it would be. Bugs and moulds aside, it was not wholly a bad thing.

On Sunday, Rachael and Shane took a spur-of-the-moment decision to drive to Durban for the day. Rachael wanted to do some decent shopping (among other things, she had run out of Woolworths frozen meals) and Shane had to collect a part for his computer.

Shane had gone back to his flat, after having spent the night with Rachael, and had promised to pick Rachael up at ten o'clock. Rachael was ready and waiting for Shane at five to ten. She locked the door of her prefab and sat down on her front step. The sky was clear and there wasn't a breath of wind, which was unusual for mid-September. It was cool in the shade, but in the sun it was blissfully warm. Rachael moved along her step slightly so that her whole body was in the sun. She felt like the snake that she had seen sunning itself earlier in the week. She thought that she could sit there in the sun forever and be perfectly content.

Shane picked her up at half past ten. He apologised as Rachael climbed into his car.

'Sorry I'm late. Bit of a family drama,' he said by way of explanation.

'Is everything okay?' Rachael asked, concerned. She had learnt that the less Shane said about something, the more likely it was to be an issue that affected him in some way.

'Yes, should be fine. My mom's a little sick and my sister was worried about her, so I had to sort that out. And, as usual, they need more money. My sister's daughter needs new school clothes or something.'

His tone of voice as he made the last statement was accepting rather than bitter, and Rachael was reminded once again of how much more complicated Shane's life was than hers – or than he always let on. Superficially he was always the joker, the player, the charmer, but in reality he was a very good doctor who was also sole provider for his mother and was partly responsible for his sister's family too. Occasionally he hinted to Rachael the extent of his familial duties, but she knew that he didn't like to speak to her about them so she never asked him more than he volunteered. Rachael often thought that she was Shane's escape, and that this was why he didn't speak much to her about his family. When he was with her, he could pretend he was someone else, someone who didn't have an extended family to support and who hadn't lost a father. Involving Rachael would destroy the pretence. And Rachael didn't mind, because in her own way she was doing the same thing. Being

241

with Shane made her feel as though she was breaking away from her parents, asserting her independence and developing ideas and an identity of her own. Yet the reality was that she had not even had the courage to tell her parents or any of her Cape Town friends that she was going out with an Indian man.

They drove in silence for a while. Rachael was glad that Shane was at the steering wheel because it gave her a chance to look out of the window at the scenery. She had not been in KZN for long enough to have grown blasé about the beauty of the countryside. The redness of the clay soil, the lime-green of the sugar cane, the impossible blue of the sea, the lushness and life everywhere still entranced her.

'The sugar-cane plantations are so beautiful,' she said to Shane. 'I know they're environmental disasters, but they do look deceptively verdant and green. I suppose they're a bit like golf courses in that way.'

'You know that the sugar-cane plantations are the reason why there are so many Indians here?' Shane asked.

Rachael didn't know what answer Shane was expecting, so she kept quiet.

'Indians were brought over as indentured labour,' he continued. 'The conditions were atrocious; they were basically slaves. It was only stopped recently, in about 1919, I think.'

Rachael didn't know how to respond. Had it been insensitive of her even to mention the plantations? She tried to think of another topic of conversation, one that was more neutral, but all she could think about now was slave labour from India.

'You know why white people call us *charous*?' Shane asked. His tone of voice was unusually, and inappropriately, belligerent.

Rachael shook her head. She didn't know. She felt awkward with the conversation, wanted to end it. This was the first time she felt that race was interfering with her and Shane's relationship, and she didn't like it. She would have preferred just to ignore the issue, pretend it didn't exist. But for some reason, Shane seemed determined to press on with it. Rachael couldn't help getting the impression that he somehow blamed her for the past.

242

'You know how the farmers burn the sugar cane before harvesting it?' Shane asked. But he didn't give her time to answer. 'It makes it easier to harvest: gets rid of the leaves and the cane rats and snakes.'

Rachael had often seen the orange flames of cane fires licking the night sky and had noticed the ash, the black snow, that fell the following morning, in sooty, grimy spots on windows and freshly laundered washing.

'The Indians that cut the burnt cane used to get covered in soot, in charcoal, which made them even browner than they were,' Shane continued. '*Char* means "brown". Some people say the *ou* is from the Afrikaans word for "man". Put them together and you get *charou*,' Shane continued.

Rachael didn't know how she was supposed to respond, what Shane wanted her to say. Did he expect an apology? Or commiseration?

'I just thought you might be interested,' Shane said at last, 'since you're dating a *charou*. It's part of my history.'

Rachael's initial impulse was to argue with Shane, to tell him it had all happened too long ago to be relevant to his life, but then she remembered how much the history of the Holocaust had been part of her upbringing, and that was just as distant. She had been reminded of it over and over again at school and at family gatherings. It was something that was integral to the fabric of her culture, and so was indelibly part of her. Shane had a point. It wasn't really right for her to accept the aspects of him that she wanted to, that she liked, and leave out the facets that made her feel uncomfortable.

'So, where do you want to go for lunch?' Shane asked, changing the subject completely.

'Let me think,' Rachael said, relieved that the tone of the conversation had been altered. As much as she realised that what Shane was telling her was important, she didn't feel like talking about it now. 'How about we find a seaside fish-and-chips place and get greasy fingers and beer bellies?'

'Mmm, sounds good,' Shane said. 'I think I know just the place.'

Rachael smiled and slipped her hand onto Shane's thigh. She was glad that once again their conversation was comfortable. But the differences between her and Shane's backgrounds lingered uneasily in her mind.

That evening, Rachael was still unable to shake the sense of discomfort she had experienced earlier in the day. It sat at the back of her mind, pricking her like an irritating splinter that she couldn't precisely locate and that wouldn't budge. She and Shane were at her house, watching a DVD she had bought in Durban. It was a romantic comedy, Rachael's favourite genre, and normally she would be enjoying it, and enjoying snuggling up to Shane on the couch. But this evening she found the DVD irritating and she couldn't get comfortable. Shane's body, which usually accommodated hers so readily, now felt hard and angular. She got up abruptly.

'What's wrong?' Shane asked.

'I don't know,' Rachael said. 'I'm irritable. I'm going to make a cup of hot chocolate; maybe that will help. Do you want?'

Shane shook his head. 'I haven't finished my beer yet,' he said, indicating a half-empty bottle. 'Do you want me to pause the DVD while you make your drink?'

Rachael shook her head. 'It's okay,' she said. 'I'm not really concentrating anyway.'

Rachael realised that she needed to talk to Shane, that they needed to discuss where their relationship was going. She knew why she had been worried earlier in the day about the large cultural divide she had felt between them. If they were going to take their relationship to a deeper level, from a casual fling to a serious partnership, they would have to address the issues that lay between them. Great sex and flirtatious banter were fun for six months, and it had given Rachael a great sense of independence and adventure, but it wasn't enough to hold them together for much longer. Rachael felt that a critical point had been reached, that they had to decide now whether to take their relationship further and make something of it, or allow it to fade away. She knew that if she and Shane ended their relationship, she would miss him terribly. She would miss his companionship and would miss the smell and taste and touch of his body. But she was still emotionally unattached enough to know that she would get over him quickly. If they decided to take their relationship to a more meaningful level, they would have to start making all sorts of commitments and promises. They would have to make an effort to learn about their differences and they would have to meet each other's families. Rachael didn't know if she was ready for that yet. She also didn't know if she was willing to risk the kind of hurt that a more complex relationship would develop.

The kettle clicked as the water reached boiling point and Rachael filled her mug. She stirred the contents vigorously until the instant powder had all dissolved. The hot chocolate wasn't going to get rid of her irritation, as she had implied to Shane that it might. Only talking to him would accomplish that. She sat down and took a sip of her drink. She would wait until the DVD was finished before broaching the topic.

Shane's phone rang just as the final credits of the movie were showing. He took it from his pocket and glanced at the screen.

'It's my sister,' he said. 'I'd better take it. Sorry.' He pressed the answer button and put the phone to his ear. Rachael could hear a high-pitched voice shouting at Shane, but she couldn't decipher if it was in anger or consternation. She looked at Shane's face to gauge his response. His expression was unreadable. He caught Rachael's eye, saw her staring at him and stood up. He walked away from Rachael and stood next to the window so that his back was facing her. Obviously he didn't want her involved in the conversation at all. He still hadn't said a word. Rachael picked up a magazine from her coffee table and pretended to start reading it.

'Well, will she be okay?' Shane eventually said. 'What have the doctors looking after her said?'

Then later: 'For God's sake, Evashni, calm down … It's nothing serious, okay? Just some fun … I can't talk now … I'll drive through and meet you at the hospital.'

Shane put his phone back into his pocket. Rachael could see he was worried, but there was something else in his expression, embarrassment perhaps.

'Everything all right?' Rachael asked. Obviously everything wasn't all right, but Rachael didn't know what else to say.

'No,' Shane said, rather abruptly. 'My mom's been admitted to hospital with angina. Apparently she's in a bit of a state. I'll have to drive through to Durbs to see what's going on.'

'Oh no,' Rachael said. 'It's a pity you didn't know earlier, before we drove all the way back. You could have stopped in to see her then.'

Shane looked at her strangely. 'But you were with me then,' he said.

Rachael had not been expecting this response and she didn't know how to reply to it.

'Sorry,' Shane said. 'I've got to go. I'll speak to you tomorrow.'

'I could have waited in the car,' Rachael said to his retreating back.

Shane was waiting outside Rachael's prefab when she got home from the hospital the following evening. She had tried to call him twice during the day, but both times he had cut off her calls without answering.

'How's your mom?' Rachael asked Shane as she let him in. 'I was worried about you … and obviously about her.'

'She's okay. She was discharged last night, about an hour after I arrived,' Shane said.

Rachael noticed that he was avoiding making eye contact. He seemed agitated and was fiddling with his cellphone in his pocket. This wasn't the collected, suave Shane she was used to.

'I need to talk to you about something,' he said bluntly.

Rachael nodded and went to sit down on the couch. Shane followed and sat down next to her. He took her hand in his and, for the first time since arriving, looked Rachael in the eye.

'This is so hard for me,' he said. 'I want you to know before I say anything else that I really don't want to be having this discussion with you.'

And Rachael knew that Shane was going to end their relationship. Although she had considered it the night before, had even been expecting it, she felt tears prick the back of her eyelids.

'Please don't cry,' Shane begged. 'Please don't make it harder for me than it already is.'

Rachael suddenly felt herself getting angry. 'Why?' she said, her voice raised. 'Why should I make it easier for you? This isn't just about you. I can cry if I want to.' As she said the words, she realised how pathetic she sounded. 'It's my party and I can cry if I want to,' she muttered, smiling sardonically. 'Sorry, I overreacted a bit.'

Shane hugged her. 'Oh, I love you so much,' he said. Rachael found it rather ironic that the first time he was saying these words to her, even in jest, was as he was breaking up with her. 'Let me explain what's happened,' Shane said. 'It's kind of out of my control.'

He told Rachael that his cousin had seen them together the previous day, at the fish-and-chips place where they had lunch. She had immediately telephoned his mother, her aunt, and told her that Shane was dating a white girl, which had precipitated his mother's angina attack.

'So your mother had a heart attack because you're going out with me?' Rachael couldn't help asking.

Shane nodded. 'I know it sounds ridiculous but it's complicated. I'm all she has and she's desperately afraid of losing me, and the fact that you're white doesn't help. A good Indian girl would know and accept my mother's place in the family hierarchy, but a white girl probably wouldn't. She's expecting that she'll live with me and be supported by me until she dies, and you threaten that paradigm.'

'So does this have to mean the end?'

'My mother told me last night that if I continue seeing you she'll have a heart attack, and that if she dies from it, it will be my fault and that it would be as good as murder. I can't live with that on my conscience.'

Part of Rachael wanted to argue with Shane, wanted to tell him that he needed to cut the umbilical cord and break away from his mother, that his mother was just manipulating him (she couldn't voluntarily have a heart attack, surely?), that it was wrong to break up with her just because she was of a different culture, but another part of her knew that Shane was right. It was her ego that wanted to fight. Her heart knew that if Shane's mother was somehow to die of a heart attack, he would never forgive either Rachael or himself.

Besides that, in her future plans she had never imagined having her mother-in-law living under her roof.

So, instead of arguing with him she put her arms around Shane's neck and cried into his shoulder. She would miss being with him.

'We can still be friends,' Shane said, and Rachael didn't rail against the cliché; it was actually true. They probably would still be friends.

She kissed Shane goodbye, a long, delicious kiss, and promised him that she would be fine. And she knew she would be.

As Shane shut the door behind him, Rachael realised that he hadn't been talking about his mother's condition on the phone the night before when he mentioned that it wasn't serious. He had been describing his and Rachael's relationship. Rachael wasn't cross with him about it; she couldn't be. She knew that if her parents had found out about their relationship she would probably have reassured them with the same words.

Seema

23

Mr Ferreira was back in the ward. He was thinner, far thinner, than he had been the last time Seema had seen him, and she could tell that he was losing the battle against his cancer. He still seemed inexplicably positive, though, asking Seema how his favourite doc was keeping as she approached his bedside. She smiled at him and looked down as she answered, afraid that he would see her concern if she looked him in the eyes.

'And how are you feeling?' she asked Mr Ferreira.

'You told me to come back if the pain was too bad, Doc,' he said. 'I'm not really coping at home. I don't want the missus to know, though, so just pretend you asked me to come back in, if you don't mind. I told her you'd asked me to come in for some tests. She's been trying so hard to make me comfortable. I don't want her to think she's failed or that I'm ungrateful, you know.'

'Your secret's safe with me,' Seema reassured him. 'And don't worry about the pain: we'll get you on a morphine drip as soon as possible. That should bring you some relief.'

'Thanks, Doc. It's unbearable, you know, this pain. It's so deep in my bones, nothing seems to lighten it. I've said my goodbyes, in my own kind of way. I know this time I've come in to die. I'm leaving this hospital one way; whether it's up or down isn't for me to decide. I've made my peace with everyone, you know. I don't mind if the drugs confuse me now, I just want an end to this pain. I've told my family they're not allowed to come and visit me. I want them to remember me how I was at home, not like this. My wife probably won't listen to me, though,' he chuckled. 'She's a stubborn girl that. Always has been.'

He carried on talking as Seema put the drip up on him. It was as though he wanted to say as much as he could before the high doses of morphine made him delirious. Or before he died. 'Did I tell you how we met? My wife and I?' he asked Seema.

She shook her head.

'I went to post a letter and there, behind the post office counter, was the most beautiful girl I had ever seen. She smiled at me and I thought she was pretty enough to be a film star. My favourite at the time was Brigitte Bardot, but I remember thinking that post office clerk would give her a good run for her money any day.' He had closed his eyes and was smiling as he spoke. Seema could see that at this moment her presence was not important, that to him she no longer existed. He was back in that post office twenty, thirty years ago. 'It took me fifty-three letters – I went and posted a letter to my poor old gran every Monday to Friday for fifty-three days – before I could pluck up the courage to ask that beauty behind the counter to come for coffee with me.'

'Did you know straight away that she was the right person for you?' Seema asked. 'That you were going to marry her?'

After she spoke, it occurred to her that perhaps she shouldn't have interrupted Mr Ferreira. She should have kept quiet, let Mr Ferreira reminisce in peace, but she was unable to control her curiosity. The way that Mr Ferreira had met his wife was so different from the way that she and Satesh had met. Satesh was the son of one of her father's business acquaintances, and he had been brought home by her father specifically to meet Seema with the prospect of marriage in mind. She had known, the first time she laid eyes on Satesh, that there was the possibility that she would marry him. It had by no means been an arranged marriage and, had she disliked Satesh intensely, Seema liked to believe that her parents would have discouraged her from marrying him, but she couldn't help thinking, retrospectively, that her perception of Satesh had been influenced by the fact that her parents *wanted* her to marry him. She remembered that she had spent over two hours with her mother in her bedroom dressing and grooming in preparation for her first meeting with Satesh. Her mother had helped her pleat her sky-blue sari into hundreds of folds and her hair had been carefully curled and piled on top of her head. She had walked down the stairs and into her parents' lounge feeling like a princess. Satesh had been sitting in an armchair drinking a whisky with her father. Her initial reaction had been one of hesitation: he appeared somehow cold to her, arrogant, but she had brushed the impulsive thought away. Surely her parents would not have chosen someone that wasn't perfect for her? Besides, he had been undeniably handsome. In many ways he had reminded her of some Bollywood star, sitting in that armchair with his slick, gelled hair and fair skin. Perhaps because of her naivety (he was the first man she had ever seriously thought about romantically), or perhaps because she had had such a strong desire to make her parents happy, she had convinced herself that it was love at first sight. She had denied her initial response and afterwards told everybody that, the moment she saw Satesh, she had known he was the man she wanted to marry. She had believed, because she hadn't known otherwise, that all relationships were fairy tales. How she wished now that things had been different, that Satesh had had to post fifty-three letters before she agreed to spend more time with him.

Mr Ferreira started speaking again, oblivious to Seema's memories. 'No, I didn't know the first time I saw her that I wanted to marry her,' he said in answer to her earlier question. 'When I first saw her, I just wanted to hop into bed with her. Remember, she looked like Brigitte Bardot,' he chuckled. The morphine was obviously removing his inhibitions. 'It was only later, when I got to know her, that I knew she was the one for me. You see, I knew by then that I could trust her to bring up my children. That was the most important thing for me: I wanted to marry someone whom I could trust one hundred per cent to bring up my children if something ever happened to me.'

It was a strange way of thinking about marriage, of deciding on a life partner, and one that Seema had never once considered during her and Satesh's brief courtship, but in many ways it made a lot of sense to her. It would be ridiculous to marry someone that one didn't trust with one's most precious possessions, and implied in that same trust would be great respect, common values, shared morals. Seema wished she had had a Mr Ferreira to speak to before she got married. Why hadn't her parents given her the same advice? But perhaps if they had, she wouldn't have taken it. During her courtship with Satesh, she probably would have deceived herself into believing that she knew him well enough to trust him to bring up her children.

'Thank you,' she said softly to Mr Ferreira. She was thanking him not only for his wisdom but also for sharing his memories with her.

'No, thank you, Doc,' Mr Ferreira replied. 'This seems to be relieving the pain.' Seema didn't know if he was referring to the morphine or to the talking.

Ten minutes later he fell asleep. The opiate was doing its job. As she stood at the end of the bed and observed Mr Ferreira's peaceful breathing, Seema hoped he was dreaming about Brigitte Bardot behind the post office counter.

The sister from the medical ward paged Seema three hours later to tell her that Mr Ferreira had died and to ask her to come and certify the body. Mrs Ferreira was standing at her husband's bedside when Seema arrived at the ward. She was a short, plump woman with greying bobbed hair. Although Seema could see no resemblance to the legendary Brigitte Bardot, Mrs Ferreira's face was attractive in an open, honest way. She smiled at Seema as she approached the bedside.

'You must be Dr Singh,' she said.

Seema nodded and, unexpectedly, Mrs Ferreira put her arms around her. 'Thank you for all you did for my husband,' she said, squeezing Seema. 'He spoke so highly of you, you know.'

'I wish I could have done more. If we'd just caught the cancer earlier we might have been able to treat it,' Seema said.

'You did more than enough,' Mrs Ferreira said, releasing Seema.

They stood in silence for a few moments at Mr Ferreira's bedside, until the sister appeared with the death certificate for Seema to fill in. Seema said goodbye to Mrs Ferreira and once again expressed her condolences. As she was walking away, Mrs Ferreira's voice stopped her.

'It must be a wonderful feeling,' she said, 'knowing that you make such a difference in people's lives. You take care of yourself now. There aren't many special people like you around these days.'

Seema nodded and hurried away because she didn't know what else to say. Mrs Ferreira's words made her uncomfortable: she didn't feel as though she was special. If she was special, surely Satesh should treat her differently? He was her husband, the man who was supposed to protect and care for her, and yet he didn't believe she was worth protecting and caring for. The realisation came to her that one of the reasons she enjoyed being at the hospital so much was that her work, caring for patients, gave her a sense of self-value that she did not otherwise have. Why did she drop that self-belief when she walked out of the hospital doors? What made Satesh so important that his opinion outweighed hundreds of other people's? Seema knew that she shouldn't be thinking about her husband in this way, but the ideas refused to leave her mind. For the first time ever, she was considering the possibility that she could be happy without Satesh, that the option of a life without him existed. What was their relationship worth anyway, if she didn't trust him enough to have children with him? She carried her emotions around with her for the rest of the day like the bag of textbooks that was slung more or less permanently over her shoulder. Sometimes her thoughts and feelings lifted her, were so liberating they made her float through the wards; at other times they anchored her to the ground, her guilt and disloyalty as heavy around her neck as the textbooks on her arm.

The giddiness affected her, the flying and the sinking, and Seema knew she had to sort out her thoughts before they made her fall. She was glad when she arrived home that Satesh was out at soccer practice. It would give her time to work through everything that had been running through her mind that day. She made herself a cup of tea and sat down at the dining-room table with a pen and an exam pad. She hoped that if she wrote something down, she would be able to start making sense of her thoughts and feelings. The comment that Mr Ferreira had made about trusting his wife to bring up his children kept coming into her mind. She scribbled a question on the top sheet of the pad, cryptically, so that if Satesh came home unexpectedly he wouldn't make sense of it: *Is S trustworthy in the same way as Brigitte Bardot?* She stared at what she had written. She didn't need to write down the answer! She tore off the piece of paper, crumpled it up and crushed it in her hand. Of course she didn't trust Satesh to bring up her children. She didn't trust the morals that he would instil in them and she didn't trust that he would not abuse them. She knew there was little chance that his behaviour would change because there were children around. He wouldn't miraculously be cured of his addiction to pornography and get rid of the graphic magazines he so carelessly left lying about. He wouldn't suddenly abstain from beating and abusing Seema just because there were tiny eyes looking on.

Satesh had spoken to Seema about having children. Often he had moaned at her, labelling her infertile and barren because she hadn't fallen pregnant in the two years they had been married. She hadn't told Satesh that the reason she hadn't fallen pregnant was the clandestine three-monthly visits she made to the clinic for a contraceptive injection. For the past two years she had managed to convince herself that she was having the injections because she didn't want to fall pregnant until she completed her community service; however, she knew there was more to it than that. It had taken Mr Ferreira to verbalise it for her: she hadn't wanted to fall pregnant because she didn't trust Satesh to bring up her children. She didn't trust that, if they had a little girl, Satesh would not rape her too.

She put the exam pad back into her bag, as if she were packing her emotions away. At that moment, without having written anything further down, she knew what she had to do.

Her parents' home phone rang twice before her mother answered it. Seema wished that it had rung for longer because it would have given her more time to think of what to say. She knew that she had to tell her mother about her decision, but she didn't know how to broach such a gigantic, foreign topic. She didn't know how to begin or even what words to use. So when her mother answered, she asked her mother for the recipe for *karanji*.

'Of course I'll give you the recipe,' her mother replied. 'Are you going to make it for Diwali?'

Diwali. Seema had forgotten about Diwali. How could she have? It was in less than two weeks' time. She hesitated. Perhaps she should wait until after Diwali to tell her parents. It wouldn't be right to ruin the occasion for everybody else and there was little that would destroy a family gathering as much as rumours of divorce. But Seema knew she was just procrastinating. She realised she needed to act on her decision immediately, before it became watered down by self-doubt, cowardice and fear. And before Satesh managed to manipulate it, to make it into her weakness, her fault, her downfall.

'Yes,' she said to her mother distractedly. 'I was thinking of making *karanji* for Diwali.' She wondered whether perhaps it wouldn't be better if she just omitted telling her parents. Maybe she should get divorced, get the whole thing out of the way, before telling them and then present them with a fait accompli. But that would be impractical because she needed their help and support. She needed her father to tell Satesh to move out and to protect her and to find her a good lawyer, and her mother to explain to the priest and to the rest of the family what was happening and why. On her own, she didn't have a clue where to start. She knew nothing of divorce and what it entailed. Her mother had started listing the ingredients for *karanji*. Seema interrupted her.

'I don't trust that Satesh wouldn't molest our daughter, if we had one,' she blurted out to her mother. It was the most pressing thought on her mind and, as such, seemed to have edged its way ahead of all her other thoughts and explanations.

'What are you talking about?' her mother asked. 'Are you pregnant? Am I going to be a grandmother at last?'

'No,' Seema said. 'I think that I want to get divorced because I don't trust Satesh to bring up my children.'

'Have you gone crazy?' her mother asked. 'You haven't got any children. And what's this mention of divorce?'

Seema realised that she must sound mad to her mother. She wasn't making sense. She needed to clear her mind, to present her case to her mother like she presented patients' cases on handover rounds.

'Mother, Satesh and I don't have a good relationship. He has morals that I don't agree with and I don't want to bring up my children, if we were to have children, according to his values. I don't think he's going to change and the only option I can see is for us to get divorced.'

'What are you talking about? Divorce isn't an option. Do you know what it actually means? Divorce is serious, not just some fashionable trend. It goes against all that marriage stands for. It betrays the sacrament of marriage. You can't just threaten divorce every time your relationship runs into trouble. If your father and I did that we would have been divorced twenty times over. You need to work at a relationship. Remember, marriage is something that's ordained by a higher power; it's not something you can take control of.'

'It's not a fashionable trend I'm following and I'm not just running away from my problems,' Seema countered. 'I've thought about this a lot. I know how serious divorce is and I know it would be devastating for the family and go against the sacrament of marriage, but I can't see any other way out. You don't know Satesh the way I do.'

'This is all because you've moved away from home. I knew it was a bad idea from the start. What would the family say if they heard you talking like this? What would the priest who blessed your marriage say? And Satesh's family? Don't you care for them at least?' Her mother broke down and started wailing.

'You're not listening to me, Mother. I know this is difficult for you to hear, but things can't carry on like this. I'm fully aware of the implications of divorce, but I think that in this case there are exceptional circumstances.'

'I've listened to enough,' her mother said firmly, her composure regained. 'You put these silly ideas out of your mind right now and you never mention this again, do you hear me? If you promise never to entertain such nonsense again, I won't tell your father.'

Seema didn't know what to say. She had expected some mild resistance from her mother but not anything this vicious (*that* she had expected from her father, and she had been counting on her mother's support to convince her father). Surely her mother realised that Satesh beat her up? Surely she didn't need to spell it out for her? Or did her mother condone the abuse? Did her mother care more for her ideals, her image and her religious beliefs than for her daughter's well-being? Seema felt anger build up inside her.

'It's easy for you to say all this, to judge me and try to tell me what's right, because you have a perfect marriage,' Seema said. 'I don't. Mine's far from perfect.'

Her mother was silent for a moment and Seema thought that perhaps she was considering what Seema had said.

'Your father is constipated,' she said at last.

For a second Seema wondered if she had heard her mother correctly. The comment was hardly appropriate. Even if Seema's mother had decided simply to ignore the issue, to pretend that talk of a divorce had never been brought up, now was not the ideal time to mention her father's medical problems.

'Every day he has to drink bitter aloe crystals so that he can go to the toilet,' her mother continued. 'Sometimes he uses glycerine suppositories. Do you know why he is constipated?'

'No,' Seema said sharply. And she didn't care. She had just told her mother that she wanted a divorce and her mother was describing her father's toilet habits to her. The whole conversation was entirely inappropriate. 'Can we get back to the issue we were discussing before?' Seema said. 'I don't think we're finished.'

Her mother seemed to ignore her. 'He's constipated because he has severe peri-anal warts. Big, ugly, scaly things that hang over his anus. Do you know why he has peri-anal warts?'

'Please, can we stop discussing this!' Seema protested. The vision that her mother was painting was beginning to nauseate her.

'Your father has peri-anal warts,' her mother continued, almost as though she was talking to herself, as though Seema was not a part of the conversation, 'because one of the whores that he visited gave him genital warts.'

Seema was shocked into silence. What was her mother saying? Her father wasn't like that. For a brief moment Seema wondered whether the news of her possible divorce had pushed her mother over the edge. She had heard of cases like that.

'That was how I found out,' her mother continued, 'about his whoring. Once the warts appeared, he had to tell me.'

She wasn't speaking like someone who had lost her mind.

'All those business meetings. All those nights he worked late. Everything. Everything was lies. At the time I found out, I was faced with a decision similar to yours. The big difference was that I had three young children and another on the way and I had no means of supporting myself,' her mother said gently. 'I had nobody to speak to about it. Eventually, like you, I spoke to my mother. She advised me that the role of the wife is to stay by the husband's side, whatever happens. The fate of a woman, she told me, is to deal with what life throws at her. Marriage is sacred, lasts for seven lives. It's not something that we, as humans, can decide the fate of. I never mentioned the prostitutes to your father again. And your grandmother was right. Look at you, you grew up quite happily without knowing any better.'

'When … when … did you find out?' Seema asked.

'When you were three,' her mother replied. 'He still goes. I know. I can smell the whores on him when he comes home.'

Seema felt as though her whole world was collapsing. Everything she had believed and trusted in had been a lie. Her whole life had been based on an untruth. Tears erupted from her in large, retching sobs.

'Don't cry,' her mother advised, misinterpreting the cause of Seema's sadness. 'You'll have tears enough of your own to cry. Don't waste them on me. My life hasn't been that bad. I've had security and a home. People respect me. I have children of whom I'm proud. My life could have been far worse.'

'But it could have been better,' Seema spluttered. 'It could have been more than "not bad"; it could have been happy.'

'My child, life is not only about being happy. It's about doing your duty and about devotion. It's about upholding certain values.'

'No,' Seema responded loudly. 'You're wrong!' She refused to believe her mother. She didn't want to live a life that was not bad, that could have been far worse. 'I won't settle for that,' she said to her mother. 'I won't settle for what you settled for. I want more from life.' And as Seema said the words, she knew that they were true. She was destined for more from life. She was destined to help people, to make a difference, to win a scholarship to Harvard, to be happy.

'If you go ahead with this, you'll not be welcome in your father's and my house,' her mother said.

'Listen to you! What are you talking about – "your father's and my house"?' Seema shouted. 'The grand delusion. How can you live with such lies? What else are you hiding from me? How hypocritical that you can condone Father's cheating on you and not accept that I have grounds to want to leave my husband.'

'Seema, Seema, listen to me,' her mother said soothingly. 'Do you think that it was easy for me to live with the pain? Many nights I've spent crying in bed. I'm telling you to do what is best for you. Do you want to be rejected by the family and the community? Do you want to be known as the divorced woman? Do you want whispers and gossip to follow you? It's far easier to live with your secret, trust me. Do you know what it means to be divorced? Who will you turn to when your family all reject you? When your religion forsakes you?'

Her mother was right: who would she turn to? She had no one, apart from her family.

Her mother took her silence as acquiescence. 'It's the right thing to do, Seema. I promise you.'

'No,' Seema said eventually. 'No, it's not. The right thing to do is to leave Satesh. The cowardly thing to do is to stay with him. You've disguised it as martyrdom, as duty and devotion, but in fact it's cowardice.'

Seema knew that her words must be hurting her mother, but she didn't care. She was angry at her mother for wanting the same unhappiness for Seema that she herself had had to endure.

'I won't listen to this,' Seema's mother said quietly. 'If you come to your senses you're welcome to speak to me. If not, I will no longer consider you one of our family. And don't bother to speak to your father about this; you know his feelings about divorce.'

She heard her mother put down the telephone.

Seema felt as though she had entered the realm of madness. This was what insanity must feel like, she thought. Nothing made sense to her any more. All the structures that had supported her throughout her life, the foundations upon which all her paradigms had been built, had collapsed in one conversation. Her belief in her parents and in her religion had tumbled down around her as all that she had taken for truth was disproved. Questions circled in her mind, making her dizzy. How could her mother have lied to her? How could her father have behaved so despicably? How could her sacred, precious religion have condoned it? How could her mother want the same misery for her daughter as she herself had lived with for her whole married life?

Seema knew that she could not face Satesh in this state. She had to get out of the flat before he arrived home. She picked up her car keys and ran down to the parking lot, praying that Satesh would not arrive home before she had left. She got into her car and started driving towards the hospital exit. Once she had left the hospital grounds, she took the road that she knew she would not pass Satesh on, the road that led away from town towards the coast.

Seema got to the sea at sunset. She parked her car and walked over the dune that led down to the beach. The sea was frothy with white water and the sand, in the light of the setting sun, was golden-brown. She had half an hour, at most, before it would be dark. She knew that it probably wasn't safe to be alone on the beach at this time of day, but she didn't care. Her life had already fallen apart. There was a cold wind blowing and she welcomed it, glad that she hadn't brought a jersey with her. She wanted the wind to blow through her, to cleanse her completely. As she stood staring at the magnitude of the sea, she imagined that her body didn't exist. She was the wind and she was the water. Her little life, with its small, mundane, human complexities, mattered little on the universal scale. Slowly, as though she were eighty and not twenty-three, she sat down.

24

The day of Seema's wedding was supposed to have been the happiest of her life. At the time she had convinced herself that it was, but now, looking back, she acknowledged that there had been small, seemingly insignificant incidents that had concerned her. It had worried her that her and Satesh's score on the astrological charts had been only eighteen. Eighteen was still an acceptable score, but it was far from the thirty-six Seema had always imagined she and her prospective husband would score. She had pushed the concern from her mind, reminding herself that were the marriage not auspicious, the astrological charts would have given a score of less than eighteen. Also, there had been Satesh's odd behaviour in the days just prior to the wedding. He had disappeared for three nights in a row; he had started arguing with Seema's parents about where he and Seema would stay once they were married; and, two days before the wedding, he had decided out of the blue that he didn't want a long, religious ceremony and that Seema and he should marry in court in order to save money and hassle. It had taken Seema hours to convince him that it was too late to change things at that stage and also that it was important to be married in a temple by a priest. Seema had attributed his change of mind to prenuptial nerves and had managed to convince herself that it implied nothing serious, but she wasn't so sure now that had been the case.

The wedding had been on a Wednesday, because that was the day ordained by the astrological charts. Seema had been dressed in a brilliant red and gold sari that was so full it had taken her mother nearly an hour to get the pleating right. Her arms were covered in an armour of gold bracelets, and gold earrings with red garnets dangled from her ears. She had worn a matching gold and garnet necklace and anklets.

She had waited with her mother and father for Satesh's arrival at the wedding hall. She couldn't help wondering now what her mother had been thinking then. Had she been remembering her own wedding and thinking about how different the reality of her marriage had been relative to her expectations? Her mother had had tears in her eyes and Seema had always presumed they had been tears of pride and happiness. Perhaps they hadn't been.

Once Satesh reached the wedding hall, Seema's mother had welcomed him and his family, who had flown down from Johannesburg for the wedding, with blessings and red turmeric *kumkum* marks. Seema and Satesh had exchanged luscious crimson and white garlands. Then Satesh had been led to the *mandap* and had been seated. Slowly the guests had filtered into the hall to watch the ceremony. Seema had taken her place at Satesh's right, and Satesh had performed *achamana* and *angasparsa*, taking a small sip of water and then touching his limbs with dampened right middle and ring fingers. Seema remembered thinking then that Satesh had beautiful hands with elegantly long fingers, hands fit for a surgeon or a pianist. Now those thin, spidery hands revolted her.

Satesh had been handed a cup of *madhuparka* and, before sipping on the rich blend of honey, curd and ghee, had recited a blessing:

May the breeze be sweet as honey; may the streams flow full of honey and may the herbs and plants be laden with honey for us! May the nights be honey-sweet for us; may the mornings be honey-sweet for us and may the heavens be honey-sweet for us! May the plants be honey-sweet for us; may the sun be all honey for us and may the cows yield us honey-sweet milk!

How many of their days of marriage had proven honey-sweet? Seema could remember few. No, instead of *madhuparka*, Satesh should have sipped on bile.

Satesh's mother, whom Seema had not met before the wedding, and who had struck her at the time as a dominating and imposing matriarch, had given Seema a *mangala sootra*, and her own family had given gifts to Satesh's family. Unconsciously she fingered the necklace that she had worn since that day. It signified her status as a married woman. Would she soon be taking it off, she wondered?

The sacred fire had been lit and Seema remembered that she had looked into the flames while the *Purohit* had recited Sanskrit mantras and she had prayed that her marriage would be as happy as her parents' had been. It seemed a sad mockery now, the worst blessing to have asked for. After exchanging vows, Seema had stepped over a stone that was supposed to represent her willingness and strength to overcome difficulties in the pursuit of her duties. Was she forgetting that now? Was her mother correct: was she being weak when she should be showing strength, forsaking her duties when she should be showing determination? Did her religion expect that of her? Were abuse and rape considered difficulties?

She had led Satesh around the fire three times, and then he had led her around one last time before marking the parting in her hair with red *kumkum* powder. Once he had marked her forehead, Satesh had stood beside her and they had walked seven steps together, reciting a prayer at each step. Of the seven vows, only one had materialised: the prayer for food. Their marriage had not been filled with strength, or prosperity, or wisdom, or friendship, or health, or progeny. One out of seven was a poor rate. Had her mother been thinking, as she watched Seema and Satesh walk the seven steps, about the failures of her own marriage, or had she been silently congratulating herself on having sacrificed her happiness to ensure the realisation of her vows?

She and Satesh had tied a symbolic matrimonial knot, yoking them together by the neck, and then, after having faced the sun and the polar star, they had been blessed as a married couple by the priest and elders. At the time, all the rituals had seemed so purposeful and significant. When they were performed, when Seema participated in them, their meaning had seemed unshakable, but now they had been reduced to childish play actions. Seema couldn't help wondering whether they were any more than simple rituals that had been passed on thoughtlessly from generation to generation. How many mothers watched their children getting married while thinking of their own matrimonial unhappiness?

Seema had imagined that thinking back to her wedding day would weaken her resolve to divorce Satesh but, paradoxically, the memories seemed to have the opposite effect. Thinking back to her wedding day, to the dreams and ideals she had had at the time, made her realise how short her marriage had fallen from what she had imagined. She wondered how her mother lived like that, knowing that she had sacrificed what she really wanted, that she had settled for second best. Seema didn't want that. She didn't want to repeat the cycle, pass it on to the next generation. If she had a daughter, she didn't want to stand at her daughter's wedding grieving the loss of her own dreams.

Seema knew that if she went ahead with the divorce, she would be left alone: her mother did not make idle threats. A divorce would bring shame on Seema's family and disgrace her father in front of his business associates. And because of that Seema would alienate herself from everyone that she loved and from all that was familiar to her. It would not be an easy path to follow, but Seema knew that she could not spend the rest of her life living a lie. She knew that she would go ahead with the divorce.

The sun had almost set. Seema was just about to get up when she sensed a presence behind her. Suddenly alert, she turned around, ready to flee should she have to. But the silhouette of the figure walking towards her was female. She relaxed a bit. She should probably leave anyway; it wasn't safe for her to be alone on the beach. She didn't know what excuse she would give for being late if Satesh was home when she got there. She would deal with it at the time. Now that she had made the decision to get divorced, every-thing seemed suddenly easier. Perhaps it was because now there was a finite end in sight. The figure on the beach came into focus and Seema recognised Rachael. She wondered what she was doing on the beach. Rachael hadn't appeared to recognise Seema.

'Hello,' Seema said, attracting Rachael's attention. Rachael's eyes were swollen, as if she had been crying. Seema wiped her own eyes self-consciously, realising that she probably looked the same.

'Looks like we both came to the beach for the same reason,'

Rachael said, smiling as she sat down beside Seema. Her smile was so open, so inviting, that Seema couldn't help smiling back. She liked Rachael and couldn't imagine what had made her cry. Rachael seemed to live the perfect life.

'Shane broke up with me,' Rachael said, as though in answer to Seema's thoughts. 'Silly that I should be crying, hey? I never expected it would be a long-term relationship; I knew he would eventually break up with me. But here I am, bawling my eyes out like a baby. That's my excuse. What's yours?'

Seema had no intention of telling anyone of her decision to get divorced, but Rachael's question was asked with such disarming good-heartedness that Seema found herself wanting to tell her everything. All at once she needed to talk, needed to let out all that she had kept secret for so long. She told Rachael about the abuse and about the phone call to her mother, about her father's philandering and about the implications that going through with a divorce would have on her life. Her story tumbled out so quickly that Seema felt as though she hardly had the time to take a breath between sentences.

Rachael was silent for a moment after Seema eventually finished speaking and Seema wondered whether she should have been more discreet. Perhaps she shouldn't have told Rachael everything. Rachael probably thought she was crazy, a real weirdo with a completely dysfunctional family. She had put Rachael into an awkward situation; they were little more than strangers, after all.

'I'm sorry I unloaded all this on you,' Seema said apologetically.

Rachael put her index finger to her lips, indicating to Seema to be quiet, and leant over to give her a hug. It was the second time Seema had been hugged by a relative stranger that day and she was surprised by how comforting it felt. She wasn't used to being hugged.

'Well,' Rachael said, 'you've certainly put my issues into perspective. I can guarantee you I'll be wasting no more tears on Shane. Where are you going to stay tonight?'

'What do you mean?' Seema asked, confused. She hadn't planned on leaving Satesh that very evening.

'You can't go back. Tonight might be the night he really goes after you. Besides, I'm scared that if you go back he'll break down your resolve and you'll end up staying with him. And what if your mother's already told Satesh? Imagine what he'll do to you then.'

Seema hadn't thought of that. If her mother had been stupid or cruel enough to tell Satesh of her intentions, he would probably lock her into the flat forever. Or worse.

'I've got a spare bed. It's not great – it's the one that came with the prefab – but you're welcome to use it,' Rachael offered. 'Your husband doesn't even need to know you're staying with me.'

'But Satesh will worry about me if I don't pitch up at home,' Seema argued. Everything was moving a bit too fast for her.

'You can write him a letter. I'll slip it under his door.'

Seema tried to argue with Rachael, giving her all the reasons why tonight would not be a good night to leave her husband: she didn't have clothes or a toothbrush; she needed to think about things a bit more; she needed to explain everything to Satesh; she had to get all her documents and personal belongings together. But Rachael seemed to have an unnervingly simple solution for every one of her objections.

'I've got a spare, unopened toothbrush for you. I always keep one, just in case I get lucky,' Rachael said. 'And you can use some of my clothes. You're smaller than me, but I'm sure we can make a plan. You can't go back or you won't ever leave.'

Seema remembered Dr Ribbentrop's prophetic words about the abused woman they had seen together: *They never leave.* Rachael was right. It had to be now.

'Thanks,' Seema said. 'Thanks so much. I'll repay you for everything, I promise.'

'No need,' Rachael said. 'That's what friends are for.' She took Seema's hand and started pulling her towards her car. 'We should probably get going,' she said.

Only then did Seema notice that it had become dark. Seema followed Rachael along the path that led back to the car park. Perhaps she wasn't quite as alone as she had thought. Rachael had called her a friend.

Nomsa

25

Nomsa had spent the past three days, the three days since she had heard about her mother's death, in a strange, dream-like state. Most of the time she had functioned on automatic, her body performing its daily functions with little input from her mind. She had followed her usual routine: put on her make-up as she did every morning; made herself a cup of sweet coffee for breakfast; gone to the hospital and seen patients; assisted in theatre. At those times it was almost as if she had forgotten about her mother's passing on, as though it had never happened.

Occasionally, however, when she was alone in her prefab with nothing to distract her, cracks had appeared and she had spewed anger around her. She was like a rumbling volcano, waiting to erupt. She found it strange that she wasn't sad, that since the evening she had heard the news she had been unable to cry. All she had felt, between the periods of numbness, was a fiery rage. She was angry at her mother for being careless, for picking up a preventable disease; she was cross with the dead prison warder who had passed the fatal virus on to her mother; and she was angry at the community that had condoned her mother's behaviour and, through that, had allowed her mother's death. The anger, when it overcame her, seemed to consume her. It made her feel alive – the only times she had felt alive in the previous three days. It burnt her body, so that she checked her temperature over and over again, convinced that she was pyrexial, and it filled her legs with a restlessness that drove them to keep on moving. She tried taking sleeping tablets to calm herself down, but they made her feel dead again and she preferred the anger to the numbness.

That evening, Noluthando, her sister, phoned her:

Noluthando: The funeral is going to be three days from today.

Nomsa: On Saturday?

Noluthando: Yes. Ma didn't have a funeral policy. We need money for the funeral.

Nomsa: What a surprise. How much do you need?

Noluthando: Four thousand.

Nomsa: I'll send the money postal order today.

Noluthando: You can bring it when you come.

Nomsa: I'll send the money. I can't make it to the funeral. I have to work.

Noluthando (*loud wail*): How can you not come to our mother's funeral?

Nomsa: Someone has to work. You've just asked me for money; I have to work to earn that money. You think money falls into my hands just because I'm a doctor? I still have to work for it.

Noluthando: But can you not work another day? It will show our mother and our ancestors great disrespect if you do not come to our mother's funeral. It will make them very unhappy, Nomsa. It will bring great misfortune on us.

Nomsa: Oh, stop this nonsense about misfortune and bad luck. You create your own misfortune. Do you think our mother died by accident? No, she died because she was too stupid to use protection.

Noluthando: How can you talk like this, Nomsa? What is wrong with you?

Nomsa: I'll send the four thousand today. In my books that's showing more respect than anyone else. Goodbye.

Nomsa's phone rang again the next morning. This time it was not her sister calling her; it was Mrs Watson. Nomsa rejected the call. Mrs Watson must have heard about her mother's death (Nomsa prayed she hadn't heard what the cause of death was) and was probably phoning to pass on her condolences. Nomsa didn't want to have to deal with the questions and polite sympathy. Mrs Watson called again later, and again Nomsa ignored the call, but when she phoned the third time, Nomsa knew that she could not put off taking the call any longer.

'Nomsa,' Mrs Watson said when Nomsa eventually answered, 'I'm so glad to reach you. I was worried about you. You didn't call on Sunday.'

Nomsa realised that in the shock of hearing about her mother's death, she had forgotten to make her usual weekly call to Mrs Watson. She immediately felt guilty. She knew how much her phone calls meant to Mrs Watson. Perhaps that was why Mrs Watson was calling; perhaps she hadn't even heard about Nomsa's mother's death. Nomsa felt her spirits lift. She decided she would wait to see what Mrs Watson knew. She wouldn't bring up the topic of her mother's death.

'I'm so sorry, Mrs Watson,' Nomsa said, trying to make her voice sound relaxed and cheerful, as normal as possible. 'I was working and completely forgot to call you.'

'Well, I hope you're not working too hard. I've seen on *Carte Blanche* how hard they make you doctors work, and under what terrible conditions. I hope you're looking after yourself. Are you eating enough?'

'Yes, I am,' Nomsa reassured Mrs Watson. 'And I don't mind working hard. I'm learning so much.'

'You always were such a diligent girl, Nomsa. Your mother must be very proud of you. How is she, your mother? I've been thinking about her so much this past week, for some reason. I keep meaning to phone her. Is she keeping well?'

Nomsa didn't know what to say. It was almost worse than if Mrs Watson had heard about her mother's death from someone else. She wanted to lie to Mrs Watson and tell her that her mother was fine, but the words wouldn't form in her mouth. She pictured Mrs Watson's frail body scooped up in her wheelchair, her short grey hair neatly combed to one side, her make-up still so conscientiously applied. She imagined Mrs Watson's alert blue eyes looking at her from beneath heavy lids, her soft mouth turned up expectantly, hopefully, as it always was. Nomsa couldn't lie to her.

'My mother ...' Nomsa hesitated. She didn't know how to say it, what words to use. 'My mother ...,' she tried again. Should she use a medical term? Would that make it easier? *My mother has suf-*

fered a cardiac arrest secondary to multi-organ failure. Or should she be blunt? *My mother is dead.* Or should she use a euphemism, as the doctor who had given her the news had? *My mother has passed away.*

Eventually the words found their own way out. '*Umama wam akasekho emhlabeni,*' Nomsa said softly.

'I beg your pardon?' Mrs Watson asked. She didn't understand Xhosa.

'My mother's dead,' Nomsa interpreted. It seemed easier to say it now, once it had been said in Xhosa.

'My dear, dear girl,' Mrs Watson said. 'I'm so sorry. No wonder you didn't phone me on Sunday. Can I do anything to help? You must be feeling devastated.'

Mrs Watson's words seemed to have released something in Nomsa. Or perhaps it had been her own words. Whatever it was, Nomsa found she could no longer summon up her anger. She searched for it, in order to contain the tears that were now threatening a flood, but it had dissipated completely.

'I'm so sorry, Nomsa,' Mrs Watson continued. 'Your poor mother. And she was so young.'

Nomsa waited for Mrs Watson to ask her how her mother had died, but she didn't. Nomsa was glad; she didn't want Mrs Watson to think any less of her mother. Then Nomsa heard something that she had never heard before: Mrs Watson crying. It rattled her, made her unashamed of her own tears. In all the years she had known Mrs Watson, she had never heard her cry. She hadn't even heard her cry after she had come home from the hospital in a wheelchair, after the accident that had killed her husband and left her paralysed from the waist down.

'Have you had the funeral?' Mrs Watson asked.

'No,' Nomsa said. 'It's on Saturday.' And as she said the words, she knew that she would go to Aliwal North to be present with her family at the funeral.

'Your mother was a good woman, Nomsa,' Mrs Watson said reflectively. 'And a good mother. She loved you more than I think you ever realised.' And Nomsa knew that Mrs Watson was thinking back to Nomsa's graduation when she said that. Nomsa had been too embarrassed to invite her mother to her graduation, too worried that she would start ululating or dancing or making a fuss. She had chosen, instead, to invite the woman who had sponsored her studies, for whom her mother had worked as a domestic servant; the woman who, even in a wheelchair, fitted in with the profile of the other parents.

'She was proud of you, so very, very proud of you,' Mrs Watson continued, and Nomsa knew she was right. Her mother had been proud of her, painfully proud of her. She realised now how hurt her mother must have been that she had not been invited to Nomsa's graduation, how she would have loved to see her daughter qualify as a doctor. Nomsa had been embarrassed about her mother's pride because it exposed the poverty of her background. In the families of her friends, her privileged white friends and her BEE black friends, it was an achievement to graduate from medical school, but at least it was conceivable. To her mother it had been something beyond her wildest imaginings.

'Could I send you some money to contribute to the funeral?' Mrs Watson asked, bringing Nomsa back to the present. 'I'd like to do that for your mother.'

'Sure,' Nomsa said. 'Thank you.'

Mrs Watson put down the telephone and Nomsa collapsed into a heap of sorrow. No vessel would have been large enough to contain her grief.

Nomsa packed a bag with some clothes and toiletries before going to the hospital for her call. She wanted to be able to leave for Aliwal North as soon as she had finished her shift. She had phoned Rachael the previous day, after getting off the phone with Mrs Watson, and had organised to swap a shift with her so that she would be able to drive to Aliwal North on Friday and attend the funeral on Saturday.

There were three patients waiting for Nomsa when she arrived in casualty. She was glad she was working because she knew the activity would keep her mind occupied. Unfortunately, the first patient she saw did not distract her from thinking about her mother. Judith Motala was a forty-five-year-old woman who presented with

271

a painful rash on her side. Nomsa recognised it immediately: it was shingles. Warning bells went off in her head. In otherwise well, relatively young adults, shingles was one of the signs of compromised immunity. Nomsa asked the patient if she had had an HIV test.

The woman looked at her guardedly. 'No,' she said, after a moment.

Nomsa examined the woman thoroughly. She had all the markers of AIDS: swollen lymph nodes all over her body; oral and oesophageal candida; an itchy rash on her trunk and limbs; the deep purple growths of Kaposi's sarcoma; chronic diarrhoea; and weight loss.

'You need to have an HIV test,' Nomsa told the woman as gently as she could. 'We need to make sure that you don't have the disease. If you do, the sooner we can start you on treatment, the better.' Nomsa knew the woman would be eligible for anti-retrovirals, as she could see clinically that the patient's CD4 count was less than two hundred.

'But I can't have HIV,' the woman said. 'My husband was killed twenty years ago and after then I have only had one boyfriend. I know that people who sleep around get HIV. I don't sleep around. I have only ever made sex with my husband and with my boyfriend.'

Nomsa struggled to keep her emotions in check. Was this what her mother had believed? Had her mother trusted her prison warder in the way that this woman obviously trusted her boyfriend? Nomsa's mother had never been happily married. Perhaps she had hoped to marry this last boyfriend of hers, the one who ended up killing her. Had she been lonely, looking for companionship now that her children had grown up? Had she been trying to find someone to grow old with? The questions whirred through Nomsa's head. She felt ashamed and heartbroken that she had never discussed these things with her mother. Were they not the types of issues that mothers and daughters discussed? She had never seen her mother as a woman in her own right, with her own feelings and emotions and dreams and desires. Nomsa had seen her mother only in relation to herself and to her own needs and disappointments. She had not known the individual who had been her mother and now it was too late. She had been a terrible daughter, a selfish, self-consumed, arrogant and pretentious daughter. She would live with guilt as close to her as her shadow for the rest of her life.

Nomsa realised that she had forgotten about her patient and drew her thoughts back to the present. 'Is your boyfriend well?' she asked the woman in front of her. She would treat this patient, and every patient that she saw with HIV from now on, with the respect and tenderness that she never gave to her mother. She hoped that her mother would look down on her actions and see that she had some remorse and had learnt from her mistakes.

'He's not too sick,' the woman responded. But Nomsa thought that the woman was lying. Something in her demeanour had changed. Nomsa could see that the woman was realising, for the first time, that HIV could be a possibility. Was this the way that her mother had found out, Nomsa couldn't help wondering?

'Does your boyfriend have any other girlfriends? Is he married?' Nomsa asked gently. She was asking not to pass judgement, but because she wanted to reveal to the woman in front of her, as tenderly as possible, that it was not only her own fidelity that ensured against HIV.

'He's married,' the woman said, dropping her head into her cupped hands. 'He has two wives.'

Nomsa could see that the woman understood the implications of her answer. She sat quietly, waiting for her to come to terms with the realisation. For once she didn't look at her watch, didn't think about the other patients that were waiting, didn't rush the consult so that she could move on to her next patient. She let the woman take as long as she needed.

'Do you think I need a test?' the woman asked eventually.

Nomsa nodded. 'Yes,' she said, 'because if we test you and we find out that you have HIV, we can start you on treatment as soon as possible.'

Nomsa spent the following fifteen minutes counselling the patient about HIV. She reiterated, again and again, the role of anti-retrovirals and their importance. Nomsa explained to her patient all the things she should have told her mother. As the woman in front of her stuck her arm out for Nomsa to draw blood for the HIV test, Nomsa couldn't help wondering if anyone had counselled her mother this thoroughly. It was unlikely. Three days ago Nomsa would never have spent more than three minutes counselling a patient about HIV. She would have drawn the blood for the test and then told the patient to go to the clinic for the result and for further HIV counselling, knowing that the clinic was understaffed and disorganised and that patients seldom actually received any information. Three days ago she would have defended her actions by claiming that it wasn't the doctor's job to sit and counsel patients; that she had more important things to do; that the patient was going to die in the near future anyway. Her behaviour in the past was not defensible and she knew that she would never make the same mistakes again, but she also knew that the changes she vowed to make were going to be difficult.

Nomsa bumped into Rachael in the doctors' office after her call. She was making herself a post-call cup of coffee and Rachael was making herself a pre-call one, so they sat and drank their cups of sugary instant coffee together.

'Thanks so much for agreeing to swap shifts with me,' Nomsa said to Rachael. 'I've got an emergency at home in Aliwal North that I have to go back for. I really appreciate it.'

'It's no problem at all,' Rachael said. 'I didn't realise you were from Aliwal North. I always thought you were from Cape Town. Where is Aliwal North anyway?'

'It's in the Eastern Cape,' Nomsa said. 'My family's from Aliwal North; I spent my early childhood there. I moved to Cape Town when I went to high school.'

It was the first time in a very long time that Nomsa had told anyone that she came from Aliwal North and she couldn't help feeling uncomfortable revealing the information. It made her seem exposed and vulnerable. When she had been asked before where she was from, she had always said that she was from Cape Town. But no longer. She had decided that she wouldn't hide her background any more. She had learnt a painful lesson and she didn't want to have

274

to learn it again. In some ways it was similar to getting pus on one's face, she thought. What surprised her the most, though, was that Rachael didn't seem at all perturbed by the news that Nomsa had grown up in Aliwal North and not in Cape Town. Rachael didn't flinch at the information. She didn't squirm in embarrassment or tell Nomsa that she had to rush off or look at Nomsa with pity in her eyes. In fact, she appeared so untouched by the information that Nomsa wondered if Rachael had heard her properly. Nomsa was hit by another wave of remorse. She had spent so many years, wasted so much time and effort, and hurt so many people in the process of creating an alternative background for herself, and now it seemed that it had all been in vain. It had been exactly for people like Rachael that she had made everything up to impress. She felt so disconsolate; it had all been such a waste.

Rachael obviously mistook the emotion in her face for exhaustion. 'Long call?' she asked sympathetically.

Nomsa nodded and got up to put her coffee mug in the basin.

'I can see you're tired but, before you rush off, do you mind if I run something by you? I promise I won't take long,' Rachael asked.

'Sure,' Nomsa said, sitting down again. She would welcome any distraction now.

'Well, actually, it's more to coerce you into something than run something by you,' Rachael confessed.

'Another paediatric ward makeover?' Nomsa smiled.

'Caught out! Almost, but not quite,' Rachael said. 'Actually, it's on a much bigger scale. I'm good at organising things and at getting people to do things …'

'So I've noticed,' Nomsa interrupted.

Rachael laughed. 'And I've got loads of business contacts through my dad. I want to get sponsorship to set up an HIV testing and counselling centre at the hospital. An NGO. Something that works and is functional and that makes a difference in people's lives. Would you be willing to help me? I'd organise all the funding and the admin stuff, but I'd need doctors to train up the nurses and the counselling staff. I know I'm probably being totally ambitious and dreaming the impossible dream, but I'm sure we can pull this off if a few of us put some effort in.'

'Of course I'd help,' Nomsa said. It couldn't be coincidence. This was fate. This was her chance to make amends, to right the mistakes that she had made. This was her mother, stretching out her arm from the realm of her ancestors and offering Nomsa her hand in peace and forgiveness.

Rachael looked shocked. 'Just like that?' she asked. 'You aren't going to tell me I'm crazy and that it will never work and that you don't have the time? You're not going to tell me I'm an idealist and that I'll never get sponsorship and that the government will never allow it?'

'Is that what other doctors have said?' Nomsa asked, guessing that Rachael was speaking from experience.

Rachael nodded.

'My mother has just died of HIV,' Nomsa said. 'I'll do whatever I can to stop it from spreading further.'

Nomsa waited to see what Rachael's reaction would be, waited for the pity or the disgust. She looked into Rachael's eyes, challenging her to hide the racism and the bigotry. But all she saw in Rachael's eyes was sympathy.

'I'm so sorry,' Rachael said, getting up and putting her arms around Nomsa. 'Is that why you're going home?'

Nomsa nodded. She couldn't talk. If only Rachael had rejected her. Now everything, all the pain that she had caused her mother, had been for nothing.

Rachael

26

The form arrived in a bureaucratic-looking brown envelope. Rachael knew that it contained the application form for the following year's community service postings because of the slightly smudged 'Department of Health' stamp on the reverse side of the envelope. Although she collected the post from her box in the morning, she waited until the evening, until after she had finished work, to fill in the form. She had been toying with the idea of staying at Prince Xoliswe Hospital for her community service for the past two months, but completing the form would take the decision from the level of contemplation to that of action, a progression with an inherent irreversibility. She didn't know if she was ready for that finality yet.

Until recently, Rachael had always presumed that she would do her community service at a less rural hospital than Prince Xoliswe (at least one at which the accommodation was not dependent on borehole water). The application process allowed doctors to choose five potential hospitals in which they would be prepared to do their community service. The chance of obtaining a post at one's hospital of choice was very likely if the hospital was rural (so Rachael was almost guaranteed a place at Prince Xoliswe Hospital if she made it her first choice) and very unlikely if one's hospital of choice was a popular tertiary or academic hospital such as Groote Schuur. At the beginning of the year, Rachael had thought she would apply for posts at smaller, urban hospitals so that she had a realistic chance of getting the post while still being able to live near a large town (preferably Cape Town). Now she was not so sure she wanted to go back to an urban setting, especially if it was Cape Town.

Rachael made herself a microwave baked potato topped with melted cheese for dinner, then sat down on the couch with her plate of food and the unopened envelope. Slowly, she lifted the gummed-down flap and removed the application form. It had been folded in half. She unfolded the form and read the top page, which turned out to be little more than a request for personal details. The following five pages were the important ones. They contained the lists of hospitals that had posts available for community service doctors. They were divided according to provinces. Rachael flipped the pages over until she got to KwaZulu-Natal and ran her finger down the alphabetically arranged list of hospitals. There it was: Prince Xoliswe Hospital. She needed to decide whether to tick the little box next to the hospital or not. She looked at some of the other hospitals that were available. There were big tertiary hospitals, like Chris Hani Baragwanath in Johannesburg and Tygerberg Hospital in the Western Cape, and then there were the smaller but still urban hospitals like Addington in Durban, Helen Joseph in Johannesburg and Somerset Hospital in Cape Town. It was tempting to tick one of those boxes as her first choice.

The form had to be completed only by the following week, but Rachael knew that putting off the choice would not make it any easier. This evening was as good a time as any to determine her future and, if she made the decision now, at least it wouldn't be weighing on her for the next week. She reminded herself that the decision was not something that she would be stuck with for the rest of her life. Community service was only one year long, so if she made the wrong choice of hospital, she would have to survive only one year. When she first moved to Tugela Bridge, a year had stretched out before her interminably. But the day-to-day experiences and frustrations of all that she was learning at the hospital, the distraction of her relationship with Shane, the new friendships she had made and the challenges of living independently had eaten up the time so quickly that Rachael found it hard to believe that three-quarters of the year had already passed. She briefly considered phoning her mother for her advice but then decided against it. She knew what her mother would say: get out of the country as quickly as possible, while you still have the chance; spend next year in a hospital in the UK or in Israel, anywhere but in South Africa; maybe you'll meet a nice husband and settle down overseas. No, the decision had to be hers alone. For that reason, she was glad in some ways that she and Shane had broken up. Now even he couldn't influence her choice.

Rachael's thoughts were interrupted by Seema's arrival back from the hospital. She greeted Rachael as she put her bag down. The lounge-cum-kitchen of Rachael's prefab had been Seema's temporary home for the past few days. Rachael had enjoyed sharing the prefab with someone else, especially since Shane no longer spent most of his time there, and Seema had hardly proved a difficult house guest. Seema's husband didn't seem to have realised that she was staying with Rachael or, if he did, he had decided to do nothing about it. Seema had written him a letter, which Rachael had placed beneath the door of Seema's flat, telling him that she needed some time alone to think about the future, that he should not worry about her because she was staying with a friend, and that she would contact him when she was ready (Rachael had helped Seema word the letter assertively). Satesh appeared to accept the ultimatum because he hadn't come knocking on all the prefab doors looking for Seema. Although Rachael was not afraid of him, Seema was visibly petrified. Rachael couldn't help noticing that Seema got twitchy as soon as she walked out of the prefab door, looking around her repeatedly as though to make sure that her husband was not watching her. And she never walked to or from the hospital alone; she always waited for either Rachael or Nomsa to walk with her. Seema was living with an inordinate amount of fear and, although she had mentioned to Rachael some of the atrocities that her husband had forced on her, Rachael knew that there were more that Seema hadn't told her about.

Seema walked over to Rachael and Rachael pointed at the pieces of paper in front of her. 'I've got the community service application form for next year,' she said. 'Have you decided where you're going to apply for yet?'

Seema looked at Rachael hesitantly. 'No, not really,' she said. 'Well, actually, that's not entirely true. I've applied for a scholarship to Harvard. Obviously the chances are really small that I'll get it, but I thought I'd try anyway.'

'Oh, wow!' Rachael exclaimed. She was surprised, not because she doubted Seema's abilities (Seema was by far the strongest intern both academically and practically and often knew more than even the senior doctors), but because Rachael couldn't imagine Seema having the guts to apply for an overseas scholarship, or to leave her family and all she was familiar with if she was to be awarded it.

'I know what you're thinking,' Seema said, and Rachael realised that an element of her thoughts must have been reflected on her face.

'I know my chances of getting the scholarship are slim,' Seema continued, 'but I thought there was no harm in trying. I didn't intend to tell anyone, but when you asked I couldn't lie to you.'

'No,' Rachael objected, 'I wasn't thinking that at all. I was wondering how you would feel about leaving your family for some place so foreign. I've got no doubt in my mind that you're the best candidate for the scholarship.'

Seema looked down before answering. Rachael noticed that she was playing with the delicate silver band on her ring finger. 'In some ways it would be better if I left,' Seema said. 'My family won't take me back once they realise that I'm serious about the divorce. Our religion doesn't accept divorce readily, so what I'm doing will bring great disgrace and shame on my family.' She paused. 'Besides, I'd like as much distance as possible between Satesh and me once the divorce goes through. You don't know what that man's capable of,' she added, with a rare note of bitterness.

Rachael nodded in understanding. 'I'll hold thumbs you get the scholarship then,' she said. She could see that what they were talking about was not easy for Seema, and that thinking about her family and her husband was making her upset, so Rachael steered the topic of conversation back to where it had started. 'You should probably fill in the application form for next year anyway, though, just in case you don't get the scholarship,' she suggested.

'Of course. I haven't had time to think about it much because of all that's been going on. And you? Have you decided where you want to go yet? I know you mentioned before that you were thinking of staying on here. Are you still considering it or are you going to go back to your family in Cape Town?'

'I'm definitely still contemplating staying here,' Rachael responded. 'There's a lot more for me to learn at Prince Xoliswe and, all in all, I've had a good year here.'

As Rachael said the words, she realised that they were true. She *had* had a good year in Tugela Bridge. She thought back to the girl who had arrived at Prince Xoliswe Hospital ten months ago, a girl who was very different from the woman Rachael believed she was now. The girl who had come to Tugela Bridge had been embarrassingly naive and innocent, not in a romantic or idealistic sense, but in a protected, ignorant way. She hadn't had a clue about the reality of what was going on in the country in which she was living. She had believed that financial hardship was not being able to afford one's own car and had not realised that some people didn't even have the money to pay the taxi fare to the hospital to visit their dying child. She had not understood that, for some South Africans, once their wallet was empty they had no more money: that was the end of the month, the end of the line. Rachael cringed when she remembered the temper tantrum she had thrown at the beginning of the year when she found out she would have to pump her own water. Now she threw temper tantrums when a seven-year-old rape victim was visited by the perpetrator of the crime. She wondered how she could have found the life that she was leading prior to her arrival at Tugela Bridge meaningful. Perhaps she hadn't. Perhaps that was why she had suffered from anxiety attacks, and searched for meaning in expensive yoga classes and psychology sessions, and spent hours creating an image of the person that she believed those closest to her wanted her to be. At Tugela Bridge, she had discovered who she wanted to be. Most importantly, she had learnt the value of making a difference in other people's lives – that this gave one a sense of self-value and self-worth that outshone anything of material value. Yes, it had been a good year. She ticked the box next to Prince Xoliswe Hospital.

Later, after finishing her hospital shift, Rachael went to the doctors' office. She had agreed to meet Seema there so that Seema would not have to walk back to the prefab alone. She had just finished making herself a cup of coffee when Nathan and Eliza Engelbrecht rushed into the doctors' office.

'Where's everyone else?' Eliza asked breathlessly. 'Come, you have to see this.'

'What?' Rachael asked.

'Just come, quickly,' Nathan said urgently. 'You'll see when we get there.'

Rachael had never seen him so animated before. She followed Nathan and Eliza into casualty, where she saw Nomsa and two of the other doctors peering out of one of the windows.

'Dr Zamla's decided to pay us one of his rare visits,' Nathan said excitedly.

Seema walked into casualty and Nathan dragged her, along with Rachael, to an unoccupied window. Because of the horseshoe shape of the hospital building, casualty looked on to the hospital entrance. Parked in the parking lot, directly in front of the hospital door, was a shiny black Mercedes with the most darkly tinted windows Rachael had ever seen. As the doctors watched, Mrs Hlope emerged from the hospital sliding doors. This in itself was odd because she rarely crossed the divide between the clean luxury of the administration building and the smelly grittiness of the hospital. She seemed to be encrusted in diamonds; her rings, earrings and necklace – even her supersize sunglasses – sparkled in the sun. Behind her walked the elusive Dr Zamla. He was a tall, broad man with a completely shaved head. He wore a black pinstriped suit and also sported large sunglasses. After reaching the car, he leant over and hugged Mrs Hlope before slipping into the back seat. He had a chauffeur! Mrs Hlope waved enthusiastically as the vehicle glided quietly from the hospital parking lot, then heaved herself back to the security of the administration block.

As the doctors dispersed back to their various posts, Rachael couldn't help wondering again how the situation with Dr Zamla could be condoned. He was earning a senior medical officer's salary from the government, a full salary with overtime and a rural allowance, and yet only made a yearly appearance at the hospital. In effect, Rachael was working to pay off his expensive car and driver. She was filled with so much disgust she wanted to spit. It was that kind of greed and corruption that threatened to undo South Africa.

'Are you still planning on setting up that HIV centre?' Seema asked Rachael as they sat down for dinner. One of the distinct advantages of having Seema staying with her was that Seema enjoyed cooking. Rachael had all but ditched her diet of ready-made meals. Somehow Seema was able to rustle up a delicious curry out of one onion and a tin of tomatoes.

'Yes, absolutely,' Rachael confirmed, lifting a mouthful of yet another mouth-watering meal to her lips. 'In fact, I'm glad you reminded me about it. I've written a template letter requesting sponsorship. I just need to speak to my dad and get some numbers and contact details from him. I'll phone him after supper.'

As soon as she had finished eating, Rachael phoned her parents. Gloria-Jean answered and Rachael made herself comfortable on the couch. She knew that she would have to spend at least thirty minutes talking to her mother before she would be able to ask to speak to her father. Gloria-Jean rambled on about some changes that were being made to the mall parking lot and Rachael examined her feet. They really were in a terrible condition. Her nails looked awful. She decided she would book a pedicure for the next time she drove to Durban. And she might as well book for a manicure, if she was making the rare effort to get to a beauty salon. She kept her nails short now, for obvious reasons, but her hands could do with some pampering.

'So, aren't you going to thank me?' Gloria-Jean asked, interrupting Rachael's salon planning.

Rachael didn't have a clue what her mother was talking about.

'Or do you still have those ridiculous ideas about staying in South Africa?' Gloria-Jean continued.

'Well, I had thought …,' Rachael began, but she was interrupted almost immediately by her mother.

'This is an opportunity you can't miss, my girl. It only happens once. It isn't just coincidence that I bumped into Lauren Greenblatt. She was only here for three days. What are the chances of that happening? I'm telling you, it was fate.'

Rachael's ears had pricked up at the mention of Mrs Greenblatt. Mrs Greenblatt was Daniel's mother – Daniel, her childhood crush. She wished she'd been listening to what her mother had been saying.

'And Donny Greenblatt has gone to so much trouble to organise the post for you,' Gloria-Jean continued. 'You'll be working at the same hospital as him, you know.'

Gloria-Jean was obviously talking about Rachael's placement for next year. Rachael thought about the application form she had filled in the previous evening. As tempting as being close to Daniel Greenblatt sounded, she had made her decision. She told her mother that she had applied to stay on at Tugela Bridge for a further year.

'Are you crazy? What's wrong with you? Is there some boy you've gone and fallen in love with who's keeping you there?' Gloria-Jean asked.

Rachael couldn't help smiling to herself. She was glad she wasn't making her decision based on Shane.

'Norman, our daughter's gone mad,' Rachael heard her mother shout to her father. Gloria-Jean spoke into the phone again. 'I just can't believe you're being so ungrateful,' she said, 'after all we've done for you. We've only ever wanted the best for you, you know.'

'I appreciate that, Mom,' Rachael said, 'but I believe that the best for me in this case would be to stay here for another year.' She tried to explain to her mother her reasons for wanting to stay at Tugela Bridge, but her mother was too angry to listen to what she was saying. Rachael could hear that Gloria-Jean had already convinced herself that Rachael would take up the post in the UK (and, hopefully, marry Daniel Greenblatt) and her disappointment in Rachael's response was making her angry. Hysterical and in tears, Gloria-Jean eventually handed the phone to Rachael's dad.

Rachael didn't even bother trying to justify to her father her decision to stay but instead starting explaining her idea of the HIV centre. She asked him if he would give her the contact details of any business associates who might consider sponsorship.

'You don't understand how this world works, my girl,' Rachael's father said, almost sadly. 'Why would they want to donate money to some far-away Africans who are dying from AIDS and who have no relevance to their lives whatsoever? No, you need to set up a nice clean charity, something like a fund for kids with cancer, something that looks good. They'll donate to that. Or to something that'll bring them lots of exposure. Exposure is free advertising. But I don't expect your little project will get much coverage.'

'And what's this bullshit I hear about your not wanting to go overseas next year?' he continued. 'You've had your year of fun playing doctor-doctor in Africa. It's time to wake up to the real world. You've got to start considering your future.'

Rachael was too outraged initially to know how to respond to her father's comments. What did he mean by 'playing doctor-doctor'? Did he have no idea of what she did, of what her life and her work entailed? And what did he know about the real world? He lived in a comfortable house with sea views, a security system and an electric fence. He drove to work in an expensive four-by-four, worked all day in the comfort of an air-conditioned office without once getting his hands dirty and then came home to a whisky, dinner and a willing wife. No, that wasn't the real world. What she experienced – what she came into contact with through each patient she saw – *that* was the real world.

'I don't need your help,' she said eventually. 'I'll manage to get sponsorship on my own. There are people out there who aren't as cynical as you. And I'm staying here. I'll play doctor-doctor for a bit longer in my fantasy world.' She slammed the phone down and vowed she wouldn't speak to her parents again until they apologised to her. The thought crossed her mind that people like her parents were probably as bad for South Africa as the Dr Zamlas were.

Seema

27

Dr Ribbentrop handed Seema the empty, washed ice-cream container as she walked into the doctors' office.

'Thanks, I think it was the best curry I've ever tasted,' he said as he handed it over. 'Sorry it's taken so long for me to bring the box back. I kept on forgetting.'

'No problem,' Seema said. 'I wasn't expecting the container back anyway.'

Seema was on call with Dr Ribbentrop for the evening. She wished she had checked the call roster before coming to work. If she had known she would be working with him, she would have worn something different, asked Rachael for something more conservative. The outfit she had on, which belonged to Rachael, was not something she would ever have chosen to wear, especially to work. She looked down at herself self-consciously. Rachael had assured her that she looked stunning in the tight leggings and low-cut knit top, but she felt suddenly awkward and underdressed. In her mind, these clothes did not qualify as suitable work clothes and she didn't want Dr Ribbentrop to think she didn't take her work seriously. Luckily he didn't seem to notice or, if he did, he was too polite to comment on her attire. Instead, he turned back to the paper he had been writing on when Seema arrived.

'I'll be with you in a moment,' he said to Seema. 'I just have to complete this application form. It needs to be in by tomorrow. I only found out about the job this afternoon, so I'm pushing things a bit.'

'Are you leaving?' Seema asked, horrified. She knew that it was impolite of her to ask, that it was none of her business, but the words were out before she had time to think about what she was saying. She couldn't imagine Prince Xoliswe Hospital without Dr Ribbentrop. He couldn't be taking a job somewhere else!

'No, no,' Dr Ribbentrop chuckled. 'The powers that be will have to work a bit harder at making my life hell before they manage to chase me away. I'm applying for a principal medical officer post that the government has at long last decided to open up at the hospital. It's about bloody time. Apparently it was advertised, but I never saw the advert in the papers. It was purely by chance that I went to fight with Mrs Hlope about something this afternoon and saw the advertisement lying on her desk.'

'I'm surprised she didn't let you know about the post,' Seema said. She could think of no one who deserved the post more than Dr Ribbentrop, except perhaps Dr Chetty. Seema wondered if she too was applying.

'Mrs Hlope and I don't have the best relationship in the world,' Dr Ribbentrop said bluntly. 'I think I'm probably the proverbial thorn in her foot.'

Seema didn't know how to respond. She wasn't used to talking to Dr Ribbentrop on so personal a level. She decided just to answer honestly. 'You may be a thorn in her foot but you're one of the biggest reasons this hospital keeps functioning,' she said earnestly. 'I don't think this place would actually survive without you and Dr Chetty. If it's worth anything, I think you deserve the job.'

'Thanks,' Dr Ribbentrop said, smiling a rare smile. 'You'd better get to casualty before my head gets any bigger.'

Seema walked to casualty thinking about Dr Ribbentrop. He would be perfect for the job of principal medical officer, she thought. He was both a good leader and a good doctor and he knew the ins and outs of the hospital like nobody else. Besides, he didn't seem to get all caught up in the politics of running the hospital. Seema was sure he would get the job; he was the obvious choice.

By eleven o'clock the mad rush of the evening was over and casualty seemed to have quietened down. Seema went to the pile of folders to call in her next patient, but Dr Ribbentrop stopped her just as she was about to pick up the top folder.

'Go have a cup of tea and grab a bite to eat,' he said to her. 'It's not that busy. I'll see these last few patients and then we can swap: you can hold the fort here and I'll make myself something to drink.'

'Are you sure?' Seema asked. The idea of a cup of tea was certainly tempting, but she didn't want Dr Ribbentrop to feel he had to treat her differently because she had fainted on a previous call. 'I'm not going to pass out again, I promise,' she reassured him. 'I've eaten a big supper.'

'Good to hear,' Dr Ribbentrop said, 'but I wasn't making the suggestion because you looked faint. I firmly believe we should all learn to relax a bit when it's not busy. It happens seldom enough. Now go, before the pace picks up again.'

Seema took Dr Ribbentrop's advice and made her way to the doctors' office. He was right: it wasn't often there was opportunity for a break on call. She went to the kettle and switched it on, then washed a cup for herself. She was just about to pour the water when she heard the door of the doctors' office open behind her. She hadn't expected Dr Ribbentrop to finish seeing the patients so quickly.

'The water's just boiled. Can I pour you a cup?' she asked without turning round.

'Expecting someone else, were you?' a voice asked.

It was Satesh.

Seema felt her hands begin to tremble, but she forced herself to continue pouring the boiling water into her cup as though she was unaffected, as though she had been expecting Satesh. She didn't want him to know that she was petrified, because it just made his hold over her stronger. She didn't feel the burn of the boiling water that splattered onto the hand holding the cup. What was Satesh doing here?

'Were you waiting for your boyfriend to come and join you for coffee?' Satesh asked. They had been married for over two years and Satesh still couldn't remember that she drank tea, not coffee. Seema heard the click of the doctors' office door being locked from the inside.

'Did you think you could hide away from me forever, you stupid bitch?' Satesh asked. 'Did you think I wouldn't find you? That I'd just leave? Turn round and look at me when I talk to you,' he ordered.

Seema gripped the cup of tea in her hands and turned round to face Satesh. He was wearing dark jeans and a long-sleeved black shirt. His face seemed haggard, and his lanky frame was thinner than Seema remembered it having been. His eyes were cold and hard, his upper lip twisted into a cruel snarl.

'Who the hell do you think you're messing with?' he asked, taking a step towards Seema. She shrank back involuntarily, pressing her body against the counter behind her.

'I'm not the kind of man whose wife leaves him,' Satesh said coldly. 'Look at you! You've been away from me for less than two weeks and already you're dressing like a slut. Do you think I don't know what you're up to? Do you think I haven't been watching you?'

'I don't know what you're talking about, Satesh,' Seema said timidly. Her body had fallen into its old habits. It was freezing up, preparing itself to be injured. Her only movement was involuntary: the trembling of her limbs and the clenching of her bladder muscles.

'Save your breath,' Satesh said. 'I've had enough of being taken for a fool. I've come to fetch you. You're coming back to Joburg with me, to my family, and you'll stop this nonsense of working and come and behave as a dutiful wife should: keep my home and have my children.'

'No,' Seema cried. Her voice sounded weak and strangled. Even though Satesh had come no closer to her, she could feel his hands around her neck, the pressure of his thin, spidery fingers pressing on her throat.

'Yes,' Satesh said firmly. 'I've had enough of you wearing the pants in this relationship. It's time I took control. I always knew I was stupid to marry a woman with a degree. They get all high and mighty, all above themselves.'

'So why did you marry me?' Seema couldn't help asking.

'Why?' Satesh asked, laughing sardonically. 'Why? I'll tell you why. Because I made a stupid mistake. I got a teenager, a little black girl, pregnant. The stupid bitch laid a charge of rape against me.

My family sorted out the charge but news leaks. It was difficult for me to find a wife after that; even Joburg is a small place. Your father needed the money for his expensive little habit.'

'What do you mean?' Seema asked.

'What? You didn't know about the prostitutes your father hangs around with?' Satesh asked with mock innocence. Obviously he had been hoping to rattle Seema with the information; he had no way of knowing that Seema had already heard about her father's predilections from her mother. But Seema hadn't been questioning her father's habits; she had been concerned about the exchange of money.

'You mean you paid for me?' Seema asked uncertainly. No wonder their marriage had been unhappy. It had been doomed from the start. It was a marriage belonging to demons. For the second time in as many weeks Seema felt as though her world was collapsing. How many other secrets were there? How many other lies? Was there anybody that she could trust? Suddenly she felt angry, angry that she had been bartered like a piece of meat, angry that her father had willingly given her to this man he knew was evil. Why should she continue to behave according to the way she had been brought up? It meant nothing; nothing was sacred; nothing was of consequence.

Satesh stepped towards her and grabbed her left hand forcefully. 'Come,' he said, 'we're going.'

Seema knew she wasn't going with him. She had no bond to him. Their marriage had been a lie. The spiritual link that she had believed would bind them for seven lifetimes was negated. She tried to think clearly. What would Rachael do in a situation like this? How would she handle it? She looked down at the cup of tea to which her right hand was still clinging and knew. As she threw the cup of hot tea at Satesh, she screamed. It was a loud and vicious scream, the culmination and expression of all her anger and betrayal. Satesh let go of her hand to try belatedly to cover his eyes and Seema dashed for the door. The collapse of her world, the shattering of all that had held and supported her for her whole life, had freed her legs. She turned the lock and screamed again. Behind her, Satesh was cursing. He lurched towards her as she opened the door. Dr Ribbentrop was standing on the other side of the door, trying to force open the lock.

'Seema!' he said. 'What's going on? I thought I heard screaming. Are you all right?'

Without answering, Seema looked behind her, at Satesh.

'What are you doing here?' Dr Ribbentrop growled.

'I've come to fetch my wife,' Satesh said. Seema could hear that he was trying to sound defiant but, like the husband of the abused patient that Seema had seen, he seemed to shrink in the presence of Dr Ribbentrop.

'You get off the hospital grounds now,' Dr Ribbentrop said icily. 'Seema, call security,' he instructed without taking his eyes off Satesh. 'I never, ever want to see you on the hospital premises again. Not in the hospital itself and not on the hospital grounds.'

'You have no right to say that,' Satesh argued though his voice sounded weak and uncertain. 'I've got every right to come to this hospital. I'll take you to court. I know good lawyers,' he said, resorting to the age-old tactic of the weak.

'Save your good lawyers for your divorce. You'll need them,' Dr Ribbentrop said calmly. 'Now get out of here. I'm sending security to your flat at lunchtime tomorrow. You'd better make sure you're out by then. Now move!' he roared.

Satesh walked quickly out of the doctors' office, mumbling something about lawyers, but Seema could see that he knew he was beaten. She also knew, instinctively, that he wouldn't stay. He would be gone the next day.

A security guard knocked on the door and Dr Ribbentrop instructed him to keep tabs on Satesh until he left the following day. He was to make sure, Dr Ribbentrop instructed him, that Satesh made no contact with Seema whatsoever.

'I'll go and check that he's left for good before you move back into your flat,' Dr Ribbentrop said to Seema. 'Actually, I'll organise with human resources to move you into a prefab. It's probably better. I think there are one or two open.'

'Thank you,' Seema said. 'Thank you. I don't know what else to say or do to show you how grateful I am.'

'Just don't go back to him,' Dr Ribbentrop said.

Seema knew she wouldn't go back to Satesh. What he had told her about their marriage had freed her. It had invalidated any vows that had been made. She had stuck to him for so long out of a sense of duty, to both her parents and her gods. Now she realised that it had been a false sense of duty, a sense of duty based on deception. No link existed between her and Satesh, on a physical or metaphysical level. She was free to create her own future.

Dr Ribbentrop stuck to his promise. The following evening he went to Seema's flat to ensure that Satesh had left. He called Seema once he had checked that the flat was unoccupied. 'I'll help you move what's left of your stuff across to the prefab,' he offered.

Earlier in the day Seema had picked up a key for the prefab she was moving into and spent most of her afternoon cleaning it. It was the prefab next to Nomsa's, the one she had once imagined staying in. She walked across to the married quarters and met with Dr Ribbentrop. As they climbed the stairs to her old flat, Seema couldn't help thinking how glad she was to be moving. The place held no good memories for her. Dr Ribbentrop unlocked the door of the flat and held it open for Seema to enter. For the first time, she walked into the flat fearlessly. Even though it had been unoccupied for only a few hours, the place smelt different, as though it had already shed the identities of its former occupants and was readying itself for the next tenants. Seema looked around her. All the furniture was missing. She opened the kitchen cupboards: they were empty; even the *masala dabba* which had been a wedding gift from her mother was gone. Satesh had taken everything. He had taken her clothes and her make-up, her shoes and her toiletries. He had taken all the furniture that didn't belong to the hospital and had taken what crockery and cutlery were theirs. He had removed everything they had owned together, including all their wedding presents. He had even taken Seema's textbooks and notes, though what use he would have for them Seema could not imagine. The flat looked exactly as it had the day they moved in.

'He's taken everything,' Seema whispered, still in shock.

'I'm sorry,' Dr Ribbentrop said, as though it was his fault. 'I didn't anticipate this. You'll get some of it back with the divorce settlement, don't worry.'

'No,' Seema said. 'Don't be sorry. I don't want any of it back. I don't want a single thing that would remind me of the time I had to endure with him.'

Seema felt as light as a feather blown about in the wind, as though the removal of all her material possessions had freed her emotionally. She no longer had any links to or any reminders of the past.

'Thank you,' she said to Dr Ribbentrop. Impulsively, without any hesitation or embarrassment, she hugged him.

That weekend Seema drove to Durban and shopped until her credit card reached its maximum limit. She bought herself new clothes and shoes and make-up and jewellery. She went to home stores and bought herself linen and curtains and crockery and cutlery. She shopped in a frenzy, buying whatever caught her fancy. It felt wonderful and liberating to buy just for herself, not to have to think about whether Satesh or her parents would approve of what she was choosing. She felt almost guilty following only her whims and desires and not taking anyone else's opinions and wishes into consideration. Shop assistants came to offer her their help and she shooed them away. She wanted to consult no one but herself.

Rachael came around to Seema's new prefab later that evening. She brought a bottle of champagne with her and, as Seema unpacked the bags filled with her new life, they toasted a fresh start. By the time Rachael left, Seema didn't know if her giddiness was the result of too much champagne or if it was the headiness of newly discovered freedom.

Nomsa

28

The trip to Aliwal North was long and, once she had crossed into the Eastern Cape, occasionally treacherous. Before leaving, Nomsa had mapped out what she thought would be the shortest route to her mother's home. Her route followed the smaller back roads instead of the main roads, but what her map had not made clear was that many of the smaller roads were untarred gravel roads replete with potholes. Not only were the roads in a state of disrepair, but they often seemed to act as the main byways for the passage of cattle, and Nomsa had to stop more than once while a herd of cows urged on by a ten- or eleven-year-old stick-wielding cowherd crossed in front of her. Only once it was too late, when she was too far along in her journey, did she realise that it would have been better to take the main tarred roads: although the distance would have been greater, the time taken to travel the roads would have been far shorter.

She pulled over to the side of the dirt road she was on and consulted the map once again. At the rate she was travelling, she calculated that she would reach her mother's house about four or five hours later than she had banked on. Part of her did not mind: the thought of going back to her birthplace and of seeing family she had not seen for many years was not all comforting to Nomsa. She was not looking forward to her mother's funeral, not just because of what it signified, but also because she was nervous about facing members of her family who were practically strangers to her. She was worried that she would not remember the correct things to say or that her behaviour would be inappropriate. Unlike Noluthando, she was not comfortable with all the rituals and practices involved in a funeral, and Nomsa was worried that her ignorance of her culture would be betrayed by a thoughtless word or action.

She turned on her ignition and noticed that a spot of rain had fallen on her windscreen. Another landed on the glass and then another. They were heavy, pregnant drops that splattered into smaller droplets when they hit the glass. Great, she thought to herself, this is just what I need. Rain would turn the roads on which she was driving into slippery, muddy death traps.

Within minutes of Nomsa's resuming her driving, the rain was pelting down so badly that she could barely see two metres in front of her. She slowed down to a crawl and wondered whether the hair-raising driving conditions were a sign that she should never have undertaken the trip. She couldn't help feeling that the storm outside her car was a reflection of the emotional turbulence within her. Nomsa didn't know whether she was ready to go back to her mother's house, ready to face her mother's death. She knew she often dealt with emotionally difficult situations by pushing the feelings away, hiding them in another compartment of her psyche until they were less evocative and easier to deal with. She would have liked to handle her mother's death in the same way, but the funeral threatened to bring those emotions to the fore, where she could not ignore them. Not only was she worried about the feelings that her mother's funeral would engender, but she was worried about how she would react to seeing her family again and to going back to the place of her childhood. Since she had left her family home, she had made a determined effort to reject the culture of her childhood. Nomsa didn't know whether she was ready to accept it back again or, conversely, whether it was ready to accept her back again.

In front of her and off to her left, she made out a sign indicating upcoming roadworks. She let out a cry of frustration. They would slow her journey down even more. It would be the fifth set of road-works that she would be passing through since turning off the main road. The pattern seemed to be that the construction crew worked on one lane, which they blocked off, and allowed traffic to flow alternately in either direction along the other lane. On each side of the section of road being worked on, the flow of traffic was directed by men who communicated by means of two-way radios. She would probably have had more patience with the roadworks had she actually seen any activity going on, but she had yet to see a single person working on the road. She approached the stop sign at the start of the roadworks and looked for the worker who was supposed to be manning it. There was nobody in sight. She wondered whether he was inside the little tin shack that had been set up next to the stop–go sign. She hooted and waited for the man to emerge. Still no one appeared. She waited a bit longer. Rain pelted down and turned the road around her car into a mud bath. She turned on the radio and started fiddling with the dial but was unable to get reception for a single station. Still nobody had appeared from within the tin hut.

Reluctantly she opened her car door. The man who was supposed to be directing the traffic had probably fallen asleep. She stepped outside the car into ankle-deep mud, ruining her new leather and cork wedge-heeled shoes. Rain pelted down on her as she made her way to the tin shack as quickly as she could in the slippery mud. In the distance she could hear the crack of thunder. Once she had reached the hut, she shouted out a greeting and banged on the door, but nobody emerged. Eventually she pushed the door open. The tin hut was deserted.

Nomsa felt like bursting into tears. Everything that possibly could was going wrong. If she hadn't been so far along on her journey already, she would have turned around and made her way back to Tugela Bridge. She picked her way over the relatively drier pieces of sludge back to her car, and then tried to wipe some of the water and mud off her body before sitting down in the driver's seat once again. She didn't know what to do. The sign told her to stop, but there was not a soul visible to change the sign. In fact, there was no evidence of anyone even working on the road. She tried to decide between taking a chance and ignoring the stop sign (while praying that no one was driving up the road in the opposite direction) and waiting for the rain to stop, which would hopefully herald the return of the workman supposed to be manning the sign. The deciding factor was the knowledge that the cold front could take days to pass. She edged her way on to the single lane. She didn't know whether it was more sensible to drive at a snail's pace to ensure that, if she hit an oncoming vehicle, it would be less of a high-impact collision or whether she should just put her foot down on the accelerator, say a prayer and get the stretch of road behind her as quickly as possible. Eventually she decided on the latter. She made a quick plea bargain with her ancestors, then put her foot down on the accelerator.

She saw the car coming from the other direction as she mounted a blind rise. Instinctively she braked and tried to turn off the road. She realised too late that that was a mistake. She lost control of her car as the locked wheels made the mud as slippery as ice. Her car skidded out of the road, on to the sodden grass verge, just as the oncoming vehicle whizzed past her. Miraculously, her car didn't roll. The moment passed in a fraction of a second and Nomsa was left watching the once-again empty road. Only she and perhaps the driver of the oncoming vehicle knew how close she had come to death. Her ancestors had kept their side of the deal.

When she tried to restart her car, her foot was trembling so much that she couldn't push down the clutch.

Nomsa arrived in Aliwal North five hours later than she had expected to, just as the sun was setting. The rain had stopped. The main town area had grown since she had last been there and was far more urbanised than she remembered it. She drove through the more populated area to the rural outskirts where her family lived. She parked just above her mother's house, which was built on the slope of a hill, and then got out of her car to negotiate the muddy path down to the front door. The place looked the same as Nomsa remembered it, as though nothing had changed since she had left thirteen years before. The sky-blue paint was still flaking off the walls of the house, the flat tin roof was still held stable against the wind with an assortment of different-sized rocks. Attached to the back of the rectangular cement and brick building was the same round mud hut with thatched roof that had been Nomsa's mother's first home, before the additional rooms were built on. Outside, chickens still pecked at the ground, their feathers scraggly and muddy from the rain, and an old yellow-eyed goat chewed at a pumpkin plant.

There had been some changes, though, and Nomsa knew where to look for them because she had paid for them: the new panes of glass in the windows; the metal security gate outside the front door; the green rainwater storage tank next to the house. Seeing the changes, what she had contributed to the house, made Nomsa feel slightly more welcome. At least she had done something. The renovations that she had paid for made her a presence in the house, albeit a small one. She had not been entirely absent from her mother's life.

Noluthando was sitting on the step at the front door, as though she had been waiting for her sister's arrival.

'Nomsa, you are here!' Noluthando shouted to Nomsa. She stood up and met Nomsa halfway up the path. 'Nomtobhoyi said you would come. When the sun started to go down and the boys brought the cows home and you had not come, I thought she had made a mistake, but now you are here. Oh, I am so pleased that you came,' she said, flinging her arms around Nomsa.

It felt odd to Nomsa to have her sister's arms around her, the sister she had not seen for over three years. Noluthando had filled out since the last time Nomsa remembered hugging her; her breasts had swollen and her back had become more sloped. She had the body of a woman now, no longer that of a young girl. Nomsa returned Noluthando's hug, tentatively at first and then, as the familiar scent of her sister drove her inhibitions away, more recklessly. Strangely, she felt no irritation at her sister's comment. Usually, mention of Nomtobhoyi's prophecies would have angered her, but now she felt only the comfort of her sister's arms encircling her.

'All of our family have already come,' Noluthando continued. 'Our brothers. All of our aunties and uncles. All of our cousins. I have emptied the house to make space for them. It is right that you, the eldest, are here too.'

Nomsa followed Noluthando into their mother's house. Her sister had spoken the truth: their home was full of people. But apart from the presence of so many bodies, the interior of her mother's house had changed little from her memories. She half expected to see her mother walk through the door to greet her. She looked for her mother among the women brewing beer in the large metal pot and between the people milling next to the big bowl of samp and beans. The presence of her mother in the house was so strong that Nomsa could almost convince herself that her mother was not dead, that she had driven to Aliwal North for a different celebration – a wedding, perhaps. Noluthando excused herself and then came back a few moments later with a toddler on her hip.

'Is … is this your child?' Nomsa asked. Noluthando nodded and held the infant up for Nomsa to see. The little child reached out her arms towards Nomsa and Nomsa instinctively leant forward to receive her. The young girl was soft and warm and burrowed into Nomsa's neck. She smelt like Sunlight soap, like their mother. Nomsa felt tears prick her eyelids. She didn't want to feel like this, hadn't expected to experience these emotions. The little girl, her younger sister's child, represented for her so much of what she despised. She had berated her sister many times before for falling pregnant, reprimanded her for not being sensible and going for an abortion when she had initially found out she was pregnant, but now, with the little girl pulling at her braids and smiling her gummy smile at her, Nomsa could not imagine how she had ever not desired the child's existence. This girl, this plump little bundle wriggling in her arms, was her flesh and blood. It was a link to her mother, its DNA so similar to her mother's. All at once, Nomsa understood the drive to procreate. It wasn't about simple reproduction; it was about seeing a little of oneself in another. This child represented not only herself, not only the future, but the past too – all the generations that had come before her. With her big brown eyes and rosebud mouth, this little girl was the physical manifestation, the combined DNA, of all Nomsa's ancestors. The realisation filled Nomsa with wonder.

'Can I hold her for a while?' she asked Noluthando hesitantly. She didn't know if her sister would want to let her hold the child whose existence she had so vehemently protested against.

'Please,' Noluthando said. 'It would help me if you would watch her for a while. I have to prepare some things. Besides, she should get to know her mother's sister.' Noluthando scuttled off, busy as the queen bee in a buzzing hive, and Nomsa settled down in a corner with the child. Nobody in the room had recognised her yet; they were too busy with their talking and eating and drinking, and Nomsa knew that she looked very different from the little girl she was when they had last seen her. She didn't mind remaining incognito for a little longer. She needed time to sort through the memories that being in her mother's home had aroused before facing the onslaught of questions that would follow in the wake of her relatives' greetings.

Noluthando's daughter seemed perfectly content with Nomsa, as though she had known her aunt for her entire short life. Nomsa bounced the infant up and down on her knee and, unconsciously, the words of a lullaby sprang from her lips. She couldn't remember ever having made an effort to learn the words of the song; they seemed to come forth of their own accord. She knew that it was a song that her mother had sung to her and, as she listened to the words fill in the spaces between other people's conversations, she thought that her mother was singing through her.

Laa! Laa! Bhabhane
Laa! Laa! Bhabhane
Laa! Laa! Bhabhane
Umama ugeza ngoku
Umama ugeza ngoku

Her mother wasn't dead, Nomsa realised. She was alive, very much alive. She lived in the child swaying on Nomsa's lap. She hadn't gone forever; she was simply hiding in unexpected places.

Later that evening, once all the aunts and uncles were asleep, Nomsa and Noluthando sat in front of the dying fire together. They talked with soft, quiet voices, careful not to wake slumbering relatives or unwelcome spirits.

'What are your plans for the future, Noluthando?' Nomsa asked her sister. 'Are you going to go back to school to complete your matric?'

Noluthando cocked her head at her sister. 'I don't know,' she said. 'I was planning to go back, but then our mother got sick and

I had to take care of her. It's expensive too, to study more. I need books and clothes. And who will look after the child?' Nomsa heard the unspoken words: *now that our mother is no longer here.*

'Leave the child with our aunt, with our mother's sister,' Nomsa said. 'I'll pay for you to study further, for you to finish school and for studying after school. You won't ever get a job without studying something else and you can't stay here in Aliwal North forever.' Nomsa had not thought about making this offer to Noluthando before coming to Aliwal North. She didn't even know if she would be able to afford to pay for her sister's studies. Again, she felt as though her words did not belong to her, as though they were her mother's words, being said through her. She didn't regret what was said, though; she didn't retract her offer. She knew it was the right thing to do.

Noluthando said nothing. Instead she got up and placed another branch into the dying fire. The sisters sat for a while in silence, staring at the glowing orange coals.

'I was always jealous of you,' Noluthando said to Nomsa eventually. 'I was always jealous that you were chosen to go live in Cape Town, jealous of your fancy clothes and the school that you went to. I was always angry that Mrs Watson paid for you and that she didn't offer to pay for me too. I used to dream, before I was old enough to understand that it would never happen, that she would send money for me to join you in Cape Town. I used to picture fashionable clothes and shoes, parties, magazines, the kind of food that I would see on television – all that I imagined you had. I was even jealous of the friends that I pictured you having.'

'She knew me; that's why she paid for me,' Nomsa said. 'She never got to know you. Mother moved back here when you were too young.'

'I know,' Noluthando said, 'but it didn't make the jealousy less.'

Nomsa didn't know how to respond. She wanted to tell Noluthando that it hadn't been easy; that it hadn't been the romantic life Noluthando had imagined and that she had had to work hard to fit in with a different culture and be accepted by people whose immediate response was to look down on her; that she had spent hours and hours studying to keep up academically with her better-educated classmates; that she too had had to give up so much. But now was not the right time to say the words.

'You knew our mother better. You got to spend more time with her,' she said instead.

Noluthando nodded. 'That is true,' she said.

'I hardly knew her,' Nomsa said sadly, 'and now it's too late.'

They watched the last branch crumble into ashes and then Noluthando went to lie down. The day ahead, the day of the funeral, would be a busy one for her. Nomsa knew that she too should get some sleep but she was unable to close her eyes. She looked around her, at the family that she was supposed to be part of. Noluthando had said that she was jealous of her. Nomsa had not told Noluthando how jealous she was of her. She didn't know, at that moment, whether by allowing Nomsa to go to Cape Town to become Mrs Watson's surrogate daughter, her mother had done her a favour or a disfavour. Nomsa had watched Noluthando during the evening. She was so comfortable with her role in the family; she knew what needed to be done for the funeral and how to do it; she was well aware of all the intricacies of ritual and tradition of which Nomsa was ignorant.

Nomsa's mother had made a choice to let her daughter go to what she believed was a better life, a better opportunity, but Nomsa didn't know if it had been. Nomsa had been left identity-less, belonging to no one. Exposed to too many cultures, she had been left cultureless. To fit in with her adopted customs, Nomsa had had to reject her own traditions and history. And now she felt like a dried leaf that could too easily be blown around in the winds of fate. Noluthando was not like that. She was like a big, old tree with ancient roots clawing deep into the ground, stabilising her. She knew who she was and where she came from. Nomsa knew only where she wanted to go. Which was better? Nomsa didn't know. Eventually she fell into a confused and restless sleep.

That night Nomsa dreamt about her mother's approaching funeral. A strange man visited her in her dream. He was wearing khaki clothes and leant on a gnarled old walking stick. His face looked vaguely familiar to Nomsa, but she was unable to place it. Noluthando told her later, when Nomsa described her dream to her, that the man was her grandfather, their mother's father. Nomsa was standing with the women, cooking the meat of a slaughtered cow in a pot of boiling water, when the old man came to fetch her. He led her away from the other women along an overgrown path to where her mother's grave was. In her dream, Nomsa could smell a strange scent and she asked her grandfather what it was. He told her it was *imphepho* burning, to keep the bad spirits away. Once they had arrived at her mother's grave, the old man lit white candles and placed them on the sandy ground. Nomsa saw her mother sitting upright in the grave. Next to her she had a bowl of unspiced meat as well as a beaded necklace. She was smoking her pipe. At this point her grandfather disappeared and Nomsa's mother beckoned her to the grave. Nomsa approached her mother, then stopped at the graveside, afraid that she would fall into the grave with her mother and be buried alive. Her mother smiled at her and Nomsa knew that her mother meant her to step into the grave with her. Nomsa took a step, expecting to fall, but the air seemed to support her. She was filled with a feeling of great love and warmth, and when she looked down at herself she realised that she had taken on the body of a child once again. Her mother extended a hand to Nomsa and handed her a necklace made from beads and the hair from a cow's tail that had been plaited on to the tendon of a slaughtered goat. Also plaited on to the necklace were gold charms: miniature keys and shoes and syringes. Her mother touched Nomsa's hand one last time and then disappeared. The grave closed up, hiding her mother's body, and Nomsa found she was standing in the middle of a kraal filled with fat cows. A small child came and led her back to her mother's house.

Nomsa told Noluthando about the dream once she had woken up. Noluthando was excited by it and urged her to go ask Nomtobhoyi for an explanation of the dream, but Nomsa refused. It was not that she was reluctant or that she distrusted Nomtobhoyi; rather, she didn't need an explanation. Her dream had made sense to her. She knew it was the spirit of her mother and her ancestors that had been speaking to her, telling her she did not need to ask for forgiveness. Her mother had never been angry with her, had never stopped loving her. Her mother had also revealed to her that she needed to make peace with the differences between the culture of her ancestors and her adopted culture if she wanted to find happiness. She realised now that the two were not mutually exclusive and that she did not need to reject one in order to accept the other. The two could be married, in the same way that the elements of the necklace were married, so that they enhanced each other instead of excluding each other. Nomsa felt a peace within herself that she had never experienced before, a kind of deep contentedness. She smiled at Noluthando. 'What can I do to help you?' she asked. 'I don't know exactly how everything needs to be done, but I'll do whatever you tell me.' She was ready to learn.

Nomsa arrived back at the hospital on Sunday evening. The journey home had been far smoother than the journey there, not only because Nomsa had taken the tarred roads but because her state of mind was far more peaceful than it had been on her previous trip. She stopped at the post boxes to pick up her mail before going to her prefab. There was only one letter for her: an official-looking document. She turned the letter over to see a 'Department of Health' stamp. Intrigued, she tore open the envelope. The application form for the following year's community service posts fell out. Nomsa realised that in the turmoil of her mother's death she had forgotten that the year was passing and that she needed to make a decision about where she wanted to spend the next year.

When Nomsa had started her internship at Prince Xoliswe, she had been convinced that the year would be a stepping stone on the path to a greater goal: to become a surgery registrar as soon as possible. At that time her plan had been to apply for her community service post at a large tertiary hospital, where she hoped she would be able to impress enough people and make the right contacts to go directly into a registrar post. Now, having spent three-quarters of the year at Tugela Bridge, she wasn't so sure that she wanted to leave. On a purely academic level, she was learning under a good master. Dr Ribbentrop was one of the best surgeons she had come across. In addition, she was doing a greater number of operations and far more variable surgery than she would ever be allowed to do at a tertiary hospital, where interns and community service doctors were the last in line for cases. On a professional level, it actually made sense for her to stay in Tugela Bridge for another year, refining her surgical skills and adding to her surgery logbook, which she knew was already pretty impressive. But she had another reason for considering staying, a more emotional reason. She knocked on the door of Rachael's prefab on her way home. Seema, not Rachael, opened the door.

'Are you still staying here?' Nomsa asked, surprised to see Seema. She had thought that Seema was moving into the prefab next to hers that weekend.

'No,' Seema said, 'just visiting. Rachael got so used to eating home-cooked meals while I was staying with her that I brought her some biryani for dinner so that she wouldn't get withdrawal symptoms. There's still some extra. Would you like it?'

After all she had eaten over the weekend, Nomsa thought she would never be hungry again, but the delicious aroma escaping from the open door was making her mouth water. Obviously her stomach had stretched.

'That would be stunning, if you've got extra,' she said to Seema.

Rachael's voice called out from inside the prefab telling Nomsa to come inside.

'Do you want some dinner?' Rachael asked as Nomsa walked in.

'Seema's already offered,' Nomsa said.

Rachael gave Nomsa a bowl and spoon and Nomsa dished up some biryani for herself.

'How was your weekend?' Rachael asked once Nomsa had sat down to eat. 'I know it couldn't have been great, being your mom's funeral, but was it nice to go back and see your family at least?'

'Yes,' Nomsa replied. 'It actually was.' Indeed, in a strange way, it had been a good weekend. She had felt closer to her mother on the weekend than she had felt for the last few years that her mother had been alive, and she had developed a new relationship with her sister.

She had left Aliwal North feeling far happier and more contented than when she had arrived. Her strange dream, her reconnecting with her family and her acceptance of her roots had seemed to satisfy a deep hunger that had previously possessed her. It no longer seemed so important to her to prove herself and to succeed materially. 'In a strange way the weekend turned out to be better than I was expecting,' she confirmed aloud. 'Anyway, I didn't stop here to score a free meal, although the dinner is most welcome. I actually wanted to ask you something before filling in my application form for next year,' Nomsa said, turning towards Rachael.

'Fire away,' Rachael said.

'I wanted to know whether you were serious about setting up that HIV counselling and testing centre and whether you're going ahead with it. If you are, I think I'm going to stay at Tugela Bridge.'

Nomsa knew that it wasn't entirely reasonable to base her decision to stay at Tugela Bridge on the possibility of helping with the establishment of an HIV centre, but she couldn't shake the feeling that it was not coincidence that Rachael had asked her to help with the centre when she did, just as her mother died of AIDS.

'I am most definitely going ahead with it,' Rachael confirmed. 'I've had a bit of a fight with my parents – we aren't speaking at the moment – but I've decided I don't need my dad's help with this. So, yes, the bottom line is that I'm going ahead with it. I've already approached a few companies for sponsorship, and I've applied for a fund-raising number and to be recognised as an official charity. And please stay on here; I'm staying and I could do with a friend. Lots of the other doctors are leaving.'

Nomsa knew instinctively that Rachael was talking about Shane. He had told Nomsa the previous week that he had decided to go overseas for a while to earn some decent money.

Nomsa unfolded her application form and put a cross in the box next to Prince Xoliswe Hospital. 'Settled, then,' she said. She put the form back in her bag. 'Just don't expect me to give up every free Saturday to paint walls,' she added, looking pointedly at Rachael. 'I'm probably going to be spending a lot more of my weekends at Aliwal North. I've got a little niece to get to know.'

Rachael

29

Rachael's day started badly, before she even reached the hospital. She had checked her emails while she was eating breakfast and had received two rejections to her requests for sponsorship. They were from large companies, companies that she had really hoped would agree to giving just a couple of thousand rands. She couldn't help wondering if her father had been right, whether her idea wasn't romantic enough to attract funding. No, she refused to think that everybody was so shallow. She'd sent off dozens of emails requesting donations and she'd only received two responses. She turned off her laptop and decided that she would not allow herself to get despondent until she had received rejections to every request. Rachael finished her breakfast, then watered the geranium stalk outside her front door before leaving for the morning ward round.

On her way to the hospital, Rachael caught sight of Sipho. He was leaning against the wall smoking a joint and examining the undersides of his fingernails. She waved him over and handed him a twenty-rand note. She'd figured out that the best way to ensure a constant supply of water in her prefab was to ensure an equally constant supply of money in Sipho's pocket, so whenever she saw him she gave over whatever change she had in her wallet. She didn't know how fair the system was, and she had noticed that the doctors who regularly supported Sipho's other business venture seemed to have to pay less for their water, but she was willing to pay a bit more to know she could have a shower when she wanted to. At least one thing she would be able to look forward to next year would be upgrading to the community service flats and, by default, to running water.

Rachael entered the doctors' office just as the handover round was about to start.

'We can all go through straight after the handover round, so try to keep brief and to the point. I don't know how long the meeting's going to be,' Nathan said as Rachael walked in. She had obviously caught the tail end of an announcement.

'What have I missed?' she whispered to Nomsa as she sat down next to her.

'Mrs Hlope's called some or other meeting after the round,' Nomsa answered under her breath.

Rachael groaned. Mrs Hlope's meetings were usually long and boring and filled with dismal news such as further staff cuts or budget restraints.

Once the handover round was over, the doctors made their way to the seminar room. Rachael was surprised to see Dr Chetty and Dr Ribbentrop arrive for the meeting; ninety per cent of the time they managed to come up with some or other excuse not to attend Mrs Hlope's meetings. Even more surprising was the presence of Dr Zamla. He sat at the front of the room, next to Mrs Hlope.

Once all the doctors were seated, Mrs Hlope stood up and welcomed everyone. 'I've called you all here for a very special reason,' she said. 'Today we are announcing our new principal medical officer.'

Rachael noticed Seema turn round and smile at Dr Ribbentrop. Did Seema know something? Rachael thought it would be fantastic if Dr Ribbentrop was made principal medical officer. He was exactly the right person for the job and he obviously needed the extra income: apart from his motorbike, he drove a battered red Citi Golf that looked like a relic of his student days. He deserved something more for the amount of work that he did.

'Our new principal medical officer', Mrs Hlope continued, 'is one of our hardest-working and longest-serving doctors.'

It could only be Dr Ribbentrop, Rachael thought.

'I gladly introduce to all of you our new principal medical officer, Dr Zamla,' Mrs Hlope announced.

Rachael thought for a bizarre moment that perhaps this was Mrs

Hlope's idea of a warped practical joke, but it appeared not to be. She had turned to Dr Zamla, whom Rachael had seen exactly twice at the hospital, and was giving him a sweaty hug. Rachael couldn't bear to look back at Dr Ribbentrop to see his disappointment. The way that Seema looked at him earlier made Rachael sure that he had applied for the job. Had he known this was coming? Then Rachael saw Seema raise her hand. Mrs Hlope hadn't been expecting any questions and it took her a while to respond to the raised arm.

'Yes?' she asked impatiently. She obviously wanted to get out of the discomfort of the hospital as soon as possible. 'What do you want?'

'I just wanted to know…,' Seema began, but she was interrupted by Mrs Hlope.

'Who are you to talk to me like that without identifying yourself?' Mrs Hlope demanded.

Rachael noticed that Seema's hands were trembling but she seemed determined to press on with what she had been saying.

'I'm Dr Singh, one of the interns,' Seema said. 'I just wanted to know how the decision was reached and on what grounds Dr Zamla was given the job. He's hardly ever present at the hospital. I don't believe that it's appropriate to have a principal medical officer who is not an active, visible presence in the hospital.'

Rachael could not believe what she was hearing. Of all the doctors present in the room, Seema was the last one Rachael would have expected to raise an objection, especially directly to Mrs Hlope. The other doctors must also have been in shock because a moment of tense silence followed Seema's question. Then, unanimously, the room broke out in applause and shouts of support for Seema's comments. Mrs Hlope appeared rattled. Obviously she had not expected this type of reaction to her announcement. She leant over and whispered something into Dr Zamla's ear, then stood up to speak.

'Quiet, quiet, everybody!' she shouted. 'Please, I will have order in this room.'

The doctors quietened down in preparation for Mrs Hlope's response.

'This is a rude and inappropriate question that I refuse to answer,' she said, scowling at Seema. 'We do not tolerate racism in this hospital and our posts are decided on a basis of equity. If you have an objection, you can take it up with the Department of Health. This meeting is ended. Any doctor who continues to misbehave will be relieved of his or her job immediately.' She stomped out of the room with Dr Zamla following closely behind her.

As soon as Mrs Hlope left, Rachael went over to Seema. 'Well done,' she said. 'What made you question her? I would never have had the guts.'

'Dr Ribbentrop applied for the job. I know he did because I was with him when he filled in the application form. He should have got the job. He's a far better candidate than Dr Zamla.'

'I agree, but you don't want to get on the wrong side of Mrs Hlope. She'll be gunning for you from now on.'

'I owe Dr Ribbentrop a lot,' Seema said softly.

The fiasco at the meeting, combined with the negative responses to her requests for sponsorship, had made Rachael despondent. She couldn't help wondering whether she was doing the right thing by staying in South Africa. Perhaps her father was right; perhaps she was living in some delusionary world far removed from reality. She walked to the outpatients' clinic wondering if she should find out about the requirements for practising in the UK.

The first patient Rachael called in was a woman in her early twenties who was complaining of chronic diarrhoea. She walked into the cubicle with a young child strapped onto her back with a towel. Rachael asked her to lie down on the bed, and the woman unravelled the towel and placed the child on the towel on the floor. The child looked even more unwell than the woman. He was malnourished, with the typical brittle bronze-tinted hair and protruding potbelly of kwashiorkor. He had blisters around his mouth and a discharging sore on one leg. Rachael dragged her eyes from the child to her mother. The woman had lain down on the bed and taken off her top. She was skeletal with protruding rib bones. Her abdomen was so concave that her jutting hip bones looked abnormal, almost deformed. One side of her chest wall was scarred from an old shingles infection. Rachael asked her to open her mouth. Her tongue was white with oral candida. She coughed, a deep, chesty cough that seemed to rattle her frail bones, and spat blood-speckled phlegm into a tissue. Rachael didn't need to ask any more questions or examine any further to know what was causing the woman's diarrhoea: she had AIDS. Her child probably did too. Rachael asked her whether she had had an HIV test before and the woman shook her head. Would she like one? She shook her head again.

Rachael couldn't help wondering about the future that was lying on the bed and floor in front of her. This woman would die before the end of the year. Her child, if he had not died before her, would be left motherless until he too died. Was the father alive to take over care of the child or had he already succumbed to the virus? But instead of feeling hopelessness, Rachael saw potential. This was why she had to stay in South Africa. This was why her father was wrong.

Potentially, the future could be so different. The woman could have been educated before she contracted the virus, could have been taught the value of using a condom. And if that had failed, she could have been diagnosed far earlier, counselled about HIV, tested regularly and started on anti-retrovirals as soon as she was eligible. If she had been diagnosed before she had fallen pregnant, she could have been given anti-retrovirals to prevent transmission of the virus to her child. And if the child had still become HIV-positive, he too could have been started on treatment at the earliest possible stage. The present would be different. Mother and child would be relatively healthy now, with few of the opportunistic infections that they were both currently riddled with. Perhaps they would not be in hospital. Perhaps the mother would still be strong enough to be working. And the future would look so different: ten, twenty or more hopeful years would stretch ahead of them, not just a few months.

Rachael realised she was probably being idealistic and a dreamer, but she believed she could be a significant part of the difference between the future that was currently facing her and the possible future. And if she made a difference in only one person's life, if she changed only one present to an alternative future, she would have done enough to warrant any energy and time spent on setting up an HIV centre. She knew she would stay at Prince Xoliswe and that she would persist with her dreams – and, hopefully, with time she would find enough other dreamers to join her to create a new future.

Seema, Rachael and Nomsa

30

Seema laid the cutlery neatly on the table and then placed small, brightly wrapped gifts at each place setting. She straightened the tablecloth for the fiftieth time and rearranged the condiments in the centre of the table. Lastly, just before her guests were supposed to arrive, she lit the candles. She had bought dozens of candles – red columnar candles, elegant white dinner candles, floating candles in the shapes of flowers, and thick, handcrafted cinnamon and vanilla candles – and had placed them not only on her dining-room table, but all over her prefab. Once all the candles had been lit, she flicked the electric light switch off. The light created by the myriad of candles was warm and soft and scented.

Seema tried to stop herself from imagining what would be taking place right now at her parents' house, but it was difficult. She wondered who would be there, whether they would be missing her. Would her father be lighting fireworks for the children now? Her mother and aunts gossiping around dishes of spicy sweetmeats? Her cousins eyeing each other's jewellery and saris and shoes? She pushed the thoughts from her mind. One day, perhaps, her parents would welcome her back into their home for Diwali, but until then she would celebrate it in her own way. She looked around her at her kitchen-cum-lounge. The flickering candlelight had softened all the edges, so that the table and chairs seemed to be floating just above the ground, the walls appeared to be patterned with shadowed wallpaper and the ceiling looked softly cushioned.

When Seema first decided to invite her friends around for a Diwali dinner, she had worried that her actions were sacrilegious, but then she had thought about the true meaning of Diwali. The festival wasn't about superficial traditions and trappings; its essence was about allowing the light of consciousness to shine. Sometimes, she thought to herself, the light of consciousness shone stronger without the external distractions. Someone rapped on her door and Seema went to open it.

Rachael handed Seema a large bunch of bought-in-Durban salmon-coloured roses and stepped into the room. Her nose was immediately overpowered by a barrage of foreign scents. There was cumin somewhere, and coriander and cardamom. There was aniseed and clove and the nose-tickling tang of black pepper. The smell was rich and multilayered, so that just when Rachael thought she had recognised all the scents she caught the aroma of something else, like camphor or sandalwood. Eventually she gave up trying to identify the different scents and allowed herself to take deep breaths of the overall composition. It was like listening to a piece of classical music, hearing the whole instead of picking out the individual instruments.

Seema had walked across the room and was putting the roses into a jug.

'I haven't bought a vase yet,' Seema apologised, 'so this will have to make do. I hope it does justice to the roses.'

Rachael assured her that the roses looked beautiful in the jug, but she was talking without thinking. Her mind was distracted. Walking into Seema's prefab, being faced with the cultural barrage of light and smell, had reminded Rachael that three weeks earlier she had not gone back to Cape Town to spend Yom Kippur with her family. Her mother had broken her silence to invite Rachael home, but Rachael had not felt like going back. She had texted her mother, explaining that she wasn't able to take leave then because there were too many other doctors on leave. That had been a lie. She hadn't wanted to go home, because she knew that she would be unable to forgive her father for the way he had treated her. His words still hurt her too much. And there was little point in asking for forgiveness and atoning for one's wrongdoings if it was done on only a superficial level. So, for the first time in her life, she had not celebrated Yom Kippur. She had worked in the hospital instead, trying to make her actions count for more than her thoughts.

Seema interrupted Rachael's introspection. 'Can I get you something to drink?' she asked.

Rachael nodded. 'I think some champagne's in order,' she said. 'I've got some good news.' Rachael wasn't going to allow herself to become melancholy. She thought about how much more difficult this evening must be for Seema than it was for her. Seema deserved all the cheering up that she could get.

'What's your news?' Seema asked.

'I got our first positive response to our requests for sponsorship. We now officially have six thousand rands towards our HIV centre from a company called Data Unlimited.'

'That's definitely news worth celebrating,' Seema said.

'What is?' Nomsa asked, walking in through the open door.

Rachael told Nomsa about the sponsorship.

Nomsa was pleased, not only because of the money itself, but because the HIV project had suddenly become a reality. Now it was not just an idea; it was starting to become concrete. It was the beginning of the transformation of the sadness and needlessness of her mother's death into something positive.

'Well, I just happened to bring some champagne,' Nomsa said, handing Seema a bottle. 'I wanted to toast the start of your new life, but the more we have to toast, the better.'

Seema took the bottle from Nomsa. It had been in the fridge and the glass was wet and slippery with condensed water droplets and for a moment Seema thought that she was going to drop it. She gripped it more tightly and placed it on the counter.

'Do you mind opening it?' Seema asked Nomsa. 'I've never opened a bottle of champagne before.' As Seema spoke, she realised that this really was the beginning, not of a new life, but of a new phase in her life. And she suddenly felt excited. There was so much for her to learn, so many experiences waiting for her. She went to fetch three wine glasses from the cupboard as Nomsa popped the cork from the bottle. The sound reminded Seema of the fireworks that would be rocketing into the sky at her parents' home, but the memory didn't cause her sadness. Instead she felt an unexpected pride. She was taking her life into her own hands, creating her own destiny. And she knew the decisions she had made over the last month were the right ones. She held a glass out to Nomsa and Nomsa started pouring the champagne. Seema watched as the golden liquid slipped down the side of the glass and then bubbled up to a frothy head.

'Thanks,' she said, looking directly at Nomsa and then at Rachael. The thanks were for far more than just the drink.

Nomsa handed a glass of champagne to Rachael and Rachael couldn't help wondering whether Nomsa felt awkward celebrating something so soon after her mother's death. She searched Nomsa's face, looking for signs of sadness.

'I miss her,' Nomsa said, understanding Rachael's look. 'But she isn't gone. She's watching me, waiting to see whether I keep my side of the bargain and help you get that HIV centre running.'

'Good,' Rachael smiled, 'because I guarantee you she's going to like what she sees.'

'Don't make the same mistake as me, Rachael,' Nomsa said, suddenly serious again. 'Forgive your parents. They're just doing what they think is best for you. You never know what tomorrow might bring with it.'

Rachael knew that Nomsa was right; she would swallow her pride and phone her parents the following day. But that was tomorrow's problem. Now was about celebrating, about celebrating the independence and freedom that all three of them had discovered that year. It was about acknowledging an unusual initiation rite that they had all, in their own blundering ways, passed. It was celebrating a coming of age, as doctors and daughters and women. And it was about celebrating the promises that the future held for them.

'To a year full of challenges successfully overcome,' Rachael said, raising her glass. 'And to new beginnings.'